Henry & Kate

BY LAURA KNEIDL

The Darlington Series

Henry & Kate
Ethan & Grace
Logan & Rose

LAURA KNEIDL

Henry & Kate

TRANSLATED BY
CHARLIE WÜHRER

An imprint of Authors Equity

Authors Equity
1123 Broadway, Suite 1008
New York, New York 10010

Cover design by Jeannine Schmelzer and Bastei Lübbe AG, using images from © Shutterstock (© Nataliia Kucherenko; © Shutterstock; © Phoebe Yu; © VectorMachine; © Lyottav)
Illustrations © Gabriella Bujdosó
Book design by Scribe Inc.

First published in Germany in 2025 by LYX, an imprint of Bastei Lübbe
First published in the United States in 2026 by LYX, an imprint of Authors Equity

Library of Congress Control Number: 2025949094
Print ISBN 9798893311648
Ebook ISBN 9798893311709

Printed in Canada
First printing

www.lyxbooks.com
www.authorsequity.com

This book contains explicit content.
For more detailed information, please see page 483.

Disclaimer: The content warning
includes spoilers for the entire book!

We wish you the best possible reading experience.

Love,

Laura & LYX

For Reshi

Women stand against Richard Darlington!
When: Monday 22nd September
Where: Westminster Bridge

Call to protest

Kate

I've always been a good runner. When I played tag as a kid, no one could catch me. I made it onto the athletics podium in Year 7, and when I was sixteen, I was the best forward on the girls' football team. That was before I'd dropped out of school. I used to run for fun, but these days, I ran to survive.

I was running now too—and fast. Running away. I didn't want to spend another night at the local police station, which was full of weirdos and drunk assholes who couldn't keep their hands to themselves. And I was afraid that if I got arrested, I wouldn't get off as lightly as I had last time. I'd been caught pickpocketing a few weeks ago, but they'd let me go with a warning. A warning I was currently ignoring.

"*Questa puttana mi ha derubato!*" roared the man racing after me, whose wallet I currently had in my pocket. I didn't have a clue what he was saying, but I assumed it wasn't friendly. The sound of his voice merged with the whistling wind and the pounding of my boots flying over the asphalt. I was lucky they didn't fall apart, given the loose soles and the cracked leather.

The tourists swarming around Parliament Square were obstacles, sure, but they were also good camouflage. I dodged a family taking a photo in front of a red telephone booth and leapt over a dropped ice cream.

"*Prendetela!*" yelled the man, who seemed unwilling to give up.

I should have known better than to glance over my shoulder—I crashed into someone, and they fell limply to the ground. I tripped over them and only just managed to catch myself. A woman glared up at me. The contents of her handbag were strewn across the ground, but she seemed uninjured.

"Sorry!" I called as I sprinted away, hoisting up the strap of my rucksack as it threatened to slip from my shoulder. A group of young men who'd been watching stepped into my path. I dodged to the side but felt the brush of a hand reaching out to grab me. I darted away before it could, making a beeline for the pier on the other side of the road.

I'd just been hit by the unmistakable scent of the Thames when I heard calls coming from up ahead of me. They grew louder by the second, countless voices chanting the same words over and over again. A protest. Perfect! Dozens of people blocked the bridge and crowded the street, angrily holding aloft placards and signs. I didn't know what they were protesting, but right now, I was on their side. Police officers loitered, but they were too busy managing the crowd to pay me any attention, and I was sure they couldn't hear the Italian's incensed shouts over the roar of the mob.

I slowed down so I wouldn't attract attention, mingling with the protestors. Most of them were angry young women, so I fit in perfectly; I'd celebrated my twentieth birthday a few weeks ago. And by *celebrated*, I mean I went around the city taking advantage of birthday offers for things I couldn't otherwise afford. Which was only possible because I had identification, a privilege not all homeless people have. Naturally, I guarded my passport like it was a treasure. In addition to the birthday offers, it gave me access to night shelters I'd otherwise be turned away from.

I wove my way through the protestors, merging with the crowd. I was breathing rapidly, less out of exertion than agitation. Taking several breaths to calm myself down, I suppressed the urge to turn and check if I was still being followed—I'd only attract attention. Instead, I let myself be swept along by the protestors. I shoved my hand into the pocket of my scuffed leather jacket and clutched the Italian man's wallet tight. I hadn't put everything on the line just to be pickpocketed myself.

"Believe the women! Believe the women! Believe the women!" chanted the people around me in unison.

I chanted along, still breathless, and scanned the placards being brandished. I realised now what they were protesting against. Or rather, *who* they were protesting against: Richard Darlington.

There couldn't have been anyone in London, except perhaps the royal family, who lived a more radically different life from mine than Richard Darlington. He and his family were part of the upper echelons of British high society. They owned The Darlington, the most expensive, prestigious hotel in the city, perhaps even in all of Europe. Politicians, nobility, and celebrities were constantly flitting in and out. I'd never met Richard Darlington, but I knew exactly who he was, what he looked like, and what he had done, like presumably everyone else in the country. He'd been in the news for months because multiple women had accused the hotel owner of sexual abuse. Their allegations had spread through the media like wildfire. He denied everything, of course.

I yelled along even louder as the protest slowly approached The Darlington, which rose majestically from the banks of the Thames. The hotel was steeped in history: We'd even learned about it at school when we'd covered the history of London.

The hotel spanned several floors and had been built in the early twentieth century, taking inspiration from the Beaux-Arts style. With its arched arcades and its pristine facade of cream-coloured limestone, it exuded pure luxury. Several pointed turrets crowned the building, presumably offering breathtaking views of London. With its fairy-tale appearance, the hotel attracted the attention of anyone strolling along the river. It embodied the essence of wealth and elegance. In short: There was no way I could ever afford to spend a single night there.

The protest stopped directly in front of the hotel, which was surrounded by police. I risked a glance over my shoulder and saw with relief that there was no sign of my pursuer. This was my chance to leave. I escaped the crowd and followed the bank to Lambeth Bridge, which I crossed to return to my side of the city.

As I walked, I pulled out the stolen wallet from my pocket to inspect my haul. As always, I checked the cash compartment first. Eighty pounds. Not bad. These days, people usually only had bank cards on them, or they stored their credit cards digitally on their phones. Inconvenient for someone like me. But there was also a credit card in the wallet. If I was quick, I could use it to buy food before the Italian man cancelled it.

I no longer felt the pangs of guilt I'd had when I first started out pickpocketing. I'd much rather not have to steal, of course, but I wasn't doing it for fun. I stole to survive. And this man—Pietro Mazzeo, according to his passport—could surely spare a few pounds, if he could afford a holiday in the most expensive city in Great Britain.

I tucked the money into my rucksack and went on the search for food. I didn't have enough time to find a supermarket, but when I spotted a Pret A Manger, I headed straight towards it. I bought fresh sandwiches, a few packaged snacks that would keep for a while, and a bottle of water. Holding my breath, I touched the stolen card to the card reader. A beep signalled that the payment had gone through. Leaving Pret with my bag of snacks, I unwrapped one of the sandwiches. I took a satisfying bite to settle my stomach, which had been rumbling for hours, and set off for the lost-and-found office. I may have been a thief, but I wasn't cruel. Money was rarely the most valuable thing in a tourist's wallet. More important were the photos and tickets, and the ID they'd need to get through airport security.

I walked down the street. Nobody paid me any attention. With my black leather jacket, my faded jeans, and my chin-length, dark-brown hair, I was as inconspicuous as a person could possibly be. Essential for someone living on the streets, especially a woman. *Don't attract attention* was the first lesson I'd had to learn. The hard way. *Be fearless* was another. Fear made you seem weak, and the weak easily became victims.

Fifteen minutes later, I arrived at the shabby lost-and-found building. The glass of the door was cracked, and there was colourful graffiti scrawled across the window. Not particularly confidence-inspiring, but anyone doing an online search for lost-and-found offices in London would be sent here.

I pushed open the door—to my relief, it didn't shatter—and stepped inside. The smell of plastic, rubber, wood, and dust hung in the air. The walls were lined with dark wooden shelves laden with an assortment of meticulously arranged items, from forgotten umbrellas to single gloves, lost books, and orphaned cuddly toys. There were also some oddities. A mannequin head, for example. And there was an accordion that had been lying on top of a cupboard for weeks.

"Hey, Kate," Mary said. She was sitting on a stool behind the counter knitting, as usual. Mary was a student at the University of London, but she helped out at the lost and found three days a week.

I approached the counter. "Hi. How's it going?"

"What with? Knitting? The job? Uni?"

"All of it," I answered nosily and took a sweet from the bowl on the counter. I unwrapped it and shoved it into my mouth.

"The knitting is going well. No updates on the job front. And uni is stressful. The semester has only just started, but I'm already drowning in work. I should really be studying, but I've opted for stress-knitting instead. I'm going to have more woolly socks than I can possibly wear this winter."

"I'm here if you ever want to get rid of some," I said, only half joking. My socks were all pretty full of holes. I could really use a new pair, especially of the warm and fluffy variety. It was the end of September, and the days were still mild, but the nights were getting colder. I wasn't looking forward to my second winter living on the streets.

Mary smiled. "How about you? Everything OK?"

"Yes. Same old, same old." I kept it short. Telling her about my problems wouldn't make a difference. There was nothing she could do about it anyway, and the less I talked about my life, the easier it was to ignore how fucked up the last year had been. I pulled out the stolen wallet from my jacket pocket and handed it to Mary across the counter. "I wanted to hand this in."

"Where did you get it?"

"I found it."

"That's the third wallet you've 'found' in the last few days."

"What can I say? I notice things. It's a skill."

Mary gave a sceptical hum and took the wallet off me to log it in her records. When she saw the empty cash compartment, she glanced at me and then at the Pret A Manger bag in my hand. A brief flash of displeasure crossed her face, but she didn't say anything. I was certain she knew what I was doing, but she never addressed it. The lost and found was city-owned, and if I confessed to a crime, she'd have to report it. "Thanks for bringing it in."

"You're welcome. Have a good day."

"Thanks. You too," Mary replied.

I smiled and waved goodbye. I sometimes wished we could have a friendship based on more than ten minutes of small talk. I missed having a real friend. But our lives were probably too different. What would we talk about? I had nothing to share, and anything I said would presumably just depress her.

I left the lost and found and was making my way to St. James's Park when a sudden shiver ran up the back of my neck. A kind of sixth sense set in when you'd lived on the streets for a while and constantly had to look over your shoulder to stay safe. A moment later, a rusty old Vauxhall pulled up next to me. A car I unfortunately knew all too well.

Shit.

This was the last thing I needed.

The car stopped, the door flung open, and Randell got out. Without a moment's hesitation, I whirled around and ran off, even though I knew there was no escape. If the bastard didn't get me today, he'd get me tomorrow, or the day after that. He wouldn't give up until he had the money that I apparently owed him.

The rucksack thumped against my back, and the bag of food smashed into my thigh. I wasn't sure if Randell was coming after me, but I didn't dare turn and look. For the second time today, I was on the run. I didn't know this part of town very well, but that didn't stop me. Looking for somewhere to hide, I ducked off into a side street, only for Edwin, one of Randell's drinking buddies, to appear out of nowhere and block my path.

Fuck!

I darted away, but his reflexes were surprisingly quick given his bulky frame. He grabbed me with his calloused hands and pulled me towards him. My bag of food fell to the ground. Edwin dragged me down a flight of stairs to a basement flat before passersby could cotton on to what was happening. I struggled but was no match for his iron grip.

"If you scream, I'll shove something into your mouth," Edwin hissed. His mouth was twisted—not in a smile but by a scar that ran the length of his lip.

He released me and tore my rucksack from my shoulders. Only now did I realise how hard he'd gripped me. There was a painful throbbing where his fingers had dug into me. Everything was telling me to run, but I couldn't leave my rucksack. It was the most valuable thing I owned.

I lifted my chin, trying not to look scared when Randall came down the steps, despite the fact that I was terrified. I knew what the man was capable of. My mum and I had lived in his decrepit, mouldy bungalow for a year. Today he was wearing black jeans and a T-shirt—no coat, as if he were immune to the cold. His light-brown hair was shaved down to a buzz cut, which made his otherwise round features appear angular. But it was the merciless look in his eyes that gave him such a menacing air, alongside the fact that it was impossible to tell how much he'd had to drink or what he'd taken. It made him unpredictable.

"Hello, Kate."

"Randell," I replied.

He came towards me, stopping an arm's length away. The acrid stench of sweat and stale cigarette smoke filled my nostrils. If nightmares had a smell, they'd smell like Randell Barker. "Where's my money?"

"At the bank?"

He snorted but didn't seem amused. "Very funny. Let me rephrase: Where's the money you owe me?"

I clenched my hands into fists. "I owe you nothing!"

"I wouldn't say four thousand pounds is *nothing*," he said, his dark eyes drilling into me. I shuddered. I hated that I was so much smaller than him and that he could look down on me. "So, where's my money, Kate?"

"I don't have it," I said, knowing there was no point in arguing. My voice sounded remorseful, despite the fact that I didn't owe Randell anything. My mum had borrowed nearly five thousand pounds from him, and since she'd died, he was convinced it was my responsibility to pay him back. I'd managed to pay off a little, but there was still a lot to go.

"Have you forgotten what will happen if you don't pay?" he asked, taking a step towards me. Up close, I could see that his pupils were dilated. He was clearly high.

I pressed my lips together and shook my head.

"So, why don't you have my money?"

"It's been a tough few weeks." It had actually been a tough few months, but the last thing I wanted was to give Randell more insight into my thoughts and feelings. He'd ruthlessly use whatever he found against me.

He tutted, disappointed, and then stepped even closer. He dropped his voice to a whisper when he next spoke, as if he wanted to let me in on a secret. "You don't have to be on the streets stealing to get my money together. You can work off your debts in a more personal way."

"How?" I asked before I could stop myself, although I knew better than to get caught up in his games.

He raised a hand to stroke my cheek. I desperately wanted to flinch away from his touch, but I had my back against the wall. Literally. His fingers traced a line down to my mouth, and he fixed his gaze on my lips before running his dirty thumb over them. His silence spoke volumes. But I'd rather end up in prison for stealing than have sex with my mother's ex-boyfriend. The thought alone made me feel sick. How could Randell not be disgusted by himself?

I jerked my head away. "Over my dead body, you gross wanker."

"That can be arranged," Edwin growled. He had stopped searching my rucksack but clung on to the stolen eighty pounds.

Randell smirked. “That won’t be necessary. Kate knows what’s at stake, don’t you?” he asked. He didn’t wait for my answer, taking the money from Edwin. “I expect another five hundred pounds from you within a couple of days. This is my interest. If I don’t get my money on time, things will get ugly. Understood?”

I didn’t reply.

“Understood?” repeated Randell more forcefully.

I nodded.

He smiled and took a step back. “Wonderful. See you around, *Kaitlynn*. And don’t bother hiding from me. I’ll find you.”

I gritted my teeth. He knew very well how much I hated that name, especially coming from his mouth. With a self-satisfied grin, he turned away and climbed the stairs. Edwin scowled at me and dropped my rucksack, then turned to follow Randell out. I didn’t move, didn’t even dare breathe a sigh of relief until I heard the roar of the car engine.

My heart raced and my legs felt like jelly. Randell had let me go with a warning this time, but I knew from experience how nasty things could get.

I crouched down next to my rucksack. Edwin had rummaged through its contents, but nothing was damaged—not the envelope of photographs nor the old children’s book my mum used to read to me back when the world still made sense. I put everything back in its place and wondered where the hell I’d find five hundred pounds.

Welcome to The Darlington!

The Darlington is London's most luxurious five-star hotel. Located in the heart of the city on the bank of the Thames, it garners international acclaim for its impressive rooms, exclusive service, and timeless elegance. Step inside!

Excerpt from The Darlington Hotel's website

Henry

My arms trembled.

My thighs throbbed.

My back burnt.

I felt incredible.

I gritted my teeth, relying on sheer willpower to resist letting go and welcoming the fall. If I did that, it would be over, and at the end of the fall, discussions and decisions awaited me, not to mention questions from the press about the protest that had blocked Westminster Bridge for hours yesterday. But as long as I kept a tight hold on the crimps and jugs on the bouldering wall, I didn't have to think about any of it. I only had to think about whether my muscles could take me even higher.

I assessed my position, picked a hold I could reach, and pushed myself up higher to grab it. My fingers were dry from chalk. The only sound in the bouldering gym was my own controlled breathing. The gym was usually still closed at this time, but I paid a lot of money to have it opened for me—and only me—because I needed it. Now more than ever.

Mornings were the only time of the day that really belonged to me. I usually worked out at my penthouse gym, but once a week, I fled from the hotel to the bouldering gym. Getting rid of excess energy in the evenings on the treadmill or the elliptical trainer helped replace my worries with exhaustion, but it was nothing compared to the kick that climbing gave me. It not only engaged every muscle in my body but also silenced my thoughts. Switching off my brain had been a challenge the last few months.

I ventured higher and higher—until I heard the beeping of my phone alarm several metres below. A reminder that it was time to leave. I let go of the grips reluctantly and landed on the mats with a groan. Sweat dripped from my forehead. I pulled off my drenched T-shirt and went to the bench to collect my water bottle and a towel to wipe my face with.

I grabbed my phone and turned off the alarm. More tiny red numbers had appeared next to the apps in the last hour: twenty-seven missed calls, ninety-two unread messages, one hundred and twenty-eight unanswered emails. I didn't have to open them to know that none of them bore good news.

I'd always known that I'd take over The Darlington sooner or later. Not only was I the oldest son; I was also the only one interested in the hotel. Logan was only two years younger than me, but he'd turned his back on our parents and the family business years ago to do his own thing. And Ethan? He was only twenty, and most of the time, his thoughts went no further than the panties of the next model he wanted to screw. So it was up to me to run the hotel. I'd initially envisioned a smooth transition, with my dad gradually stepping back from the business. I hadn't reckoned with being handed the responsibility all in one day while a massive high-society scandal steamrollered my family.

I draped my towel over my shoulders and headed for the changing room, nodding in greeting at the janitor, who had the thankless task of letting me into the gym this early. He returned the gesture wanly and wished me a nice day—something I could only dream of. My day was chockablock with appointments, and I just knew all kinds of disasters awaited me. Thanks to the workout, though, I at least felt halfway prepared to face it.

My phone vibrated. A message from Logan. If there was anyone who had an even more fucked-up sleep cycle than me, it was my brother. He owned one of the hippest restaurants in the city and was often there until late at night—before getting up early the next morning to buy fresh ingredients for the evening. He had sent me a photo of today's page of his mindfulness calendar, as he did every day.

Love yourself
and you will never be unhappy.

ME:

Is this a call to masturbate?

LOGAN:

Make fun of me all you like. This calendar is awesome.

ME:

You only say that because it's encouraging you to have a wank.

LOGAN:

You're just jealous.

ME:

You keep telling yourself that.

I'd given Logan the calendar with its nuggets of pseudowisdom last Christmas. It had become a tradition to buy him something silly, because for eight years, he'd been giving me the same present for every occasion: a DVD of *London Has Fallen*, the most terrible film in existence. We'd gone to the cinema to watch it together, but I'd hated it so much that I'd left early, leaving Logan to sit through the rest alone. He had never forgiven me for that. And to make sure I didn't get the idea of selling the DVDs or even throwing them away, he left me personal messages inside the cases.

I pushed open the door to the changing room. As I was the only person at the gym, I left my sports bag on the bench instead of in a locker. I undressed and showered in the adjoining bathroom, turning the water temperature all the way down to cool my hot body. I felt a headache brewing behind my temples. Back in the changing room, I popped a pill to keep me half functioning for the next few hours. And after drying my hair, I removed my suit from the clothes bag. I planned to go straight from working out to work.

I pulled on my trousers and a shirt, tied my tie, and slipped into my jacket. I squared my shoulders and scrutinised my reflection in the mirror hanging between the scratched lockers. Everything fit perfectly. The dark suit, my black hair, even the three-day beard I'd been cultivating, much to my mum's irritation. It was my little rebellion against a well-oiled system. The only flaw was the dark rings under my blue eyes, which hadn't been there the year before. But I assumed I was the only one who noticed them, because no one actually cared. People didn't really see me. They saw only what they wanted to see.

My dad: a businessman.

My mum: a beacon of hope.

The press: an heir.

The rest of the world: a guy with power.

I, on the other hand, saw a man trapped in a golden cage he couldn't break out of without leaving his family and the hotel in the lurch. A hotel he loved above all else. The Darlington Dynasty stood on the brink of collapse—and it was up to me to save it.

THE BLACKROOM

Welcome to the Blackroom, the place of
Richard Darlington's nightmares.

Men with too much power and even more money traditionally get off scot-free, but we believe that none of them deserve a free pass—not even Richard Darlington. Which is why we've created the Blackroom: an independent blog that stands in solidarity with Richard Darlington's victims.

We have connections at The Darlington Hotel and contacts in Richard Darlington's family and inner circle . . . and we're poised and ready to bring his darkest secrets to light.

Because this isn't just about Richard Darlington. This is a structural problem. This is about the safety of women, about justice, about consequences. This is about the fact that no one is above the law, regardless of their gender, wealth, status, or position in society. We will follow the Richard Darlington case closely, bringing you reports from the Blackroom.

Beware of pickpockets! Keep a close eye on your personal belongings. If you see something suspicious, report it to the police immediately!

Warning to tourists

Kate

"The Red Lady has been causing trouble in St. James's Park for centuries. According to legend, she was murdered by her husband, who decapitated her and threw her head into this very lake. She's been wandering through the park ever since, searching for her missing head," said the guide of the haunted walking tour. He spoke in an eerie tone, although there was nothing spooky about his story in broad daylight, even with the dark rain clouds hanging overhead. It was actually pretty boring, but I couldn't complain, since I had not paid for the tour. I'd been following the group for a while, hoping to steal a wallet or something else of value. I'd not had any success so far.

I'd stolen two hundred pounds in the last few days. It wasn't bad, but the worse the weather, the harder it was to get at money. The tourists' coats became bulkier, which complicated picking their pockets. And they were more likely to mill around in restaurants and shops, which made begging even more futile and unappealing. As if it weren't already humiliating enough. Most of the time, people like me, with our cups and baskets for begging, were ignored. People pretended we didn't exist and clung on to their change with misplaced concern as they swept past us, assuming we'd spend anything we got on alcohol and drugs. But in reality, most of us were just hungry.

"People have reported seeing the Red Lady near the lake. If you come here at night, you might just get lucky too," said the tour guide and motioned the group to move on while he cast me a warning look. I didn't know whether he'd seen through me or just didn't want me listening for free to a monologue he'd clearly learned off by heart. Either way, it was my cue to leave. I adjusted the straps of my rucksack and made my way to the public restroom.

Getting in cost a few pence that had to be paid with a credit card, but the people who cleaned the facilities knew me. Today it was Ada who opened the barrier and let me slip through. I washed my hands thoroughly before pulling my toiletry bag out of my rucksack so I could brush my teeth and wash my face. I used a public shower occasionally, if I could afford it.

After I was finished, I said goodbye to Ada and wandered through the park in the hope that I'd come across some heedless tourists walking around with their wallets in their trouser pockets. St. James's Park had been my home for a while, and I knew its paths like the back of my hand. I'd tried out various new sleeping places in the last few months, but of all the outdoor locations, this park was my favourite. It was central, and there were the public restrooms and St. James's Café. They knew me at the café too, and every so often, I got free food at the end of the day. The park was beautiful, with centuries-old trees and lovingly tended flower beds. Wherever I looked, there were birds and squirrels preparing for winter, and in the summer, the lawns were littered with peanut shells, evidence of tourists feeding the park's wildlife.

A little snack kiosk caught my eye as I walked around the lake. I usually paid it no attention—everything was so expensive—but today I didn't ignore it. There was a queue, and last in line was a man who looked like he'd been born grasping hundred-pound notes. I had him sussed out immediately. If you lived on the streets long enough, you developed a sharp instinct for people. This man wasn't just acting like he was important; he really was. He clearly didn't come from new money either. He wasn't someone who walked around sporting flashy brand logos. No, this man wore elegant leather shoes and a tailored coat that fit his broad shoulders like a glove. The guy clearly came from old money.

I got in the queue behind him. He smelled good. Not of expensive perfume, but something else, something more subtle. Perhaps his shampoo, or the fabric softener his housekeeper used. He had thick black hair and good posture, and he was relatively tall. At five foot one, I barely reached his shoulders.

The man's phone rang, and he reached into his coat pocket to pull it out. It was a brand-new iPhone and must have cost a small fortune. He hesitated before answering.

"Yes?" His voice was warm and deep. Soothing.

The person on the other end said something I couldn't hear.

"I'm taking a break," the man said.

". . ."

He sighed. "No, I'm not at the hotel."

". . ."

"Because I had to get out," he answered, irritated, and I wondered if I'd made a mistake. Yes, he blatantly had money, but perhaps he wasn't as important as I'd assumed him to be. Important people didn't justify themselves. They were arrogant enough to believe they didn't have to.

". . ."

"I'll be back in time," the man promised before hanging up. He sighed again and slid the phone back into his coat pocket before pulling out a little box. He opened it and popped something into his mouth. A sweet or a piece of gum, I assumed.

I observed the man's movements carefully until he reached the front of the queue, where he ordered a coffee to go. I glanced around. When I was sure no one was watching me and that he was distracted, I slipped my hand into his coat pocket and nimbly pulled out his phone. Quick as a flash, I dropped it into my own pocket before he noticed.

He said goodbye to the man behind the kiosk and left with his coffee, and then it was my turn. I treated myself to an overpriced cookie and paid for it without a hint of remorse, thanks to my loot. Because if I sold the treasure now stowed away in my coat pocket, I could pay off most of the money I owed Randell.

I cast a glance behind me and watched the man walk away obliviously. I felt an unexpected stab of guilt for having taken an expensive phone rather than the usual handful of cash. But I forced myself to brush the feeling aside. The guy was practically drowning in money, and if he wanted to, he could probably buy ten iPhones without batting an eyelid. My safety, on the other hand, depended on me paying Randell.

"It's terrible what his father did to those women."

I glanced at the kiosk owner and noticed he was also watching the man walk away, shaking his head indignantly.

He caught my confused look. "You don't know who that was?"

"No." I hadn't seen the man from the front.

"Henry Darlington. Richard Darlington's son."

"Oh," I said.

I looked back again, but Henry Darlington had disappeared. So his father was the monster I'd inadvertently ended up protesting against a few days ago. Still, I couldn't stop a smile from spreading across my face. If it really was Henry Darlington's phone I had in my pocket, it was worth far more than I'd initially thought.

4

Richard Darlington Denies Accusations: "This Is a Smear Campaign Against Me and The Darlington!"

Guardian headline

Henry

Journalists loitered outside The Darlington, eager to snatch up the next sensational headline. They chatted idly, but the moment they saw me coming, they leapt to their feet. Less than a minute later, I had four microphones and a camera shoved in my face. I ignored the journalists tussling for a statement about the protest that had taken place earlier that week, walking past with my head held high. Stanley swung open the double doors, their golden handles gleaming. He was a second-generation concierge, and it was his job to prevent unwanted guests from entering the hotel.

The press had been stationed outside The Darlington, trying to get statements from the family and staff, ever since the first allegations against my dad had been made eight months ago. Every employee had been asked to sign a confidentiality agreement. No one was allowed to talk to the press without permission, not even me, even though I ran the hotel now.

After consulting with my dad's lawyers and crisis manager, we had decided it would be best if he took a step back from actively managing the hotel, so he couldn't further harm its reputation. Were The Darlington just any hotel, public interest would probably have died down quickly. But it wasn't just any hotel. It was *the* hotel, a landmark of London. It was just as integral a part of the skyline as Big Ben, Westminster Abbey, or Buckingham Palace. There probably wasn't a London travel guide in existence who didn't mention The Darlington.

My dad hadn't been happy about stepping down, but he'd reluctantly followed the advice of the consulting team and handed over control to me. Unfortunately for me, he'd kept enough shares in the hotel to still hold sway behind the scenes. If it had been up to me, he wouldn't have any authority at all. Even if nothing came of the accusations against him, the rumours would linger for years, casting a shadow over the family name like a storm cloud. Not to mention that being in the same room as my dad disgusted me. What these women had accused him of was despicable, and I didn't have a shadow of a doubt that they were telling the truth. If I loved the hotel just a little less, I would have thrown in the towel and spared myself the stress.

I felt an immediate calm settle over me as I stepped into the foyer, despite the hustle and bustle. The hotel exuded an inviting warmth. The beige-and-golden wallpaper, the sage-and-terracotta carpets, the cosy bergères and récamiers, the fireplace with a piano in front of it: All of it encouraged guests to linger in the foyer with a cup of tea. By day, Theodore, the hotel's pianist, filled the room with soothing music. Golden chandeliers hung from the stucco ceiling, which was supported by marble columns. A gold statue of two smiling women stood in the middle of the foyer, welcoming the guests.

For me, The Darlington was so much more than this obvious beauty. It was my heart, my soul, and above all, my home. Everything about it was familiar. Even blindfolded, I'd easily be able to weave my way through the corridors without bumping into anything. As children, Logan and I had used every spare minute to explore the hotel. We had drawn maps, wonky floor plans we marked with crosses that represented not treasures, but the best hiding places. The Darlington had hardly changed since then, so I still knew them all.

"Hello, Philippa," I greeted the receptionist behind the marble front desk. She was wearing a trouser suit with the hotel's logo embroidered on it: a *D* framed in golden flourishes, surrounded by a circle decorated with leaves and the hotel's five stars.

Philippa smiled at me. "Hello, Mr. Darlington. How are you?"

"Good. And you?"

"Same. My boyfriend and I finally found an apartment. Thanks again for the tip."

"I'm glad to hear it," I said with a nod and walked past the reception to a door with a sign that said "Staff only." Mr. Boyd, one of my dad's three lawyers, had requested an urgent meeting, but I decided to first make a detour to Rakesh's office to pick up the latest crisis report in person. I stopped at the door with a "Management" plaque and knocked.

"Come in!"

I pushed open the door to find Rakesh hunched over the desk. He had been working at The Darlington for years before being promoted to hotel manager. Together, we ensured that the hotel ran smoothly. Although he was only forty, today he looked a decade older. His black hair was dishevelled, the dark circles under his eyes rivalled mine, and I could smell the acrid stench of cigarettes underneath the floral room spray. Smoking was banned in the hotel, but Rakesh had always been a stress smoker.

"Hello, Henry," he greeted me in surprise, although he should have grown accustomed to my visits by now. My dad had never visited Rakesh; he'd always had his assistant summon him. I'd never forget the look of astonishment on Rakesh's face the first time I turned up at his office.

"Have you been out?"

"I went for a walk around the park to clear my head," I answered. "Do you have a moment?"

"For my favourite Darlington brother? Always."

I snorted. With Logan's absence and Ethan's antics, which caused Rakesh more of a headache than anything else, it wasn't a hard accolade to win. I wordlessly opened a window before sitting down in the chair opposite him. His desk was buried beneath a mountain of documents, but the rest of his office was immaculate.

"Shoot," I said and steeled myself for the worst.

"Do you want the good or the bad news first?"

I raised my eyebrows. "There's good news?"

"Not really," Rakesh said, wringing his fingers nervously. He was probably craving a cigarette. "There's bad news, and *very* bad news. I just wanted to make it sound more palatable."

"I feared as much. Give me the very bad news first."

"The BBC has withdrawn its request."

I nodded slowly. It didn't surprise me. The broadcaster had planned to make a documentary about The Darlington's rich and historic past and significance in the media to mark the hotel's centenary. In the past, the hotel had often served as a location for films and TV shows and had also been booked frequently as a location for photo shoots. And until recently, The Darlington had been an integral part of London Fashion Week. At the beginning of the month, however, we'd had to pull out of this year's event. The designers had all jumped ship, fearing their collections would suffer from negative media coverage. Even Natalia Asterdam, my best friends' mother, had pulled out.

"OK. And the bad news?"

Rakesh wrinkled his nose. "That wasn't all of the very bad news."

I held back a groan. "Is it too early for a drink?"

"Not under these circumstances, but I don't have anything here."

"Shame," I muttered, but it was probably for the best. It was enough that my mother had developed a predilection for drowning her sorrows in wine. Plus, it wouldn't make my headache any better. "What else?"

"Diana D'Angelo gave an interview."

I frowned. "The actress?"

"Yes. She spoke with the *INsider* about her experience with your dad. She said that he was very pushy at the last film festival, and 'accidentally' brushed against her breasts with suspicious frequency," Rakesh said, tight-lipped, attempting to stay professional. It was clear he and I had the same opinion of my father, but I couldn't tell him how I felt. Vivian Edwards, my dad's crisis manager, had instructed me not to say anything negative about my dad in the presence of employees. If any of them decided to breach confidentiality, it could come back to haunt us. I wouldn't have minded if it only affected my dad, but he was inextricably tied to the hotel, which I didn't want to damage—it was the only reason I kept my mouth shut and listened to Vivian, my dad, and his lawyers. For the time being, at least.

"Was that the last of the very bad news?" I asked.

"Yes."

I sighed with relief. "And the bad news?"

Rakesh shrugged and rifled around in the chaos on his desk. "The usual. Negative coverage. Two new resignations, which brings the total to almost forty. And more cancellations. The hotel is sixty percent booked this week, but next week, it's only fifty-five. I've emailed you the report."

"Thank you. Who resigned?"

"Priya and Sahra. Two room attendants. But it won't really affect us."

"Especially if we're only sixty percent booked," I muttered, concerned.

"Perhaps it's just a postsummer dip."

I murmured an agreement, although we both knew it wasn't true. Yes, bookings usually dropped in the autumn before picking up again in the winter months leading up to Christmas, but even in the off-season, The Darlington had always been at least eighty percent booked up. "Do we need to start thinking about redundancies?"

"Not yet. The resignations are taking care of that."

"That's . . ." I started, but I had no idea how to finish the sentence. *Good* didn't seem to be the right word. The fact that our employees were leaving—whether out of sympathy for the victims or fear for the future of the hotel—wasn't good news. In fact, it was very bad news. "I have to go now. Thanks for the update. Don't let your wife catch you smoking."

Rakesh pursed his lips. "I won't. Hang in there."

I left his office and made my way to the conference centre to join the meeting with my dad and one of his lawyers.

As a kid, I'd always been creeped out by this room, its walls lined with portraits of deceased Darlingtons. Logan and I had firmly believed that the room was haunted, and the pictures of the dead were watching us. But today, I was more afraid of the living who were waiting there for me: my dad and Mr. Boyd. Vivian would presumably also be in attendance. My dad had hired her several months ago to clean up his image, a feat she'd achieved once before with a professional athlete who had fallen into disrepute after similar allegations.

"You made it," my dad snapped, irritated, when I stepped into the room. He sat grimly at the head of the table, which was now technically my place. His dark-grey suit was the same shade as his hair. Looking at him was like looking into my future, only I hoped my eyes would be less embittered. "What took you so long?"

"I was busy," I answered evasively, hanging my coat on the coatrack next to the door. I sat down in a chair to his right; I didn't want to start a debate about which seat belonged to whom. "What's so urgent?"

The mood in the room soured at my question, like a glass of milk left out in the sun for too long. My dad's expression grew even darker. For a split second, worry flickered across Vivian's face, before it was replaced by her usual steely resolve. It seemed the update about the BBC and Diana D'Angelo hadn't been the only very bad news today.

Mr. Boyd spoke up. "I got a phone call this afternoon. Apparently, it has been decided to take your father's case to court. The authorities say there is enough evidence for a lawsuit."

"The audacity!" my dad objected. The vein on his forehead popped—something I'd always feared as a child, because it meant I was in trouble. "I did nothing that those women didn't want. To make out now that I assaulted them is outrageous. This is defamation! Can we file a libel suit against them?"

I bit back a snide comment. My dad pretty much asked the same question at every meeting. His default response to criticism was to silence the other party using his money or power instead of reflecting on himself. Self-reflection was a concept that I only understood thanks to Shelley, my old nanny. She had set great store by making Logan and me aware of our privilege and liked to bring us down to earth.

"I'd counsel against it at this moment in time, Mr. Darlington," replied Mr. Boyd. His hair had been sparse since I'd known him, but in the last few months, it seemed to have grown even thinner. Presumably because of my dad and this case, which was enough to make anyone want to pull their hair out. "A defamation suit could reflect poorly on you. We can think about that once we've won the case and the full extent of the situation is clear."

The vein on my dad's forehead continued to pulsate. He wasn't used to not getting what he wanted, but he should have thought about that before he'd crossed a line with those women. He argued that he was innocent, but I didn't believe a word he said. Once upon a time, long ago, I had looked up to him, but now I knew that Richard Darlington was a cold, ruthless bastard.

"We could try again with an out-of-court settlement, if you'd be willing," Mr. Boyd suggested. My dad had already whittled down the allegations from seven women to three with out-of-court settlements. The two million pounds he had offered each woman had proven too tempting.

"You promised there'd be no trial," Vivian said, without responding to the suggestion. Her dark hair was gathered in a tight plait, and she wore a blue suit that looked like a uniform. At our first meeting, I'd been surprised that she was only a few years older than me—her CV was just as impressive as her clientele was questionable.

"I made no such promise, Mrs. Edwards," said Mr. Boyd. "I said it *probably* wouldn't go to trial. Statistically, less than five percent of reported sex offences end up in court. There usually isn't enough evidence. The indictment was only filed because of media pressure. The Metropolitan Police and the Crown Prosecution Service can't afford bad press or to be accused of sloppy work. This is just theatrics."

"You don't seem particularly worried," I said as I patted my suit, looking for my phone. Perhaps I had another appointment that would get me out of this one. I had nothing to contribute anyway. But my phone wasn't there. It was probably still in my coat.

"I'm not," Mr. Boyd said, head held high. "Your father hired the best law firm in town. My colleagues and I know this case inside out, and there's no solid evidence. It's their word against ours. We have the law on our side."

I would have said the same in his position—and with his wage—but Vivian seemed satisfied with his statement and made fervent notes on her tablet. My dad looked smug.

"What's next?" he asked.

"The prosecution has submitted an indictment to the Court of Justice. Based on this, the judge will decide at the first hearing whether the evidence is as airtight and whether there will be a trial or not. If he decides there will, the case will be referred to the Crown Court. Should this happen, we would push for immediate bail. It shouldn't be a problem. There'd presumably be a fine, and they'll take your passport to prevent you from leaving the country. You might also get a court order for electronic monitoring or a curfew."

"Unacceptable!" my dad hissed.

"Could we circumvent that?" Vivian asked with a businesslike tone.

Mr. Boyd took off his glasses and cleaned them with a cloth he drew from his trouser pocket. "We can plead that Mr. Darlington is an upstanding member of society, and that the company and family domicile prevent him from being considered a flight risk. But ultimately, it's for the court to decide."

Vivian shook her head. "A photograph of Richard wearing an ankle monitor is the last thing we need. It would only cast him in a negative light. We need to create positive momentum."

"Positive momentum is your job, not mine," replied Mr. Boyd with a tight-lipped smile. He explained the next steps in the proceedings, which could, in the worst-case scenario, take several years. But, he speculated, public interest would likely make sure the case was dealt with swiftly. When he was done, Vivian went through possible measures that would make my dad look like a better person than he really was.

I only half listened to the discussion. While my dad was focussed mainly on himself, I was thinking about the hotel, about the cancellations and our employees. I drummed my fingers nervously on my knee. My thoughts snagged on the day's to-do list. Unsurprisingly, I realised I wouldn't have enough time to do everything. I glanced with irritation at the heavy Audemars Piguet strapped to my wrist. My mum had given me the watch as a present after my dad had appointed me CEO.

"Henry?"

I raised my eyes. I had been staring into space, lost in thought, drafting an email to the BBC in my head. I knew I wouldn't be able to persuade them to make the documentary after all, but I wanted to write a dignified response to their rejection. "Yes?"

My dad scowled at me. "Did you hear what Vivian said?"

"No, sorry. What was it about?"

"The Pearl Gala."

I frowned. "What about it?"

The Pearl Gala was a fundraising event that my grandmother Selma had started forty-three years ago. Every year in the last week of December, we invited people to The Darlington to raise money for a charity. The guest list was exclusive, and the red carpet was not only one of the most significant but also the final one of the year for most stars and celebrities. The media often reported that the Pearl Gala set the tone for the following year. But for the first time since its inception, no gala was planned for this December.

"Vivian thinks we should still hold it."

My eyebrows shot up. "Seriously?"

She nodded resolutely and stabbed at her tablet with her stylus. "Yes. The Darlington is in desperate need of good press, and cancelling a charity event is the opposite of good press. The gala would give the family an opportunity to present itself as a unit. Your mother, Ethan, and you—you can all show your support for Richard and make a public display of your generosity. A particularly lavish donation is a must, of course."

"Of course," my dad echoed with a smile. "I think that's an excellent idea."

My frown deepened. "You were the one who cancelled the gala."

"Don't talk nonsense." He gestured dismissively and stood up to walk over to a trolley in the corner, which held carafes of tea and coffee, along with a jug of water filled with floating cucumber and lemon slices. "The marketing team pushed for the cancellation. I was always on board."

It was a barefaced lie. I'd been at the meeting where Dad had insisted on cancelling this year's Pearl Gala. I'd even argued against it, but he hadn't wanted to hear it. He didn't care about the gala, though he'd been taking credit for it for years.

"It's almost October," I remarked, choosing not to argue further about his erratic behaviour.

He poured himself a glass of water. "What are you trying to say?"

"We usually start preparing in March." I had started managing the gala two years ago. It had been my segue into the family business after I graduated, and it had given me a chance to prove myself after my grandmother died. "It's almost impossible to organise an event like that in three months."

"*Almost* being the operative word."

"I don't have time."

My dad cast me a warning look intended to put me in my place, but I wouldn't let it intimidate me. He'd clearly forgotten that his former role was now mine. "And *we* don't have time to hire someone new to take this on. You're familiar with the event, and the only one who knows the processes, suppliers, and sponsors. Vivian and Rakesh can give you a hand."

What about you?

The question was on the tip of my tongue, but I kept it to myself. I would organise the Pearl Gala, even if it became stressful. Because I wanted to, and because I loved the gala. I would carve out time for it in my already busy schedule, but I would do it without my dad's sceptical comments and criticisms. And I certainly didn't want to spend any more time than necessary in his presence.

"I'd be happy to help with the planning as much as I can," Vivian chimed in. Which realistically meant she wouldn't lift a finger. Confirming my suspicions, she said, "I'm sure your mother would be willing to help too. She likes to organise events."

"A brilliant idea," my father agreed.

Suck-up.

"You'd be doing the hotel an enormous favour," Vivian added, her smile triumphant. She knew how much I loved The Darlington and that I'd do anything to save it.

"Fine," I heard myself saying. But I wasn't doing it for Dad or Vivian. I was doing it in memory of my grandmother, and because the gala could help a lot of people. Besides, my dad was right: We couldn't hand the planning over to someone else this last minute without risking the event being a disaster. The last thing The Darlington needed was yet more negative press.

James threw a party on Dad's boat yesterday. Ethan got drunk and fell into the water. Luckily there was someone sober enough to fish him out.

Message from Olivia to Henry

Henry

The highlight of every conversation with my dad was its end, but today, I didn't feel my usual relief. How could I organise the Pearl Gala with so little lead time? I'd have to cram ten months' work into three and grovel to suppliers, service providers, and sponsors, since we'd already called off our arrangements for December. I could only hope our usual contractors still had capacity. Bringing in anyone new on such short notice carried risks I'd rather avoid.

I reached into my coat pocket for my phone to text Rakesh the bad news so he could kiss his free time goodbye. But my hand encountered an empty pocket. I tried the other one but found only a packet of tissues and the little tin I always carried with me. Confused, I patted down my suit and then my coat again. I tried to remember when I'd last had my phone in my hand. The call with my dad in the park. So where was it now? The answer was as clear as it was unpleasant: I had lost it. It must have fallen out of my pocket on the way back to the hotel.

Fuck.

Just what I needed. Could this day get any worse? Probably not, but I didn't want to tempt fate. I really needed my phone back. My data was backed up in the cloud, but some of it was pretty sensitive. I could only hope that whoever had found the phone was honest or that they couldn't get past the screen lock.

I strode purposefully to my office, which was at the other end of the corridor. It had once belonged to my grandfather, and I hadn't found the time yet to decorate it to my liking. The room was elegant but gloomy. Sometimes when I inhaled deeply, I thought I could still smell my grandfather's stale cigar smoke. The imposing chandelier that my great-grandfather had chosen still hung from the ceiling, and the walls were lined with glass cabinets full of old books with cracked leather bindings that probably hadn't been touched in decades.

I tossed my coat onto the burgundy velvet sofa in the corner and slipped behind the desk to log into my laptop. I opened the Find My app nervously and sighed with relief when I located my phone. It was still in St. James's Park, and it wasn't moving. I took the lift up to my apartment to get the key for my Bentley. I'd usually walk to the park, but there was no time to lose.

I grabbed the key from the sideboard and headed straight back downstairs. The doors of the lift were just about to close when my brother Ethan appeared from around the corner. He was wearing a grey hoodie and dark jeans, and his dishevelled black hair stood on end. I couldn't tell if it was a carefully put-together look or if he'd just rolled out of bed.

"Wait," he called when he spotted me.

I instinctively pressed the button, and the doors of the lift slid open again. A moment later, I regretted my decision. Ethan didn't speed up but walked slowly, with all the arrogance of a man used to others waiting for him. In the time it took for him to make his way down the corridor, I could have gone down and sent the lift back up again.

"Thanks," he said when he finally reached me. At least he hadn't entirely misplaced his manners.

I pressed the button for the first floor, and the doors slid shut. Ethan stood beside me, arms crossed in front of his chest. Although he was now twenty, it still surprised me that he was almost as tall as me.

"What happened to your eye?" I asked, not wanting to let on that my best friend Olivia had already told me about his wild night on the Asterdams' boat.

Ethan refused to look at me, staring instead at the metal door in front of him, but he couldn't hide the bruise standing out deep purple against his pale skin. "Nothing."

"It doesn't look like nothing to me."

"It was an accident."

"An accident involving you and a door, or you and a fist?"

"What do you care?" Ethan asked dismissively, and I couldn't blame him. We'd never been particularly close. Ethan had been a toddler when our parents had sent me to boarding school in Crawley. Unlike Logan, who had followed shortly after, Ethan remained at home, spending the next few years with a private tutor, receiving more personalised support. We'd only seen each other sporadically at the weekends. By the time our parents had finally let him go to Crawley, I'd already started at Oxford. We'd been living under the same roof again for just over a year now, but thanks to my new position at The Darlington, I hadn't had much time to get to know this new, more adult version of Ethan. He was rarely at home, spending most of his time with his friends or at clubs. And when he was at the hotel, he was usually throwing parties here.

To my surprise, Ethan said, "It was Charles's fist."

"Charles Eddington?"

He nodded.

"I thought you were friends."

"He gets aggressive when he drinks." He shrugged and pulled something that looked suspiciously like a joint from his hoodie pocket. He looked at it with wonder, as if he'd forgotten he had it.

"Sounds like he should drink less. What are you doing here, anyway?" I asked. "Shouldn't you be at a lecture?"

Ethan slipped the joint back into his pocket. "I wasn't in the mood for uni."

"Do Mum and Dad know you're skiving?"

He finally raised his head and looked at me. In that moment, he looked so much like our father that my blood ran cold. It wasn't just his dark hair, his high cheekbones, and the blue eyes we both had—it was the icy detachment in his expression. "As if they'd care. Dad's life is going to shit because he couldn't keep his dick in his pants. And Mum is probably on her third glass of merlot in some corner of the hotel, reading erotica and dreaming of getting a divorce."

"Ethan," I warned.

"Henry," he imitated me as he had done when we were kids, only without the trace of lightheartedness in his voice. In that moment, the lift doors opened. Ethan made to dash out as if he couldn't get away from me fast enough, but first, he turned to me: "Relax. And enjoy your luxurious life while you still can. I've read the indictment against Dad, and it doesn't matter what his lawyers say. We're fucked."

6

Please don't feed the pelicans!

Sign for tourists in St. James's Park

Kate

"We're certainly not going to pay you for a stolen phone that may or may not belong to Henry Darlington," said the woman from *INsider*, her voice crackling loudly from the broken speaker of my ancient phone as it cut in and out. "Deliver it . . . directly to . . . and then . . . talk again, but don't waste . . . time. Goodbye."

The woman hung up without giving me a chance to say another word. I removed the prepaid phone from my ear, and a piece of the shattered case fell to the floor. Fuck it, it belonged in the bin anyway. That had probably been its last call.

Henry Darlington's gleaming, brand-new iPhone pinged. Something it seemed to be doing every three minutes. This time, it was a message from *Richard Darlington*. Who the hell saved their dad's contact with his first and last name? But what did I know? I didn't have a dad, only a faceless progenitor.

I put my own shabby phone aside and pressed the button on the side of the fancy smartphone. The lock screen lit up and told me that—surprise, surprise—facial recognition wasn't working. The background image was an abstract pattern, giving zero hint of a personality. Perhaps it was even a default background. I was asked to enter a code, but I didn't bother trying my luck. I wondered if Henry Darlington had noticed yet that his phone was missing. Without all the notifications that kept coming in, his life must be pleasantly quiet right now. He may even have been grateful for the theft.

The display had just lit up with another message when suddenly a telltale prickling at the back of my neck put me on my guard.

I raised my eyes—and froze.

Henry Darlington.

He was back.

And he was heading straight for me.

7

Henry Darlington's Epic Battle: Can He Save The Darlington, or Will the Scandal Surrounding His Father Destroy Everything?

INsider headline

Henry

It was the young woman from the kiosk.

I had only glanced back at her briefly while walking away, but I recognised her instantly. A face like hers was hard to forget. She was incredibly pretty in a raw, natural way. She wore no makeup, but her eyes were framed by thick lashes. Her dark-brown, almost-black chin-length hair was cut wonkily, but the haircut didn't diminish her beauty. She'd probably still be stunning if she were bald. She wore a tatty leather jacket, and the only jewellery I could see were several silver rings and studs in her ears.

Her shoulders tensed as soon as our eyes met, and her legs twitched as if she wanted to stand. She was sitting on the grass, hidden between several bushes that had already started losing their leaves. Next to her lay a rucksack, and behind her was a heap of unidentifiable rubbish, probably left behind by teens. It was a strange place for her to decide to sit.

The wet grass made squelching sounds as I approached her to ask about my phone. The location app wasn't that precise, and I'd already been searching the area for fifteen minutes. I couldn't rule out that someone had taken it in the last few minutes, although the park was surprisingly empty given the time. A handful of people wandered around the lake, but the forecast of rain seemed to have scared most of them off.

"Excuse me . . ." I started but stopped when I saw that the woman was holding my iPhone. Relief replaced my confusion. "I was about to ask you about my phone, but I see you've already found it."

I stopped in front of the woman, and she tilted her head back to look at me. I smiled at her gratefully, but she didn't smile back or give me my phone. Instead, she shoved it into the pocket of her tattered jacket. "I'm sorry," she said. Her voice was soft. "I don't know what you're talking about."

Her answer rekindled my confusion. "My phone. You have it."

"No, I don't. It's mine."

I faltered. It was possible that she had the same model, of course, but given the tatty rucksack and her threadbare jacket, it didn't look like she could afford it. Besides, it was the same colour and didn't have a case, like mine, which seemed like too big a coincidence. I had just opened my mouth to say so when I registered that what I'd taken for a pile of rubbish behind her was actually blankets. Why hadn't I noticed it before? She wasn't merely spending an afternoon off in the park. She was homeless, and she lived here. And she hadn't found my phone. She'd stolen it. She'd somehow managed to take it without me noticing. If I weren't so furious, I'd be impressed.

My smile disappeared. "Give me my phone back."

The woman remained silent and examined me, her gaze sliding from my polished shoes made of imitation leather and my tailored coat up to my face, where her eyes lingered for a moment. And then she looked away indifferently. "Like I said, it's not . . ."

"You stole it," I interrupted.

"I didn't!"

My jaw tensed. "Yes, you did."

She jutted out her chin petulantly. "I didn't."

"It's my phone. Just give it back," I demanded. But she didn't move. I sighed, irritated, and massaged my temples. The conversation was going round in circles, and I'd already lost too much of my precious time to drag the situation out any longer. I took a deep breath. "What do you want?"

"I want you to leave me alone." Her voice was firm as she fixed me with an astonishingly piercing gaze. The brown of her irises was so dark that the pupils almost got lost in them. I felt an unexpected tugging in my stomach. It didn't feel like anger at all. Strange.

"I mean for the phone. What do you want for it?" I couldn't believe that I was offering her money for something that was already mine. She was probably planning to sell it to some shady dealer who'd restore it to factory settings and then sell it on, but the risk of someone getting hold of my data and messages was too great.

The woman looked at me thoughtfully. Up close, she was even prettier. Freckles dotted the bridge of her nose, and she had the kind of voluminous lips that many women I knew suffered painful procedures for. But beautiful or not, she was still a thief.

"Let's say I take you up on your offer and I give you this phone," she said, slapping the pocket of her leather jacket. "Would you call the police if it turns out to be yours after all? Hypothetically speaking."

My mouth twitched, despite the situation not being funny at all. The audacity of her question was a little, though. "No. No police. We'll settle it between us. So, what do you want?"

"Money."

A gust of wind swept over us, whirling up leaves. "How much?"

"Four thousand pounds," she said without hesitating. "And you'll take me out to a restaurant of my choice."

I raised my eyebrows. "Four thousand pounds? Are you out of your mind? I can buy myself two new phones for that amount and still have some to spare."

She shrugged. "That's my price."

"For *my* phone," I snarled.

"You don't know that."

My eyes drifted from her to the mound of blankets behind her. I couldn't help but wonder what her life must have been like so far for her to end up here. She had to be the same age as Ethan. I suppressed my rage. I wasn't really angry at this woman. I was stressed and irritated after the meeting with my dad.

"Agreed," I heard myself say, because I didn't want to come across as an arrogant snob. Besides, she clearly hadn't stolen from me out of malice, but because she evidently had nothing but a heap of tatty blankets. Four thousand pounds meant nothing to me. I had more than enough money.

Her eyes widened. "Really?"

"Yes. But you have to come with me to the cashpoint."

"The wealthy hotel heir doesn't carry four thousand pounds around with him in cash? Disappointing," she teased.

So she knew who I was. I wasn't sure how I felt about that, but I shouldn't have been surprised. Since the first allegations against my father, my family had constantly been in the media. The only face that didn't keep showing up in the tabloids was Logan's, and that was because he avoided being in the public eye at all costs.

"Also, you owe me a meal."

I looked at her, taken aback. I'd assumed it was a joke. I didn't have time for a late lunch with some stranger. Even if she was a very pretty stranger. "Is that really necessary?"

"Yes."

"Can't you buy your own food with the money?"

"No."

She got up and brushed off her trousers before stooping to pick up her rucksack. It had been patched up so much that it looked like it might fall apart at any moment. She shouldered it carelessly and adjusted her leather jacket. I hadn't noticed when she was sitting, but she was small, tiny, and barely reached my shoulders. It was incredible that I was letting this pip-squeak fleece me out of four thousand pounds.

"One more thing," she said suddenly.

My gaze jerked from the pocket that held my phone to her face. "What now? You want me to buy you a designer handbag? Take you for a spin in the Bentley? Let you fly in my private jet?"

"No."

"What, then?"

She took a step towards me. Her pleasant, slightly earthy smell surprised me. She looked up at me and smiled. Two dimples appeared in her cheeks, which frustratingly made her even more adorable. My heart faltered. She held out her hand to me as if nothing had happened. As if she hadn't just stolen from and blackmailed me. "I'm Kate."

For a moment, I was too stunned to shake her hand, but then her fingers clasped mine. They were warm and a little rough, but most of all, they were delicate. "I'm Henry, but you already know that."

Her smile broadened. "It's nice to meet you, Henry. Do you like burgers?"

8

According to the latest sources, the Darlington family's fortune is estimated at 1.7 billion pounds.

Excerpt from an article in *Forbes UK*

Kate

When you live on the streets and pick pockets, every day is a surprise. No day is the same as the last, and no one week is like another. Something unexpected could always happen. But when I'd gone out that morning to find the money for Randell, I couldn't have imagined I'd end up at a McDonald's with Henry Darlington. I knew there were better places to eat in London, but I loved McDonald's. My mum and I had hardly ever been able to afford to eat out, but whenever we'd had a little cash to spare, it was where we would end up. The food was mediocre, but the memories I associated with the place made it a five-star restaurant in my eyes.

I approached the digital order kiosk. "Do you want anything?"

"No, thanks," Henry replied, looking around. In his tailored three-piece suit and tie, he looked completely out of place among the cheap decor.

Henry paid for my order with a credit card he pulled from the inside pocket of his jacket. The kiosk churned out the receipt with an order number, and we joined the other diners waiting for their food. The smell of fried meat made my stomach rumble in anticipation.

I looked up at Henry to see if he'd heard, but he wasn't looking at me. He was tensely watching the order numbers on the digital display and looked like he couldn't wait to leave. Perhaps it would have been wiser to take his money and run. He had promised not to call the police, but what if he changed his mind? I wasn't keen to get arrested, but my desire for company was greater than my fear of going to jail.

Living alone on the streets could be pretty lonely, even though there were people everywhere. And I was curious too. I'd never met anyone like Henry. Someone who was so rich that money didn't matter. I couldn't imagine it.

"Do you really have a private jet?"

When he turned from the orders board to look at me, I saw that he had the bluest eyes of anyone I'd ever met. They'd often looked out at me from screens and magazines in the last few months, but the pixels disguised how bright and colourful they really were.

"Yes. It belongs to my family."

"And you can fly in it whenever you want?"

He nodded.

"Wow," I murmured. "It must be so freeing to go wherever you want, whenever you want."

"Yes." His mouth twisted into a smile, but it seemed forced, as if the corners of his lips had been weighed down. I couldn't tell if his sombre mood was because of my presence or the glances of other diners who had, unsurprisingly, recognised him. At a table just a few steps away, a woman was pointing him out to her companion.

"Do you fly a lot?" I asked to distract him.

"No, not anymore. I used to go on holiday with my friends a lot, but I don't have time for that anymore."

"What kinds of places did you jet off to?"

The number on the display changed, and a man standing behind me jostled me as he rushed to collect his food. I stumbled forward into Henry.

"Sorry."

"It's OK," he said.

He didn't let on if I smelled bad. It had been a few days since my last shower, which I now regretted. For not only was Henry nice to me—nicer than he should have been—but he was also incredibly good-looking. He had outrageously long eyelashes, black hair that curled around his ears, and neatly trimmed stubble that seemed at odds with his otherwise polished appearance. I, on the other hand, probably looked like a scruffy stray dog.

Henry cleared his throat. "Everywhere. Monaco. New York. Sardinia. Paris."

"Wow," I murmured again. "I've never been outside of England. Or London, even. Although . . . that's not exactly true. I went to Watford once, but only because I fell asleep on the train. It was late, and super annoying to get back."

"You've never left London?" Henry asked with surprise. I shook my head, and he shrugged. "You haven't missed anything. I've been to a lot of cities, and honestly? None of them holds a candle to London."

"You're just saying that so I don't feel like an uncultured loser."

"No, I'm saying it because it's the truth. London is the best city."

"Prove it."

"How?"

I pursed my lips. "Tell me what you like about it."

He hesitated. "*Everything* won't cut it with you, will it?"

"No. I want details."

It was a strange question, but Henry seemed to give it serious thought. "I love the parks, and that the Thames is right on my doorstep. I like all the restaurants where I can eat food from around the world even when I'm stuck here. But the best thing about the city is how many different kinds of people and possibilities there are. There's nothing here that you can't do."

I smiled. His answer was so heartfelt, even if it wasn't true. There was a lot you couldn't do in this city if you didn't have the money for it. But that was my problem, not his.

Before I could answer, my order number showed up on the display. I'd bought so much food that Henry had to help me carry it to a free table by the window. As soon as we were sitting, I hastily unwrapped the first of five burgers and took a big bite.

"Oh my god," I groaned appreciatively. It was by far the best thing I'd eaten in a long time, even if it was just because I was famished. I took a second bite before I'd even swallowed the first and gave another rapturous sigh.

"It sounds like you're really enjoying that."

I froze. I was so fixated on my food that I'd managed to forget Henry for a brief moment. He watched me, bemused, and my cheeks flushed. Where he came from, people probably ate burgers with knives and forks and didn't hoover them down.

"Sorry," I mumbled, cheeks bulging.

"You don't have to apologise."

I dabbed at my mouth with a napkin and told myself to eat a little slower. I'd also be doing my stomach a favour. "Sure you don't want any?"

Henry leaned back in his chair and opened the top button of his jacket in one fluid motion. "Thank you, but I don't eat meat."

"I can't afford to not eat something. Apart from peanuts. I'm allergic to them." I tore open several ketchup sachets and squeezed their contents into the lid of my burger box. "Are you allergic to anything?"

"Wasps."

"Have you been stung before?"

Henry looked at me appraisingly. "You're pretty nosy."

"I'm just making small talk," I answered with a shrug.

"Yes, I was stung once when I was a kid."

"Was it bad?"

"Pretty bad. Shelley had to take me to hospital."

"Is Shelley your mum?" I asked. If his dad's contact was saved in his phone with his full name, it was possible he called his mum by her first name.

"No, she was my nanny."

I drowned a chip in a lake of ketchup. "Was?"

Henry's mouth twitched. "Yes. I'd say being twenty-six makes me a little too old for a babysitter, don't you think?"

"Oh. Of course. I just thought . . ." I fell silent and felt myself blush for the second time in several minutes. "Never mind. Forget what I said."

"Don't worry, I already have. Shelley now lives with her husband near Bristol, and . . ." Henry broke off when a group of women sat down at the table next to us—all of them looking at us. Strictly speaking, they were looking at Henry. I slid down lower in my chair, but Henry didn't move. If anything, he straightened his shoulders and raised his chin a little, as though projecting strength was his way of facing uncertainty.

"Doesn't it bother you when people stare at you like that?" I asked quietly.

"No. What bothers me is the reason why they stare."

"You mean your dad?"

He grimaced slightly. "So you know about that."

"Of course. I live on the streets, not on the moon." I unwrapped my second burger and lifted the top bun to put several chips on it. "In fact, I ended up at the protest outside your hotel earlier in the week. Unintentionally, though."

Henry looked suspicious. "How do you end up at a protest unintentionally?"

I hesitated, weighing up whether or not to tell him the truth. I decided that he'd sussed me out by now anyway. Besides, we'd probably never see each other again after today. Who cared what he thought about me. "I stole a wallet, and the guy noticed. I ended up caught in the protest when I was running away from him, so I just joined it until the coast was clear."

"How long have you been doing that?" Henry asked, ignoring the women at the next table and fixing his attention fully on me.

"I don't really know. It snowballed over the years. It started with shoplifting just every once in a while. Sanitary products my mum and I couldn't afford. But after getting caught two or three times, I switched to pickpocketing. I don't like doing it, but I don't have any other choice."

"Why don't you find a job?"

"Oh my god! Of course! What an excellent idea. Why didn't I think of it sooner?" I replied with exaggerated enthusiasm, something in my chest tightening. Henry had no way of knowing that I constantly got asked things like that. People acted as though being homeless was a fate I'd chosen freely, one I could change with enough motivation and determination.

Henry grimaced apologetically. "Sorry, I didn't mean to . . ."

"It's OK," I interrupted. It wasn't his fault, after all, that he'd been born with a silver spoon in his mouth. "I don't expect someone like you to understand. Believe me, I want a job, and I'd work hard, but there aren't many employers queueing up to employ a homeless high school dropout." I kept my explanation simple, although that wasn't the full story. I didn't have the tools or resources to even fill out a job application, and I couldn't do anything without a permanent address, which I would need to get both a contract and a new bank account, now that my old one had been blocked. It was a vicious circle, hard to escape. It wasn't an excuse; it was a fact.

Henry cleared his throat. "You dropped out of school?"

I nodded. "I bet you went to uni."

"Yes. Oxford."

"Where else? And I'm guessing you did well." I took a sip of my cola and silently slid my cup towards Henry. To my surprise, he took it and drank from the same straw. I wasn't contagious, but sometimes people treated me as though a homeless person could single-handedly bring back the plague.

"Yes. If I'm honest, I was top of my class."

"Nerd."

"That's just what my brother Logan always called me, even though his grade average in school was only slightly lower than mine. Why did you drop out?"

Nervously, I started folding the paper wrapper my straw had come in. "I had to make money. My mum and I weren't doing so well financially, and I wanted to help pay rent so we wouldn't lose our apartment. It didn't work, obviously."

"Is your mum homeless too?"

I tightened my lips into a joyless smile. "Not anymore. She lives in an underground two-square-metre apartment."

"What?" Henry asked, confused, and then it dawned on him. "Oh, shit. I'm sorry."

I feigned indifference and shrugged. I didn't like to talk about my mum, even though she was always on my mind. A part of me wished I could take back my macabre comment, because today was a good day, and I didn't want to ruin the mood.

Henry touched his tie as if he wanted to loosen the knot. But when he noticed what he was doing, he dropped his hand. He had nice hands. I didn't know if other people paid as much attention to hands as I did, but as a pickpocket, my own were my most important tool. Henry had long, elegant fingers with perfectly filed nails. They were marred only by a scratch on his left thumb.

"How did you get that scratch?" I asked, pointing at it.

Henry turned his hand. "Oh, it's from bouldering. I slipped."

"You boulder?" There had been a bouldering society at my school, but I couldn't afford the gym membership, so I had joined the athletics team for free instead.

"Yes, for a few years now. You sound surprised."

"I thought people like you played polo or golf."

He raised his eyebrows. "People like me?"

"Well, rich people."

Henry snorted. "Not all rich people have the same hobbies."

"But most of them, right?"

"Yeah," he admitted reluctantly. "But I'm not like most of them."

I laughed, although I got the sense that he might be telling the truth. Sure, he was wearing a smart suit and an outrageously expensive watch, but the longer we sat there, the more I suspected it was all for show—another Henry was lurking beneath the layers of fancy fabric.

"Of course not. You're a very unique snowflake."

"I am, and it's high time someone acknowledged it," he grinned.

"Don't worry. I see you, Snowflake," I hammed it up, sliding my hand across the table and placing it on his in feigned sympathy.

I'd intended it as a joke, a casual gesture, but my smile faded when my fingers touched his. An electrifying tingle shot up my arm to my chest, and my heart raced. Taken aback, I looked up at Henry's handsome face. He was watching me with an odd expression that I couldn't quite read, which sent the tingle in my chest lower down my body. It threw me. I hadn't felt anything like it in years—perhaps ever. I was under no illusion that someone like Henry could be attracted to me. I looked all right, aside from the tattered clothes and wonky haircut. But people like him cared about those things. And I was pretty sure I'd read on the cover of some gossip magazine that he was dating the daughter of a famous fashion designer.

Another vibration in my jacket pocket ended the moment. Henry's phone had been buzzing nonstop over the last few minutes, but so far I'd ignored it. I let go of his hand and pulled out his phone. Olivia Asterdam had messaged him.

"I don't know how you stand it. Getting constant notifications would really stress me out," I said, sliding the phone across the table to him.

He looked from me to the phone. "You're giving it back?"

"It keeps vibrating," I said, and as if it had heard me, the phone lit up again. "It's annoying. And I trust you to give me the money anyway."

Slowly, almost as if he wanted to give me time to change my mind, he reached for his iPhone. "I could just get up and leave now. You know that, right?"

"Yes, but you won't."

He raised his eyebrows. "How do you know?"

I pushed a chip into my mouth. Chewed. Swallowed. Smiled. "Because you, Henry Darlington, are an honest person. Far more honest than I am."

He looked even more surprised. "You can't know that. You barely know me."

"Perhaps not, but I have a gut feeling."

"A gut feeling," he repeated, as if he'd never heard the phrase before.

"Yes. Gut feelings shouldn't be ignored. If you're a woman living alone on the streets, you really have to watch who you trust."

"And you trust me?"

"Yes."

"Given the allegations against my dad, most people would probably think trusting me is a mistake." His tone was matter-of-fact, but I could detect a hint of pleasure in his voice.

"Well, I'm not most people. And you're not your dad."

Henry didn't reply but fixed me with a blank stare. His gaze was sharp and probing, as though he were no longer merely looking at me but peering deep into my soul. I didn't like it. As good as I was at reading other people, I hated being read in return. Only someone who knew the real me could truly hurt me, and my life was dangerous enough without me putting my feelings on the line.

"I think I'll save the rest for later," I heard myself say, feeling an urge to flee. I began stuffing the leftovers into one of the paper bags. "There's a cashpoint right around the corner. And then you'll be rid of me."

Henry hesitated. "OK."

Was I imagining it, or did he sound disappointed? No, it couldn't be. My imagination was running away with me.

We left the restaurant without a word and walked to the cashpoint. I stepped back as Henry withdrew the money. Moments later, he was beside me, brandishing a gigantic wad of bills.

"Here," he said, holding it out to me.

His voice was entirely devoid of emotion, as if four thousand pounds meant nothing to him. Which it probably didn't. My heart, on the other hand, did somersaults at the sight of it. I'd never had so much money in my life, let alone held it in my hands. My fingers tingled as I reached for it, and I felt uneasy. Four. Thousand. Pounds. I could get Randell off my back for good. The thought briefly crossed my mind that Henry could have given me more money. He had enough of it, after all. But I didn't want to use him. More importantly, I never wanted to owe anyone anything ever again. Not Randell, not Henry. I just wanted to be free.

"Thank you," I said, which seemed inadequate. We both knew I hadn't earned the money, but it didn't stop Henry from smiling at me as though I had done him a favour. "I'm sorry I stole your phone. I'm not a bad person. I . . ."

"I know, Kate," he interrupted before I could pour my heart out to him. He reached into the inner pocket of his jacket, pulled out a little card, and gave it to me. A business card. It had the logo of The Darlington embossed on it in gold, and beneath it were Henry's name and contact details. "For emergencies. If you ever find yourself in trouble . . . Call me, or come to the hotel."

Stunned, I looked up at Henry when I realised what he was offering me: his help. But taking it was out of the question. I'd already taken more from him than I was entitled to.

I shook my head and held out the card to give back to him. "Thanks, but I'll be fine."

He didn't take it. "Keep it. Please."

"I don't need it."

"Then don't use it," he answered, and with that, he'd won.

With an annoyed sigh I hoped would conceal how much his gesture meant to me, I stuck the card into the pocket of my leather jacket. Even if I knew I wouldn't call the number printed in gold on my own accord. "Thank you. For the money, the food, and . . . the card," I said, swallowing hard. There was a lump in my throat that hadn't been there before, and I had no desire to analyse it. I took a step back. I'd got what I wanted, and there was no reason to stay any longer. But I didn't really want to leave. It was probably the odd tug in my stomach that prompted my next move: I saluted.

I saluted. At Henry. As if he were the King of England and I was a member of his royal guard. But what else was I supposed to do? Shake his hand? Give him a high five? Hug him?

"Have a nice life, Snowflake."

He smiled. "Thanks. You too, Kate. Look after yourself."

I liked how he said my name. He made it sound soft and familiar despite his deep voice. As if we'd known each other for much longer than an hour. It made it even harder to leave, but I had no choice.

"I will," I promised, turning away before the situation could become any more embarrassing.

I strode away, feeling Henry's eyes on me. I didn't turn back, afraid of what I might feel if I did. If I was being honest, I thought it was a shame I would probably never see Henry Darlington again.

THE BLACKROOM

Rich. Beautiful. Popular. The Darlingtons! But who are the people behind the family name—a name worth billions?

Richard Darlington—The Tyrant

Old money and shrewd investments have made Richard (62) a billionaire, but a shadow hangs over his success. The path to wealth for the head of the family hasn't always been entirely legitimate. His business practices are surrounded by ongoing controversies, including allegations of bribery, corporate espionage, and labour exploitation. Employees at the hotel where Richard lives with his wife report frequent mood swings, outbursts of anger, and gaslighting.

Amanda Darlington—The Trophy Wife

Richard's wife, Amanda (52), has stood by her husband for almost thirty-three years. The former catalogue model met the billionaire, ten years her senior, when she was eighteen. They married when she was just nineteen. She has no authority within the hotel, playing a purely symbolic role at Richard's side. She has not yet commented on the allegations made against her husband, but a divorce seems out of the question for Amanda. Did she already know about her husband's transgressions? Is she letting herself be blinded by all that money? Or is she just another of her husband's victims, trapped in a loveless marriage she can't escape?

Henry Darlington—The Heir

Henry (26) is the eldest son. After the initial allegations against his father earlier this year, he was appointed CEO of The Darlington. But other than the occasional headline about his love life, Henry has stayed out of the limelight in recent years. Now he has been tasked with salvaging The Darlington's reputation by playing up his spotless image. But how can he stand by a man who so recklessly destroys the lives of others with a clear conscience?

Logan Darlington—The Lost Son

Logan (24), the middle son, has been estranged from his parents for years. As a teenager, he was sent away to boarding school in France and distanced himself from the family upon his return. He now keeps to himself, comanaging The Meridian, a restaurant located in Covent Garden, alongside Maxton Prescott. Unsurprisingly, he has also not yet commented on the allegations against his father. He has refused to make a statement about his family for years. We ask ourselves, why?

Ethan Darlington—The Fuckboy

Ethan (20) is the youngest of the Darlington brothers. Expensive alcohol and loud parties are part and parcel of everyday life for him and his wealthy friends, and he leaves a trail of used condoms and broken hearts in his wake throughout London. Although he studies at Imperial College, it remains unclear whether he possesses the intellect or emotional maturity to fully grasp the accusations levelled against his father. The arrogant baby of the family considers himself invincible—but pride comes before a fall, as the saying goes.

9

London Rent Prices Shoot Through the Roof: New Record Highs Make Housing Unaffordable—Homelessness Rates Rise!

The Times headline

Kate

I'd promised myself I would never again set foot in the shabby housing area that had been my home for a year—yet here I was. This place held so many of my worst memories, most of which were associated with Randell. I'd lost count of how often I'd stood here, between the oak tree and Mrs. Smith's bungalow with its heart-shaped letter box, putting off walking the last steps to the front door so I could avoid Randell for just a few moments longer.

I'd never understood what had drawn Mum to him. She'd been a stunning and charming woman, despite her problems. Randell, on the other hand, was ugly inside and out. His face was puffy from alcohol, and his skin was sallow and blotchy. But it was his sexism, racism, and uncontrolled rage that made him a monster. I could count on my fingers the number of days he hadn't been drunk and raging. He'd always had a beer in his hand—or his belt, which he had used to beat respect and gratitude into me and my mum, after he'd taken us in and saved us from homelessness. His bouts of rage had mainly been targeted at my mum. In the weeks before her death, she had new bruises almost every day, and to avoid drawing attention to them, she had hardly left the bungalow.

A deep sorrow washed over me when I thought about how my mum's life had ended in the same way it had begun. She'd had a tough childhood, growing up with a violent father who had beaten her too. It was why I'd never met my grandparents. Her crappy childhood was probably also the reason she'd never truly found her footing in life. Fear and depression had caused her to lose one job after another, and in the end, I'd had to drop out of school to support her financially. It hadn't made a difference. We'd been evicted from our flat and had ended up at Randell's place. She'd fallen in love, both with him and with the bittersweet numbness she felt when they took drugs together.

I missed her. Watching Randell and the drugs destroy her had broken my heart. But I couldn't have saved her. I'd tried. I'd *really* tried. I'd talked to her again and again. I'd begged her to leave Randell and had hidden her drugs. I'd even flushed them down the toilet once, which got me a good beating from Randell. My ears rang for days after that, and the hearing in my right ear had never fully recovered. But none of it had helped. A few weeks later, my mum had died of an overdose.

I let out a heavy sigh. My heart was racing, and I wanted nothing more than to turn and leave. But I had to be brave one last time and face that arsehole so I could give him his money. Then it would be over, and I would never have to see him again. The thought gave me the courage to start moving. The branches of the oak tree bent in the wind of a coming storm, and the leaves rustled like pompoms cheering me on.

As I slowly made my way towards the dilapidated bungalow, I shoved my hand into the pocket of my leather jacket and toyed nervously with Henry's business card, which was already pretty tatty. The facade of the building was yellowing and its windows dirty—they probably hadn't been cleaned since I'd moved out almost a year ago. The fly screen was crooked in the window frame, and a bin bag buzzing with flies had been tossed right in front of the door, despite the bins being just a few steps away. Wrinkling my nose, I walked past the bag and knocked on the door. I desperately wanted to put this behind me.

"You can do this," I muttered.

I heard the tinny sounds of Randell's ancient television set, then footsteps. A moment later, he opened the door. He was wearing jeans, a T-shirt, and a Manchester United cap that my mum had given him for Christmas. My stomach tied itself in knots, and I suddenly wished I hadn't come alone. But who could I have brought with me? I *was* alone.

Randell leaned against the doorframe. "Kate. What brings you here?"

"My debt."

"So you've decided to work it off?" he asked. He eyed me up in a way that no man of his age should look at a woman of mine and gestured obscenely at his crotch.

"No. I have the money."

Randell frowned, puzzled, as if he hadn't reckoned on me getting together so much money in such a short time. "You have it?"

"Yes. Five hundred pounds, like you said." I let go of Henry's business card and took out the first of two bundles from my bag. I knew better than to give Randell all of it in one go. He took the bundle I held out and stuffed it into his trouser pocket. There was a loud bang behind him, as if a gust of wind had slammed shut a door.

I cleared my throat. "How much do I still owe you?"

"Three thousand five hundred pounds."

"Are you sure?" I asked. I needed to be certain before I put all my cards on the table. I didn't want Randell to come for me later demanding more, claiming there was interest or inventing some other flimsy pretence.

He nodded, irritated. "Yes. And not a penny less."

"If I give you the money, you'll leave me alone?"

"Of course. Do you really think I enjoy chasing after a brat like you?"

"I'm glad to hear it." After a final hesitation, I reached into my other jacket pocket and pulled out the rest of the money. Randell's eyes widened when I held out the notes. "Three thousand five hundred pounds, and not a penny less. Like you said."

He grabbed the money from me and counted it with his dirty fingers. Once. Twice. Three times. His self-satisfied grin grew wider each time. My heart bled as I watched. He didn't deserve it. I could have rented myself a little room for the winter with the money, and then I wouldn't have to be outside in the cold. But I knew Randell wouldn't ever leave me alone unless I paid him, and it was worth it for that alone.

After he'd counted the notes a fourth time, he looked at me with a gratified glint in his eyes. "How did you get the money?"

I shrugged my shoulders. "Does it matter?"

"It will if the police turn up here."

"It's legit." As legit as it could be when blackmail was involved. But even if Henry decided to send the police after me, which I doubted, it would be pretty much impossible to trace the money back to Randell. Unless I ratted him out, which I wasn't planning on doing. I was happy never to have to think his name again, let alone speak it.

"If you're lying . . ."

"I don't lie," I interrupted. "It's my money."

He hesitated. "Did you spread your legs for it?"

I was about to deny it, but why should I? I didn't care what a loser like Randell thought about me. If he wanted to believe I'd sold my body for the money, then so be it. I pressed my lips together and let my silence speak for me.

"I always knew you were a dirty whore," he sneered, entertained. "I kept telling your mum too, but she didn't want to hear it. She always thought you were such an innocent angel."

My hands instinctively clenched into fists. I hated this guy, and I hated the idea of him trying to turn my mum against me. If he hadn't thrown me out without warning after her death, I wouldn't have had to do many of the things I'd done.

"So are we even now?" I asked.

I didn't want to talk to Randell any longer.

I just wanted to leave.

He didn't move or speak for a moment, and my heart stopped out of fear that he would find some ridiculous excuse to keep me in his debt. But then he nodded. "Yes. Now get lost."

I couldn't think of anything I wanted to do more.

10

Dream Couple Alert! Henry Darlington and Olivia Asterdam Spotted Kissing in Front of The Darlington After a Hot Night of Passion!

Old *INsider* headline

Henry

Perhaps the unrelenting stress, countless overtime hours, and many sleepless nights were slowly driving me nuts. Either that, or Ethan was a genius. I'd asked my dad's lawyers to give me the indictment so I could see for myself if we were, to quote Ethan, *fucked*, but I didn't understand any of it. The lengthy sentences with their technical terms and references to legal paragraphs didn't offer a shred of enlightenment. I gathered that it wasn't good, but did I really know what any of it meant? Nope.

Perhaps I could ask Ethan to explain the indictment, if he ever sobered up. As far as I knew, he'd been away all weekend, getting hammered with his friends. I liked to pretend I was judging him for it, but truthfully, I was envious. I longed to possess his carefree recklessness, a feeling I no longer even remembered. But I couldn't afford a lifestyle like his anymore. Yesterday I'd stayed at the office past midnight trying to come up with a concept for the Pearl Gala.

It had to be perfect. The hotel was under scrutiny, and the papers were watching our every move for the smallest thing to turn into their next scathing headline.

I leaned back in my chair with a sigh and realised how dark it had grown in my office. A glance at the clock told me it was just after 2 p.m. I switched on my desk lamp and turned my back on the city. Dark clouds hung over the London skyline. A storm was brewing. It would clearly be a big one. The trees bowed in the wind, which whipped up surprisingly large waves across the surface of the Thames. The London Eye had closed for business, even though it was built to withstand any weather. Seeing it standing still in the daytime gave me an uneasy feeling.

My thoughts wandered—unsurprisingly, since they often had lately—to Kate. Not a day had gone by in the past week that I hadn't thought about her. About her frankness, her situation, and the things she had to do to survive. But above all—and this was probably the worst thing—I couldn't stop thinking about her smile. About the little dimples in her cheeks and the dainty freckles on her nose. I wondered if they were visible all year round or if they faded in the winter. Right now, I was wondering how she would fare in this storm and whether she had shelter for the night. I hoped so.

Sighing, I turned back to my desk and reprimanded myself for not concentrating on my work. Kate would get by. She'd been living on the streets for a while. She didn't need someone looking after her. With this mantra in my head, I opened September's financial report, which Rakesh had sent me an hour ago. But the moment I began to read, my phone rang.

It was Olivia. I accepted the call, and her face appeared on the screen. Behind her was the bathroom of her new flat in

Mayfair—she'd moved in a few weeks ago. She was in the process of applying her makeup, her blond hair twisted up in curlers.

"Tell me," she said without a hello, propping up her phone.

I raised an eyebrow. "What's to tell?"

"Don't pretend you don't know what I'm talking about."

"No need to pretend. I really don't know."

She groaned as if she were annoyed at me and dabbed some cream under her eyes. There was constant speculation about what cosmetic procedures Olivia Asterdam, heiress to the Asterdam fashion empire, had undergone to achieve her flawless appearance. But Olivia was a natural beauty. I knew because I had watched her grow up. Sure, she invested more time and money than most people on her appearance and had some compulsions when it came to her diet and exercise. Then again, we all had compulsions in our circles. We called them routines, habits, or traditions, but in the end, it all boiled down to the same thing.

"I'm your best friend, Henry," she finally said. "Correction: I'm your *only* friend. Why didn't you tell me? I had to find out from my brother sending me a link to the *INsider*."

I still wasn't following. "I don't know what you're talking about."

She stopped moving. "Hold on. I'm confused."

"That makes two of us."

"So you haven't seen it?"

"Seen what?"

"Check the *INsider*."

I rolled my eyes. The *INsider* was a tabloid that financed itself by printing lies and rumours. If there was anyone I disliked as strongly as my dad right now, it was William Hunt: an editor at the *INsider* who had made it his mission to terrorise my family with lies about us. Just three months ago, he'd insinuated that Ethan had gotten a woman pregnant, just because he'd been photographed on the street walking next to a pregnant stranger. Olivia and I also regularly made it into the *INsider* gossip column together, because William Hunt loved nothing more than speculating about our alleged relationship.

Olivia and I had known each other since childhood and had been friends right from the start. We'd admittedly gone on a few dates three years ago—it had seemed like the natural progression of our friendship, and uniting the Asterdams and the Darlingtons would have been a strategically clever move. But it hadn't felt right. I was a businessman through and through. I loved negotiating contracts and closing deals. But if there was one thing I felt should be more than a profitable business deal, it was love.

Luckily Olivia had been on the same page, and we concluded unanimously that we were better as friends. Unfortunately, the media had continued to write about our "relationship" ever since, much to our mutual aggravation. So I anticipated yet another fabricated relationship drama as I opened the website on my laptop. What I most definitely didn't anticipate was a photo of Kate and me on the homepage.

"What the hell?" I muttered.

The photo showed the strangely electrifying moment when Kate had placed her hand on mine. The camera had caught the second before her smile faded. There was a bright gleam in her dark eyes, and although my face was barely recognisable from this angle, there was no mistaking that I was smiling too—just moments after she'd given me that ridiculous nickname. We looked intimate and close, enough so that the headline didn't come as much of a surprise:

Is Henry Cheating on Olivia?
Who Is the Mysterious Woman He's Been Spotted With?

I opened the article uneasily. It consisted mainly of eyewitness reports of how close Kate and I had seemed. People claimed that we were obviously on a date and had left the restaurant holding hands. Hunt accused me in the article of cheating on Olivia, and the last paragraph was dedicated to speculations on who Kate was, indicating that he'd failed to unmask her true identity.

The article sparked two contradictory feelings. I was furious at William Hunt, who had nothing better to do than present these lies to the world, and annoyed with myself for not being more careful. At the same time, though, I felt a strange heat flood my stomach as I examined Kate in the photos.

"Fuck," I mumbled.

"Is that all you have to say? Who is she?"

I looked from the laptop to my phone. Olivia had been applying her eyeliner as I'd been reading, but now she was looking at me expectantly. "Just a friend."

"A friend," she repeated sceptically and gave me a look that warned me not to lie. She knew me all too well—and she didn't know Kate at all. It was enough to rouse her suspicion. Wealthy people liked to keep to their circles. Everyone knew everyone else, and if an unfamiliar face came along, it often meant scandal.

I sighed. "Her name is Kate."

"Uh-huh."

"And we met last week."

"Ohhh. Where?"

"St. James's Park."

"And how did you end up at McDonald's?"

I hesitated. There was no good explanation. For one, Olivia knew how much I hated that kind of fast-food chain. Not because they were beneath me, but because of how appallingly they treated animals. "I'll tell you, but you have to promise not to tell anyone else. Not even your brother. He'll just tell Ethan, and then everyone will know."

"I promise," Olivia said, so I told her the whole story. How Kate had stolen from me, blackmailed me, and more or less forced me to take her to lunch. Olivia listened to me with curiosity, but I couldn't figure out what she was thinking. She seemed surprised, disappointed, and amused all at once.

"Did you really give her the money?"

I nodded. "Yes."

"She stole from you," Olivia stated the obvious. She'd finished her makeup and was in the process of taking out her curlers. Her hair fell in gold waves over her shoulders.

"Didn't you hear the bit where I said that she's homeless?" I asked, leaning back in my chair. "Kate has nothing. Just a few dirty blankets and an old leather jacket. We've had champagne that cost more than four thousand pounds a bottle."

"OK, OK. I can get behind that. But it doesn't explain the photo."

I stopped short. "It doesn't?"

"No. You look totally relaxed. Almost happy. I haven't seen you look like that in . . . no idea. Months, if I think about it. Kate must be special if she got you to lose that brooding frown."

I hastily smoothed out my expression. "I don't have a brooding frown."

"You really do. It's already given you wrinkles."

I rubbed my forehead. "I don't have wrinkles."

Olivia exhaled heavily. "Fine, you don't. But you will, if you keep going around looking at everyone—Kate aside—like that. Maybe you should see each other more often, given she has the same effect as an antiwrinkle cream."

I didn't know how to respond.

Olivia took her phone from the bathroom shelf and went into the kitchen. "When are you seeing each other again?"

"We're not," I replied, turning towards my window. The sky had grown even darker and the wind stronger. "Like I said, I only went to lunch with her because she asked me to."

It was Olivia's turn to frown. "But you like her."

"What makes you say that?"

Olivia laughed. "Henry, we've been talking about this woman for fifteen minutes. When I tried to set you up with my friend Sandy a few weeks ago, you got up mid-conversation to make yourself a cup of tea."

"Maybe, but I don't have time for something like this," I said, avoiding the point and deciding it was for the best that I didn't tell Olivia how often I'd thought about Kate since we'd met. I told myself it was because of my worries about her living situation, but if I was honest, my thoughts about her were unrelated to that.

Olivia tutted. "You don't have time for anything anymore."

"It's true. I have to organise the Pearl Gala."

"I thought it was cancelled?"

"Not anymore," I replied, and told her about my dad's decision to hold the gala after all at such short notice. Olivia ranted about his erratic behaviour and cursed him for putting even more work on my plate. But I was only half listening. The article was still open on my laptop. I studied Kate's delicate features, her warm gaze, and her adorable smile, which I hadn't been able to get out of my head.

But it didn't matter how often I thought about her or how much I had enjoyed talking to her. Even if I found time to see her again between all the crisis reports, bad news, and organisational chaos, it wouldn't be anything more than a one-night stand. My life was already complicated enough without the scandal that would inevitably follow if I got involved with someone like Kate.

11

> Henry Darlington took his date to McDonald's? Perhaps the hotel really is doomed. Good! #BoycottTheDarlington

Online comment by ShyAndroid

Henry

Lightning flashes lit up London's skyline in rapid succession. The glare turned night to day, despite the dense apocalyptic clouds obscuring the sky. Rain dashed against the windows of my penthouse apartment, and every time a gust of wind hit the panes, I felt tremors beneath my feet. A loud rumble of thunder came from the distance. The storm was about to get even wilder.

It was just after 11 p.m., and usually at this time of night, I could watch from my sofa as people scuttled around below, on the hunt for entertainment. But today the streets were deserted. I was sipping a whisky when another flash lit up my dark living room. I'd already tried going to bed, but sleep had eluded me. It wasn't the storm that kept me awake—it was my restless thoughts, as usual. I'd spent an hour on the treadmill, but I was still filled with a nervous energy.

My thoughts wandered again to the *INsider* article. I'd stared at it for a long time, not because of the headline, but because of the photos of Kate. She had stirred something inside me, not just because she was incredibly pretty, but because she was also funny, entertaining, and refreshingly honest. I kept replaying our conversation, trying to figure out if I'd been a jerk. I knew I could be pretty standoffish. Sheer abundance in my social circle often led to boredom, which resulted in youthful hijinks. As we got older, it fuelled gossip, so we were overly cautious about the things we said. I was worried I'd been distant with Kate out of habit, even though our meeting had been one of the highlights of my last few weeks. In spite of the fact that she had cheated me out of money.

I supposed this was why I couldn't stop worrying about her—there was no way she could sleep in the park in weather like this. The radio had advised people to stay away from open spaces and avoid sheltering under trees due to the risk of lightning strikes and falling branches. A chill ran down my spine at the thought of Kate huddling, drenched and freezing, under her pile of blankets in St. James's Park, the world ending around her.

I shook my head to dispel the image of her getting struck by a tree. She was fine. She had probably used my money on a hotel room or an Airbnb, and she had my business card for emergencies. Still, I was consumed by worry and absolutely certain that I wouldn't sleep a wink until I knew Kate was safe. If I woke up tomorrow to the news that a homeless woman had been killed in the storm, I'd never forgive myself.

I grabbed my phone from next to me on the sofa and called reception. A few seconds later, Philippa, the unlucky employee assigned to night duty, answered. "Good evening, Mr. Darlington. How can I help you?"

"Is the chauffeur service still available?" I felt sober despite the whisky, but I didn't want to risk anything, especially in this weather.

"Mr. Hammond is still here."

"Tell him that I'll be down in a moment," I said, making my way to my bedroom to get dressed. Since I'd already been in bed, I was wearing only the boxers I'd quickly pulled on when I got up. I normally slept naked—another small act of rebellion against a silk-pyjama-wearing society.

"Of course, sir," Philippa said. "What is your destination?"

"St. James's Park."

She fell silent. "Mr. Darlington," Philippa said, sounding alarmed. "The rain is torrential, and this storm is forecast to get worse. Are you sure this is the right time for a nighttime walk?"

"Absolutely," I said and hung up. What else was I supposed to say? I was well aware that it was a ridiculous idea to go outside, especially as Kate could be anywhere. But the park was the only place I could think of, and so I would try my luck.

Ten minutes later, I was sitting in the back seat of Mr. Hammond's car, watching the rain run in rivulets down the windows.

The windshield wipers flew back and forth, and we could barely see a metre ahead, so although ours was the only vehicle on the road, we crept towards St. James's Park at less than twenty miles an hour. The drive felt like a test of my patience, but we eventually made it. Mr. Hammond stopped the car as close as he could get to the spot where I'd first met Kate last week. I pulled the hood of my black raincoat over my head and pressed a button that ejected an umbrella from a door compartment of the car.

"Sir, are you sure you want to go out there?" Mr. Hammond asked, glancing at me in the rearview mirror. The look in his eyes indicated that he was questioning my sanity. And to be frank, so was I. But that didn't stop me from opening the door.

"Yes. I'll be right back," I said and ventured out into the storm.

The wind was bitingly cold and whipped at me so forcefully that it tore my hood down and made it impossible for me to open the umbrella. My hair was soaked through in seconds, and my tracksuit bottoms were plastered to my legs. I swore, tossed the umbrella back into the car, and trudged off.

Battling the wind and rain, I made my way to St. James's Café, which was close to where Kate had set up camp. It was dark in the park despite the streetlights, and now that I'd veered off the path, the storm engulfed everything in gloom. I regretted not bringing a torch. I'd have to make do with the one on my phone.

"Kate?" I called into the dark.

The storm swallowed my words, and the lawn squelched under my feet. My socks became soaked through almost as fast as my hair. Branches torn from the trees by the wind cracked underfoot.

"Kate?" I called again.

But again, there was no answer.

I'd reached the spot between the bushes where Kate had hidden her things, but there was no trace of her or her blankets. Perhaps she really had checked into a hotel. I regretted not asking her more questions about her life on the streets and what she was planning to do with my money. But it was too late for regret. I decided to do a lap around the café. If I didn't find her, I'd go back to the car.

"Kate?"

The only response was the howling of the wind.

I shivered, blasted by a particularly forceful gust of wind, and wondered if I'd lost my mind. It was freezing cold, and I was drenched from head to toe. I couldn't get sick. Every day I'd lose at the office would be a disaster for the hotel and the Pearl Gala. And yet here I was, risking it all for a woman I barely knew.

"Kate?!"

"Snowflake?"

I stopped. Had I imagined it? I spun around, but I couldn't see Kate anywhere.

"Over here!"

It was definitely Kate! I turned in the direction her voice had come from. At first, I couldn't make her out, but then I saw her on the café veranda. Although it had a roof, she looked just as wet as I was. I ran towards her and leapt over the wooden balustrade to join her under the roof. I stopped in front of her. Her wet hair was plastered to her head, and instead of the leather jacket, she was wearing a raincoat that was far too big for her.

"What . . . what are you doing here?" she stuttered. We stood face-to-face, but she still had to shout to make herself heard above the storm.

"I came to pick you up."

"What?"

"You can't sleep out here tonight."

Kate looked at me with confusion. She tried to blink away the fat raindrops caught in her eyelashes. "And where should I go, in your opinion?"

"To the hotel. You can stay there for the night."

She shook her head. "I can't."

I frowned. "Why not?"

She didn't reply. She didn't have to. Even in the darkness, I could see the uncertainty in her eyes, the caution that a life on the streets had instilled in her. Kate knew my name, but at the end of the day, I was a stranger. I could take her anywhere, do anything to her.

I took a step back, aware that my size and stature might seem threatening. A flash of lightning bathed us in bright white light. "I don't want to hurt you, Kate. I just want you to be safe. The storm is going to get worse. This is just the beginning."

She crossed her arms and looked at me. In her bedraggled state, she seemed younger than she had when we'd first met, probably because of her big, round eyes. "Why are you helping me?"

I smiled. "Because I'm a good person. You said so yourself."

"I said you're an honest person. That's different."

I paused. "But you said you trusted me, didn't you?"

Kate bit her lower lip and hesitated, then nodded. Despite the cold, I felt an unexpected jolt of warmth in my belly.

"So come with me," I said. "If I really wanted to kidnap you, I wouldn't be standing in the rain arguing. I could just throw you over one shoulder. There's no one here to stop me, after all. Come on. You must be cold. You can have a hot bath at the hotel."

Kate took notice at my last words. Her gaze drifted from me to the dark clouds. A loud rumble sounded, no longer distant. It was close, very close. It wouldn't be long before the eye of the storm reached us. "OK, but we have to take my things with us. I'm not going without them."

"Sure. There's room for them in the car. Where are they?"

She led me around the veranda to her sleeping spot. She had pushed together three tables that had been chained together, along with the chairs. The structure was covered with a tarpaulin made of bin bags, which she had weighed down with rocks. It was crafty, but it probably wouldn't withstand the storm for much longer. Kate had stowed her blankets and rucksack beneath it.

"Come on, let me help you," I said and grabbed a couple of blankets.

For a moment, it looked like she would stop me from touching her belongings, but she didn't protest. We gathered them and ran to the car, tossing everything onto the back seat instead of in the boot so we wouldn't have to spend a second longer than necessary in the rain. Mr. Hammond had turned the heating up full blast, and Kate let out a contented sigh next to me.

"Take us back to the hotel," I said as I fastened my seat belt.

Mr. Hammond's eyes wandered from me to Kate and back again in the rearview mirror. I wondered if he'd seen the photos of us and whether he recognised her. If he did, he didn't let on. "Of course, sir."

I glanced at Kate as we drove off. The air from the heater was pleasantly warm, but she was shivering as if chilled to the bone. I longed to pull her close to me and warm her with my body, but I sure as hell wasn't going to touch her without her consent.

"Why didn't you call me?" I asked sternly. I was angry, not at her, but at myself for delaying the search, even though I'd had a bad feeling for hours.

"My phone is broken." It was dark outside, and the interior lights were so bright that I could see her face, which she'd turned away from me, in the window's reflection.

"You could have come to the hotel." I had offered her that too.

Her reflected eyes narrowed, and she turned to me abruptly. "I can look after myself."

"You clearly can't," I said and promptly regretted my words when her face darkened. I understood. She'd been too proud to ask for help, and as a result, she'd unnecessarily put herself at risk. However, there was no point in telling her off. Worst-case scenario, it would scare her away, and that was the last thing I wanted. "I'm sorry. You obviously know far more about surviving on the streets than I do. But I wish you'd reached out instead of letting me look for you in the rain."

"I didn't ask you to look for me."

"You didn't. But I wanted to."

At these words, something flashed across Kate's face. She turned away to look out the window again, even though there was nothing to see in the rain besides blurred lights.

I sighed, closed my eyes, and leaned back against the headrest. The conversation could have gone better.

"Thank you."

I blinked and looked at Kate again.

She watched me in the reflection. Her gaze was steady, but the anger had disappeared from her face. "For looking for me. The next few hours would have been terrible otherwise."

I smiled. "You're welcome."

12

> The patient was admitted to A&E after being attacked by two men on the street. She sustained severe bruising and abrasions to her head, face, and body, and reported chest pain. Initial examinations revealed no fractures.

Excerpt from Kate's medical records, dating six months back

Kate

I was afraid.

To be unafraid would have been foolish.

I knew many criminals, jerks, and shady characters who had no moral qualms about hurting women. Henry didn't seem to be one of them, but my experience over the last few months had taught me to be cautious and never trust anyone. Which is why I clutched the pocketknife in my raincoat in a painfully tight grip as Henry's chauffeur drove us to The Darlington. If the wind had been slightly less icy or the rain not quite as torrential, I probably wouldn't have taken up his offer, but the storm was bad. Worse than I'd expected it to be.

I had initially planned to spend the night in a homeless shelter, something I rarely did, but when I had arrived, they had already been full for hours. I was sent from one shelter to another until I finally gave up. I had even briefly considered calling Henry, but I couldn't bring myself to ask him for more. He had come anyway, which meant I was now indebted to him. Which I hated. Especially since I'd paid off my debts to Randell just a few hours ago. All I wanted was to be free.

"We're here," Henry said, as if I could have missed the hotel. Our little fight from a moment ago had been forgotten. The chauffeur drove the car with its expensive leather seats into the underground garage and parked it among a row of similarly luxurious vehicles.

Before I could get out with my belongings, the chauffeur opened the door for me. He was older, with brown hair and thin lips that gave a friendly smile despite the late hour and the terrible weather.

I smiled back. "Thank you."

"You're welcome, Miss . . ." He hesitated.

"Kate," I helped him out.

His smile broadened. "You're welcome, Miss Kate."

"Thank you for the safe ride," Henry said, holding an armful of my belongings.

"Of course, Mr. Darlington. Do you need help carrying up the luggage?"

"No. We'll manage, thank you. You should finish for the day."

The driver nodded and stayed with the car while Henry and I made our way past dozens of luxury vehicles to the lifts. The gleaming black Mercedes, parked next to a fancy Bentley, was probably the least expensive car in the garage. I suddenly felt shabby in my stolen raincoat and wet shoes. My feet were ice-cold, because my socks had been soaked for hours.

We got into the lift, which was so much more than a gleaming metal box. The floor was carpeted, the ceiling mirrored, and the walls wood-panelled. A painting of a lake sparkling in the sun hung on the back wall. Henry pulled a key chain from his coat pocket and scanned the attached ID chip before pushing the button for the penthouse.

I held back a gasp of astonishment when the doors slid open to reveal a wide corridor. It exuded wealth and luxury, with old oil paintings in heavy frames adorning the walls. The sage-green carpet was spotless, and dozens of gilded wall lights illuminated the corridor, which was lined with solid wooden doors. Everything was so immaculate that it almost seemed unreal.

"Are you coming?" Henry asked when he noticed I'd frozen in the lift.

I nodded and followed him down the corridor. "I'm sorry. I'm making everything wet." I tried in vain to stop my sopping body and blankets from dripping.

"Don't worry. Me too," said Henry. Even now, he was devastatingly attractive. The rain that pearled off him seemed to intensify the blue of his eyes. "Anyway, there are no guests up here who'd be bothered. This floor is private. It belongs to my family."

"Your whole family lives here?"

"Not all of them. My brother Logan isn't here. But I'm the only one who can access my apartment, so don't worry about running into anyone if you need to get a glass of water from the kitchen tonight."

"OK," I muttered.

Henry paused in front of one of the dark wooden doors and unlocked it using the same ID chip he'd used in the lift. He pushed it open, gesturing for me to go in first. My steps faltered as I stepped inside, and I was instantly struck by the fact that Henry's apartment was nothing short of a palace. The entrance opened into an enormous, unexpectedly modern room. The far wall was made entirely of floor-to-ceiling windows, which, if not for the stormy darkness outside, would probably have offered a sweeping view of the city. A sectional sofa upholstered in luxurious fabric stood in front of the glass, while an open-plan kitchen occupied the opposite side of the room, featuring light-toned cabinets, gleaming white marble countertops, and a double-door fridge. The ceiling was several metres high. An imposing stainless-steel chandelier bathed the suite in soft light, and a staircase led up to a mezzanine. The room could easily have felt cold and uninviting, but the plush carpets, the large plants in every corner, and small details like the sports bag lying on the floor made it feel homey.

"You live here?" I asked in disbelief as it sank in how wealthy Henry really was. He wasn't just rich—he was filthy rich. Henry set my wet things down on the floor near the door, and I resisted the impulse to pick them straight back up to avoid getting anything dirty.

"Yes," he said, oblivious to what I was thinking.

"Wow," I breathed, adding the items I'd carried to the heap. I kept hold of my rucksack, just in case I had to make a quick getaway, but I doubted I would have to. I couldn't say why, but I'd had a good feeling about Henry from the very beginning. Still, although I was comfortable in his presence, I felt uneasy surrounded by so much luxury.

"Shall I show you to the guest room?"

I nodded wordlessly, unable to find the right words for the situation. I could handle contempt, hatred, and ignorance. But Henry's generosity and helpfulness left me at a complete loss. Especially since I deserved neither. A familiar pressure built behind my eyes, and I fought back tears as I trailed Henry around his apartment.

He led me to a closed door. A light turned on automatically when he opened it, revealing a room no less impressive than the living area. In the centre stood a large king-size bed with a padded headboard and silk covers. A wooden desk and several substantial bookcases lined the room, along with a walk-in wardrobe featuring integrated lighting and recessed cupboards. But the cherry on top was the adjoining bathroom, complete with a spacious rain shower *and* a freestanding bathtub. A warm shiver coursed through me at the thought of soaking in it.

"I should have asked for more in exchange for your phone," I said with a forced chuckle, playing down my spiralling anxiety. Everything was impossibly chic and fancy, and I felt completely out of place.

"You'll know better for next time," Henry replied with a smile that had a strange effect on my heartbeat. "You'll find slippers, a dressing gown, and towels in the cupboard in case you want to have a bath. I'll get you some dry clothes."

I nodded. My mouth felt incredibly dry. The pressure behind my eyes grew stronger at the thought of spending the night here, in a real bed. In a warm, dry room without insects buzzing around me. Without strangers scrutinising me as they walked by. The thought not only filled me with relief and gratitude but also restored a sense of humanity that I'd lost during my time on the streets, when most people either treated me like rubbish or completely ignored me.

"Are you hungry?" Henry asked.

"I'm always hungry."

He frowned at my answer. He was probably wondering what had happened to his four thousand pounds, given that I'd spent it on neither accommodation nor food, but he didn't ask. "Is toast OK?"

"Of course. I'm not picky."

"OK. Wait here," Henry said and left the room. I hardly dared to move until he returned with a bundle of clothes in his arms. "They're probably too big, but at least they're dry."

"Thank you."

"You're welcome. Take your time," he said. He closed the door behind him when he left the room.

I stood rooted to the spot for a moment before I locked the door. Not because I didn't trust Henry specifically, but because I'd learned to not trust anyone. I walked around the room. Was I dreaming? It felt like it.

I went to the bathroom and turned on the bathtub taps. On the rim were small bottles bearing the hotel's logo, including bubble bath. I undressed and showered briefly to rinse off—I had no desire to stew in the grime of the last few days—then tipped the lavender-scented liquid into the tub.

I slid into the warm bathwater. The bubbles prickled at my skin, and I felt my icy limbs thaw and warm up slowly, my muscles relaxing. I was permanently tense on the streets, always alert to danger. It was exhausting. But here in this beautiful apartment, submerged in warm water and unafraid, my tension melted away.

I began to cry.

At first it was just a single tear, but it soon became an unstoppable flood. I didn't usually let myself cry—tears made you seem weak—but here, in this moment, I'd allow it.

I was safe.

I was unhurt.

I was alone.

For a brief moment, it was OK not to be Kate but Kaitlynn. A version of myself I would have been in another life, one in which I had a family. Friends. A little money. In which I had dreams that didn't shatter on the hard asphalt of reality as soon as I dared to hope.

Kate was tough, unfazed, confident.

Kaitlynn, on the other hand, was simply afraid.

This storm is intense. Send me a message when you're home from the restaurant.

Message from Henry to Logan

Henry

I finished showering long before Kate was done. As I waited, I stowed away the sports bag I'd taken bouldering the day before and took Kate's dirty blankets down to the hotel laundry. They were wet and caked in mud. I returned and waited for Kate to emerge from the guest room. The *locked* guest room. I'd heard the click of the key right after I'd left. I didn't mind her locking it—the room was hers for the night, after all, and she could do as she pleased. Still, I couldn't help but wonder what she'd been through to make her so tense and cautious. She said she trusted me, but her body language told a different story.

Half an hour later, I finally heard movement from the guest room, and I knew Kate had finished her bath. I retrieved a frying pan from the cupboard and got to work in the kitchen. I hadn't thought it was possible, but the storm had grown even worse in the last few minutes. The rain beat almost horizontally against the windows, and the wind whistled through every little crack. Thunder rumbled and lightning flashed directly overhead, as if a portal to the underworld had opened up and was ready to devour London.

"I hate storms," I suddenly heard Kate say.

I looked up from the frying pan and froze at the sight of her in the doorway, dressed in my clothes. She was wearing my old high school rugby team hoodie, which was now far too small for me. I'd kept it purely for sentimental reasons. On Kate, however, it was too big, and the trousers looked ready to slip from her narrow hips. She had the build of someone who was naturally slender, yet she still looked underweight. Unsurprising, given her circumstances.

She approached cautiously and perched on a barstool at the kitchen island. Her towel-dried hair was dishevelled, and a delicate blush coloured her cheeks. My chest tightened. Kate was utterly enchanting. I, on the other hand, was an insensitive arsehole . . . I couldn't help but think how her hair would be even more dishevelled and her cheeks even rosier if she spent the night in my bed instead of the guest room.

Kate craned her neck to squint at the frying pan. I had sautéed tofu, peppers, and onions before adding Himalayan black salt and soy yoghurt. On the plate next to the cooker, I'd arranged toast with vegan cream cheese and grapes. Kate looked at me, her surprise evident. "You cooked for me?"

"Isn't it a bit of a stretch to refer to making toast as cooking?" I asked, ladling the golden scrambled egg substitute onto the plate. Kate watched me with wide eyes, and I saw that they were slightly dull, as if she had been crying.

"I thought you'd order something from the kitchen."

I frowned. "Would you prefer to have something else?"

"No! It's just that . . ." She hesitated and bit her lower lip, as if she wasn't sure whether she should voice what was on her mind. She stopped biting her lip and met my eyes. "I don't get it."

"What don't you get?"

"You," she said, uncertainly. "I don't get you."

"I'm not that complicated."

"You are. You don't make any sense." She frowned and watched me so intently, it felt as though her gaze had cut through my skin and bones, baring my soul. "Why the hell are you so nice to me?"

"Because . . ." I began, but I wasn't sure how to end the sentence. The truth was that I didn't know either. I liked Kate, and I liked even more how normal I felt around her. Maybe I was just trying to prove I was a better person than my dad, even if helping Kate was only a drop in the ocean.

She sighed. "It doesn't really matter. You should know I have nothing to give you, even though I am grateful. I can't even pay you back. The money is all gone. I used it to settle some debt."

I stepped closer and, placing my hands on the countertop, I leaned towards her until our eyes were level. Her gaze searched my face expectantly. But I waited to speak until her eyes finally locked with mine. "I don't want my money back. And I don't expect anything from you. I chose to bring you here. All I want is for you to eat the damn tofu scramble before it gets cold, because I really made an effort."

Kate's stony face relaxed. "Fine."

I straightened up. "Are we good?"

She nodded.

"Great." I pushed the plate toward her. "Do you want something to drink?"

"Do you have orange juice?"

Wordlessly, I turned to the fridge and poured two glasses of orange juice before setting one down next to Kate, who had started to eat. I had no idea if she really liked it or was simply famished, but she ate as though she was afraid I'd take the plate away.

"I took your blankets down to the laundry service. I've flagged them as priority, and you should have them back by midday tomorrow. If you want, we can send your clothes down too."

"I already washed them in the bathtub."

"It really wouldn't be any trouble," I assured her.

"Thanks, but it's not necessary," she said with a terse smile, and I understood. It wasn't about the effort or inconvenience—it was about control. She wasn't willing to part with her clothes any more than she was ready to let go of her rucksack, in case she had to make a sudden getaway. Whether from the hotel or even from me.

I leaned back against the kitchen counter. "Can I ask you a question?"

She looked up from her food. "Sure."

"How old are you?"

"Twenty."

"And how long have you been homeless?"

"Almost a year." Her answer turned my stomach. "My mum and I lost our apartment two years ago. After that, we moved in with her boyfriend. When she died, he kicked me out. I've mostly been sleeping in parks since then. I had a tent until a few weeks ago, but some kids destroyed it."

"Aren't there homeless shelters?"

Kate snorted. "There are, but they're usually overcrowded. And even if you're lucky enough to get a place, they're not exactly safe places to be. Especially not for women. Most people just want a warm, dry place to sleep, but not everyone."

"I'm sorry. I had no idea."

She took a sip of her juice. "Why would you? I bet you've never had to worry about where to spend the night."

I shook my head. "You mentioned your mum. What about your dad?"

"I never got to know him. My mum had a tough childhood. Her dad hit her. She ran away when she was seventeen and ended up homeless for the first time. She found shelter in the beds of random men and got pregnant by accident when she was eighteen. My biological father didn't want to know."

"Did you ever try to contact him?"

"No, why would I? I don't need someone in my life who doesn't want me in his." She shrugged and popped the last bite of food into her mouth. "That was really good, by the way. You should think about becoming a chef."

I laughed. "Better not. That's pretty much the only thing I know how to cook."

"So you admit it qualifies as cooking?"

"Call it what you like, but it's all you'll ever catch me making. Logan is the chef in my family," I said as I stacked the dirty plates into the dishwasher, empty aside from two protein shake bottles.

"Logan is one of your brothers?"

I added the two glasses to the dishwasher. "Yes, the middle one. Ethan is the youngest."

"And Logan is a chef?" she asked with interest.

"Yes. He owns a restaurant. The Meridian."

"Are you close to your brothers?"

"It depends. Ethan is six years younger than me, and our lives couldn't be more different right now. I'm closer to Logan, but it's not like it used to be. We both work a lot, and we only manage to see each other for a couple of hours every month." I could see in Kate's eyes that she had more questions, but I steered the conversation away. "Enough talking. It's late. We should sleep. I have to wake up at five."

Kate slid from her stool. "Oh, I'm sorry. I didn't want to keep you up."

"You didn't. I'm sleeping pretty badly at the moment," I admitted.

Kate offered a sympathetic smile. "Me too, but something tells me tonight will be different."

I made my way around the kitchen counter, catching Kate giving me a once-over. We crossed the living room together, and at the point where our paths diverged, we stopped simultaneously, almost as if we'd agreed on it. Kate stood right in front of me, and without the kitchen counter as a buffer between us, I could smell the delicate scent of the hotel's lavender soap. I'd grown so used to the smell that I hardly noticed it anymore, but I was acutely aware of it on Kate. We stood in silence, neither of us seeming ready to say goodnight.

I cleared my throat. "Sleep well. I'll see you tomorrow."

Kate smiled. "You too, Snowflake. And thank you for everything."

The Darlington dress code: Men are required to wear a jacket and tie in our in-house restaurant, Darlington Dining. Women are expected to dress elegantly. In all other areas of the hotel, tasteful attire is required. Please note that shorts, jeans, trainers, and sportswear are permitted only when leaving the hotel, and should not be worn within it.

The Darlington house rules

Henry

Kate appeared to still be asleep. Not a sound came from the guest room. I knew this because I'd been standing at my kitchen counter for the past five minutes, sipping my coffee and listening to the silence. I'd hoped to see Kate before going to the office, but waking her was out of the question. It was probably the first time she'd slept in a proper bed in weeks, maybe even months, and I didn't want to rob her of that. Our conversation the night before had kept me awake for a while. Especially what she'd said about homeless shelters and the fact that she was always hungry. It was unimaginable to me. Although we hardly knew each other, I couldn't shake the ridiculous urge to ease her troubles, simply because I could.

But perhaps the feeling was also driven by the guilt that had been gnawing at me for months.

I wasn't my dad, and I was disgusted by what he had done to those women. Yet because I ran the hotel now, people seemed to think I was on his side. Still, I couldn't bring myself to pack my bags and leave as Logan had done years ago. The hotel was part of me. It was my home, a place tied to my most cherished childhood memories. I wanted to save it, even if that meant appearing to support my dad, which couldn't be farther from the truth. If it were up to me, he'd have no say in anything. But he had shares in the hotel, and given the recent drama and media attention, now wasn't the right time to force him out of the business.

I swore silently and rubbed my forehead. It was too early for these kinds of thoughts. I gulped down the rest of my coffee and decided to leave Kate a message. I tore off a note from the magnetic notepad on the fridge and hoped that she'd be able to decipher my handwriting. Logan was the only person who had no trouble reading it, and he joked that it was his god-given talent.

I put the note by the sink and hoped that Kate would find it. After unplugging my phone from the charger, I made my way down to the morning meeting about the Pearl Gala. When I checked my emails, I saw that I had received several in the night. Unfortunately, none of them were spam I could simply delete. I resolved to reply to them later and read my personal texts as I walked. I had a new one from Olivia:

OLIVIA:

> You listened to me.

ME:

What do you mean?

OLIVIA:

You met up with Kate.

ME:

Who told you that?

OLIVIA:

James. Ethan told him.

ME:

And how would Ethan know?

OLIVIA:

No idea. But is it true?

I resisted the urge to swear. So Mr. Hammond had recognised Kate after all. And if Olivia already knew, it was only a matter of hours before the entire hotel did too. By the end of the day at the latest, every member of staff would know that Kate had spent the night with me. Great. Discretion and privacy were apparently too much to ask for when you were a Darlington.

ME:

Yes, I brought her to the hotel yesterday.

OLIVIA:

Oooh!

ME:

It's not oooh-worthy. I just didn't want something to happen to her in the storm.

OLIVIA:

Awww, you were worried about her.

ME:

Looks like it.

OLIVIA:

You like her!

ME:

I just wanted to help.

OLIVIA:

Sure you did. And it's pure coincidence that she's super cute and totally your type.

ME:

I don't have time for this.

OLIVIA:

So you're not denying that you like her?

ME:

I don't not like her.

"Henry!"

Against my better judgement, I stopped. The shrill way my mother called my name, insistently and an octave too high, was a good indicator of what she wanted to talk about.

I turned to see her striding towards me in her high heels. She was ten years younger than my dad, but whereas his age showed, she looked a lot younger than her fifty-two years, thanks to the cosmetic work she'd had done. Not to mention the considerable time and money she, like Olivia, dedicated to maintaining her appearance. She dyed her hair blond as soon as there was even a hint of grey, and her weekly facials were a sacred ritual. As were the green smoothies in the morning, the mud masks in the evening, and the afternoon yoga sessions to stay in shape. If my dad took a leaf out of her book, he might be more balanced and less of a bad-tempered jerk.

"Good morning."

My mum stopped in front of me. She was a tall woman, and thanks to her heels, our eyes were almost level. "Don't you have something to say to me?"

I smiled. "You look lovely today."

She clicked her tongue scornfully. "You know what I'm talking about."

"Do I?" I replied with feigned innocence, refusing to give her leverage. She could bring up the *INsider* article if she wanted, but I sure as hell wasn't going to make the first move.

"The photos, Henry! I saw them."

"Oh, the photos. They weren't particularly flattering. It was a bit of a shock, because usually the camera loves my face."

"Could you be serious for once? What were you thinking?" my mum demanded, her voice dripping with indignation, as if the photos showed not Kate and me at lunch, but the two of us gleefully shooting at chained-up puppies.

My smile faded. "I don't get the issue. I had lunch with a friend."

My mum shook her head uncomprehendingly. "My god, Henry. Did you look at the woman? Did you see what she was wearing? And that dreadful restaurant! What will people think? Let alone the press! Barbara called to ask if we're having financial problems. And Margaret wanted to know if the photos show you buying drugs."

"No, I always meet my dealer in Hyde Park," I replied, my voice dripping with sarcasm.

"Henry! This is a serious issue. Are you sleeping with her?"

"No."

"Thank god. It's enough that your father is the way he is."

I gritted my teeth. If Kate and I were ever going to have sex, it would be consensual, unlike dad's predatory escapades. But I kept the thought to myself. Things were hard enough as it was for my mum. Half the world knew that my dad had cheated on her with much younger women—and without their consent. I didn't have to rub it in.

"What do you want me to say?" I asked instead, eager to end the discussion. "I'm not happy about the article either, but it exists. I can't change that."

My mum thought for a moment. "Let me set up a date for you, and the press will see that you're not involved with that woman. I heard Mr. Walsh's daughter is back in town. She's apparently been single for a few months, and she's open to a new relationship."

"No."

"Why not? If you were with a respectable woman . . ."

"I said no," I interrupted, biting back the urge to defend Kate. She wasn't a worse person than us, or worth less, just because she couldn't afford expensive clothes, but my mum would never understand that. At least she wasn't pushing me to date Olivia again.

"OK, but promise me you won't see her again."

"I can't do that."

"Why not?"

"Because she's in my apartment right now."

My mother's expression was a mix of disappointment and barely contained fury. "You just said you're not sleeping with her."

"I'm not. She's just a friend."

"A friend," she repeated, as if she wasn't familiar with the word. I wasn't sure whether her blank face was deliberate or the result of her latest Botox treatment. "Couldn't you have found yourself a classier friend? This is Logan all over again."

"Thank you."

"That wasn't a compliment."

"It sounded like one to me," I said, deciding it was high time to end the conversation. "We should get going. Vivian and Rakesh must be waiting for us, and we have a lot to talk through."

My mum pursed her lips thoughtfully, as if she had something to add. But instead she nodded, and we made our way to the conference room. My mum was on the Pearl Gala organisation team too.

The TV was on. Vivian and Rakesh barely noticed our arrival, their attention glued to a morning show. The host was interviewing William Hunt, a self-proclaimed expert on high society.

"What do you think his strategy is?" the host enquired. Photos of Kate and myself appeared on the screen as William began to answer. Damn.

"It could be a distraction tactic, to draw attention away from the fact that a solid indictment against Richard Darlington has been submitted to the court," William replied. The photo collage disappeared, and the moderator and William reappeared. "It could also be a message to Olivia Asterdam: *I don't need you.* No one knows if they are currently on or off, and Olivia was recently spotted dancing with another man at a party. That must have been quite the blow to Henry's ego."

The host nodded, clearly impressed by William's response. She let it sink in for a moment while she sorted her flashcards. "It's pretty unusual for someone like Henry to date a woman who's so outside of his usual circles. No one seems to know who she is, at any rate. As an expert, can you say how likely it is that this unknown woman is Henry's one true love?"

"It's very unlikely. It would—"

"Hey, I wanted to hear that!" Rakesh protested as I turned off the TV.

"You shouldn't be watching that nonsense. Anyway, it wasn't a date. Kate was hungry, so we got food," I retorted, taking my place at the head of the table. Vivian took a seat, and my mum perched on the empty chair beside her.

Rakesh raised his eyebrows. "So her name is Kate?"

I changed the topic before Vivian felt compelled to weigh in. She might have been my dad's crisis manager, but she loved meddling in my business—apparently it was also part of her job. "Eighty-four days. That's how long we have to get this year's Pearl Gala off the ground. The gala takes place on the 27th of December, but because of how little planning time we have, some of the suppliers we've used in recent years are booked out. Rakesh and I are already looking for replacements. We've called this meeting to talk about which charitable organisation we want to support this year."

"We could donate to one that supports victims of violence against women," my mum suggested. "The press has often accused us of not taking a clear enough stance on the allegations against Richard. This way, we could speak out against sexual violence without making a public statement."

"That's a good idea," Rakesh agreed.

Vivian shook her head firmly. "Absolutely not. Given how controversial a subject this is, it could look like we're trying to buy forgiveness, with Richard paying to clear his name. I suggest we donate the money to an animal protection organisation instead. Everyone loves animals—it's a safe, uncontroversial cause that no one can criticise. And Henry can play his vegan card."

"We donated to an animal protection charity last year," my mum said. "The unspoken guideline is that we never support the same charity cause two years in a row—it might make us seem biased. How about donating to a children's charity instead?"

"Absolutely not!" Vivian objected again.

Rakesh frowned. "What's wrong with helping children?"

"Children evoke too much sympathy. It might give people the impression that Richard is trying too hard to be liked. And the combination of sexual abuse allegations and children could lead to unfavourable search results."

"So what do you suggest?" my mum asked.

"Animals," Vivian replied.

"Absolutely not," my mum mocked, prompting a scowl from Vivian. Rakesh attempted to stifle a laugh. I might have laughed too, if I'd slept for more than three hours and wasn't nursing a headache.

I took a pill from the small box in my jacket pocket and washed it down with a big gulp of coffee. Only after returning the box did I finally speak. "I know that we usually donate to big international organisations, but what do you think about raising money for the homeless in London this year? I did a bit of research last night. The rate of homelessness has shot up in the last few years because of inflation and rising rents. The homeless shelters are overflowing, and even worse, they're often not safe places for women and children."

A silence followed. I considered it a small victory that Vivian was thinking about it instead of crowing, "Absolutely not."

Rakesh broke the silence. "I think it's a good idea."

"Me too," my mum said.

We all turned to Vivian. I could practically see the cogs turning in her head as she ran through every possible outcome and implication. Finally, she nodded. "That could work. Plus, it gives the gala a more humble feel. Richard could profit from that."

I couldn't have cared less about my dad when it came to the decision. I wanted to help Kate and people in similar situations.

But if this is what it took to convince Vivian to agree with my idea, it didn't matter. "Is everyone on board?"

"I think so," Vivian said, sounding as satisfied as if it had been her idea.

"I'll come up with a list of organisations we could work with by the start of next week," said Rakesh, seeming to have read my mind once again. "Should I inquire to see if they'd even be willing to work with The Darlington, or does it make more sense to wait?"

"Reach out to them," I said, just as Vivian told him to wait. I ignored her. "Reach out and offer a generous donation on our behalf. Make sure you emphasise that my father has no involvement in planning the gala, and remind them that, as always, the charity will remain the primary focus."

"Of course," Rakesh said, casting Vivian a smug look.

She turned to me. "Do whatever you want. Now that's settled, let's move on to something far more important in my eyes: the announcement. I've looked through the archives, and you've always announced the gala through a newsletter. That strikes me as too impersonal and detached. This year, I'd like to invite journalists to a press conference at the hotel to show we have nothing to hide."

I shook my head. "My dad won't be holding a press conference."

Vivian smiled. "I'm not talking about Richard. I'm talking about you. It's your first Pearl Gala as CEO. Aside from a few youthful indiscretions and the speculations about your love life, you have a flawless reputation. You're a good guy. People like that. You'll give a speech about how much London means to you and how you want to give something back to the people, and then you'll announce the organisation you've decided on. It'll be fantastic. People will love it, and it'll give the press something new to talk about."

"We've never done it like that before," I replied dryly.

"There's a first time for everything."

"I don't think it's such a bad idea," my mum added.

I unfortunately didn't think so either, even though I wasn't keen on standing in front of a horde of journalists and being subjected to an assault of camera flashes. But I'd do it. I would have done pretty much anything for the hotel. And if there was one thing I wanted, it was for the Pearl Gala to be a success. It was exactly what the hotel, its employees, and I needed: a glimmer of hope and a reminder that The Darlington was more than just my dad's scandals.

> Good morning. I hope you slept well. I'm afraid I had to go to the office, and I didn't want to wake you. You can order breakfast, or take cornflakes and milk from the kitchen.

Note from Henry to Kate

Kate

I leapt up in a panic. Even before I was fully awake, a sense of dread washed over me, accompanied by a familiar tingle that told me that something was wrong. Something was different . . .

. . . Everything was different.

I wasn't in St. James's Park. And I wasn't lying under a pile of blankets, with twigs from last night's storm tangled in my hair. I was at The Darlington, the most luxurious hotel in London, lying in the softest, warmest, cosiest bed of all time. It hadn't been a dream. I was really here. Henry had picked me up from the park in the middle of the storm and let me shelter in his penthouse.

My heartbeat slowed as I pieced everything together. Taking a deep breath, I surveyed Henry's guest room, which was probably bigger than most London apartments. I hadn't figured out how to close the blinds, and the bright poststorm sun streamed into the room. I squinted against the resplendent blue of the sky. According to the digital alarm clock on the bedside table, it was already past ten. I couldn't remember the last time I'd slept so long. I usually woke to the sound of early morning joggers or, at the very latest, to the hum of rush-hour traffic. But today, nothing and no one had disturbed me—not even Henry.

A part of me wanted to stay put and savour the snug bed for as long as possible, but most of me wanted to find Henry. I headed to the bathroom and slipped into the clothes I'd washed the night before in the bathtub. The heating had dried them overnight. I brushed my teeth and then stuffed the hotel shower gel and shampoo into my rucksack. They smelled amazing, and I figured that Henry wouldn't leave them for the next guest, given that I'd already used them. They'd probably just end up in the bin.

I shrugged on my rucksack and unlocked the door. The open-plan living area seemed even bigger in the daylight, perhaps because of the incredible view visible now that the clouds had cleared. I could see Westminster Bridge and Big Ben, and the Thames sparkled below in the sunlight. It took my breath away. After a moment, I remembered that I was looking for Henry.

I turned on my heels. "Henry?"

When no one answered, I turned my attention to what I assumed was his bedroom door. It was open. I approached it cautiously and knocked, but I was met with silence. It looked like he was gone. I didn't know what to make of the fact that he'd left me—someone who'd stolen his phone—alone in his apartment. The man was a complete mystery to me. He confused me in a way no one had before. Especially last night. I replayed the memory of how he'd cooked for me in his T-shirt and jogging bottoms. The sight of him had sparked a heat in me that I hadn't felt for a long time.

I glanced around, unsure of what to do now. My blankets were probably still with the laundry service. Should I wait here? Crossing the room to the kitchen, I spotted a note next to the sink. I picked it up and squinted at the scrawl of writing. What the hell did it say? Something about *offense*. Or was it *office*? And something that looked like *breakfast* and *milk*. Beyond that I couldn't decipher much, except for Henry's signature. Oddly, it was neater than the rest of the note. So maybe he was at his office.

I decided to wait for my blankets. There was nothing else to do. I scanned the kitchen, found the cornflakes, and poured myself a bowl before settling onto the sofa. Beside it stood a DVD shelf holding no fewer than twenty copies of *London Has Fallen*, a Gerard Butler film. Odd.

My gaze wandered from the shelf to the breathtaking view. I snuggled up in a blanket that lay on the sofa and ate my cornflakes, enjoying the warmth. The sun was shining, but I suspected a biting cold awaited me outside. I knew whatever came next wouldn't be as idyllic, safe, and peaceful as I felt right now. I should have been making the most of it, but instead a creeping bitterness and envy was taking hold. Henry had so much, and I had so little. It wasn't fair. I knew that it wasn't his fault that he'd been born into wealth. But it wasn't my fault, either, that I was the product of a one-night stand and the daughter of a drug addict who had died of an overdose.

The sound of the apartment door jolted me from my bleak thoughts. I turned on the sofa, expecting to see Henry, but instead, a young woman stood in the doorway. She had plaited blond hair and was wearing a dark uniform with a name badge I couldn't quite make out pinned beneath the embroidered Darlington Hotel logo. Her features were pretty, the expression on her face mirroring my own surprise. She stood rooted to the spot, staring at me as though uncertain of her next move. That made two of us.

"Hey," I said, waving awkwardly.

"Hi," she replied and stepped tentatively into the room. She pulled in a cart bearing various cleaning products behind her. "I'm sorry, I didn't know anyone was here. Mr. Darlington is usually at the office at this time."

"Yes, he's at the office. Or is committing an offense." I smiled, but my joke was met with no more than a tired frown. "Forget it. Are you returning my blankets?"

"No. I'm just here to clean. Should I come back later?"

I looked around at the apartment. It seemed pretty spotless to me. "No, don't let me stop you. I'm just waiting to get my things back from the laundry."

"It'll probably take another two or three hours."

"Oh, OK. Then I guess I'll make myself at home," I said, wishing Henry were here. It felt strange to be in his apartment without him.

The woman, who looked only a couple of years older than me, pushed the cleaning cart into the kitchen and wiped down the already pristine kitchen counters. I watched her for a moment, but the silence between us felt strange.

I cleared my throat. "I'm Kate. What's your name?"

The woman looked up, her face softening into a warm, inviting smile. I immediately felt less tense. "Grace."

"It's nice to meet you, Grace." I got up from the sofa and took my cornflakes to the kitchen counter so we wouldn't have to shout across the room. Only now did I notice the rings adorning Grace's fingers. They were all silver, but each was unique in shape and cut. Although they looked mismatched, together they exuded organised chaos.

Grace looked at me. "You're the woman from the photos."

"What photos?"

Her eyebrows shot up. "From the *INsider*. Wait." She typed on her phone and then held it out to show me a photograph. It was of Henry and me at McDonald's, capturing the moment I'd placed my hand on his. The headline read, "Is Henry Cheating on Olivia? Who Is the Mysterious Woman He's Been Spotted With?"

A pang shot through my gut. I didn't care much that I was in the photo—nobody knew me. But I was worried about Henry. He was a decent guy, and I was sure he wouldn't cheat on his girlfriend. I hated that people might think he would.

I looked up at Grace, who was watching me inquisitively. "Henry and I aren't together. He's just a friend. I slept in his guest room. Really! You can check. The bed is a mess. From sleeping!"

Grace smirked. "You don't have to justify yourself to me."

"I know, but I . . ." I hesitated for a moment to order my thoughts. My mouth was suddenly dry, and my hands were sweating. "I'm nervous," I said, wiping my palms on my trousers. "I didn't expect someone to come into the apartment. And it feels weird even just being here. I don't usually hang out in fancy hotels with room attendants and chandeliers."

The look in Grace's brown eyes softened, and her expression became more understanding. "Yes, The Darlington is special. I've been working here for almost two years, and I'm still not used to all this grandeur and luxury."

I stirred my mushy cornflakes. "Do you like working here?"

She shrugged. "It could be worse."

"You're not really selling it."

Grace hesitated for a moment. "Things have been overwhelming lately because of the allegations. The other day, a reporter followed me home trying to get a statement. He even ambushed my dad and asked if he was afraid that Richard Darlington might sexually abuse me too. It's all so surreal."

I nodded. That did sound surreal. I couldn't imagine how much more difficult it must be for Henry. "Do you always clean Henry's apartment?"

"Not always, but pretty regularly for the past three or four months, after Tanya quit. She used to take care of the Darlingtons' apartments," Grace explained as she emptied the rubbish into a bin on her cleaning cart.

"And what's Henry like?" I asked, hoping to discover something about him that would help me understand him better.

Grace moved on to the living area, where she plumped the sofa cushions. "If you ask me, he's the nicest of them all. His brother Ethan is an arrogant shit, and his friends are even greater arrogant shits. And don't get me started on Richard. Mrs. Darlington is OK, but quite fussy. She told me off once because I'd accidentally moved a vase a few centimetres when I was dusting."

I spooned cornflakes into my mouth. "Henry isn't like that?"

"No, not at all. He even knows my name."

I furrowed my brow. "Is that unusual?"

"It is. In our black uniforms, we all look the same to them. But it doesn't really matter. The pay is good, and that's what matters most, isn't it?" said Grace. She didn't seem to expect an answer. "How do you know Mr. Darlington? Henry, I mean."

"From bouldering," I lied. "We go to the same climbing gym."

Grace took out her duster. "Lucky you. I came across him at the gym once, at the weekend. He looks even better in workout clothes than he does in a suit."

My thoughts drifted to last night, to Henry standing in the kitchen wearing his black jogging trousers and grey T-shirt. How the fabric had clung to his muscular biceps. I had allowed myself the briefest glance, but it was still enough to make me blush at the memory. Grace noticed.

"You really aren't together?"

"No. We haven't known each other for long."

"Well, anything could happen," Grace philosophised.

"Isn't Henry with Olivia?"

"No, they're just very good friends."

Grace's answer inexplicably made my heart race. The feeling was totally irrational. Henry clearly liked me enough to help me, but he most definitely wasn't interested in me in that way. "What about you? Do you have a boyfriend?" I asked, trying to steer the conversation away from myself.

"No. I broke up with my ex a few months ago. I just want to focus on myself for a bit. This job is supposed to be a temporary solution, until I find out what I really want to do. What about you? What do you do?"

"I'm looking for a job," I answered. I could hardly tell her I made my money pickpocketing.

Grace and I talked as she cleaned. She was friendly, and we were on the same wavelength. She had a lot of anecdotes about the hotel, from special guest requests to the unsettling things she had seen and heard while she was cleaning. I followed her like a shadow through the rooms and onto the mezzanine, stopping only at Henry's bedroom. Going in there without his permission seemed like a breach of trust.

Grace eventually had to leave to clean other rooms. We said goodbye, and suddenly I was alone again in a huge apartment that didn't belong to me and where I felt like an intruder. As much as I wanted to be here, I didn't belong. It wasn't my world. It was Henry's.

16

> Thanks for your help, Snowflake.
>
> I'll never forget it.
>
> All the best, Kate

Note from Kate to Henry

Kate

The words on the note seemed completely insignificant in light of everything that Henry had given me. Not only had he saved me from the storm, but thanks to him, I'd also felt like a proper human for a few hours. I would miss that feeling even more than I would miss the luxury. I had grown so used to having no home, no security, and no comforts that I hadn't questioned my extremely precarious state of instability over the past few months. Now that I knew it could be different, the thoughts I'd successfully repressed since my mum's death came flooding back.

"Stop it," I chided myself, and drew a little heart in the top right-hand corner of my note. I put it on the kitchen table in the exact same spot where Henry had left his own note earlier that morning. Part of me wanted to wait and say goodbye in person, but leaving felt hard enough as it was, harder than it really should have been. It was best this way. I only wished I knew if and when I'd see him again.

I shouldered my rucksack and the clothes bag with my blankets. They were clean, dry, and folded neatly, and smelled like lavender. At least their scent would remind me of The Darlington and Henry for a couple of nights. I scanned the penthouse apartment one last time before stepping out into the wide corridor and pulling the door shut behind me. There was no going back now.

I made my way to the lift, with its old vintage display. I pressed the call button and watched the needle move from left to right as the lift ascended, until finally the door slid open with a ding. I stepped inside and pressed the button for the first floor. My stomach dropped as the lift descended. The ride took no more than a few seconds, but it felt like minutes. By the time the lift door opened, the weight of my rucksack seemed to have doubled.

I took a deep breath and exited, but my steps faltered as I entered the foyer for the first time—last night, Henry and I had entered the hotel through the underground car park. Not even Henry's lavish apartment could have prepared me for the sight.

The sheer grandeur of The Darlington's lobby took my breath away. The ceiling soared impossibly high, adorned with intricate stucco details accented by golden elements. I had to tilt my head back to fully take in the tops of the marble columns. They were awe-inspiring, majestic in a way that made me feel even smaller and more insignificant. Massive chandeliers lit the foyer. They were made not of modern stainless steel like the ones in Henry's apartment but of matte gold. Despite their size, the metal flowers and vines entwined around them made them seem delicate and gave them a graceful charm. Everything in the foyer gleamed and sparkled in their light, especially the imposing gold statue at the centre of the space. It depicted two women in flowing dresses, so lifelike that I felt an irresistible urge to touch them, curious about whether their skin would really be cold.

Clusters of armchairs and sofas in beige and gold made the foyer feel cosy despite its splendour. These were flanked by side tables adorned with lavish floral arrangements, with not a single wilted leaf among them. This must have been the source of the sweet scent that filled the foyer, mingling with the gentle strains of music coming from a man playing a gleaming grand piano near the fireplace.

I'd already felt out of place in Henry's apartment, but this wasn't just another world—it was another unfathomable galaxy. I cautiously placed one foot on the sage-and-terracotta carpet, identical to the one I had seen on the top floor. It stretched across the entire lobby, leading to a grand staircase that ascended to a set of polished wooden double doors. What lay behind them? I crept towards the exit, my steps barely audible against the backdrop of the soft music.

"Miss!" a voice called suddenly.

It was clear that I was being addressed, because besides an older woman wearing the same uniform as Grace, I was the only person in the lobby. I turned to face reception, with its counter of gleaming marble. Behind it stood a man in a suit. He rounded the desk and approached me, looking so impeccable that had it not been for a name tag pinned to his lapel reading "Mr. Gardner," I might have mistaken him for a hotel guest.

"Where are you going?" asked Mr. Gardner.

I pointed at the exit. "Out."

"And who are you?"

"Kate."

Mr. Gardner looked at me, waiting.

"Hamilton," I added. I hadn't said my last name in a long time. Where I came from, last names weren't important.

He scrutinised me. "You aren't a hotel guest."

"No, that's why I'm leaving."

"Hold on a moment, please."

"OK."

Mr. Gardner turned on the heels of his highly polished shoes and hurried back to reception to make a phone call. He didn't take his eyes off me, speaking so softly that I couldn't hear his words. He remained behind the counter after hanging up. Had he called Henry to let him know I was leaving?

"Miss?"

I whirled around. Another man had slunk up to me as silently as a cat. Something like this would never have happened under normal circumstances, but I'd grown careless in the face of such an abundance of luxury. This man was bulkier than Mr. Gardner, but no less elegantly dressed.

"Yes?"

"Come with me, please."

"Where to?" My heart sank to my knees.

"Follow me, please," the man replied firmly, ignoring my question. He pointed the way, but I didn't move.

I didn't know this man, nor did I trust him. Henry had been an exception, but I did not like this guy. I stood frozen in place and weighed up whether I should make a run for it. I was sure I was faster than him. "Please, Miss."

I got ready to sprint. "What do you want?"

"I have to check your bag," the man explained calmly.

"Why?"

"Because you entered the hotel without permission."

So that's what this was about. They thought I'd broken in and was trying to smuggle out stolen loot through the main entrance. If I really had stolen something, I'd have climbed out through a window, but I didn't say that. "I was with Henry."

The man frowned. "Mr. Darlington?"

"Yes. Henry Darlington," I said. "There are photos of us!"

The man's gaze flicked from me to Mr. Gardner, who had overheard our conversation. Wordlessly, Mr. Gardner picked up the phone again, but this time he didn't lower his voice. "Good afternoon, Mr. Darlington. Apologies for disturbing you, but we have a Kate Hamilton here at reception who claims to have been your guest."

For a split second, I feared irrationally that Henry would deny it, but at his answer, Mr. Gardner nodded. He hung up and approached me with graceful steps, offering a friendly yet somewhat stiff smile. "Please excuse the misunderstanding, Miss Hamilton. Mr. Darlington will be here in a moment. May I offer you something to drink while you wait?"

I shook my head.

Mr. Gardner inclined his head in a slight bow before returning to his position behind the reception desk. The dapper brute who had appeared so suddenly had now vanished just as quietly. I shifted uncomfortably, unsure of what to expect next. As I debated whether to sit down, the door marked "Staff Only" near reception swung open, and Henry stepped into the lobby. Grace's words flashed in my mind, but I had to disagree with her. Sure, Henry looked good in a T-shirt and jogging bottoms, but in the blue suit he was wearing now, he was even more attractive.

He stopped before me. "What are you doing?"

"You tell me. I was trying to leave when your receptionist and his bouncer stopped me," I answered, gesturing at Mr. Gardner. He was staring intently at his computer, clearly listening to us.

Henry eyed me. Only now did he seem to register my rucksack and the clothes bag full of blankets. He frowned. "You want to leave?" he asked, as if I hadn't just told him.

I nodded. What other options did I have?

"Why?" His surprised tone confused me.

"Because the storm is over?" I said, my inflection making it more a question than an answer. As happy as I was to see Henry again, the pain of saying goodbye, something I'd been trying to avoid, was growing stronger by the second.

He took a half step towards me, slowly, as if he wanted to give me time to flinch back. For some reason, though, I felt no need to run from him. "Stay," he said.

I was sure I'd misheard. I looked at him, bewildered. "What?"

"Stay," he repeated.

"Here? At the hotel?"

"Yes. We have a couple of free rooms. You can have one."

"You're kidding," I said, resisting the urge to pinch my own arm. Perhaps I'd fallen asleep on the sofa and was dreaming. Henry couldn't possibly want me to stay at The Darlington. But his next words proved me wrong.

"Yes. I'm serious. Stay with me."

"Why would you ask me something like that?"

"I don't know." He shook his head as if he didn't quite understand either. "Because I can?"

I shouldn't stay. I wanted to, but I shouldn't. This wasn't my life, and it wasn't a good idea to become dependent on Henry like this.

Leaving felt far too difficult already, and that was just after one night together. "You know I can't afford to stay here, right?"

"I don't want your money, Kate."

"So what do you want?"

"Nothing. Just for you to stay." He reached for the strap of my rucksack. Not to take it off me, but because it had become twisted and he wanted to fix it. He barely touched me, and yet I felt a tightness in my chest as his fingers brushed against me.

"But why?" It just didn't make sense. *He* didn't make sense. He was Henry Darlington. The whole of London was talking about him and his family. Perhaps even the whole country. But me? I was a nobody. Just some homeless girl with problems he'd never understand.

"Because I'll feel better knowing you have a roof over your head," he explained matter-of-factly, as if I should have figured it out myself. But we barely knew each other, and there were thousands of other homeless people in this city. Why me?

"Kate . . ." Henry stepped even closer to me. His smell washed over me, and I felt the warmth of his body. I looked up. His blue eyes were hypnotic, and I didn't know how I would ever tear myself free of them. "I said it last night and I'll say it again: I don't expect anything of you. This hotel has one hundred and thirty-seven rooms, around fifty of which are vacant right now. We have plenty of space, and you're pretty tiny."

"I'm not that small," I protested.

Henry smiled. "You go ahead and tell yourself that, if it makes you feel better."

I didn't smile back. I was still too preoccupied with his offer. I wasn't used to getting anything for free. Everything came at a price. And most of the time, I didn't pay in pounds, but with my conscience and morals. Yet Henry had made it very clear he wasn't asking for either.

"If I stay here, I'd like to earn my room," I said. I never wanted to owe anyone anything again. "I could help clean rooms. Or work in the kitchen."

"You don't have to do that. We have enough staff," Henry assured.

"Perhaps. But I want to help."

"So you'd stay if I let you work," he said, sounding almost hopeful, which made no sense to me. He was doing me a favour, not the other way round.

I swallowed hard. His gaze was so intense that I felt I should avoid his eyes—but I didn't. My heart raced uncontrollably, drowning out all logic. "Yes, I . . . I think so."

> The Darlington offers luxurious rooms starting at around eight hundred pounds per night. It's not cheap, but still a bargain compared to the most expensive suite, whose nightly cost is a whopping twelve thousand pounds.

Excerpt from a London guidebook

Kate

"You're kidding me," I murmured. "This is your cheapest room?"

Henry nodded and placed the room key on the desk. It had a heavy, metal tag engraved with a golden "107." Despite its vintage appearance, the key used state-of-the-art technology. It was fully digital and worked like an ID card, but the key had to be inserted into the lock rather than just scanned. Not only were the rooms secure as a result, but the hotel's timeless style was preserved.

"This is your cheapest one?" I repeated incredulously.

I had asked Henry to give me the least expensive room. I didn't expect a storage room, of course, not at The Darlington, but the room we were standing in now—*my* room—was about as far from a storage room as you could get. Warm daylight flooded through the sheer curtains and lit up the space. The beige carpet looked so plush that I gave in to the urge to take off my shoes. There was a lounge area with a sofa, two armchairs, and an antique-looking side table. Further into the room stood a dark-stained wardrobe and a desk, on which lay stationery and a gold pen, both emblazoned with The Darlington logo. The room was a dream. Everything matched, and the result was an effect of absolute perfection that I was afraid to destroy. Still, that didn't stop me from placing my rucksack down next to an enormous four-poster bed piled high with meticulously arranged pillows. If Henry hadn't been with me, I'd probably have thrown myself onto the cloud-like heap without a moment's hesitation.

"Yes. It's not as well situated, and it's smaller than the other rooms."

Smaller? The room was huge, and that didn't even include the bathroom, which was at least half as big as the bungalow where I'd lived with Randell and my mum. There were two sinks, a rain shower, a bathtub, and a dressing table. Next to the toilet was a bidet. Mirrors lined three of the four walls, and I could see myself from every angle. Apparently rich people had no reservations about seeing their reflections in any and all circumstances.

"How much does the room cost for one night?"

Henry opened his mouth to speak.

"No. Wait! Don't tell me. I think I'd rather not know. I can keep deluding myself about how it's just two hundred pounds or something."

Henry's snort indicated I was way off the mark.

The luxuriousness of it all left me feeling lightheaded. My eyes wandered to a glass door that led to a little balcony. I pushed it open and stepped outside. Despite the sun, the cold prickled at my skin. My room didn't have a view of the Thames, like Henry's apartment did, but looked out onto a courtyard that almost completely blocked out the noise of the city.

I took a deep breath and let the calm wash over me, even though things in my head felt loud and chaotic. I was looking for a catch—it all seemed far too good to be true. Henry claimed that he didn't expect anything from me, but where I came from, nothing was free. On the contrary, if you weren't careful, you'd be tricked and robbed or, worse still, end up in the bad books of the wrong people.

"So you like the room, then?" Henry asked.

I felt his eyes on me. It wasn't the kind of look that made my flight instinct kick in. It made me want to stay. "It's incredible."

"I'm glad."

I stepped back into the room and closed the balcony door to keep out the cold air. The change in temperature made me shiver. Or perhaps it was just the anticipation of a warm bath, the soft bed, and my favourite TV show, which hopefully I'd finally get a chance to watch.

I turned to Henry, who was watching me with his hands shoved into his trouser pockets. His outrageous good looks briefly distracted me from what I wanted to say. The tailored suit clung perfectly to the contours of his body, and the navy blue of its fabric accentuated his bright eyes, which stood out against his thick, raven-black hair.

I cleared my throat. "Thanks, Snowflake."

"You're welcome, Shorty."

I shook my head vehemently. "Oh, no. Forget it."

"What?" He glanced at me with feigned concern, but I caught the unmistakable twitch of his lips. "Don't you like the nickname?"

"It's not a nickname. It's an insult."

"I'll have another think."

"Or just leave it," I suggested.

"No, I don't think I will." There was a hint of a challenge in his voice, and I knew he wouldn't give up until he'd found a nickname for me. For some reason, I liked the idea of it.

"Thank you," I said again. I didn't just mean for the room, but for everything that had happened since last night. I plucked up the courage to step right up to Henry and resolutely wrapped my arms around his waist, hugging him with all my might.

And the best part?

He hugged me back without a moment's hesitation.

I buried my face in his chest as he held me close, his body warm against mine, sending tingles across my skin. He smelled comfortingly of laundry detergent and soap. A feeling of security I hadn't felt in months, perhaps even years, coursed through me. I could feel the rhythmic beating of Henry's heart in his chest. It was steady and strong, whereas my own fluttered erratically. My fingers dug into the thick fabric of his suit jacket, and against all reason, I snuggled closer to him, because his closeness quieted the chaos in my head. And his touch made me believe that everything made sense.

"Kate . . ." He whispered my name.

I released him and took a step back. My cheeks were glowing, and I didn't dare look at him. I fixed my gaze on his chest. "Sorry, I didn't mean to ambush you like that."

"You didn't." His voice sounded a little scratchy, but not angry, which gave me the courage to raise my head. Perhaps I was imagining it, but I thought I saw the same heat that had risen to my cheeks burning in his eyes. Before I could interpret his expression, his phone vibrated. He glanced at it. "Shit. I've got to go."

"Sure. Don't let me stop you." He'd already given me more of his time than I'd expected him to. "I think I'll take a bath."

A dark flicker passed briefly over Henry's face, but then he took a step back. He adjusted his cuff links and his suit jacket, creased by my enthusiastic hug. "I have a favour to ask."

"Anything."

"Please don't tell anyone how we met. It would be good if no one here found out about your past."

I blinked. "Oh . . . OK."

Henry rubbed his neck. "Don't get me wrong. I don't have a problem with it, but other people might, and things are quite tricky right now. Every little thing makes the headlines, and every tiny slipup is blown up into a scandal. I don't want you to get caught up in it, and—"

"It's OK, Henry," I interrupted. "I can lie."

He sighed with relief. "Thank you."

"It's fine," I replied with a smile.

Henry lingered for a moment longer before wishing me a nice day and turning to leave.

I didn't move. My heart pounded wildly, and my thoughts raced as I watched the door close behind him. With his departure, the chaos in my head returned, bringing back my doubts about whether there really was a place for me here at The Darlington.

THE BLACKROOM

Miranda McCloud
Chloe Lawrence
Amiyah Marsh

These are the names of the three courageous women who—despite numerous insults, attempts at intimidation, and online death threats—have filed charges against Richard Darlington.

Miranda McCloud worked at The Darlington six years ago as a room attendant and was assaulted by Richard while cleaning a guest's room alone. **Chloe Lawrence** accused Darlington of sexual abuse after a company event a few years ago. She says she kept quiet for fear of professional repercussions and continued to work at the hotel until the end of last year. **Amiyah Marsh**, a former receptionist, has made similar allegations that Richard Darlington made advances towards her during a night shift. The night's footage from the hotel foyer was suspiciously never retrieved.

A coincidence? We don't think so.

18

I have employed a new room attendant, Kaitlynn Hamilton. The HR department is to finalise the contract as soon as possible. We will provide Miss Hamilton with a room as compensation for her work.

Excerpt from Henry's email to Rakesh

Kate

"Do you have any more questions?" Giulia asked as we sat in The Darlington's housekeeping office. She had just finished giving me an overview of what to expect in my new job.

It was Monday, my first day as a hotel employee. I'd already been to the HR department, where I'd had to sign an NDA that forbade me from talking to the press about the hotel, the Darlington family, or the rape accusations. I'd also signed an employment contract that guaranteed me not only a room at the hotel but also a small salary of three hundred pounds a month to cover everything The Darlington didn't provide. It wasn't a lot, but it was enough to get me started. Perhaps I could find a second job when I got the chance. But for now, I had a place to live and, thanks to Rakesh's help, a new bank account. I might even be able to start saving money. The thought was wonderful and frightening at the same time. I'd learned the hard way how deceptive hope could be.

"I don't think so," I replied.

Giulia's warm smile etched dozens of fine lines onto her face. Her black hair was gathered up in a bun. Despite the British weather, she was tanned, as if she'd spent the summer in a country much further south. "OK. But if you think of any questions or have something weighing on your mind, you can come to me," she reassured, rising from her chair. "Let's find Grace. She's one of our most reliable employees, and she'll spend a couple of days training you. You've already met, right?"

I followed Giulia out of the office. Even behind the scenes, everything at The Darlington was sleek and fancy, with heavy wooden doors and elegantly curved wall lamps. Only here, instead of carpet, there was dark parquet. "Yes, we ran into each other in Henry's apartment."

"Have you known Mr. Darlington for long?"

I shook my head as I tried to memorise the route we were taking, confused by the many corridors and hallways. "No, we've only just met. But he's very nice."

Giulia gave me a knowing look. It was as if she could hear what I was thinking: that Henry was ridiculously hot and that I'd spent far too much time thinking about him over the weekend. "Mr. Darlington is a good guy, and he's doing pretty well given the circumstances. I've worked at the hotel for thirty years, and I've never experienced anything like the last few months."

"Wow, thirty years? That's a long time."

Giulia clicked her tongue. "Well, I'm old."

I held up my hands defensively. "I didn't mean it like that!"

She gave a cheerful laugh. "I know, but it's the truth. I started working for the Darlingtons right after I finished school. First as a temp, and then I got a permanent contract as a room attendant. After a while, I oversaw Mr. and Mrs. Darlington's private apartment, and a few years after that, I was promoted to housekeeping manager. Since then, I've been responsible for all things hygiene and cleanliness here at the hotel."

"And do you like the job?"

"Very much so. It's probably hard for you young people to imagine. You all want to be rich and famous, but this is my dream job. I hope I get to keep doing it for as long as possible. Oh, Grace, here you are! We were just looking for you."

"Congratulations, you found me," Grace said with a grin.

Giulia pointed at me. "You already know Kate. She's working for The Darlington from today. I want you to train her."

"Sure, no problem. This is going to be fun!"

"You're not here to have fun, you're here to work," Giulia admonished, not sounding at all stern. I decided I liked her. The Darlington may have been grand and intimidating, but both Giulia and Grace seemed down-to-earth and warm, which instantly made me feel at ease.

"Why can't we do both?" Grace asked.

Giulia rolled her eyes like an exasperated mother. "I'll let you get to work. Let me know if you need anything. My door is always open."

I smiled. "Thanks."

Giulia nodded and turned to leave. Grace and I didn't speak until she'd disappeared around the corner. "I'm glad you're working for Darlington now too," Grace said. "I have to admit, I was hoping you would when you said you were looking for a job."

"Yes. It was a pretty spontaneous decision."

"I heard you're living here at the hotel. Is that right?"

"Yes."

"With Henry?" Grace asked inquisitively.

I laughed. "No. I have a room on the first floor."

"Wow. But you're not paying, right?"

"Oh my god, no. Henry is letting me live there in exchange for me working here."

Grace gave a dreamy sigh. "I'm envious."

"I get it. It's a really nice room." On Friday night, after Henry had left, I'd taken a bath and gone straight to bed. Aside from trips to the bathroom, I hadn't left my mountain of pillows, catching up on months of lost sleep. When I woke, I watched TV and scoured the hotel for snacks, taking apples, pears, and bananas from the golden bowls on small tables I found in almost every corridor.

"Do you have your uniform yet?" Grace asked.

"No, not yet."

"Let's pick that up first, and then we can start." She led me to a room that was a combination of a utility room and a laundry. The washing machines clattered loudly, and the clean smell of fabric softener hung in the air. "Towels and bed linen, as well as the cloth serviettes and tea towels from the restaurant, are washed externally. A van comes by once a day to pick them up. We take care of the guests' clothes and our uniforms in-house. That's not part of your job, though. We have Patricia and Estrella for that."

I made a mental note not to forget their names.

Grace examined me. After a moment, she went to one of the many cupboards and pulled out a dark uniform. "Small," she said, handing it to me. "It should fit. When you need a fresh set, you can just take that one to the laundry service and help yourself to a new one. Come on, I'll show you the changing room."

"There's a changing room?" I asked, surprised.

"Yes. Employees have their own space, with a kitchen and a dining table. There are a few beds too, but you won't be needing those," Grace replied, and led me on through the corridors. "There are three shifts: early, late, and night, so there's always someone here to take care of the guests. But only one room attendant is assigned to the night shift, since it's not very busy. You're mainly on call in case there's a spillage or something like that. So it's cool to have a place where you can hang out. I actually don't work the night shift anymore, because I take care of the Darlingtons' private rooms during the day. We always get our work schedule a month in advance."

"I don't have one yet."

"You'll get one." Grace opened the door to the staff area. It smelled of coffee and air freshener. There was a large table in the middle of the room next to a kitchen and even a sofa with a TV. "Over there is the room with the beds, here is the restroom, and this is the changing room with the lockers."

The changing room was empty, presumably because the staff assigned the early shift had long since started. I took off my leather jacket and put it in a locker. I kept on the top I was wearing underneath, because I didn't own a bra.

Grace sat down on a bench.

"Where do you live?" I asked, slipping on the uniform shirt. It felt incredibly soft and comfortable. Would anyone notice if I took an extra uniform for myself? I didn't have many clothes at the moment, and it would come in handy.

"With my parents," Grace replied. "I'd love to live alone, but London is too expensive, and I'd rather save until I know what I want to do."

I untied my boots so I could swap my jeans for the trousers. "Do you get on with your parents?"

"Yeah, they're great. But it's a bit crammed in the house with the five of us. I have two siblings, Amy and Jason. Amy is my twin sister, and Jason is fifteen." Grace's voice had softened. It was clear how much she loved them, even if she craved more space for herself. "Do you have siblings?"

"No."

"And your parents?" Grace asked.

I pulled on the new trousers and wondered how much of the truth I could tell Grace without breaking my promise to Henry. "My mum died at the end of last year. And I've never met my dad."

Her eyes widened. "So you're all alone?"

I straightened up and tensed my shoulders. It was reflexive, a gesture intended to make me look more resilient. "I got used to it," I lied.

In reality, I'd just learned to ignore my feelings. Randell had left me no other choice. I was still grappling with the fact that my mum was dead when he'd thrown me out, leaving me to suddenly navigate a harsh new reality. I hadn't had a second to grieve or come to terms with my loneliness. I'd found myself in survival mode, where I'd been for the last few months. I could feel that mode deactivating now, slowly but surely. Not just because of my new sleeping arrangement, but also because of Henry, and people like Giulia and Grace, who had welcomed me so warmly to The Darlington.

19

Hot. Hotter. Ethan Darlington. What Does the Coveted Bachelor's Dream Woman Look Like? We Know!

Shout Magazine headline

Kate

"We have to be as discreet as possible when we clean the rooms so we don't disturb the guests. They deposit their keys at reception when they leave the hotel, and as soon as that happens, we get a notification," Grace explained, showing me her tablet. "If you have time to clean the room, you press the green button. And we also get notified when the guests go down to the restaurant."

"So you only clean the rooms when there's no one in them?"

"We try, but it doesn't always work out that way, of course," Grace answered. "When you click on the room number, you can see who's staying there. Remember their names, because it's company policy that we greet every guest personally when we run into them. And under the name, you'll see a list of special requests, if there are any. Most of them are relatively normal—they might have a preference for a particular colour of bed linen, for example—but sometimes we get some pretty weird stuff. We once had a guest who wanted a different colour of lightbulb every day. On Wednesdays, he wanted purple; yellow on Thursdays; and red on Fridays."

"And you do it?" I asked, amazed.

"Of course," Grace said with amusement, and pressed a button on the tablet to dim the display. "We do everything for our guests. They spend a lot of money to stay here. If I'm honest, with prices like that, you're not just paying for the room. You're paying for the service, for integrity, for privacy. We get a lot of celebrities and politicians here. Don't share their special requests with anyone. That includes friends."

It was an easy promise to make, because I had no friends. The only person I'd talked to in the last few weeks was Mary from lost and found.

After Grace had explained how the tablet worked, we started cleaning. Every day, each room at The Darlington was cleaned as thoroughly as if a new guest were arriving. We aired the room, straightened the curtains, emptied the bins, made up the bed, replaced the towels, vacuumed, restocked the minibar and the toiletries in the bathroom, cleaned the mirrors, and polished the surfaces until they gleamed. Each room took at least half an hour, maybe longer, but The Darlington prioritised quality over speed.

With every room we cleaned, it became clearer to me that Henry really hadn't been lying when he'd said I was staying in the least glamorous room in the hotel. The rooms I cleaned with Grace were all quite a lot bigger and even more luxurious. A few even had fireplaces. But no two rooms were the same; each was uniquely furnished and decorated. In some rooms, shades of pink and purple dominated, while others featured accents of blue, orange, or green. We even cleaned a suite with a separate living and dining area.

Grace and I talked nonstop as we worked. She raved about the hotel's indoor pool and about the rooftop bar where a summer party for employees was held every year. But she also talked about how the mood had shifted since the first allegations against Richard Darlington had become public at the beginning of the year. Hardly anyone at the hotel believed he was innocent. There'd been enough conversations among staff since then, with female employees sharing stories of uncomfortable encounters with Henry's dad.

Grace had fortunately never experienced harassment herself, but the knowledge that Richard was capable of it, coupled with the bad press, still affected her. There'd been several resignations in the past few months—staff left both in solidarity with the victims and because they feared that being associated with the hotel could harm their careers. Even if the court declared Richard innocent, the allegations and the memory of them would linger. They were a permanent stain on The Darlington's otherwise spotless reputation.

Grace's work schedule eventually led us to the hotel's private penthouses on the top floor.

"Keep your fingers crossed," Grace said after we'd finished with Henry's apartment. It had felt strange to be there, as if I were invading his privacy, especially when we'd cleaned his bedroom. Grace had assured me it was OK, but I'd felt an overwhelming urge to ask Henry for permission to be there. We now stood before the door of another apartment. Since Logan didn't live at the hotel and Grace didn't have Richard and Amanda Darlington's apartment on her rota today, this had to be Ethan's suite.

"What for?" I asked.

"That it's not total mayhem in there."

Grace unlocked the door with the golden ID card that gave her access to every room on the private floor. The stench of alcohol and the acrid smell of weed hit me as soon as the door opened. I wrinkled my nose. I hated the smell—Randell and my mum had smoked weed together sometimes. In comparison to some of the other stuff they'd taken, joints were harmless, but in general, it had been enough to turn me against drugs completely. The bitter, slightly rotten smell brought back a lot of unpleasant memories.

The state of Ethan's apartment was worlds apart from Henry's, which had been immaculate. It looked like there'd been a rave here over the weekend. Nothing seemed to be where it belonged. There were cups and bottles everywhere, crockery-laden trolleys in the middle of the room, and several pizza boxes lying around. Glow sticks were scattered across the floor, and I even came across a shoe and a pair of boxer shorts someone had obviously lost on the way to the bedroom.

"Crossing my fingers obviously didn't work," I muttered.

Grace snorted. "It could be worse."

"Is it always like this?"

"Not always, but often enough," she said, wrinkling her nose when she spotted a thong. "You collect the bottles, I'll do the cups, and then we'll take care of the rest."

I grabbed a bin bag and made a start, scanning the apartment for clues as to who Ethan really was. So far, all I knew about him was that he was six years younger than Henry and that he loved parties. But that couldn't be all. A gleaming black piano stood in the corner of the living room, but I couldn't tell whether it was decorative or regularly played. And there were several game consoles under the TV.

A sudden sound came from the bedroom. I froze as the door swung open and Ethan Darlington came into the living room, half naked.

"Morning," he said, his voice raspy. He was wearing only a black pair of boxers, which accentuated more than they concealed. I blushed. Ethan could easily have been one of the underwear models I sometimes saw plastered across the bright ads at Piccadilly Circus.

"It's after twelve," Grace said.

Ethan squinted at her tiredly. "I didn't ask, but thanks."

He made his way to the kitchen, which we'd already cleared of rubbish, and turned on the coffee machine. Ethan winced as it came to life, as though a nail were being driven into his head.

"Fucking hangover," he muttered to himself.

Maybe it was all the bare skin, or perhaps it was because Ethan, with his black hair and blue eyes, looked like a younger version of Henry, but my brain short-circuited for a moment. It was the only explanation I had for my next words. "Maybe you should drink less."

That caught Ethan's attention. He had ignored me so far, but now he turned to me. His gaze was alarmingly sharp for someone who had just complained of a headache. "Who are you?"

"Kate."

Ethan studied me closely. "Oh, wait. I know you. You're the woman from the photos. You must be quite something in bed if Henry's willing to go to McDonald's for you. But hey, I'm glad he's finally found someone to fuck."

My face flushed hot. The mere thought of sleeping with Henry sent electric heat shooting through me. "Your brother and I are just friends."

Ethan placed a cup under the coffee machine. "Ah, I see. So you're one of his charity projects. He's always had quite the hero complex."

"Better than an arsehole complex," Grace whispered beside me, but Ethan heard. His face darkened. He crossed the room silently, coming to a stop directly in front of her. Grace was just a few centimetres taller than me, and Ethan towered above her, but she didn't seem intimidated.

"What did you say?" he asked in a tone that made the hairs on the back of my neck stand on end.

Grace was unfazed. She lifted her chin defiantly and returned his gaze without flinching. "You heard me, Beelzebub."

Ethan didn't seem taken aback by the nickname, as if it wasn't the first time Grace had used it.

"Give me one good reason why I shouldn't fire you for that."

"Easy. You can't. I work for the hotel, not for you."

Ethan snorted. "That's a lot of ego for someone who cleans up my trash."

"I'd rather clean up trash than be trash."

"In that case . . ." Ethan grabbed the bin bag from Grace's hand and turned it upside down, sending the cups she'd just collected clattering to the floor.

I held my breath.

Grace clenched her hands into fists as Ethan gave her a smug grin. For a few seconds, they stared each other down, locked in a silent battle of wills, until Ethan finally turned and went back into his bedroom. Grace didn't move until the door shut behind him, and only then did she exhale sharply and drop to her knees to clean up the mess a second time.

I went to help. "What an arsehole."

"You can say that again," Grace replied, and held open the bin bag for me. "Ethan's just the tip of the iceberg. These people are all the same. They think they're at the centre of their tiny little universe. It's best you don't get too caught up in it."

I nodded, even though I wasn't in any real danger of that happening. I'd never be a part of this world. *Stay with me*, Henry had said, but sooner or later, he'd lose interest in me and disappear from my life again. That was just how it went. People like him didn't associate with people like me. I belonged to the dregs of society and he to the absolute elite. He was letting me peek behind the gilded curtain for now, but it was probably only a matter of time before he realised how little I belonged here and pulled the golden curtain shut before my face.

20

The smell of flowers is a reminder of how sweet the moment can be.

Logan's mindfulness calendar

Henry

I stared at the blinking cursor on my laptop. I couldn't focus on my work. If I had been distracted in the past, it had usually been because I was worried about the hotel. But this time, I had a new distraction. A woman. Kate, to be precise. I couldn't stop thinking about her. We hadn't run into each other since I'd reluctantly left her in her room last week to go to yet another meeting with my dad and his lawyers. Throughout the meeting, I couldn't help but think about Kate, picturing her lying in the bathtub, immersed in warm water that lapped at her naked body.

I would much rather have stayed with her than listen to my dad talk, for the hundredth time, about wanting to file a defamation lawsuit. His insistence that he was innocent was draining, and it was pushing me closer and closer to the breaking point. Kate, on the other hand, had a strangely calming effect on me. Not only was she the most intriguing woman I'd met in a long time, but she was also by far the most attractive. Ethan, with his preference for tall, slender supermodels who looked like they'd stepped right out of a vintage Victoria's Secret catalogue, would probably have disagreed, but I liked Kate just the way she was. I couldn't pinpoint exactly what it was about her that captivated me—I barely knew her, after all. But something about her grabbed my attention, despite this being the worst possible time for such a distraction. I needed to focus on the hotel and the Pearl Gala, but that didn't stop my mind from lingering on memories of our embrace, which had felt far too intimate and meaningful.

I wondered constantly how Kate was doing, what she was doing, how her first day of work had been. Was she still cleaning somewhere in the hotel? Or had she finished work for the day and was now back in her room? My offer to let her stay at The Darlington indefinitely had surprised her. To be honest, it had surprised me too, although I'd already briefly considered it. Not least because it would have been hypocritical to set her out on the street while raising money for the homeless. What had confused me, though, was how urgently I found myself wishing Kate would accept my offer.

"Henry?"

Rakesh's voice was insistent, as if he'd been trying to get my attention for a while. I looked up at the hotel manager, who was standing at my desk, studying me with interest. How long had he been there?

"Yes?"

"I need your signature." He pointed at a document he'd placed on the desk in front of me. The newly negotiated contracts for one of the hotel's suppliers.

I grabbed a pen. "I'm sorry. I was lost in thought."

"I noticed. Are you worried about the gala?"

"Yes," I said, grateful for the excuse. It would have been pretty unprofessional to tell him that I couldn't stop thinking about Kate.

"It'll be OK," Rakesh said. "The last Pearl Gala was great, and this isn't our first rodeo. I've set aside two days in this week's schedule just for the gala. Vivian and I will put together the guest list."

I frowned. "You and Vivian?"

"Yes."

"Who authorised that?"

"Vivian."

Of course.

I gave him the signed contracts. "The two of us will put together the guest list. Without Vivian's input."

"Are you sure you have time?" The concern in his voice alarmed me. Things must have been bad if our hotel manager was so openly worried about me.

I ran a hand over my face, as if I could wipe away the tension, stress, and overtime that had written themselves across my features. "No, but I'll make time." Vivian would put together a guest list that worked in my dad's favour, but I wanted one that served the hotel, the gala, and most importantly, a good cause. I wouldn't allow the Pearl Gala to become the Richard Darlington show.

"OK, so I'll call the meeting off with Vivian and schedule time for the two of us."

I nodded. "Thank you."

"Do you need anything else from me?"

"No, you can go home. I'll call it a day soon too."

Rakesh's eyebrows shot up in surprise, and his eyes darted to the clock hanging on the wall. It was just before 7 p.m., and usually I stayed at the office until at least 9 p.m., sometimes longer. "Already?"

I shut my laptop. "Yes. I have plans."

Rakesh tapped away on his tablet, which he guarded like a treasure and took with him everywhere in the hotel. I'd even caught him in the bathroom with it once. "There's nothing in your calendar. Have I forgotten something?"

"No, it's private," I answered curtly. The entire staff was already speculating about me and Kate, especially since it had become public knowledge that she was working and sleeping at The Darlington. I pretended not to get wind of it, but I was neither deaf nor blind. I heard the muttering and caught the inquisitive looks. But no one had brought it up with me besides my mum. Probably because it was more fun to talk *about* the boss than *with* him.

I stood and took my suit jacket from the back of the chair. "Have a nice evening."

Rakesh had just left my office when my phone vibrated with a new message notification. I considered ignoring it, fearing there was some emergency that would require me to stay at the office, but I couldn't resist checking.

LOGAN:

You'll pay for this.

The next message was a photo of the facade of his restaurant. Someone had written the word "Rapist!" on the wall in red paint. The photo also featured Maxton, Logan's business partner, awkwardly wielding a sponge that didn't seem to have made an impression on the graffiti.

ME:

I can contribute a little.

LOGAN:

Are you serious? Did you just PayPal me five pounds?

ME:

Yes. Doesn't that cover it?

LOGAN:

Very funny, loser.

ME:

Pay for your own shit. Or ask Dad.

LOGAN:

I'd rather lick the paint off myself.

ME:

I don't think that'd be good for your health. But seriously, do you need money?

LOGAN:

No, I was joking. The restaurant's doing great.

ME:

I'm glad. Do you have a table free tonight?

LOGAN:

Dude. It's 7 p.m. No.

ME:

Not even for your brother?

LOGAN:

Especially not for my brother. You never pay the bill. Anyway, evenings are booked out for the next three weeks.

ME:

Congratulations.

LOGAN:

Thanks. You can come by for lunch sometime.

ME:

I'll see. There's a lot to do at the moment.

LOGAN:

Isn't there always?

ME:

Yes, but the Pearl Gala is back on now.

LOGAN:

Didn't Richard call it off?

ME:

Yes, but Vivian wants it to go ahead. And when she tells him to jump, Dad just asks how high. He really thinks she can save his bacon.

LOGAN:

And you don't think she can?

Twice, I started typing a response, only to delete them both immediately. I didn't know what I thought. On the one hand, I only wanted what was best for the hotel, and the best outcome would be for the court to dismiss the prosecution's charges next week and drop the case due to a lack of evidence. On the other hand, I wanted justice. I found it hard to accept that my childhood hero was a sex offender, but I had no doubt that he was guilty. Still, no matter what happened, The Darlington would have to live with the stigma for years to come. There was no good outcome to this situation, only a bad and a very bad one. Nothing would ever be the same again, for the hotel or my family. But I wasn't ready to accept that yet, so I avoided answering Logan's question.

ME:

I have to go, sorry. We'll talk some other time, OK?

LOGAN:

Sure. Do your important things, you important man.

ME:

I will, Dickface.

LOGAN:

Buttface!

21

> Indulge in unparalleled comfort at The Darlington, thanks to our exceptional room service. Every room is meticulously cleaned and maintained to the highest standard, ensuring a pristine and welcoming retreat. Our dedicated team is on hand to meet your every need.

Excerpt from The Darlington Hotel website

Kate

I'd underestimated my job at the hotel. I had figured tidying a couple of rooms couldn't be too hard, but I'd been wrong. Every muscle in my body ached. I definitely wasn't used to so much movement. I had walked around the city, of course, but most of my time had been spent sitting in St. James's Park, watching over my belongings and waiting for an opportunity to steal from unsuspecting tourists. Today, however, I'd put in a hard day's honest work. It felt extremely satisfying and was definitely worth the exhaustion, especially when the reward was this incredible room.

I peeled off the hotel uniform and was placing it neatly over a chair so it wouldn't get creased when I spotted the black envelope I had left on the table.

On Saturday night, I had been lying unsuspectingly in bed when my doorbell rang. People didn't knock at The Darlington; every room had its own bell. A hotel employee had been standing at the door and handed me an envelope with a golden wax seal embossed with The Darlington logo. I hadn't had a clue what to expect as I opened it. The very last thing I was anticipating was a letter from Henry. I hadn't seen him since he'd taken me to my room, and I assumed that, given his many responsibilities and duties, he'd long since forgotten me.

After opening his letter, I had read it at least half a dozen times with a racing heart and a broad grin. Even now, I smiled as I reached for the envelope again to pull out the letter.

Dear Kate,

I hope you've made yourself at home at The Darlington. I'm sorry I've not had time to check on you, but there's an overwhelming amount to do at the moment. If you have questions or need help, though, you know where to find me.

—Henry

I would have liked to go and find Henry. I wanted to see him. A shocking realisation, given that I'd spent months working on not being dependent on anyone, financially or emotionally. Especially not emotionally. Which is why I forced myself to put the letter back in the envelope.

I ran a bath to distract myself, waiting until the tub was full before I slid into the water with a sigh of pleasure. I loved taking baths, but I never had that luxury because my mom and I never owned a bathtub. I meant to seize every opportunity while I still had the chance.

As I closed my eyes and leaned my head back to enjoy the blissful warmth, my thoughts turned again to Henry. I wondered how and what he was doing and if he knew that people were talking about us. Most were just curious, and others were sceptical, but a few seemed genuinely enraged over our alleged relationship. They shot me dirty looks and gossiped nastily behind my back, as if I couldn't hear. But I didn't care. Words couldn't hurt me anymore, not after everything I'd experienced.

I stayed in the bathtub until the water turned cold and the bubbles disappeared, and then I wrapped myself in a towel and slipped into the fluffy pair of slippers I'd found in the wardrobe. The steam that had fogged up the mirror was gone, and I could see my reflection clearly—my cheeks were rosy red, and the damp ends of my hair curled into ringlets. In recent months, several days had sometimes gone by without me seeing my own reflection, and the sight now was strange. It was like looking at someone who resembled me, but had a terrible haircut. Perhaps there was a pair of scissors here somewhere so I could at least give my hair a trim.

Suddenly, the doorbell rang. I frowned, surprised. I wasn't expecting anyone. Perhaps it was another letter from Henry. I went to the door, leaving a trail of bathwater in my wake. But it wasn't another letter. It was Henry himself, standing in the corridor with his hand raised as if he had been about to ring the doorbell again.

"Hello, Sunshine."

"Hi. And . . . no," I replied, trying to hide how happy I was to see him. He was wearing jeans and a dark hoodie and was holding two pizza boxes.

"What's your objection to Sunshine? Snowflake and Sunshine sound good together."

"Sounds cheesy."

"Fine. Can I come in, anyway?" he asked. At the same moment, he seemed to notice that I was only wrapped in a towel. I was partially concealed behind the door, but it must have been obvious. His gaze moved from the wet ends of my hair to my neck and then further down to my chest.

An electric tingle coursed through me, and I pressed my lips together hard. I couldn't help but think about Ethan's obscene words—Henry had finally found a woman he could *fuck*. But that wouldn't happen. We didn't make sense together. The women Henry usually dated were probably as rich, smart, and elegant as he was. They had flawless CVs and even more flawless behaviour. I couldn't compete. I knew it. And Henry knew it too.

He cleared his throat. "Am I interrupting?"

"No, not at all," I answered, my throat dry, even though it wasn't strictly true. I'd planned to put on my fluffy hotel bathrobe, get into bed, and watch the next episode of my favourite TV show. But that was before I'd known there was a chance I'd get to spend time with Henry.

"Shall I wait out here, or . . . ?" He trailed off.

I pulled the door open with one hand and held on to my towel for dear life with the other. "No, come in. I'll get dressed in the bathroom. I'll be right back."

I grabbed my clothes from the chair in the corner of the room and hurried into the bathroom. I swiftly dressed and attempted to tame my damp hair before returning to the bedroom.

Henry had settled on the floor beside my bed with the pizza boxes and two bottles of cola from the minibar. His feet bounced restlessly, as if he couldn't sit still, and he had taken off his shoes. His left sock had a hole, which inexplicably made me smile. Sitting there in his jeans, hoodie and tattered sock, he looked almost normal, not like a filthy-rich person. Just some guy in his twenties trying to figure it out like everyone else. The only difference was the shadows under his eyes, which were so dark, they suggested he'd already lived a whole lifetime.

"Are you OK?" I heard myself ask.

Henry's nervous foot-jiggling stopped, and he glanced at me, startled. His eyes met mine, and for a moment, he simply stared at me, seemingly overwhelmed by my question. He hesitated for a long time before he answered. "Yes. Are you?"

"I am," I said. And in my case, it was actually the truth. But I didn't want to force him to talk about his problems. Perhaps he'd come to me to forget them, and I was happy to let him—he'd solved many of my own.

I sat beside him on the floor, the smell of the pizzas between us making my mouth water. The work had made me hungry, and pizza for dinner was so much better than the fruit I'd taken from the bowls in the hotel corridors.

"I got us vegan pizzas. One margarita and one with mushrooms. If you don't like them, we can get something else," Henry said, opening the boxes.

The sight made my stomach rumble. I grabbed a slice and took a bite, and the flavours exploded in my mouth. The crust was crispy, the tomato sauce perfectly seasoned and the vegan cheese melted deliciously on my tongue.

"So tasty," I mumbled with my mouth full.

"I'm glad. I was thinking about taking you to The Meridian, Logan's restaurant. But after you forced me to pay for your food at McDonald's, I wasn't sure if it'd be your thing," Henry paused, then added, "Also, the arsehole can't even get a table for his own brother."

I laughed. "Pizza is perfect. I'm usually roaming the streets at about this time, looking through bins for something edible that isn't mouldy."

Henry had taken a slice too, but now he stopped short and stared at me. Not in surprise, as he had earlier when I'd opened the door to him, but in dismay. A wave of embarrassment washed over me. I thought I'd shaken off my shame about being homeless, since it didn't get me anywhere, but Henry's appalled expression brought the feelings rushing back to the surface.

I lowered my eyes. "I'm sorry, I didn't mean to be a downer."

Henry's gaze softened. "You're not."

"Oh, really? You should have seen your face just now," I said, wrestling my shame and the pain I'd felt at his response back into the box it had escaped from.

"I'm sorry. I just didn't expect you to say something like that."

"It's fine. Forget it."

"No, I'm interested."

"Why? Is your luxurious life boring you?" I couldn't hide my bitterness, but Henry didn't seem to take offence. I didn't want to be this way, especially not towards him—he wasn't responsible for my situation.

He snorted. "I wish it were boring."

"Grace told me a bit about it," I admitted. I'd always assumed that rich people didn't have problems, because money would have solved all of mine. But Henry was facing very different challenges.

He looked up from his pizza. "What about?"

"The thing with your dad, and what it means for the hotel. Sounds terrible."

Henry laughed mirthlessly. "It is terrible."

"And you're running the hotel all by yourself?" I asked curiously.

"Yes. I have people who help, of course, and my dad has kept enough shares to make sure I can't push him out, but since he's taken a step back from actively running the hotel, I make most of the decisions."

"Would you do it? Push your dad out?"

"Yes." The resolve in Henry's immediate response was unexpected. "If the situation weren't so delicate, I'd definitely have done it by now. But the way things are at the moment, it would do too much damage."

"So you believe he raped those women?"

He pressed his lips together. Something dark flashed behind his eyes—anger, frustration, disappointment—but he didn't let it out. "I'm sorry, but I can't talk about it. Can we change the topic?"

"Sure," I said, even though I believed it was unhealthy to bottle it all up. I could practically see Henry grabbing hold of his feelings one by one and locking them away, until all that remained was his exhaustion.

"How was your first day of work?" he asked.

"Tiring, but nice," I responded honestly. I could tell that he was genuinely interested, and that the question hadn't just been a distraction ploy. "I was a bit unsure at first, because I don't have any hotel experience, but Grace explained everything really well. She's super nice and doesn't care that you and I know each other. Some of the others think it's strange."

"Have they said something to you?" he asked, and shifted slightly to find a comfier position. His leg briefly touched my knee.

"No, but people are talking about us."

"I know."

"Do you mind?" I asked, trying to sound indifferent despite wishing more than anything that he didn't care what anyone said about us.

"Do *you* mind?" Henry echoed.

"I asked you first."

"No, I don't mind. People always talk about me. It can't be helped. I'm Richard Darlington's son, after all, and their boss. But I'd much rather they talk about us than about the other shit. If it bothers you, though, I can . . ."

"It doesn't," I interrupted. "I don't care."

Henry's light eyes met my dark ones, his gaze piercing. "Good. But if that changes, or someone gives you shit because of it, will you tell me?"

"I promise," I said, and the warm tingling I often felt in his presence returned. God, I liked this man more with every minute I spent with him. "Grace and I cleaned the private family floor today," I said to distract myself from the feeling.

He raised his eyebrows. "Oh, yes?"

"Yes. It was a bit strange to be in your apartment," I admitted. "Especially your bedroom. I felt like I was snooping around."

"And did you snoop around?" Henry asked, amused.

"Of course not! But . . . I don't know." I shrugged and took another slice of pizza. I'd already eaten half of mine, while Henry was still nibbling on his second slice. "Aren't you afraid I might steal something? It wouldn't be the first time."

"I'm not. And even if you did, I'd just buy it again. There's nothing in my apartment that can't be replaced."

"Nothing? Not even sentimental things?"

Henry opened his cola with a bottle opener and took a sip before answering. "No. All my memories are of the hotel itself. For the guests, it's just a stopgap, but for me it's my home. They just see the fancy interior with its antique, handpicked furniture and its elegance. Whereas I see . . . everything. My whole life. I only know this hotel. Take the lobby, for example. You noticed the fireplace, right?"

I nodded.

"Perhaps you thought it looked cosy. But when I look at the fireplace, I think about Logan, and about how when I was a kid, I threw his favourite action figure into the fire because he called me Fartface. The burnt plastic stunk out the whole hotel. Every guest got a complimentary bottle of Moët & Chandon, and I was grounded for a week," Henry told me with a smile. "There are dozens—no, *hundreds* of memories that I associate with the hotel. Logan and I got up to so much shit here. You can't imagine."

I grinned at the image of young Henry running amok in this sophisticated setting. "Do you have a favourite place in the hotel?"

"Many!"

"Will you show me some?"

Henry's eyes lit up at the question, as if he'd been waiting for me to ask. "I'd love to. After dinner?"

"I don't have any plans."

We talked for a while about the hotel and my first day of work. I confessed that I'd already forgotten the names of most of the people Grace had introduced me to. Henry then took out his phone and showed me some Instagram profiles and photos of company parties, and explained who everyone was. Grace was right: He really did know everyone's names. It was impressive and showed me once again how important the hotel was to him.

I could hardly wait to see it through his eyes.

22

Club Owner Demands Compensation! Ethan Darlington Parties with Friends and Premium Spirits, Leaving Chaos and Destruction in His Wake!

INsider headline

Henry

What the hell was I doing here? I shouldn't be wandering around the hotel with Kate, further feeding the rumours. I'd told the truth—I didn't care if the staff talked about us. I'd grown used to having barely any privacy. It couldn't be avoided when home and the workplace were one and the same. I'd been born into the situation, though, while for Kate, this was all new. The people who were talking about us worked *for* me, but she had to work *with* them, which was a huge difference. I wanted to keep her life at the hotel from becoming uncomfortable. Kate might not have told me much about herself yet, but what I did know suggested she'd been through a lot. I didn't want her time at The Darlington to be yet another shitty experience, especially not because of me.

Yet here I was, standing next to her and pressing the button to call the lift. Because I couldn't help myself. Because I wanted to spend time with her. Because I wanted her to get to know the hotel through my eyes. Even if there was a real chance she'd regret it tomorrow when she heard the whispers, I was placing the palm of my hand on Kate's back, guiding her into the lift. She didn't resist. My fingers brushed the fabric of her T-shirt—only lightly, but even so, the touch stirred something I shouldn't be feeling. Especially after Kate had opened the door earlier. I could already tell with absolute certainty that the sight of her, covered only with that tiny towel, was something I would think about tonight while lying alone in my bed.

In the foyer, we ran into Mrs. and Mr. Crocombe, an older, elegantly dressed couple who had been regular guests at The Darlington for years and frequently attended our events. They eyed us suspiciously. Our casual clothing was technically not allowed at the hotel. I said hello, but they didn't greet us back. Then again, I wasn't sure if they even recognised me in my hoodie.

A few guests had settled comfortably into the lobby armchairs and were listening to Theodore play piano. A waiter, Terry, was doing the rounds and serving drinks. Through the open glass door of the hotel restaurant, Darlington Dining, I could hear the voices and laughter of the diners. Breakfast and lunch were served only to the guests staying at the hotel, but in the evening, the restaurant was open to the public.

I led Kate to reception. Naomi was working tonight.

"Good evening, Henry," she greeted me with a beam that grew even brighter when she saw Kate at my side. Her warmth didn't surprise me. Naomi was one of the most kindhearted people I knew, and she'd only grown more so over the years, especially after the birth of her daughter. "You must be Kate. I'm Naomi, Rakesh's wife."

"They met each other here at the hotel," I added.

Kate shook Naomi's hand. "That's lovely. I met Rakesh earlier today."

"I know. He told me about you at lunch."

"How long have you been married?"

"For three years, but we've known each other for ten," Naomi replied, pushing a strand of light-brown hair behind her ear. "We married here at the hotel, up on the roof."

Kate smiled. "Wow, that sounds amazing."

"And where did the two of you meet?" Naomi asked and looked from Kate to me and back again with bright eyes. I was certain she hadn't learned about us from Rakesh alone—she must have also read the numerous articles now circulating on the internet.

"In St. James's Park," I replied.

"Bouldering," Kate said at the same time. There was a silence, and then Kate laughed nervously. "We met each other bouldering, but we didn't really start talking until we ran into each other again in the park."

Fuck.

Naomi narrowed her eyes. "You met at the bouldering gym?"

"Yes," Kate said, just as I said, "No."

Kate stiffened beside me, and Naomi began to look sceptical. Shit. We should have agreed on a story. Anyone who knew me at all knew that when I went bouldering, I rented out the entire gym for myself, so there was no way I could have met someone there. But Kate couldn't have known. "Kate used to clean there sometimes," I lied.

Naomi frowned. "Rakesh said you don't have any housekeeping experience."

"Not in the hotel business," Kate answered a little too swiftly, shifting nervously from one foot to the other like she was itching to leave. "A bouldering gym and a luxury hotel are pretty different, aren't they?"

Naomi looked at us silently and then hummed in agreement, but it was clear she wasn't entirely convinced by our far-fetched lie. I changed the topic before she had the chance to ask more questions. "I wanted to show Kate the ballroom. Can I have the key?"

"Maybe, if you say please."

I gave her my brightest smile. "Please."

"See, that wasn't so hard." Naomi retrieved a key attached to a large fob from a drawer. "Can you bring it back later?"

"Of course. Can you turn on the light for us, *please*?"

Naomi nodded, and Kate and I turned to leave. We walked in silence to stairs that led to a wide double door. I felt Naomi's wary eyes on my back. She'd probably tell Rakesh about our conversation as soon as Kate and I were out of earshot and eyesight.

"Sorry," Kate whispered to me as I unlocked the door. She leaned towards me so that no one else would hear, and I felt her warm breath on my skin as she spoke. "I didn't know that the bouldering thing was a bad answer. I already told Grace last week when she found me in your apartment, and I didn't want to change my original story."

"It's OK," I answered, just as quietly. "You couldn't know that I rent out the whole bouldering gym once a week. Grace wouldn't know either, so it's all good. We just have to be a bit more careful."

Kate looked worried. "What if Grace talks to Naomi?"

"Then that's just how it is," I said with a reassuring smile. The world wouldn't end if someone found out the truth, but the small lie would make our lives a little easier. Kate wouldn't have to answer any questions about her past, and I wouldn't have to face my mother's outrage. She'd been upset enough when she'd seen the photos of me and Kate; she would probably have a heart attack if she found out that Kate had been homeless for the past few months.

I unlocked the door and pushed it open a crack with my shoulder so we could slip in. The light was already on, and I heard Kate gasp as she took in the ballroom. Even I still found it awe-inspiring. Marble columns soared up to meet the ten-metre-high ceiling, beneath which hung a vast Renaissance painting we'd had restored five years ago to make its colours gleam with renewed brilliance. Crystal chandeliers hung from the ceiling, and there was a large stage at the front of the hall with heavy curtains on either side. The tables and chairs, usually decked out for festive occasions, had been pushed to the side and draped in white linen cloths so they wouldn't gather dust.

"I thought this kind of ballroom only existed in films," Kate murmured reverently. Her steps echoed through the empty hall, which was otherwise completely silent. The soft music in the foyer and the voices from the restaurant couldn't be heard from in here, and not even the noises of the city made it through the high windows.

"I often forget how big the ballroom is until I see it empty," I confessed.

"Do you often have events here?" Kate asked without looking at me. She was gazing up at the ceiling, walking backwards slowly as she admired the painting.

"Yes. Pretty often, actually. You can rent it out for birthdays, company parties, and weddings. But we also organise our own events. In June, we have our summer solstice party, and at the end of October, we throw a masked ball for Halloween. The Pearl Gala takes place here too, of course." The blank look on Kate's face told me that she had no idea what I was talking about. "It's a charity event. We invite a lot of very, very wealthy people to raise money for a charitable organisation."

"Oh, wait! Wasn't there a scandal a few years ago when that drunk boy-band member threw up on the red carpet?"

"Finnian Gomez." I remembered the incident clearly. It had happened at the first Pearl Gala I'd ever organised. Finnian and his band had been celebrating their breakout, which had been swiftly followed by their downfall. "I'm so glad that that stuck with you, of all things. We raised almost twenty million pounds for charity that year, but more importantly, Finnian puked."

Kate's eyes widened. "Twenty million?"

I nodded.

"Wow, that's a lot of money. It's cool that you do things like that."

"The gala was started by my grandmother, but I've been responsible for organising it since she died," I said, running my fingers through my hair. Somehow, Kate seemed to sense that something was on my mind, as she stopped and gave me her full attention. "This is probably a good moment to say that you inspired this year's Pearl Gala."

Kate furrowed her brow. "What do you mean?"

I took another step towards her. "The morning I left you alone in my apartment, I had a meeting about the gala. It was about which charitable organisation we want to raise money for this year. I couldn't stop thinking about what you told me. That there aren't enough sleeping places for homeless people in London. So I suggested it."

Kate blinked. "You want to raise money for us?"

Us.

I nodded. "I hope that's OK."

She didn't say anything. I thought I could hear my own heartbeat in the silence. The idea had seemed like a stroke of genius at the time, but now it felt like a mistake to not have asked Kate before.

She moved, stopping right in front of me. She smelled of lavender bath bubbles. The scent would, from now on, forever remind me of Kate. Although we hadn't known each other for long, the circumstances of our meeting had permanently etched her into my memory.

"I don't know what to say," she murmured.

"Are you angry at me?"

"Angry?" The furrow in her brow deepened. "No, grateful."

I exhaled in relief. "Really?"

"Really!" she confirmed, and I could hear her smile. "Do you know how many people you can help with that money? How many shelters could be built? How much food you could buy? Or clothes for the winter? Just ten pounds a day would change my life. And there are so many ten pounds in twenty million."

There were tears in her eyes. Tears of joy. Shit. I hadn't expected this.

She tried to blink the tears away, but one escaped and tracked its way down her cheek. Before it could fall to the ground, I caught it with my thumb. Without thinking, I had reached out and touched Kate. Her breath caught as my cool finger brushed her warm skin. For a brief moment, the world seemed to stop. Her expression was sombre, but I could also see her gratitude. And there was more. Another feeling, one that made me withdraw my hand. I stuffed it hastily into my hoodie pocket before I could do anything silly, like pull her towards me.

I cleared my throat. "Come on, I want to show you something." I walked to a seemingly random spot in the hall and pointed at the floor. "Do you see that?"

Kate stopped next to me, her shoulder brushing against my arm. The touch was fleeting but electric. "Do you mean that scratch?"

"Yes. That was me. I fell off my bike," I answered, trying to forget the touch as fast as I could.

"You rode your bike in here?"

"Yes, all the time. Bike. Skateboard. Rollerblades. Our parents technically forbade Logan and me to do any of it, but there's so much space here, and it was the perfect place to race around when it was dark and cold outside," I explained. "I like this hall because it's so grand and impressive, but also because it reminds me of my childhood and all the mischief we got up to. We used to hide here from our parents, until the staff told on us."

"It sounds like you had a good time here," Kate said. Her eyes shone, despite the fact that her brown irises were so dark that even the chandelier light seemed to get lost in them. "You talk a lot about Logan."

"Do I?" I said, surprised. I hadn't noticed it, and I didn't usually talk about him. My parents didn't like it when I mentioned him, and Ethan and Logan were practically strangers to each other who coincidentally shared DNA.

"Yes. Far more than you talk about the rest of your family anyway."

"Probably because he's the only one I really know," I confessed, and sat down next to the scratch on the ground. My dad had ordered for it to be sanded down and polished a few times over the years, but it was too deep, and it had never fully gone away. "My mum has always been very reserved. She's used to being a trophy wife and leaves all the talking to my dad. He, on the other hand, has always worked a lot. That's what he says anyway. It's possible he was just too busy with other women to spend time with his sons. Logan and I were alone a lot—we were best friends. We *are* best friends, even if the last years have been a little difficult."

Kate sat down next to me. "Why were they difficult?"

"Logan and I went to the same boarding school in Crawley, but our parents sent him to France unexpectedly when he was thirteen. From then on, he was only home for the holidays. I still don't know why they did that. After he graduated, he broke off contact with the family."

"But not with you?" Kate pressed.

I shook my head and ran my finger along the scratch. "No. We wrote to each other a lot, especially in his first few weeks in France. He was pretty lonely. But at some point, he made friends, and then we stopped speaking so often. Looking back, I wish I'd stuck up for Logan, or that I'd gone with him."

Kate placed a hand on my knee. I could feel its warmth even through my jeans. "You were practically a child yourself. What could you have done? It was your parents' decision, not yours, and Logan knows it."

I avoided her eyes. I didn't feel like I deserved her pity. "Perhaps, but it ruined a lot in our relationship. When Logan came back to London, I was already studying at Oxford, and then I started working for the hotel while he was pretty busy getting his own thing off the ground. We still get on well, but it's not like before. Whatever inspired our parents to send Logan to France is still a wedge between us. It's like he's the black sheep and I'm the golden child of the family."

"That doesn't sound fair."

"It isn't." I sighed. "Logan doesn't deserve it."

"Neither do you," Kate interrupted, her hand pressing more firmly against my knee. I looked up, drawn into her dark eyes as completely as the chandelier light had been. How could something so dark radiate such warmth? "It must be exhausting, having to carry the weight of your parents' expectations."

"I got used to it." *Have you really?* mocked a voice in my head, but I ignored it. "Still, sometimes I wish Logan were here to help me out, especially with all the shit that's going on right now."

"Couldn't you get him to come back? Now that you run the hotel?"

I snorted. "Oh, believe me, I've tried, but he doesn't want to. And I get it. The hotel isn't Logan's home like it is mine, and his restaurant is doing really well. He's even considering opening another location with his business partner," I said, full of pride for what my brother had accomplished—he had managed to build his own little empire. As much as I wanted him by my side, I didn't want him to sacrifice any of that for the hotel, especially after the way our parents had treated him. Even if that meant I had to put out all the fires single-handedly.

But I'd take care of that tomorrow.

This evening belonged to me and Kate.

The people still staying at The Darlington are part of the problem! #BoycottTheDarlington

Comment by Angry_Escape02

Kate

Henry led me around the entire hotel, showing me nooks that weren't on Grace's tour. This included the cigar room, the only place in The Darlington where smoking was allowed, and the game room, with its cupboards full of board and card games, some of them decades old. We went out onto the roof terrace with the bar Grace had raved about, and now I could see why. The view was breathtaking. All of London sprawled out below, and lights glinted everywhere, almost as though the city created its own starry sky. Despite the cold, the bar was busy—part of it was in a heated dome, and the chairs and tables outside were warmed by heating units. As we had a drink, Henry told me more stories about the hotel and him and Logan, and explained what the deal was with the uniformity of his DVD collection.

Later, we took the lift from the roof down to the basement, which was anything but musty and damp. It had been converted into a wellness area with several saunas—Henry explained the difference between a Finnish sauna and a steam room—and a heated indoor pool modelled on a grotto, with turquoise water and a small waterfall. The plants dotted throughout the wellness area gave it a tropical atmosphere. According to Henry, he'd had many water fights there with Logan, all of which Henry had won.

"Ready for the last stop of the tour?" Henry asked.

No. I didn't want the evening to be over. I liked spending time with Henry and wanted to hear more stories about the hotel. I hadn't had a proper home in a long time. I'd never felt comfortable in Randell's rundown place, and even the flat where my mum and I had lived before hadn't really felt homey. Hearing Henry talk about The Darlington, though, made me feel at home. He loved the hotel, and I hated that it took so much of his strength for him to save what he loved.

"Yes," I replied after a brief hesitation.

"This was my grandfather's favourite room," said Henry as we stopped in front of a massive door on the first floor, not far from my room. The door was adorned with intricate carvings that made it look like a bookcase.

As it happened, there really was a room full of books concealed behind the door. A library.

Inside, it smelled of paper, glue, and the dust that had collected between book pages. The walls were lined floor to ceiling with built-in shelves made of dark, solid wood. The books on the upper shelves could only be reached with sliding ladders attached to cabinets. In the middle of the room were several cosy winged armchairs next to tables with cast-iron reading lamps on them.

"I think this will be my favourite room too," I said, and ran a finger over an old leather binding. Judging by the spines, there was also a large collection of modern literature. I spotted novels by Stephen King, Jojo Moyes, and Nora Roberts, and it looked like there were books in languages other than English.

Henry closed the door behind us. "Do you like reading?"

I nodded, even though it was a hobby I'd neglected in recent years. My mum hadn't been able to afford to buy me books, so I'd made good use of the school library. But after I'd dropped out of school, I hadn't been able to go anymore, and I'd been too busy trying to make money to find time to register at the public library.

"What's your favourite book?" Henry asked. His voice was low even though we were alone—the room exuded a kind of serenity.

I had my back turned to him as I browsed the books, but I could still feel his eyes on me. My skin prickled. "*The Brave Cloud Princess*."

"Isn't that a children's book?"

"Yes, by Evelyn Fairchild," I answered, thinking about the tattered copy I had in my rucksack. The cover was stained, the paper water-damaged, and some of the ink had run in the rain, but I wouldn't exchange it for a new copy even if I could afford it. "My mum used to read it to me, and it was also the first book I read by myself. Although I was cheating a bit, because I knew almost the whole story off by heart."

"Perhaps I should read it too."

I turned to him, and our eyes met. The warmth in my stomach returned. "You definitely should. It's great. Do you have a favourite book?"

"Not really."

"That's a shame."

Henry sat on an armchair and looked around the room. "My granddad always tried to get me excited about books. He hosted a lot of readings here, and he was a real fanboy when it came to his favourite writers. He had told us at least thirty times about the time J. R. R. Tolkien stayed at the hotel and read from *The Hobbit*. But for some reason, his passion for books never rubbed off on me. I think I read my last book when I was at Oxford."

I wandered over to Henry and sat in the armchair next to his. I sank deep into the upholstery. "Your granddad and I probably would have got on well. I've not read very much in the last few years, but I love reading. It used to be my biggest wish to be a children's book writer, because I wanted to be like Evelyn Fairchild."

"You don't want that anymore?"

"No, it was just a brief phase."

"What would you like to do instead?"

"No idea," I answered honestly. I really didn't know and hadn't thought about it for a long time. Manifesting self-fulfilment was a luxury I hadn't been able to afford until now. "When I was a teenager, I wanted to do some kind of social work and help people living in precarious situations, but instead, I became one of those people."

"I'm sorry," Henry said, and for a brief moment it seemed as though he wanted to reach out his hand to comfort me. I wished he would. Instead, he picked a bit of lint from his hoodie.

"What about you?" I asked, making an effort not to let my disappointment show. The part of my face Henry had touched with his thumb earlier was still tingling pleasurably.

"What about me?"

"Have you always wanted to run The Darlington?"

"Yes, only I imagined the job being pretty different. And it would have been nice to get into it under different circumstances. I guess you can't always choose how things pan out."

"No, you can't," I agreed. If I'd had any agency when it came to my life, I'd definitely have opted for a different version. "Can I ask you a question?"

"Of course, Pumpkin."

I grimaced. "Nope."

Henry knit his brow. "Why not? It's cute."

"I don't want to be a vegetable."

"So Sweet Potato is also a no-go?"

"Totally."

"Shame," Henry said. I heard his phone vibrate in his hoodie pocket. He retrieved it and sneaked a glance at his display, before returning it. It was by no means the first message of the evening. "So, what did you want to ask me?"

"Who was that?" It wasn't the question I'd wanted to ask.

"No one important. Just a business contact."

I raised my eyebrows. "At this time?"

"Yes. I'm usually still at the office now."

"Doesn't it annoy you?" The constant notifications had stressed me out in the short time I'd had his phone, and they hadn't even been intended for me.

He shrugged. "Yes, but that's part of it. It's why I try to leave my phone in the kitchen at night, rather than taking it into the bedroom with me. It doesn't always work."

"I can steal it again if you want, and then you'll have your peace. And I'll finally have a phone again," I joked. And it was a joke: I'd never steal from Henry again, or from anyone else if I had the choice. I wanted to take the opportunity The Darlington was offering me.

Henry tilted his head. "You said yours was broken?"

"Yes, but it was never *not* broken. It was ancient. I bought it years ago for a few pounds. So it was only a matter of time before it fell apart," I answered. In the past months, I'd hardly needed it. There hadn't been anyone in my life who I wanted to call or message. But now that I had Henry and Grace, it might be nice to have a phone again.

"I have an old phone somewhere," Henry said.

I snorted. "Show-off."

He rolled his eyes. "What I'm trying to say is that you're welcome to have it if you want it."

"Are you serious?"

"Sure. I don't need it anymore."

I raised my eyebrows sceptically. Henry had already given me so much without getting anything in return. Apart from my service of cleaning rooms, which I'd more or less forced him to arrange for me. I still didn't get it. "Are you telling the truth?"

He laughed. "I am. I have a contract, and I get a new phone every year. I gave Rakesh the one I had last year for his cousin. But I should still have the one from the year before. It's yours, if you want it."

I bit my lower lip and saw Henry notice, his eyes lingering on my mouth. Warmth flooded my belly. "I'll take it. But only if you really don't need it. And if you want it back, just say."

"That won't happen, but fine."

"Thank you," I said, just as Henry's phone vibrated again. We locked eyes and started laughing. This time, Henry didn't check to see who had messaged. His gaze remained fixed on me, only fuelling the heat in my stomach.

"But you actually wanted to ask me something else, right?"

It had already completely slipped my mind. I cleared my throat, sensing that my voice might betray me and reveal what was happening to my body. "Yes, but you don't have to answer if you don't want to."

Henry's mouth twitched into a quick smile. "Ask away."

"Where does your money come from? Your family's, I mean. I don't know anything about it besides that The Darlington is pretty expensive to stay at. But do you really make so much money from it? I mean, you're not just rich, you're *really* rich."

"The hotel is pretty lucrative," Henry admitted, seeming keen to satisfy my curiosity. "The most expensive suite costs over ten thousand pounds a night, and it adds up to quite a lot. And when you make a lot of money, it's easy to make even more. My grandparents invested wisely in shares and other companies, and they also bought land and property. When they died, half of their assets went to my parents, and the rest was divided between Ethan, Logan and me."

"So you earn your money by having money?" I summarised.

Henry nodded. "So to speak."

"I'm envious," I confessed, which made him smile. "I have one more question, and then I'm done. I promise." He looked at me expectantly. "You've told me a lot about Logan, but what about Ethan?"

"What about him?"

"Do you get on?"

Henry distractedly ran his hands over the armrests of his chair. "It's hard to say. We don't have much to do with each other. He was a little kid when I left for boarding school, and by the time he was sent there himself I'd already started at Oxford. We've been ships in the night for most of our lives. So yes, we get on, but we don't spend more time than necessary together. Not that Ethan would want to. I sometimes worry about him."

"Why?" I asked, thinking about the smell of weed in his kitchen. Did Henry know that his brother smoked? Perhaps he was just as worried about Ethan's drug habit as I had been about my mum's.

"He parties a lot. Too much. He's constantly skipping seminars at university, and he hangs around with the wrong sort of people. Ethan has a lot of potential. He's more intelligent than he makes out, and incredibly talented. But he's lost his way. I hope he finds it, before it's too late."

"I'm sure he will," I assured him with a smile. Perhaps I'd mention the weed to him sometime, but not today. We'd had enough deep talk for one night, and I didn't want him to ask uncomfortable questions about my past. I got up and continued examining the library, even though I knew it would take me days to look at every single book. I pulled an old fairy tale from a shelf and leafed through it carefully. The pages were yellowed and the font was ornate, as was often the case in very old, very valuable books. It was hard to decipher, so I put it back to look at some of the newer ones.

"You can borrow something, if you want."

I turned, only now realising that Henry had also stood. He was right behind me. Damn, I really abandoned all caution when it came to him.

"Really?"

"Sure. That's what they're there for. As long as you promise not to steal them."

I grinned. "I wouldn't dream of it."

THE BLACKROOM

There are new developments in the Richard Darlington case: Darlington has to stand trial.

Despite his efforts to make evidence disappear, enough has been secured to press charges against him. The date of the trial is as yet undecided, but bail has already been set. Richard Darlington's conditions include house arrest in London. He must remain within a three-mile radius of The Darlington Hotel. In addition, he has lost access to his bank accounts, and must pay a seven-figure sum to avoid incarceration. He faces imprisonment if he violates any one of these conditions.

The road to justice is often long, but these recent developments are a step in the right direction. We will continue to report on the progress of the trial.

24

EXCLUSIVE: Richard Darlington to Stand Trial!
The Billionaire Faces Up to 25 Years in Prison!

INsider headline

Kate

"We're going for a drink. Are you coming?" Grace asked.

We meant Grace and Rose from the kitchen. Grace had introduced us last week. Rose had been working as a kitchen aide at Darlington Dining for four years. She was quiet and often sat back to listen and observe while Grace and I talked. Rose reminded me of the person I had been on the streets. Always alert, always on guard.

"No. Maybe some other time," I answered. I had my own work schedule now, so Grace and I didn't see each other as often as we had at the beginning. But I still needed to get used to spending money for fun. I could probably spare the four pounds for a pint of beer, but I couldn't bring myself to do it, even though I'd be paid my first salary at the end of the month.

Grace wound a scarf in the same shade as her lipstick around her neck. "Are you sure? Amy is coming too."

"I'm not in the mood. Sorry."

"Leave her, if she doesn't want to," Rose stepped into the changing room and came to my rescue. She had dark-brown, almost-black long hair and green eyes. They were beautiful but extremely intense, and I sometimes found it hard to maintain eye contact with her.

Rose came over and placed two takeaway boxes next to me. Since she'd found out I'd been living off the fruit from the corridors for days, she insisted on giving me food. There was always something left over at the restaurant. Sometimes she brought it to the changing room after her shift, or else I picked it up from the kitchen.

"Thanks. What is it today?"

"Smoked sweet potato gnocchi with a pepper and cream sauce and morels. And crêpe suzette for dessert," she said, with an enthusiasm I rarely heard from her. Rose dreamed of becoming a Michelin-star chef and was working at The Darlington to save up for culinary school, which cost a small fortune.

I smiled. "Sounds delicious. But what are *morels*?"

"Mushrooms."

"And what's *suzette*?"

"Crepes in an orange-liqueur-and-orange-juice sauce."

Thank god. I never complained about food, especially if it was free, but these rich people ate a lot of weird stuff. Yesterday Rose had brought me something with caviar, and the day before, it had been duck liver. Neither was in the running to become my favourite food.

Grace sighed. "OK, I'll let you off the hook today. But next time, you're coming with us."

"I promise," I said, and retrieved the room key from my locker. It was the only thing in there. I'd started taking my uniform up to my room and changing there. "Have a nice evening."

"Thank you, you too," Grace and Rose said almost in unison.

I left the changing room and waved goodbye to the people in the break room. I knew almost everyone by name now, and I felt very at home at The Darlington. Probably mostly due to Henry's tour last week. No matter where in the hotel I was, I couldn't help but think about his stories. His memories had somehow become mine. Which meant, wherever I was, I was always thinking about him and wondering what he was doing. We'd run into each other a few times in the corridors, but Henry had always been with important-looking people, and we hadn't had a chance to talk. He had a lot on his plate, and his life had been tumultuous since the judge had approved the indictment against his dad late last week. It meant that Richard Darlington would have to face trial. The news had spread through the media like wildfire, and the scandalous headlines kept coming. There were more journalists than ever camped out before the hotel, hoping to get a photo or even a statement from the family.

I took the stairs up to the first floor, unlocked my door, and went into my room. I'd cancelled the cleaning service, so the room looked exactly as it had when I'd left it in the morning. My bed was unmade, my jeans were hung over the armchair, and a jumper lay on the floor. Yesterday's takeaway boxes were on the bedside table. I placed the new boxes next to them for later, then went to the bathroom and ran a bath. Taking baths had become part of my daily routine. I'd been living at The Darlington for two weeks now, but it still sometimes felt surreal, like a dream I could wake up from at any moment, shivering and hungry in St. James's Park. If it was a dream, I had no desire to return to my reality.

After I'd checked the water temperature, I poured in a splash of the fragrant bath bubbles. The scent of lavender filled the bathroom. I inhaled deeply and went back into the bedroom to choose a new book. I'd read more in the last few days than in the last three or four years combined. I was on my way back to the bathroom with the book I had picked out when I stubbed my foot on the desk chair.

"Fuck," I swore and grabbed my little toe. It throbbed intensely.

My rucksack had fallen from the chair in the collision, and some of its contents had spilled onto the floor. I rubbed my foot until the pain subsided, then knelt to pick up my belongings. They had seemed so vital to me for months, but I hadn't touched them since I'd arrived at The Darlington. I crammed everything back into my rucksack until all that was left was an envelope. I pulled out the old photos of me and my mum. They were faded and well-thumbed, because of how often I'd looked at them in the past year.

The first photo was taken in hospital after my birth. My mum held me—a tiny bundle—in her arms and smiled at the camera, exhausted but happy. The second photo showed me a year later taking my first steps as I held my mum's hand. I had no idea who'd taken the photo, but I seemed happy, and my mum looked like she was bursting with pride. In the third photo, we were in a café sharing a slice of apple cake, my mum's favourite. We hadn't been able to afford cake often, but every time we splashed out, it was a highlight.

I looked through the pile until I got to the last photo. It had been taken only three years ago. In it, we were sitting in St. James's

Park feeding a couple of insistent pigeons. My mum was laughing heartily while I pulled a face. I'd been convinced back then that I was too cool to enjoy the moment. Today, I would have given anything to relive that moment with her. I missed her every day and wished she were still with me. I wanted to tell her about Henry and The Darlington. She would have freaked out if she knew I lived here and would have insisted on meeting Henry. I was sure she would have got on well with him, at least the version of herself she'd been before the drugs had changed her. They had transformed her from a kind and compassionate woman, albeit one with struggles, into a selfish, dull shadow of her former self. It had been terrifying to watch her personality slip away bit by bit, along with everything else that had once defined her. Drugs were pure poison.

Suddenly, the doorbell rang.

"Coming," I shouted.

I crammed the photos back into the envelope, and instead of returning it to the rucksack, I placed it in the bedside table drawer. I limped to the door, my toe still throbbing.

I opened it to find Naomi in her receptionist uniform. She had tied her hair up into a neat bun.

"Hey," I said. I hadn't been expecting her.

She tilted her head and looked at me with concern. I probably still had tears in my eyes. Partly because of the pain, and partly because I missed my mum. "Is everything OK?"

"Yes, I just stubbed my toe."

Naomi pulled a face. "Ouch. That hurts. Shall I bring you some ice?"

"No, it's fine," I said with a smile. "What's up?"

"I'm supposed to give you this from Henry," she said and handed me a small white box and a black envelope, its wax seal embossed with The Darlington logo, just like the one he'd sent me on my first weekend at the hotel.

"Thanks for bringing it over," I said as I took it.

"Henry wanted to give them to you himself, but he's stuck in a call. He wanted you to get them today," Naomi said with a knowing smile. "I have to get back to reception. Have a nice evening."

"You too," I said, and closed the door. I broke the wax seal on my way to the bed and took out the letter, which once again bore Henry's barely legible scrawl.

> Sorry for making you wait so long for the phone. The last days have been hell, and I just didn't have time. Have fun with it. Message me.
>
> Henry

A broad grin spread across my face, and my heart started beating faster. Knowing that Henry was sitting in his office waiting for a message from me made something in my chest flutter. I set the letter aside and reached for the box. It was the phone's original packaging, and I lifted the lid to reveal a sleek device. It had a few small scratches, but otherwise it looked good as new.

"Shit!" I exclaimed when I remembered the bathwater was still running. I tossed the phone aside and ran into the bathroom, reaching the bathtub just in time. The water had reached the top of the overflow drain, and foam was already spilling over the edge of the tub. I wrenched the tap shut and wiped the foam from the floor. Before undressing and slipping into the warm water, I fetched my phone from the bedroom.

I dried my hands on a towel. When I turned it on, the home display lit up immediately. It had already been set up. I instinctively checked the contacts, and sure enough, a name had been saved.

I grinned and wrote *Snowflake* a message.

ME:

Thank you.

I wasn't expecting a reply, since Naomi had said Henry was stuck in a call, but to my surprise, I got one right away.

SNOWFLAKE:

You're welcome. I hope you like it.

ME:

It's perfect, so much better than my old one.

SNOWFLAKE:

I'm glad.

ME:

You really don't need it?

SNOWFLAKE:

No, you can have it.

ME:

OK. I just don't want to take advantage of you.

SNOWFLAKE:

You're not. Anyway, it's not like I'm getting nothing out of it.

ME:

Oh, really?

SNOWFLAKE:

Yes. Now I can message you.

ME:

That doesn't sound like a fair exchange.

SNOWFLAKE:

It is. Believe me. I need to talk to someone who doesn't make me want to rip every single hair from my head.

ME:

Is it that bad?

Henry was typing, but it took a while until he sent his answer.

SNOWFLAKE:

Worse. We've had another resignation and more cancellations. And my dad is furious because his case is being taken to court. He's mad about how much the bail is, even though his wife has gone on shopping sprees before where she's spent more than the bail. He's fired and rehired his lawyers at least seven times in the last six days. Vivian, his crisis manager, is going berserk about the media coverage, and she's trying to talk me into doing interviews and photo shoots so they can report on me instead of on him. Like I'm his fucking shield. And as if that weren't enough, there are even more journalists loitering outside the hotel now. I had to hire a security company today to make sure they don't harass our guests.

ME:

I'm sorry.

SNOWFLAKE:

It's not your fault.

ME:

But it's not yours either.

SNOWFLAKE:

I had all these grand plans for when I'd take over the hotel one day. I wanted to open a second location in Edinburgh, and perhaps one in Birmingham too. I wanted to put in a little cinema in the basement for exclusive screenings. I had so many ideas, and now all I'm doing is fending off press enquiries about my dad's sexual inclinations.

ME:

You'll be able to do all those things one day.

SNOWFLAKE:

If the hotel is even still around then.

ME:

It will be.

SNOWFLAKE:

How do you know?

ME:

Because I've seen how much you love it.

SNOWFLAKE:

Sometimes love isn't enough.

I couldn't help but think about my mum and about how my love for her hadn't been enough to save her. She had chosen Randell and the drugs over me, even though I'd sacrificed everything for her. My time, my education, my money. Even my friends, because I'd spent my time going to work and shoplifting to keep us afloat instead of meeting up with them. So maybe Henry was right. Maybe sometimes love just wasn't enough.

SNOWFLAKE:

Let's talk about something else.
I've had some more thoughts about your nickname.

ME:

Go on.

SNOWFLAKE:

What do you think about Bambi?

ME:

You're only saying that because I have big brown eyes and my mum is dead.

SNOWFLAKE:

Not true, but . . . forget it.
What about Bunny?

ME:

Nope.

SNOWFLAKE:

Kitten?

ME:

Only if you want me to scratch out your eyes.

SNOWFLAKE:

You're not making this easy for me.

ME:

Perhaps it's your imagination and not me that's the problem.

SNOWFLAKE:

I don't think so. I'll give it some more thought . . . How are you? How was your day?

ME:

Life is treating me pretty well right now.

I took a photo with the phone's camera, capturing the bathroom and a mountain of bath bubbles with my knees rising from it.

I sent it to Henry, but this time he didn't write back straightaway. He'd probably received a call. I took the book I'd picked out earlier and began to read. I'd only managed one paragraph when my phone vibrated with a new message. I reached for it so fast that I splashed water and foam onto the display.

SNOWFLAKE:

Shit, Kate.

ME:

What?

SNOWFLAKE:

Your photo.

ME:

What about it?

SNOWFLAKE:

You're naked.

ME:

Yes, I'm taking a bath.

SNOWFLAKE:

I see that. But you're naked beneath all those bubbles!
And now I'm imagining it.

I bit my lower lip. It hadn't been my intention, but . . . I also didn't mind. On the contrary. Knowing that Henry was thinking about me sent a wave of heat through me that had nothing to do with the warm bath.

SNOWFLAKE:

Fuck, Kate. I'm sorry! I shouldn't have written that.
Completely inappropriate.
Can we put it down to me being totally overworked?

ME:

Don't be sorry. I hope you're enjoying the image.

Three dots appeared, signalling that Henry was writing again, but then they disappeared. A moment later, they reappeared. Then disappeared. After a moment, I finally got my reply:

SNOWFLAKE:

I am.
It's a very nice one.

I made a noise I was sure I'd never made before in my life. It was a cross between a squeak, a laugh, and a shout of joy. Henry was picturing me naked—and he liked it. Holy shit.

SNOWFLAKE:

Is it OK that I said that?
Please don't report me for sexual harassment.

ME:

I was about to start looking for a lawyer . . .

SNOWFLAKE:

My dad knows a couple of good ones.

ME:

I can't afford them.
Perhaps we should settle this out of court.

SNOWFLAKE:

How?

ME:

You owe me a photo.

SNOWFLAKE:

Sounds like a fair deal.

I grinned at my new phone, but my smile disappeared when Henry's photo suddenly appeared. I assumed he'd take one in his office and that it would feature stacks of files and folders. Instead, he had sent me an older picture of himself at the beach. He was smiling at the camera with his feet buried in the sand and the sea behind him, wearing only a pair of swimming trunks. *Wet* trunks that clung to the contours of his body. He didn't look like Ethan. No six-pack, no muscles honed at the gym just for the aesthetics. Henry's muscles were less showy, more practical, made to support his body when he was bouldering. Personally, I found that much more attractive. The heat inside me moved down to between my thighs, where it grew even more fiery when I thought about the bulge in Henry's trunks.

SNOWFLAKE:

Let your imagination run wild.

25

> Write to M about V.

Note on Henry's phone

Henry

The first journalists were arriving at the press conference where I was about to announce the Pearl Gala. I could hear their voices, the clicking of their cameras, and the snapping of their tripods being tested and set up. I paced restlessly back and forth in a small room behind the stage, using a ballpoint pen to correct the speech that Vivian had handed me this morning to read out. It wasn't an announcement, though. It was a bad joke. Twenty-five percent of it was about the hotel and the gala, the other seventy-five waxed lyrical about my dad's dedication and commitment, as if he gave a shit about the gala. He only cared about how it could restore his reputation. He hadn't even asked me what organisation we were supporting this year.

"Mr. Darlington?" came a bright voice from next to me.

I looked up to see a woman with auburn hair and gold-rimmed glasses. She was wearing a colourful jacket adorned with a rainbow broach. This could only be Matilda Gallagher from Hope

Harbour, a national organisation dedicated to helping the homeless. Its headquarters were in Glasgow, but it had branches across Britain and Ireland.

"Mrs. Gallagher?"

She nodded. "Yes, but you can call me Tilly."

"Henry." I shook her hand. "I'm glad you're here."

She pushed her glasses up the bridge of her nose nervously. "Thanks for having us. Everyone at Hope Harbour is completely over the moon. It's incredible that The Darlington chose to raise money for us at this year's gala. We thought at first that the request was a joke."

I laughed, which, thanks to my headache, felt terrible. "No, we're completely serious."

"I can tell," said Tilly, glancing in the direction of the journalists' voices, which were growing ever louder. "Still, it really surprised us. We asked your grandmother a few years ago, but she turned us down because she thought it would be better to support international charities."

"Yes, Hope Harbour is the first local organisation we're supporting."

"Can I ask how this has come about? Rakesh told me on the phone that it was your suggestion."

"A friend, Kate, gave me the idea."

The door opened, and my dad came in with Vivian. My shoulders tensed and the atmosphere in the room changed immediately. But perhaps I was just imagining it. Vivian put on her most charming fake smile and made a beeline for Tilly, who nervously adjusted her glasses again even though they were sitting perfectly.

"You must be Mrs. Graham from Hope Harbour."

"Gallagher," Tilly corrected. "But you can call me Tilly."

"I'm Mrs. Edwards, and this is Mr. Richard Darlington," Vivian said, as if my dad were incapable of introducing himself. "We're so happy that the Pearl Gala can support Hope Harbour this year. Mr. Darlington chose your organisation himself. The well-being of Londoners is a matter very close to his heart."

"I know, we were just talking about it," Tilly said and gave me a warm smile, a stark contrast to the cold looks Vivian and my dad were shooting me. They'd become even icier when they noticed that I'd cut the praise for my dad from the speech.

"Henry suggested it, but it was Mr. Darlington who made the final decision to support Hope Harbour." Vivian's voice was sweet, but her words were bitter and laced with an unspoken warning that I hold my tongue.

I ignored her. "That's not true."

My dad let out a hollow laugh, and the wrinkles around his joyless eyes deepened. "Henry, let's be honest."

"In which case, you should try telling the truth for once," I retorted. I wasn't interested in praise. Rakesh was welcome to take all the recognition from Hope Harbour. He'd selected and contacted the organisations, and all I'd done was give my approval at the end. My dad, on the other hand, hadn't lifted a finger in the last weeks, neither for the gala nor the hotel. Meanwhile, I'd been working eighteen-hour shifts for days, hunched over my desk until late at night, cleaning up his mess. The Darlington now had an average occupancy of just 50 percent, and the numbers were trending downward. If reservations didn't pick up soon, we'd have to lay off even more staff despite the many resignations, because there just wasn't enough work to go around. The hotel was a service business, and if there was no one to use the service, the staff were paid to do nothing. On top of that, I was frustrated—I hadn't seen Kate in days while my dad had been off doing god knows what. He was probably screwing Vivian. How else could I explain their mutual sucking up?

"Mrs. Gallagher . . . Tilly," Vivian said, "how do you feel about getting a coffee?" Before Tilly could answer, Vivian grabbed her by the arm and pulled her away from me and my dad. He waited until the two women were out of earshot before speaking.

"What the hell are you doing?" he hissed.

"I could ask you the same thing. *You* chose Hope Harbour? I bet you didn't even know the name of the organisation until Vivian whispered it to you at the door," I retorted, defiantly looking him in the eye. The vein on his forehead stood out more with every word I spoke.

My dad took a step towards me, and a cloud of his heavy, musky aftershave hit me in the face. We'd been the same height just a few years ago, but he'd shrunk a couple of centimetres with age. "We agreed that we'd communicate it that way."

"You and Vivian agreed. I never did."

My dad's eyes narrowed, and he looked at me with more disdain than a parent should feel for their child. I didn't want it to hurt, but there was a stabbing in my chest that was hard to ignore. "It looks like running the hotel has gone to your head," he said, his voice cutting through me like a sharpened blade. "I hope you know that you're only in this position because a couple of sluts think they can fuck me over. As soon as I've taken them down in court, I'll take over running the hotel again. You should bear that in mind before you start playing the big man."

I clenched my teeth. The Darlington was *my* hotel, and he would get it back over my dead body. Regardless of what happened in court, my dad and his reputation were the reason why there might soon no longer be a hotel. If I managed to save it, I sure as hell wouldn't let him have it without a fight. But telling him that would have been a waste of breath, and I had to prepare for the press conference. I needed to impress the journalists, and I couldn't do that in my current state.

"I'm going for a piss," I said, bumping him with my shoulder as I pushed past him. It was a childish move, but it gave me a small sense of satisfaction.

"Henry!"

I stopped and immediately regretted it. I waited with my hand on the doorknob, refusing to turn around.

"While you're at it, ask your mum if she has concealer she can give you. You look like shit."

Because of you, I thought, but I wasn't about to open up the discussion again. I swallowed down the words and left the room.

I met Tilly in the hallway. She was holding a coffee, but Vivian was nowhere to be seen. I told her I'd be right back and headed for the nearest men's restroom. I quickly checked if the stalls were empty—I needed a moment to myself.

I was alone. After using a urinal, I washed my hands. I caught my reflection in the mirror. My dad was right—I couldn't sugarcoat it. I looked like crap.

I had had a sleepless night. I hadn't been able to get Kate and the image of her in the bath out of my mind. And after that, I couldn't shake thoughts of the upcoming press conference, and how much I wanted the Pearl Gala to be a success. Not just for the sake of the hotel but, more importantly, for Hope Harbour, who could put the money to good use and create meaningful change in the city. Sometime well past midnight, I had given up trying to sleep and got on the elliptical trainer to quiet my thoughts and burn off all that destructive energy. But even that hadn't helped. After taking an ice-cold shower to shock myself even more awake, I'd finally gone to the office—at 4 a.m. So yeah, I looked like shit.

At least I wasn't a piece of shit like my dad.

I breathed deeply to gather myself, preparing for a barrage of unpleasant questions. Vivian had informed the journalists that I wouldn't be making a statement about my dad, but they would probably still dig for answers. A few weeks ago, I'd thought we'd survived the worst of the media frenzy, but I had been wrong. It had been a shitstorm before, but we were now about to be hit by a shit hurricane. I knew I would have to face it.

I let go of the sink I had been clinging to as if it were a climbing hold at the bouldering gym, but my balance was short-lived. I tensed my shoulders as a sudden wave of wrenching dizziness hit me and I staggered, grabbing the porcelain sink again for support.

Fuck!

I squeezed my eyes shut, but even in the darkness, the world still seemed to be spinning wildly. Again, I concentrated on my breathing. It took a while for the dizziness to subside. The throbbing in my head had intensified, and I carefully let go of the sink to reach for the pillbox in my suit jacket pocket.

In that instant, a sudden knock sounded at the door.

I withdrew my hand as Olivia came in. I had told her about the conference, but I hadn't thought she'd come. We'd not seen each other much lately. We'd both been busy with our own lives.

"Hey," she greeted me.

I smiled weakly. "You came."

"Yes. I thought you could use a friendly face," Olivia said, taking a step towards me. As always, she looked fantastic. She was wearing elegant trousers and a tight-fitting olive-green top that accentuated her athletic figure. Several gold chains hung around her neck, and her blond hair cascaded down her back in perfect waves. "Why are you hiding back here?"

"I needed a moment to myself."

"Understandable." She leaned against the wall. "That Vivian woman is awful."

I grinned, but even that was enough to send a stab of pain shooting through my head. Perhaps I'd overdone last night's workout. "What did she do?"

"She was bossing your mum around when I arrived, as if Amanda works for Vivian and not the other way around. And then she had a go at me for letting you date that grungy girl, Kate. Her words, not mine," Olivia clarified immediately when she noticed my scowl. "Have Commander Vivian and your parents even realised yet that she works at the hotel?"

I had told Olivia before Kate's first day of work that I'd given her not just a room at the hotel but also a job. Olivia had been thrilled and regularly asked me for updates. Not that there'd been much to report until last night's chatting. I'd barely spoken to Kate, even though I'd thought about her a lot.

"No, they wouldn't notice unless there was a headline about it," I answered, attempting to straighten up my twisted tie.

"Which there could be if someone from the press spots Kate here."

"Then so be it. They'll find out sooner or later anyway."

"How is it going with her?" Olivia asked. My mouth twitched, and a spark appeared in my best friend's eyes. "Tell me everything!"

"We messaged for a while yesterday."

"Messaged?" She sounded disappointed. "You both live in the hotel."

"Yes, but I don't leave the office before ten these days. I gave her one of my old phones so we can at least write to each other."

"So what did you message about?" Olivia asked. She pushed herself away from the wall and came to straighten my obstinately wonky tie. She smelled of expensive perfume—vanilla with a hint of coconut.

"She sent me a selfie of herself in the bath," I said with my eyes on Olivia, who was loosening my tie to retie it. "And I replied that I was imagining her naked."

Olivia looked up abruptly. "You're kidding! How did she react?"

"She said she wanted a photo of me."

"Wow. Which one did you send her?"

"The one you took on the Côte d'Azur."

"That's a good one. You look very fuckable."

I grinned. "I know."

Olivia laughed. She had finished with my tie and took a step back to assess her work from a distance. Satisfied, she nodded and gestured for me to look in the mirror. I still looked like shit, but at least my tie was straight. My thoughts turned from Kate to the journalists, who were probably already waiting for me impatiently.

"Thanks for sorting out my tie."

"You're welcome."

"Can you tell Vivian that I'll be there soon? I need a minute."

Olivia nodded and patted my arm before she left the bathroom. I'd initially liked the idea of a press conference, but that had been before the shit hurricane had blown into my life, and now I wasn't so sure anymore. All I wanted was to run the hotel and carry out the plans I'd told Kate about. I didn't want to deal with journalists. But it was too late to pull out now. I took a deep breath to brace myself, and took out the box from my jacket pocket once again. I swallowed a pill without water, hoping it would cure my exhaustion as well as my headache. Unfortunately, I didn't have time to wait around for it to work its magic.

I straightened my suit one last time. Then I stepped out into the corridor . . .

. . . to meet my fate.

> Good luck with the press thing. You've got this!

Message from Kate to Henry

Kate

I sat in the break room at The Darlington watching the press conference that was taking place just a few rooms away. One of the local channels was broadcasting it live, as if it were a sporting event. I clung to Henry's every word. He announced which organisation the gala would be raising money for this year and then handed the mic over to a woman wearing large glasses and a colourful jacket. She had friendly brown eyes and a broad smile. Her name was displayed at the bottom of the screen: Matilda Gallagher, chairwoman of the Hope Harbour foundation in London.

She introduced herself and started talking about the organisation, but I only had eyes for Henry, who had taken a step back. Unsurprisingly, he looked phenomenal in his dark suit. Knowing what was concealed under his jacket and shirt only made it better. Our conversation last night had kept me awake for a while, and when I'd woken up this morning, the first thing I'd done was reach for my phone and reread our messages to make sure I hadn't dreamed our exchange.

The door to the break room swung open and Giulia came in. Her gaze swept the room and finally landed on me. I was ready to be admonished for sitting around instead of working—I'd been desperate to watch the press conference, even though my lunch break had ended half an hour ago. But Giulia seemed more stressed than angry. "Kate, I'm glad you're here!"

I smiled. "Hi. Is everything OK?"

"I really need your help. Can you clean room 316 right away? Mr. Fleming checked in half an hour ago and complained that the bathroom wasn't properly clean. We'd move him, but he insisted on his regular room."

"Sure, no problem."

Giulia sighed with relief. "Thank you, you're a gem. Please apologise to him again on behalf of the hotel, and tell him that lunch at Darlington Dining is on us. I've reserved a table for him. He can wait there while you're cleaning the room."

I nodded and made my way out. I could watch the press conference later. Or, better yet, Henry could tell me about it. I took the lift up to the third floor and got a cleaning cart from the housekeeping room. When I arrived at room 316, I rang the doorbell and put on my friendliest smile.

The door was opened by an older man of around fifty with thinning black hair. He was wearing a suit, and the buttons on his jacket strained over his belly as if he'd been indulging a little too much lately. He scowled at me.

"About time," Mr. Fleming snapped.

"I'm sorry to have kept you waiting," I said, although I had arrived as quickly as I could. "I apologise sincerely on behalf of

The Darlington for any inconvenience caused. I'd like to clean your room, if that's OK. You can enjoy a complimentary lunch at Darlington Dining in the meantime."

Mr. Fleming grunted and pushed the door open wider. He didn't step aside, so I had to squeeze past him to get in, my arm brushing his chest as I rolled the cart into the room behind me. He sat down on the bed to put on his shoes as I started working. Instead of leaving when he had finished tying his laces, Mr. Fleming remained seated. I could feel his eyes on me, watching me through the open bathroom door. His gaze wasn't controlling, though, but lascivious. Like he was touching my bum and breasts with his eyes. I didn't mind at all when Henry looked at me like that, but now it made me shudder.

"Are you new at The Darlington? I've not seen you before," Mr. Fleming piped up suddenly.

I had no desire to talk to him, but I put on my friendliest smile anyway. "Yes. I've been working for the hotel since the beginning of the month. But don't worry, I'm aware of the high standards here, and I'll make sure to clean the bathroom to your satisfaction."

"I really hope so."

From the corner of my eye, I saw him stand and come towards me. His gaze seared my skin.

He stopped a few steps away and watched me spray cleaner onto the water-stained tap. "How does a pretty girl like you end up working at The Darlington?"

It was a strange question. "I needed the job," I said, concentrating on polishing the tap until it gleamed. If I didn't engage in the conversation, perhaps Mr. Fleming would get bored and leave.

"What's your name?"

"My name's Kate, sir."

"Kate," he repeated in a guttural tone, moving even closer. The bathrooms in The Darlington were spacious, but when Mr. Fleming stood next to me, this one suddenly felt tiny. "You're very attractive, Kate."

My shoulders tensed. It wasn't an innocent compliment. There was something threatening about it that turned my stomach. I'd naively believed that I was safe at The Darlington, but I wasn't safe from arseholes anywhere. I swallowed hard. "Thank you, sir."

Mr. Fleming didn't move, but remained standing very close to me. His harsh scent cut through the cleaning spray—a combination of sweat and too much cologne, which intensified the uneasy feeling in my stomach.

Mr. Fleming lowered his voice. "What do you say, Kate—I forfeit my complimentary lunch, and you give me a personal apology?"

The hairs on the back of my neck stood on end when, without warning, Mr. Fleming's clammy fingers touched my chin. He forced my head up to meet his gaze. The pressure of his fingers was deeply unsettling.

"Let me go, please." I barely recognised my own voice. If we'd been on the street, I'd have defended myself and kicked Mr. Fleming in the balls without hesitating. But we were in The Darlington, and he was a hotel guest. I didn't want to cause trouble or make things difficult for Henry. He had enough going on. "I just want to do my job."

"And I just want you to be a good girl." Mr. Fleming ran his thumb over my lower lip. His fingers smelled just as disgusting as the rest of him. "You'll like it. I promise. Anyway, this is how things are done here at The Darlington, isn't it?" Mr. Fleming laughed as if he'd said something funny. Bile rose in my throat.

"There's a table reserved in your name at the restaurant," I said, trying to talk myself out of the situation. Perhaps Giulia would come and check on me if Mr. Fleming didn't show up. But he didn't move, not even to relax the grip of his fingers on my chin.

"I'm not hungry."

"Please, just let me clean."

"As soon as we're done here," Mr. Fleming said, his free hand reaching for the waistband of his trousers, which had a telltale bulge at the crotch.

"I'll scream if you don't let me go," I threatened.

Mr. Fleming laughed derisively. The sound went through me. "If you scream or try anything else, I'll file a complaint against you. I'm sure you know how important it is to The Darlington that its guests are happy. It would be a shame if you lost this new job you need so badly. So pull yourself together."

I raised my chin. My confidence was an act, hopefully a convincing one. "No."

"You're pretty sassy, aren't you?"

"And you're overstepping the line," I said, feigning more courage than I felt. I didn't want to lose my job. For the first time in a long time, I wasn't hungry. I had a roof over my head, and I had friends and a shot at a future. I didn't want to lose those things, but I also couldn't let a bastard like Mr. Fleming strip me of my dignity.

"I'll show you overstepping the line," Mr. Fleming hissed. His expression, overly friendly a moment ago, darkened. He let go of my chin and placed his hand on my shoulder. His fingers dug into me painfully hard as he forced me to my knees. It was clear what he expected of me. I didn't know if it was pain, disgust, or fear that drove me to let go of the rag I'd been holding and reach for the cleaning spray next to the sink. I didn't stop to think before spraying Mr. Fleming right in the face.

He screamed and released his grip to rub at his eyes.

I didn't waste any time. I squeezed past him and fled from the room.

"You nasty little slut!" I heard him call, but his enraged voice faded when the door to his room shut behind me.

I hurried down the corridor without turning back and pressed the lift buttons in a panic until the gleaming doors opened and I was safe. Pressing the button for the first floor, I leaned back against the cool metal wall. My breath was jagged, and my entire body was trembling. Regret flooded me, twisting my stomach into knots. What had I done?

"Fuck," I said under my breath.

Maybe I had just jeopardised my job at The Darlington. Mr. Fleming was probably calling reception to complain at this very moment, and rightfully so. I'd sprayed him in the face with cleaner. He had deserved it, but I was sure he would omit how he had harassed me. Perhaps I should go straight to Giulia and beat Mr. Fleming to it. But would she believe me? Mr. Fleming was a well-respected and loyal guest at the hotel, and I was a nobody. Expendable. Even if Giulia believed me, would that help me if Mr. Fleming threatened to go public? The Darlington couldn't afford more bad press, not on my account.

God, Henry would be so disappointed.

Hot tears welled up in my eyes, but I willed them away. I didn't want to cry now. I knew if I started, I wouldn't be able to stop, and I had work to do. As long as I still had a job.

No Comment: Henry Darlington Cuts Press Conference Short.

INsider headline

Henry

Heavy raindrops lashed against the window. The night was pitch-black. Dark clouds obscured the sky, as gloomy as my mood. Thunder rumbled, and the occasional flash of lightning lit up the sky. Sweat ran down my forehead, neck, back, and chest. I ran. And ran. And ran. But I couldn't escape my thoughts, which once again were keeping me from sleep. The brutal beats of Lorna Shore pounded in my ears as I pushed myself on the treadmill, but not even the singer's animal growls could drown out the negative voices in my head.

The day had been a total catastrophe, starting with the press conference. I'd opened my speech with a joke that had made the journalists laugh, and afterwards, I'd announced the plans for the Pearl Gala. The news that this year's event was raising money for a local organisation had been well received, and Tilly had briefly introduced Hope Harbour. So far, so good—until that jerk William

Hunt had suddenly started asking questions about my dad's case. I'd refused to answer, but his boldness had shattered everyone else's restraint. Every question from that moment on had been about Richard Darlington: the trial, his bail, and his house arrest. I'd reluctantly cut the press conference short, which the media had eagerly pounced on in their coverage.

I had assumed the day couldn't get any worse, but I was wrong. Vivian and my dad had given me a hard time after my speech for daring to deviate from the agreed script. Their tirade hadn't stopped until we learned that a group of activists had hung a giant banner along the parapet of Westminster Bridge during the press conference. It was clearly visible to the hotel guests. Not to mention to the rest of the world. On the banner was an unflattering photo of my dad, accompanied by the words "The Face of a Rapist."

The image had become grotesque in the darkness of the night, and my dad's face watched me mockingly as I worked out on the treadmill. I couldn't wait for the banner to be removed in the morning, even though hundreds of photos were already doing the rounds on social media. As if that weren't enough, Giulia had informed me just before the end of the day that Mr. Fleming, one of the hotel's most loyal guests, had filed a complaint against Kate. She'd apparently treated him with disrespect.

I didn't know what to think. It didn't seem like Kate, but we had to take every complaint seriously. Especially one coming from someone like Mr. Fleming, who had been a regular guest at the hotel for over ten years. The Darlington relied on the satisfaction of its guests, and I was sure my dad would have fired Kate without batting an eyelid. And perhaps that was just what I should do. My priority should be the hotel, not some woman I barely knew. But it wasn't quite that simple. Not when it came to Kate.

Gasping for breath, I stopped the treadmill. My heart was racing. I pulled off the heart rate monitor from my upper arm and headed to the kitchen, thighs burning. I chugged a glass of water, waiting for the hammering of my heart to slow. But the calmer my body was, the louder the thoughts in my head became. It infuriated me that I had to deal with this shit. I knew I could help The Darlington more without all these obstacles in the way. No, they weren't just obstacles. They were entire mountains, and they were growing bigger and steeper by the day.

I filled the water glass and drained it again before making my way through my dark apartment to the bathroom to take a shower. Showering was a necessary evil in the mornings, something to be accomplished swiftly so I could get to the office as fast as possible. All that was waiting for me right now, though, was my bed, and I wasn't in any rush to get there. I stood motionlessly in the shower and enjoyed the feeling of hot water raining down on my skin, washing away the sweat and relaxing my overworked muscles.

Fifteen minutes later, I was right back where I'd been two hours ago: sleepless in bed. Lost in thought, I stared up at the ceiling and watched the flashes of lightning come in through a crack in the curtains. I felt like I was losing my mind. Another sleepless night would be fatal. Still, I caught myself reaching for my phone instead of closing my eyes.

ME:

Hey.

I wasn't expecting an answer, but one pinged in a few seconds later.

KATE:

Hey right back at you.

I hesitated briefly before tapping the little camera symbol.

Kate answered the video call immediately. When her face appeared on my display, I saw that she was also in bed. Her hair was tousled, as though she'd been tossing and turning. Her eyes were tired, and the only light in the room came from the reading light on the bedside table next to her.

"You're still awake," Kate said.

I smiled. "You too."

"So we're both still awake," she concluded.

"It looks like it, Troublemaker."

"Nope."

"Shame," I said, as determined as ever to find the perfect nickname for her. I leaned back against my pillow. "How was your day?"

"Good." Kate's reply came a little too fast, but it wasn't this that told me she was lying; it was the silence that followed. If there was one thing I knew about Kate, it was that she enjoyed talking—and that even more than talking, she liked to listen. Talking to her was always effortless. Normally she would have asked about my day now to keep the conversation going, but she didn't. Her silence spoke volumes.

"Kate?"

"Yes?"

"What happened with Mr. Fleming?" I asked, because the topic was unavoidable.

For what felt like an eternity, the only sound in the room was the rustling of my duvet and the drumming of the rain against the windowpane. Finally, a single word crackled through my phone's speaker: "Nothing."

"So Mr. Fleming complained to Giulia about nothing?"

Fear flickered across Kate's face. "Am I fired?"

"That depends."

"On what?"

"On what happened," I said, which was a lie. Nothing Kate could say would make me fire her, risking her giving up a warm bed at The Darlington. I just wanted to know what had happened with Mr. Fleming. Whatever it was, it was apparently preoccupying Kate enough to keep her awake until 2 a.m.

"I'm sure Mr. Fleming has already explained."

"I want to hear your version."

Kate's face lit up as a flash illuminated the sky, and I could see the doubt and uncertainty in her eyes. Her lips were pressed firmly together, as if she didn't want to talk about it. But then she did. "He harassed me."

"He what?" I gasped, even though I'd heard her clearly.

"He harassed me," she repeated, but that only made it worse. I clenched my hands into fists.

"Tell me about it," I demanded.

She avoided my gaze and turned onto her side, so that half her face was buried in her pillow. I guessed she would have liked nothing more than to disappear entirely into the mountain of down feather bedding.

"Giulia asked me to clean Mr. Fleming's room, because he'd complained. At first he just watched me, but then he started asking me personal questions." She spoke so quietly that I had to turn up the volume on my phone to catch her next words. "I kept my answers short because I didn't want to talk to him, but he didn't care. He kept talking, and he told me how pretty I was." I thought I detected a glimmer of tears in her eyes, but it was hard to be sure—her camera shook as if her hands were trembling. "I reminded him that a table had been reserved for him in the restaurant as compensation for his room not being clean, but he wanted me to apologise *personally*. When I said no, he grabbed my chin and told me that I'd like it, and that it was how things were done at The Darlington."

My heart was racing, pumping pure rage through my veins. The bastard hadn't just assaulted Kate—he'd also used my dad's misconduct as justification. And then he'd had the audacity to file a complaint against Kate! Was he out of his mind?

"I made it clear that I didn't want that, and that he should let me go, but he didn't," Kate went on. Her voice was shaky, cracking as though something inside her had broken. She was showing me the shards she'd swept under the rug to hide them from the world. "He undid his trousers and tried to force me onto my knees so that I would . . . you know. But I managed to get away just in time."

I wanted to storm over to Mr. Fleming's room and wring his neck with my bare hands, despite the fact that I didn't usually resort to violence. "I'm going to kill him."

"Henry . . ."

"Or better yet: I'll tell his wife and let her kill him."

"Leave it," Kate begged.

My jaw clenched. "He wanted to rape you!"

"But he didn't." I was sure now that I wasn't imagining the tears. She wiped her face with the back of her hand before they could fall, but not before I saw them. "I sprayed bathroom cleaner at his face before anything could happen, and then I ran away."

I shook my head. "How can you stay so calm?"

"Maybe because I've gotten used to situations like this. When you're a woman living alone on the streets, you're confronted with this kind of thing all the time."

"Fuck, Kate."

I rubbed my forehead and felt the knot deep in my gut grow even tighter. I hated that Mr. Fleming had done this to Kate. And I hated even more that a part of Kate had resigned herself to being treated so terribly, with so much disrespect. No one should have to put up with shit like that and get used to it. But it was over now. I would make sure she never got into another situation like it. From now on, I would look after her.

"Can I come to you?"

Kate blinked. "What? Why?"

"I want to be there for you in person, not just on a video call."

She hesitated then nodded. "OK."

"I'll be there in a minute," I promised, before ending our call.

I leapt out of bed and got dressed, then hurried down the corridor to the lifts. The entire hotel seemed to be asleep. I didn't encounter a single person in the corridors, not stopping until I reached Kate's door. The door swung open before I could even lift my hand to ring the bell, and there she was, standing right in front of me. Kate. My beautiful, brave Kate, who had endured more in the last year than most people had to in an entire lifetime.

She was wearing a shirt that was several sizes too large, emblazoned with The Darlington logo. Her legs were bare except for socks, and her eyes were glassy with unshed tears. Even now, she was still trying to be strong. I wanted to hug her. Desperately. Perhaps more than I'd ever wanted anything before. But I also didn't want to scare her off.

Kate opened her mouth as if to speak, but all that came out of her mouth was a pitiful sound that broke my heart. She pressed her lips together, struggling to compose herself, but she'd been fighting for too long and had no strength left. She whimpered again, and I felt I had no choice but to give in to my urge. I took a cautious step towards her, and when she didn't flinch away, I pulled her into my arms, creating a space for her where she didn't have to be strong. A space where she didn't need walls for protection, because I was her wall. She gasped for air—and then she began to cry, as if she'd been waiting to finally let go.

28

> The conference was a shitshow, but holy fuck. How hot is Henry? What about a topless calendar for a good cause? I'd buy it. Anyone else?

Online comment by Anna_red02

Kate

Henry held me as I broke down and shed all the tears I'd held back since this afternoon, when I'd stormed out of Mr. Fleming's room. Or maybe even longer than that. I'd cried only two or three times the past few months, most recently in the bathtub on my first night at The Darlington. But it was different today. More intense. In the past, I'd been very careful about which feelings I allowed myself to feel, worried that the wrong ones might make me seem weak and defenceless. But in the safety of Henry's arms, suddenly none of that mattered anymore.

"Everything will be fine," he whispered into my ear.

He held me so tight it felt like he'd made it his mission to squeeze the pain of the past few months out of me. I couldn't remember when I'd last felt as secure with another person as I did with Henry. Perhaps that was the reason I'd poured my heart out to him. Since we'd met, he hadn't dismissed my feelings once. He had validated them instead. His lips brushed my forehead consolingly as I sobbed in his arms. It was probably just a friendly gesture, but his mouth on my skin and his arms around me felt unbelievably good. For a brief moment, I gave in to the illusion that there could be something more between us, despite our differences.

"I'm sorry," I mumbled into Henry's chest when I was finally capable of speaking again. He steered us into my room as I cried, to keep the entire hotel from witnessing my breakdown.

"You have nothing to apologise for." His hands were still on me, ready to pull me back into his arms at a moment's notice.

"I cried all over you," I remarked, pointing to the spots on his shirt where my tears had soaked into the fabric. I ran a finger over them, as if I could wipe them away. Now that I was regaining my composure, I was a little embarrassed by how I'd lost control.

"Don't worry. It'll dry." He brushed a strand of hair behind my ear. It was a tender, caring gesture that eased some of the shame I had felt. "How do you feel?"

"Better," I replied. "Sorry, I didn't mean to bring the mood down like that."

"You didn't, Peach."

I shook my head, and he looked disappointed. I hated nicknames, but I loved that he wasn't giving up on finding the right one for me. Encouraged, I raised my head. "Will you stay for a bit?"

"If you want me to . . ."

I nodded and reached for his hand, guiding him to the bed. I didn't want him to sit on the floor again. I felt a brief resistance when I pulled him onto the mattress next to me, but it didn't last long. We crawled under the covers together, and I rolled onto my side to look at Henry. The only light in the room came from the reading lamp, and it cut through the dark to trace harsh edges and soft contours onto his face. A flutter stirred in my chest when I realised I was lying in bed with one of the most handsome men in London. My own bloodshot eyes and swollen features were probably no pretty sight, but that didn't stop Henry from giving me his undivided attention.

"I was watching your press conference on YouTube when you messaged," I said, drawing the attention away from me. "I have no idea who William Hunt is, but I hate him."

Henry grinned. "Why do you hate him?"

There was a clap of thunder.

"He's a prick."

"What makes you say that? Not that I disagree."

"The way he interrupted when you were talking about Hope Harbour to ask about your dad was just disrespectful. And he didn't let up when you said that you didn't want to comment. It made me really mad. I wouldn't have stayed so calm if I'd been you."

He snorted. "I was furious, believe me."

"You hid it well."

"I had to, to avoid sparking another scandal."

"You did a pretty good job."

His eyebrows shot up. "Do you think so?" He sounded surprised, as if mine were the first positive words he'd heard about the press conference.

"Yes, you were really professional and confident and . . ." I stopped, not sure if it was a good idea to voice what I was thinking as we lay in bed together. But Henry was looking at me so expectantly that I couldn't leave him hanging. "And sexy."

"Sexy," he echoed, but I didn't buy his innocent tone. He knew exactly how good he looked, as proved by the knowing smile playing on his lips. He was fishing for compliments, and I was ready to give them to him. Especially as he didn't seem to be getting them from anyone else.

"Yes. You looked really hot in your suit. It's not just me saying that; people are talking about it online. I upvoted all the *Henry is sexy* comments so they'd rank higher than the mean ones."

"Thank you. I appreciate it." There was a sparkle of amusement in his eyes. "Vivian and my dad were pretty pissed after the conference, because I didn't stick to the speech they'd prepared for me. They wanted me to sing my dad's praises and pretend that he was the brains behind the Pearl Gala."

I frowned. "But that's not true."

"Which is why I didn't stick to the script."

"Shouldn't your dad be happy if you get recognition for organising the gala? Isn't that what parents do? Praise their kids?" I asked carefully. My mum hadn't been perfect. We'd had our issues, and the last years with Randell had been particularly challenging, but she'd always stood by me and supported me as best she could. She'd often told me how proud she was of me and had waited at the finish line at all my athletics competitions, cheering me on. She had also tried to stop me from dropping out of school. Deep down, she only ever wanted the best for me.

Henry shrugged. "That's not how my dad works."

"Has he always been like this?"

"I looked up to him when I was a kid, before I realised how cold, distant, and calculating he is. No idea if he's always been like that. If so, I had to grow up to realise it. Now I see it all the more clearly. All that matters to him is his own success."

I hadn't encountered Richard Darlington yet, but no one at the hotel seemed to have anything positive to say about him. That made it hard for me to associate him with Henry. "But you're his son."

"First and foremost, I'm a means to an end. I'm there to save the hotel."

"Doesn't that bother you?"

The mattress moved under me as he shifted his weight. "It mainly bothers me that it looks from the outside like I'm supporting my dad. I'm not. Everything I'm doing is for the hotel, not for him."

"One day, it'll be all yours."

Or not.

Henry didn't say the words out loud, but I could read them in his eyes. He seemed genuinely afraid that the hotel would go down with his dad. He couldn't see how brilliant he was or how much his staff appreciated him, unlike his father. But then again, how could he see all that when Richard, Vivian, and the press constantly made him feel like he wasn't good enough, that he was doing something wrong? Who wouldn't doubt themselves under those circumstances, under this amount of pressure?

"What's that?" Henry asked suddenly.

Surprised by the sudden change of topic, it took me a moment to realise he was referring to the notepad on my bedside table. Shit. I had started making a list of other jobs I was qualified for, and it definitely wasn't intended for Henry's eyes.

"Nothing," I replied evasively, trying to shove the small notebook with The Darlington logo into a drawer, but Henry got to it faster.

"*Stacking shelves at supermarket. Costa or Pret A Manger till. Barista training? Cinema ticket counter.*" He read out only a few of the ideas I'd written down. His expression darkened as he looked back at me. "Are you looking for a new job?"

I lowered my gaze. "Maybe."

"Because of Mr. Fleming?" Henry asked through gritted teeth.

"He said he was going to file a complaint against me, and I wasn't sure if you'd kick me out. I'm new here, after all, and he's a regular guest," I confessed. "But it's not just that. I like working for The Darlington, but a second job would give me more security. I could build something up. That way, if you get sick of me and fire me, I wouldn't be left with nothing again. I'd have something to fall back on."

Henry looked at me silently. I couldn't read his expression in the darkness. Was he disappointed? Or angry? I didn't want to seem ungrateful—I was more grateful to him than I could ever express. But I'd been through too much shit in my life to throw caution to the wind. I didn't want to risk becoming dependent again—on anyone.

"Are you angry at me?" I asked tentatively.

Henry seemed to realise that he'd been silent. He blinked and shook his head resolutely. "No, not at all. If anything, I'm impressed."

My heart pounded. "Really?"

"Yes. I think it's amazing how you're taking your life into your own hands," he answered with a faint smile that only intensified the pounding of my heart. "I promise that your job at The Darlington is safe, no matter what happens between us. I didn't hire you because I expect anything from you, but because I want to help you. However, it's healthy not to trust anyone blindly, including me. It shows you're looking after yourself. Which is important."

My throat constricted again, but this time not from sadness or rage, but relief. I hadn't realised how desperately I needed to hear the words Henry had spoken so easily. "Do you know how glad I am that I met you?"

Henry smiled and touched my cheek, as if to catch my unshed tears. He ran his fingers over my skin tenderly, sending electricity sparking through me. "I'm also very glad to have met you."

A comforting warmth enveloped me. The feeling of no longer being alone. I'd had no family or friends before I'd come to The Darlington. For months, there had been no one who mattered to me, and it had left a gaping void in my heart. Now Henry was starting to fill that void, and he seemed to know it.

A longing look flashed up in eyes as his thumb brushed gently across my lower lip, fuelling the heat in my chest. My response was the complete opposite of the revulsion I'd experienced with Mr. Fleming earlier. I remembered how good it had felt to be held by Henry. I was certain it would feel even better to be kissed by him. I felt the pounding of his heart when I placed a hand on his chest. My nipples hardened, and I knew that if his gaze were to stray from my lips for even one second, he'd see them pressed against the fabric of my shirt. We were so close that I felt his breath on my lips, our noses only centimetres apart.

I leaned in towards him, and he leaned in towards me . . .

. . . and touched his lips to my forehead again.

"We should try to sleep. It's late," Henry said.

Why? I didn't want to sleep. I wanted to be kissed!

He removed his hand from my face and pulled back.

I missed his warmth even before I realised what had just happened. I looked at him in confusion, searching in the dim light for an explanation for why he wasn't pressing me into the mattress, kissing me greedily. But I saw nothing but affection in his eyes, which irritated me even more.

"But you'll stay?" I heard myself asking.

He nodded. "I'll stay for as long as you want me to."

I was relieved. I didn't want to be alone with my thoughts. If Henry were to leave now, my doubts would come flooding back. I switched off the light, snuggled into my blanket and turned away from Henry onto my other side. I didn't want him to notice how disappointed I was that he hadn't kissed me.

Why had he pulled away? Had I read the situation wrong? Or had Henry reminded himself in the last moment who we both were? That I was beneath him? That we'd never truly fit together?

"Kate . . ." He whispered my name in the dark. "I can practically hear you thinking. Stop worrying."

"I'm not worrying," I lied, my voice wavering.

"Yes, you are. And it's not necessary."

Isn't it? The question was on the tip of my tongue, but before I could voice it, a strong arm wrapped around me from behind. A jolt shot through my body as Henry pulled me close, my back pressing against his firm chest. One of his legs slid between my knees. I held my breath.

"We've both had a long day. Try to sleep," he murmured into the nape of my neck. He was close again, his warm breath brushing the sensitive skin behind my ear with every word. I shivered. When I dared to breathe again, Henry's familiar scent filled my nose. I couldn't help it—with a sigh, I melted into his touch, as warm and secure as his earlier embrace had felt. It wasn't a kiss, but it wasn't nothing. It was an acknowledgement that there was something between us, something we both felt. It calmed me.

I snuggled closer to Henry. "Sleep well, Snowflake."

He grunted tiredly. "Good night, Kate."

THE BLACKROOM

Who would have thought it? The Pearl Gala is making a comeback in a desperate bid by The Darlington Hotel to salvage its reputation. Once upon a time, the rich and famous considered it a highlight of the social calendar. Celebrities and socialites alike vied for an invitation to the charity event, which not only raises money for good causes but also serves as the perfect opportunity for self-promotion.

This December's gala was initially cancelled, but now it's back on the agenda, with the surprise announcement coming just a few days after it was made public that Richard Darlington will be going to court.

Is someone trying to polish their tarnished reputation? Does the Darlington family truly believe we'll be fooled by this cheap PR stunt? As if a little glitz could make people forget that Richard Darlington has ruined lives . . .

The decision to go ahead with the Pearl Gala after all might be a noble attempt at making reparations and will undoubtedly benefit the organisation Hope Harbour, which advocates for homeless people in England. However, we can only hope that this one good Darlington deed doesn't blind the public to Richard's many wrongdoings. The gala should be seen for what it is: his desperate attempt to cover up his guilt.

Good morning. I hope you slept just as well as I did. Unfortunately, I had to go to the office, and I didn't want to wake you. Have a great day. Message me, if you like.

Note left by Henry on Kate's pillow

Kate

The next day, I heard angry voices coming out of Henry's office. His dad was furious at Henry for banning Mr. Fleming from the premises. I was still asleep when Henry had sneaked from my room. By the time I started work three hours later, the entire hotel was already talking about it. I would never have asked Henry to ban a regular guest from The Darlington on my account, but it was a relief to know I'd never run into that perv in the hotel corridors again. Still, I felt bad that Henry had to confront his dad, who voiced his disapproval of Henry's decision loud and clear, for everyone to hear. I sent Henry a message asking if everything was fine, but all I got in response was a terse *Yes*.

Over the course of the day, my thoughts kept drifting back to Henry and last night. How he had lain in my bed and held me.

It had felt just as intimate as if we'd known each other for a very long time. It was no wonder I had wanted to kiss him—he made my body tingle and my heart race. Looking back, though, I was glad it hadn't happened. A kiss would only have complicated our relationship, which was already far too complicated. He was Henry Darlington, after all. Rich. Powerful. Influential. The whole world lay at his feet, while I was being trampled by it. No matter which way I looked at it, it just didn't fit, and probably never would.

Lost in thought, my work took considerably longer than it usually did. Fortunately, no one seemed to mind. I cast a final glance around the room I had just finished cleaning to make sure I hadn't missed anything, then confirmed on the tablet that I was done so reception would know the room was ready for new guests. I returned my cleaning trolley to the housekeeping room and made my way downstairs—my shift was finally over.

After retrieving my room key from my locker, I headed to Henry's office. I had walked past it more times today than I'd like to admit, hoping to run into him. I could have knocked, of course, but I hadn't wanted to disturb him. The door had been closed every time I passed—but this time, luck seemed to be on my side. Just as I turned into the corridor, the door opened. Henry stepped out. Just one glance at his face was enough to confirm that he'd had a bad day. His skin was pale and his eyes were dull, but he was smiling. Next to him was a woman who seemed vaguely familiar. She must have been around forty, with auburn hair and gold-rimmed glasses. They were heading straight towards me but hadn't spotted me yet.

"Are you sure you don't want to come?" Henry asked.

"Definitely. It's not my scene."

"That's a shame. Let me know if you change your mind."

The woman smiled. "Thanks, I will."

Henry looked up as if he had sensed my presence, and the intensity of his gaze hit me hard. The fake, tired smile from just a moment ago transformed into something more alive and warm. I paused, not sure what to do. Should I greet them and risk interrupting their conversation? Or should I leave?

Henry decided for me. "Hi."

"Hey." Why did I sound so breathless?

They stopped in front of me, and suddenly, I realised where I had seen the woman before: yesterday at the press conference with Henry.

"Kate, allow me to introduce Matilda Gallagher from Hope Harbour," he said, confirming it. "Tilly, this is Kate Hamilton, the friend who gave me the idea of raising money for local homeless charities."

A broad smile spread across Tilly's face, etching fine wrinkles around her eyes. She shook my hand enthusiastically. "It's really nice to meet you, Kate. Thanks for thinking of Hope Harbour. It means a lot to us."

"Oh. I . . . I didn't do anything," I said awkwardly.

"Don't say that." Tilly placed a hand on my arm, an unexpectedly maternal gesture. "Thanks to you, the organisation will receive a very generous donation at the end of the year. We'll be able to help a lot of homeless people. You can't imagine what that will mean to them."

I *could* imagine—very well, in fact. But I wasn't sure how much Henry had told Tilly or how much she was allowed to know. I looked at him hesitantly and saw only openness in his eyes. He seemed to be leaving it up to me to decide what I wanted to share with her. I had promised him I wouldn't tell anyone at the hotel the truth about my history, but Tilly wasn't part of the hotel. And if anyone would understand, it was her.

"I was homeless myself until recently," I confessed, keeping my voice low even after I had made sure no one was listening. "I even went to the Hope Harbour soup kitchen a few times. You really do an amazing job."

Tilly raised her eyebrows in surprise. "Really?"

I nodded. The soup kitchen had often helped me in the last few months—when luck had been on my side. Although the meals were portioned to keep things fair, I was often turned away empty-handed because there wasn't enough to go round for everyone who needed it. But that wasn't Tilly's fault—it was a systemic problem.

"And now you work here at The Darlington?" she asked.

"Yes, Henry gave me a job."

"How wonderful! He told me that you really care about helping the homeless, which is why he wants to raise money for Hope Harbour, but I didn't realise you had such a personal connection to the cause. Can I ask how you met?" She looked from me to Henry and back expectantly.

I let Henry do the talking.

"Kate pickpocketed me," he said.

Tilly's eyes widened. "She did what?"

"Pickpocketed me," he repeated, smiling. "I was in St. James's Park, and she took my iPhone when I was buying myself a coffee. But she forgot to turn off GPS tracking, so I tracked her down and confronted her. I hadn't reckoned with how . . . convincing she can be, though."

"And after all that, you offered her a job?"

Henry shook his head. "Not straightaway. We parted ways after I got my phone back, but I couldn't stop thinking about her and everything she told me. So a few days later, I went to the park to bring her back to the hotel. It was the best decision I've made in a long time."

At his last words, he turned from Tilly to me. Our eyes did more than just meet—they collided. The expression in his blue eyes changed, giving his last words a significance that I felt at my very core.

Tilly sighed. "What a beautiful story. Once again, it just goes to show that all people need is another chance. Someone who will stand up for them. No one chooses that kind of life, and with the donations from the gala, we'll be able to make a real difference. So thank you, both of you."

"You're welcome," Henry said, while I smiled modestly.

"I'd better make a move," Tilly said, adjusting the strap of her bag. "Thanks for the meeting, Henry. I think I can see myself out. As soon as I'm back in the office, I'll send you the email I promised." She shook his hand. "It was nice meeting you, Kate. You should come and visit us at Hope Harbour sometime, if you like."

"I'd love to," I replied. I admired Tilly for the work she did and how she helped others on a daily basis.

"Great. Henry can give you my number."

"I will," he promised, and we said goodbye to Tilly.

I watched her leave, then turned to Henry. "She's really nice."

"Yes, she is. I only hope she won't end up being disappointed."

"You mean by the gala?"

Worry flashed across his face. "Yes."

I took a step towards him. The scent of his aftershave had faded over the course of the day, and now he just smelled like Henry. It was the same smell that had lingered on my sheets long after he'd left my bed. "I'm sure that won't happen. It'll be amazing. You're making such a huge effort, and I'm certain that Tilly and the rest of Hope Harbour will be grateful for any and all donations. It doesn't take twenty million to make a difference," I said with a shrug. "Nineteen million is totally enough."

My words did the trick. All doubt disappeared from Henry's face. "Thank you. I needed that."

"Thank *you*," I replied with a smile.

"What for?"

"For banning Mr. Fleming from the hotel. It wasn't necessary."

Henry's jaw tightened, as if the mention of Mr. Fleming's name alone was enough to enrage him. "Yes, it was."

"I could have handled him."

"Maybe you could have, but I couldn't. The idea that at any moment, that arsehole could run into you and try to touch you again drove me mad. He's lucky all I did was ban him from the premises," Henry said, his hands clenched into fists. The ferocity of his expression was proof of how serious he was. He would protect me, no matter what it took, and that was a wonderful feeling.

30

> I remember running into Richard in the corridor once. I said hello to him. He said hello back, and that should have been it. But then he followed me into the housekeeping room and started asking me uncomfortable questions. He wanted to know if I had a boyfriend and if I was into older men.

Extract from an exposé interview in *The Blackroom*

Kate

"There are more cancellations rolling in for the Pearl Gala, the charity event hosted by the well-known Darlington Hotel," announced the morning show host on the break room TV. I was sitting at the table with Rose, eating leftovers from the restaurant's breakfast service. My shift hadn't yet started, but Rose was already halfway through her workday. Grace had the late shift today and wouldn't be arriving at the hotel until around noon.

"The hotel came under fire earlier this year when its owner, Richard Darlington, was accused of sexual misconduct by several women," the host continued. "It's now been confirmed: The case is going to court. And that seems to be scaring off many of the A-list attendees. More on this from our favourite INsider, William Hunt!"

The camera panned across the studio and zoomed in on the self-proclaimed high-society expert, whose face I'd seen far too often in recent days. He reported almost daily on The Darlington, Henry, and his family. And unfortunately, on me as well.

Three days ago, I had appeared in the news again when reports emerged that the mysterious woman in the photos worked at the hotel. We didn't know if Mr. Fleming had outed me or if one of the journalists from the press conference had spotted me, but the story spread quickly and reignited speculation about Henry and me. Some people theorised that the secretly photographed meeting had been a job interview, while others thought we looked far too intimate for that to be the case. Henry's parents and Vivian wanted him to release a statement leaning into the job interview theory, but he refused to lie to the press.

I turned off the TV, and Rose gave me a sideways glance. "How are things going in the kitchen?" I asked.

"Fine. There's not much going on in the restaurant at the moment, but it means we have time to prepare for Halloween," she answered, stabbing at a slice of pepper in her hummus.

"What's happening on Halloween?"

"The masked ball."

"Right, Henry mentioned that," I said, recalling how we had sat on the ballroom floor and Henry had shown me the scratch he and Logan had made. "Is it a big deal?"

"We're catering a flying buffet for two hundred guests, so yeah, it's a pretty big deal."

"Two hundred? I thought people were boycotting The Darlington."

That was what I had read online, at least. I had downloaded several news and social media apps onto my phone to keep up with everything. There had been regular news items about the Darlingtons even before the allegations against Richard, but the headlines had been harmless, focussing on the Pearl Gala and the Darlington brothers' love lives. Logan had been exempt—I could find nothing about him besides a few very old photographs and references to his restaurant. Ethan, on the other hand, was everywhere, pictured alongside various women. The articles about Henry usually concerned his relationship with Olivia Asterdam, but since the allegations against Richard had surfaced, media coverage had blown up and every tiny detail of the Darlingtons' lives was being scrutinised and picked apart.

"These people like to make out that they sympathise with Richard's victims, and claim they're avoiding The Darlington because it goes down well with the press," Rose responded, looking disgusted. "But when no one's watching, those hypocritical pricks treat themselves to overpriced tickets to the ball so they don't miss out. And they know it won't damage their reputation, since there won't be press there to document their presence."

"Just be glad 'those hypocritical pricks' are buying tickets at all. Their money keeps us in our jobs," George said from the sofa. I had ignored him until now, assuming he was asleep, but now he sat up. He worked in the kitchen with Rose and wore the same white uniform. "If you think they're all so hypocritical, why are you still here?" he asked. "Why aren't you out there looking for another job? Plenty of kitchens in London are hiring."

Rose's jaw tightened. "Because I wasn't born with a silver spoon in my mouth, and this hotel pays well. Believe me, if I could afford it, I'd be out of here before you could count to three."

"Hey! No more resignations," Rakesh protested, entering the room with a mug in his hand. The smell of cigarette smoke hit me as he headed past the table towards the coffee machine.

"As if you haven't considered quitting yourself," George said.

"Not once."

"Liar," Rose muttered so quietly that only I could hear.

"Have you read the latest interview on *The Blackroom*?" asked George.

Rose nodded. Rakesh grunted miserably before pressing buttons on the coffee machine, which awoke with a rattle.

"What's *The Blackroom*?" I asked curiously. My online research hadn't gotten me that far yet. Given the deluge of reports, it was hard to keep track of everything—I was sure I must have missed a few things.

His blond hair tousled from his nap, George rose from the sofa to sit at the table with me and Rose. "It's an anonymous blog that went online a few weeks ago. It reports exclusively on the hotel and the Darlingtons. Not very positive reports, I might add. Whoever runs the blog has insider knowledge. Probably someone who works at the hotel."

"Or a former employee," Rakesh interjected.

"In any case, it's someone with contacts inside the hotel," George said, reaching across the table to take a tomato from Rose's plate. She batted his hand away, but he was too fast.

"What's the interview about?" I asked.

"It's anonymous, but whoever it is was talking about their experience with the family," George said with his mouth full. He pulled out his phone. After tapping on it briefly, he slid it across the table to me, *The Blackroom* interview open.

I skimmed it. Richard was eviscerated, described as aggressive and condescending. Ethan didn't come off much better either—the interviewer referred to him as a selfish brat devoid of empathy, which I couldn't entirely disagree with, thinking back to my first and only encounter with him. Henry's name came up as well. The interviewer was a little gentler on him, but he was still accused for not taking the allegations against his dad seriously and failing to critically distance himself from them.

I gave George his phone back. "If the interview is anonymous, isn't it possible it's all lies?"

"Everyone who has worked for The Darlington for any length of time knows everything that's being said is true."

"But Henry isn't ignoring the allegations." Even if he wanted to, it wouldn't be possible. They had taken over his life.

Rose snorted. "Of course you'd say that."

"That's not fair of you," I answered hotly, my stomach clenching. I felt an overwhelming urge to defend Henry. "You don't know him—at least not the way I do. He's taking the matter really seriously, and he's doing his best."

Rose grimaced. "And his best is to keep silent about what his dad has done?"

"What do you think he should do?" I asked. She made it sound trivial, like something that could be easily fixed. But if it were that simple, Henry would have done it already. "Is he supposed to tell the press that his dad is a monster, and then stand by as the hotel—his home—goes under?"

"You don't know that would happen. Perhaps people would admire his courage and rally to save the hotel. It would be worth a shot, instead of dismissing the victims and indirectly hoping they'll lose in court."

"If Henry takes a public stance, it would ruin the hotel," Rakesh said. He sipped his coffee and joined us at the table. "I've been at The Darlington for twenty years, and I spent five of those as a manager under Richard's leadership. I know the man and how he operates. If Henry openly defies him, he would see it as an unforgivable humiliation. He would take his son and the hotel down with him, no matter the cost. His ego wouldn't allow for anything else. Henry is doing everything right."

Rose's lips parted as if she wanted to speak, but either she had run out of arguments, or she didn't want to fight with a superior. Instead, she rose from her seat and left the break room. George, Rakesh, and I followed her with our eyes, but none of us commented on her silent departure.

31

The Cat's Out of the Bag: Henry Darlington's McDonald's Date Is a Hotel Employee!

INsider headline

Kate

I wasn't in the mood to talk after Rose's abrupt departure, and George seemed to feel the same way. When Rakesh excused himself, presumably to sneak a smoke in his office, I pulled out my phone to take a closer look at *The Blackroom*. The blog published regular posts about the hotel, which ranged from anonymous interviews and updates on the ongoing lawsuit, to old stories that had faded into obscurity. One article covered an assault charge that had been filed against Richard Darlington twenty years ago. Another was about a conspicuous black eye that Henry's mum had attempted to conceal under a thick layer of makeup several years ago. Even back then, suspicion had fallen on Richard.

It was a mystery to me how the blog could have escaped my notice until now. There were dozens of comments beneath each post, and it even had its own hashtag—#theblackroom—which people used on social media. Whoever ran this blog had clearly invested a great deal of time and effort in portraying Richard in the worst possible light. Each word dripped with hatred and contempt, sparking curiosity about who was behind the blog. In the comments, people speculated that the blog might have been started by some of the women who had filed assault charges against Richard but hadn't joined the lawsuit for whatever reason. It seemed plausible, especially since most of the allegations came from women who had worked for the hotel at some point. Which would explain the detailed insider knowledge.

Did Henry know the blog existed? I decided to talk to him about it when I got the chance, and put my phone away to get to work.

Just as I stepped out into the corridor, I heard Giulia call my name. "Kate?"

I glanced up. "Yes?"

"Grace has just called in sick. I need someone to cover the private floor. Could you take care of it? No one else is available right now." Giulia asked, but it wasn't really a question so much as an order. She held out the golden ID card expectantly. Room attendants needed the card to be granted access to the family's private quarters, which Grace was usually assigned to. She had to return the card at the end of every shift to prevent it from being misused.

"OK. But I've never done it alone."

"You'll manage. And don't worry, Mrs. Darlington is at brunch with her friends, and Mr. Darlington is in a meeting with his lawyers."

"What about Ethan?"

"He's probably nursing a hangover in some lecture. But what do I know?" Giulia shrugged. "If you run into any problems, you know where to find me."

I nodded and headed off. In the lift, I sent Grace a quick get-well-soon message, and she wrote back straightaway, assuring me it was just period cramps and she'd be fine by tomorrow. After retrieving the cleaning trolley from the housekeeping room on the top floor, I decided to start with the penthouse belonging to Henry's parents before they returned. So far, I hadn't run into either of them, and after everything I'd heard—and what I'd just read on *The Blackroom*—I had no desire to change that.

The Darlingtons' penthouse apartment was enormous, even bigger than Henry's, and surprisingly cosy. Crowded bookshelves lined the walls, a large corner sofa was adorned with an abundance of cushions, and colourful floral arrangements brightened up the space. The decorative houseplants and statues had presumably been picked out by Henry's mum or an interior designer—I couldn't for the life of me picture his dad browsing antique shops or designer furniture shops for them. The walls were decorated with family photos from a variety of locations, according to the small plaques on the frames: St. Moritz, 2006; Bora Bora, 2007; Venice, 2007; Shanghai, 2008. Even though I was surrounded by the Darlington family's luxury on a daily basis, I sometimes forgot how wealthy Henry was, because it didn't matter when we were together. But small reminders like these photos brought his money into sharp focus, hammering home the fact that our worlds were millions of pounds apart. I had never set foot in any of these places and probably never would. Meanwhile, Henry had visited them all before he'd even turned ten, without his family having to think twice about the cost. For him, it was normal. For me, it was unimaginable.

Logan wasn't in any of the photos. It was as though he had been erased from the Darlington family history. The most recent photo was taken in 2019 and showed Ethan, around thirteen, with a younger, less exhausted-looking Henry.

"Those photos won't dust themselves."

I jumped and whirled around to see Amanda Darlington standing in the doorway. My street instincts were clearly failing me—I hadn't even heard the door unlock.

She stepped inside and removed her coat, revealing an outfit that others would have worn to a gala rather than a brunch. Her blond hair was shoulder length, and her gold jewellery gleamed under the overhead light.

"I'm sorry," I mumbled, and went back to my cleaning trolley before Mrs. Darlington noticed that I hadn't even been holding a duster.

Mrs. Darlington looked good—too young to have a son in his mid-twenties. Perhaps she'd had some cosmetic work. If so, it was expertly done. Her face looked natural, with fine lines around her eyes and on her forehead, but they weren't as deep as one would expect in a woman over fifty.

"You're the girl from the photos."

I nodded.

She looked me up and down as if I were an insect—a pest in her beautiful apartment. I wished I had checked myself in the mirror before I'd come. "I was wondering when I'd finally meet you."

She made it sound as if she hadn't had plenty of opportunities to find me in the hotel over the past few weeks—she could have found out my room number at reception. But Mrs. Darlington was presumably not someone who chased people—she waited until they came to her. And here I was. I wasn't sure what she wanted to hear, so I kept my mouth shut and subjected myself to her scrutiny.

Ethan and Henry took after their father—I couldn't see much of Mrs. Darlington in them.

"Are you sleeping with my son?" she asked suddenly.

I almost choked on my own saliva. "No," I croaked.

Mrs. Darlington tilted her head and examined me impassively. "Are you sure? He seems pretty besotted with you."

"We . . . We're just friends," I stuttered, but it didn't feel quite right. If he was just a friend, I wouldn't have butterflies in my stomach every time I saw him.

"But you like him?"

It seemed like a trick question. If I said no, it would be a lie. If I said yes, she'd probably think I had lied before.

I hesitated and considered my words. "Your son is very good to me. He got me this job, and has given me one of the rooms here until I find my own apartment." Not that I was actively looking. Not yet. I needed a second job first. The three-hundred-pound wage I received from The Darlington wouldn't even get me a shabby studio apartment in London.

Mrs. Darlington's eyebrows shot up in surprise at my last words. Could it be she hadn't known I was living at the hotel? But she didn't comment on it. Instead, she approached me with measured steps, stopping directly across from me on the other side of the cleaning trolley. She was tall and slender, and towered several centimetres above me.

"Henry is a real gem," she replied, wiping the surprise from her face in a bid to restore her composure. "He's a good person—sometimes too good. So good, in fact, that I see it as my duty to make sure no one takes advantage of him. Henry likes you, Miss Hamilton," she added, reading my name from the badge pinned to my chest. "But I doubt he's thinking with his head when it comes to you. So let me make one thing clear: I'm keeping an eye on you. I won't stand by and let you use my son or damage his reputation. He may be having fun with you right now, but don't get too comfy. Your kind will never truly belong with someone like him."

Stunned and unsure how to respond, I stared at Mrs. Darlington. For a moment, the room was so silent that I could hear the wind blowing against the windowpane. Then she smiled, so sickly sweet that it felt like a trap meant to ensnare an insect like me.

"Get back to work," she said before turning on her heel. With her head held high, she marched into the bedroom.

I stood rooted to the spot, trying to process Mrs. Darlington's words and what they implied. Only after the door had closed behind her did I get back to work. I cleaned the penthouse quickly and less thoroughly than I should have done, before slipping quietly into the corridor without saying goodbye. Mrs. Darlington's words lingered. Was I using Henry? The only thing I'd ever asked him for was the four thousand pounds to get Randell off my back, but I hadn't known Henry back then, and I hadn't asked him for anything since. The room, my job, and the phone—he'd given it all to me of his own free will. But his mum and the others didn't know that, of course. Did they all think I was taking advantage of him? I hadn't considered it before, but for some reason, I hated the idea that people might think I only liked Henry because he had nice things to offer me. It wasn't true. Even if he threw me out of the hotel, fired me, and asked for his phone back, it wouldn't change the fact that I liked spending time with him.

Feeling uneasy, I made my way to Henry's apartment. As soon as I stepped inside, my thoughts grew calmer, and his mum's words faded into the background. When I'd cleaned here with Grace for the first time, it had seemed wrong and strange—I had felt like an intruder. But today, his apartment seemed familiar, because Henry was familiar. I knew him. I knew what it was like to fall asleep next to him. I knew how it felt to have his breath brush my neck. And I knew how safe and protected I felt when he cuddled up to me.

As I reminisced about being with Henry, I got to work. I started upstairs in the mezzanine and made my way through the kitchen, living room, guest room, gym, and finally, his bedroom. It smelled of him—warm and safe—and I had to stop myself from inhaling deeply. His bed was unmade, and the curtains were drawn. Even though it was Saturday, Henry had probably left for the office so early that opening them wouldn't have made a difference. I flicked a switch, flooding the room with light. I was just about to shake out the bedding when my gaze landed on Henry's bedside table.

There was a book lying on it. And not just any book. I didn't need to read the title to know it was *The Brave Cloud Princess* by Evelyn Fairchild—I recognised the cover instantly. The colours were brighter and more vivid than on my own copy, but the illustration was the same. My heart swelled, and a wide grin spread across my face. I pictured Henry in bed thinking about me—and reading a children's book, just because it happened to be my favourite.

I pulled out my phone, took a quick photo, and sent it to him with a heart emoji. A quiet *ping* sounded from the living room, followed by approaching footsteps. I turned just as Henry appeared in the doorway.

He looked up from his phone. He was also grinning. "Are you snooping around my apartment?"

"I wouldn't dream of it," I said, batting my eyelashes innocently. "What are you doing here?"

"In my own apartment, you mean?"

"Why aren't you at the office?" I clarified.

He took a step closer. I was certain I hadn't seen the petrol-coloured suit he was wearing before. Just how many suits did he own? Perhaps I *should* snoop around a little when I got the chance and take a peek inside his walk-in wardrobe.

"I was looking for you. Giulia said you'd be here." He stopped an arm's length away, and I had to resist the urge to step forward and snuggle up to his chest. It was as if the night I'd spent in bed with him had got me hooked on being close to him. He studied my face intently. "Is everything OK?"

"Yes. Why?"

"I don't know." As he scrutinised me, I noticed the light sheen of sweat on his forehead, as though he were deeply stressed. "You seem tense," he continued. "I was only joking about the snooping."

"I know. It's just . . ." I hesitated. I briefly considered telling him about the conversation I'd had with his mum, because I couldn't shake the thought that she might be right. But it would only upset Henry, and I didn't want to drive yet another wedge between him and his family. "I had a fight with Rose."

"The kitchen assistant?" Henry asked.

"Yes."

"What did you fight about?"

"That blog. *The Blackroom*," I replied carefully, testing the waters. I could tell from his expression that he knew exactly what I was talking about. "I said that the anonymous interviews might be fabricated. Rose didn't take it well. She's convinced I only said it to protect you. I don't think she likes you very much."

"Hmm. That's fine."

"Is it?"

"Sure. As long as you like me."

It wasn't a question, but I answered anyway. "I like you. A lot."

Henry's laugh was low and unguarded, and it sparked a warm glow in my stomach that took my breath away. I noticed the exact moment he realised the effect he was having on me—his laugh faded, his posture shifted, and with it, the air between us did too. It heated up suddenly, as if someone had cranked up the thermostat. Warmth flooded through me, bringing back memories of our night together. It wasn't my tears I was remembering, however, but how safe I had felt in Henry's arms. I recalled the way his body had pressed against mine, how his hands had rested on my stomach, how his fingers had brushed my cheek.

My body seemed to move of its own accord when I took a step towards him. His familiar scent, so present in his bedroom, grew stronger. I was so close now that I had to tilt my head up to look at him. But Henry didn't meet my eyes—his gaze was fixed firmly on my mouth. It was as if he could read my mind. I licked my lips. A shadow passed across his face, and the longing in my chest intensified.

"I'm glad to hear that, because I wanted to ask you something," Henry said roughly. "There's a masked ball at the hotel next Wednesday, and I'd like it if you came with me. As my date."

There was a brief silence.

"You . . . You want me to go with you to the ball?"

"Yes."

I bit my lower lip hesitantly. "Are you sure you want to go with someone like me?"

Henry's expression darkened. "What is that supposed to mean? *Someone like you*?"

I didn't want to rat out his mum, but I couldn't deny that she had a point. Henry and I were too different. Even right now, we were like day and night. Henry in his expensive designer suit. Me in my room attendant uniform—which happened to also belong to him. I didn't even own it. I had nothing, while he had everything. People looked up to him and down on me. "Nothing. But do you really think it's a good idea?"

"I think it's an excellent idea."

"People will know who I am."

"My stunning date?"

"Your employee."

Henry raised my chin with two fingers, making it impossible to avoid his gaze. He gently stroked my face with his thumb, before running it over my lower lip. When I inhaled sharply in response, his own breathing grew jagged.

"Kate, if you don't want to go to the ball with me, that's fine. But you'd better not believe for a second that I care what others think. This . . ." he gestured between us, "is a thing between you and me. It's no one else's business. *I* want to go to the ball with you, and that's all that matters. So, do you want to be my date or not?"

I didn't need to think about it for long. If I ignored the headlines, the gossip and the conversation just now with his mum, it was simple. I wanted nothing more than to go to the ball with him. But before I accepted his invitation, I raised a practical question. "I have nothing to wear."

Henry grinned. "You could come naked, and then no one would talk about the fact that you work for me. The perfect diversion."

"OK. But only if you go naked too."

He wrinkled his nose. "I'll be shaking a lot of hands. It could get pretty awkward without trousers. Imagine: I'm greeting the

Chancellor of the Exchequer, someone jostles me—and suddenly his hand ends up somewhere it shouldn't. It would traumatise everyone involved. Maybe we should stick to clothes after all."

I laughed. "Fine. But that brings us back to my original problem."

Without a word, Henry turned and made his way to the wardrobe across from his bed. He pressed on a drawer, and it slid open smoothly. Reaching inside, he pulled out a sleek black credit card, as if it were the most normal thing to keep between his socks and underwear. "This should solve your problem."

I didn't take the card. His mum's voice echoed in my head. I hadn't meant to hint that he should buy me something—I had simply been stating a fact. These events had a dress code, and I didn't have the right clothes.

I shook my head. "I can't."

"Why not? There's no limit on the card."

I snorted, not sure if he was joking or not. "It's not about that. I can't let you keep spending money on me. I don't want to take advantage of you."

Henry looked at me. His expression was sceptical, as if he suspected someone had put the thought in my head. "Kate, I think you're the only person in this hotel who *isn't* currently taking advantage of me. Whether it's because of my reputation, my expertise, or my connections—everyone wants something from me. You're the only person who isn't asking me for something. And you don't have to, because I already want to give you everything."

Everything. The word sent a warm heat spreading through me, and once again the overwhelming desire to be kissed by Henry came flooding back with full force. "You . . . I don't want you to think I'm just interested in your money."

"I didn't think that for a second."

"Not even when I blackmailed you for four thousand pounds?"

"No, not even then. Although that was pretty naive of me," he answered with a smile so charming that the butterflies in my stomach fluttered even harder. "Let me buy you a dress, Kate. I wouldn't just be doing it for you. I'd be doing it for myself too. I want you by my side at the ball. You can wear your leather jacket, for all I care, but something tells me you won't want to. So . . ." He held out his sleek black credit card insistently.

It was his expression rather than his words that convinced me. He genuinely seemed to want me there with him at the ball, and I wanted to be there for him. Just as he was there for me.

"Fine! But I won't buy anything expensive, and I'm only borrowing the money. I'll pay you back as soon as I get my first paycheck." Which would be soon. I had been working at The Darlington for nearly a month, and October was almost over.

"You don't have to," Henry assured me.

"But I want to. It's important to me."

He nodded. He understood. Just like he'd understood about the second job. I didn't just want to stand on my own two feet; I *had* to. So that I had a choice. And so that I could choose him without doubting my own reasons for doing so.

"Does that mean you'll be my date?" His voice was so hopeful that I refused to think about his mum's accusations any longer. I wanted to see Henry happy, and for whatever inexplicable reason, the prospect of going to the masked ball with me of all people seemed to make him happy. Which in turn made me happy.

I smiled. "That's exactly what it means."

Every day is a blank canvas.
Paint it with the colours of your soul.

Logan's mindfulness calendar

Henry

In the last few weeks, I'd hardly had a moment for myself. My calendar was crammed with appointments. Rakesh had taken a lot off my plate, yet most of the workload still landed on me. The temptation to cancel today's bouldering session was strong, but I knew I'd feel better afterwards. I felt like the walls were closing in on me at the hotel—which wasn't much of a surprise, given that the precious little time I had away from my office, where I sat from dawn until well past dusk, was spent arguing with Vivian or my dad.

I loved the hotel, but right now, I hated my work. The only highlight of my dreary routine was Kate. We messaged a lot, but that only got me through her waking hours, because she had to sleep at some point. And I didn't want to rob her of her sleep, even if I often fantasised about us keeping each other up at night. But as much as I longed to be in bed with her again, something held me back from going to her. Probably the same part of me that had held back from kissing her that night in her bed, even though she had clearly wanted me to.

Maybe it was my fear of dragging Kate even further into the maelstrom of my family's problems. Or maybe it was just my guilty conscience. Kate had been completely on her own for months. I could only imagine the horrors she must have endured on the streets. She had come a long way since then, but deep down, the frightened woman I had found in the park that day was still there. I had sensed that all too clearly when she had told me about Mr. Fleming.

Despite everything that had happened to her, she trusted me, and I didn't want to break that trust, let alone take advantage of it. Kate needed a friend more than a lover—someone who would support her, stand by her, and help make her world a fairer place. She deserved a shot at a decent life. That was what I should have been focussing on, not how good she felt in my arms, how incredible she smelled, or how adorable the little sounds she made when she slept were. But despite knowing all that, it hadn't stopped me from asking her to accompany me to the masked ball. As my date.

Because I couldn't stop thinking about her.

Because I wanted to spend time with her.

Because I wanted to dance, wrapped in her embrace.

Because I needed her close to me, even if it was just as a friend.

Sweating, my muscles burning, and my head a little clearer, I wrapped up my bouldering session. The only sounds in the gym—which I'd had to myself this morning, as usual—were those of my footsteps and heavy breathing. I showered quickly, and ten minutes later, I was behind the wheel of my Bentley, driving back to the hotel. It wasn't quite rush hour yet, and the streets of London were still relatively empty. A Sleep Token song played over the speakers, and my fingers drummed rhythmically against the steering wheel, as if they had a life of their own. Suddenly, the music was interrupted by an incoming call.

Logan.

I accepted the call, and my brother's face appeared on the dashboard screen. Unlike Ethan and I, who were the spitting image of my dad, Logan took after our mum. He had brown eyes and blond, shoulder-length hair that he usually wore in a top-knot or a plait to show off his undercut.

I stopped the car at a red light. "Good morning."

"Morning," Logan replied. He was sitting in his usual café—I recognised the counter and the slate menus in the background. He often had breakfast there before heading to the market. Sometimes, Maxton joined him, but today, he seemed to be on his own. "You're already out and about?"

"I was bouldering."

Logan sipped his coffee. It was probably so strong that it would have given anyone else a heart attack, but he gulped it down like water. "Perhaps you should have stayed in bed. You look like crap. Did you sleep at all?"

"Not much. There's a lot to do right now."

"You sound like a broken record: *I'm Henry, and there's a lot to do right now*," he mimicked. Much to my annoyance, he perfectly captured my tone.

The light turned green. The old Kia in front of me struggled to get going, and it took a moment before we were moving.

"Is there any particular reason why I have to put up with your annoying personality this early, or are you just trying to piss me off?"

Logan laughed. "Someone's touchy today!"

"I think I'll hang up now."

"Don't you dare!"

I rolled my eyes. "So make your point."

"There is no point," Logan said, and although I had my eyes fixed on the road, I sensed he had grown serious. "I just wanted to see how you're doing. You said you were thinking of coming by for lunch, but you never followed up. Is everything OK?"

"Yes, it's fine. There's just—"

"Don't you dare say that there's just a lot to do, or I'll have to come over there and set you straight," Logan interrupted.

"OK, I won't. But I promise I'll come and see you when things calm down a bit."

"And when will that be? In two years?"

"After the masked ball?" I suggested. The Pearl Gala would be looming on the horizon, requiring far more organisational effort than the ball, as it would be in the media spotlight—but I doubted Logan would be willing to wait until next year. Anyway, I wanted to see him too. I missed him. And even though he refused to help me with the hotel, he always made time to listen when I had problems or needed to vent.

"Sounds good," Logan said. "Are you going with Olivia again this year?"

I suppressed a smile. "Not this year, no."

"Did she bail on you?"

"No, I bailed on her," I replied, turning a corner. The London Eye came into view on the other side of the Thames. A lone boat drifted past The Darlington Hotel, which, with its pillar arcades and small balconies, had looked unchanged from the outside for decades.

Logan snorted. "As if!"

"It's true."

I stopped at another red light, Big Ben ahead of me. On the dashboard display, Logan raised a sceptical eyebrow. "Are you seriously telling me that you, someone who never has time for anything, have found someone who is not Olivia Asterdam to be your date for the ball?"

"Yes."

"Did Amanda set you up with the daughter of one of her friends again?"

Amanda. Not *Mum*. Logan never called our parents Mum and Dad.

"No. I'm capable of finding my own dates."

"What's her name?" Logan asked.

"Kate."

"Last name?"

"Hamilton."

"Kate Hamilton," Logan repeated slowly, his expression thoughtful. I knew exactly what was happening in his head: He was trying to link her name to a respectable family. We didn't usually date outside our social circle—it was snobbish, but it was the truth. Before Kate, I had never dated a woman whose last name wasn't associated with wealth. Not because I wanted to date only wealthy women, but because doing so was the path of least resistance. "It doesn't ring a bell."

"It would have surprised me if it had. She's not from a wealthy family."

Logan's second eyebrow shot up. "Oh, oh. A mere mortal?"

I nodded and turned left onto Westminster Bridge. An ambulance with flashing lights raced past me to St. Thomas' Hospital.

"Do Richard and Amanda know you're taking her to the ball?"

"No, and it's none of their business."

Logan let out a bitter laugh, as if I'd told a joke with a macabre punchline. "I'd really like to see their faces when you introduce Kate to them. It would almost make coming to the hotel worth it."

"The Darlington doors are always open to you."

"I'll think about it."

"Do that," I answered, even though we both knew that he wouldn't. Logan avoided the hotel like the plague, and our parents would rather starve than step foot in The Meridian. I had tried everything over the last few years to bring my family together again, but nothing had worked. The media speculated that my dad's atrocities would tear our family apart, but the truth was, it had already happened long ago. Something had been broken when our parents sent Logan away, and there was no fixing it.

There's no way that was just an interview between Henry and an employee! That touch. That eye contact. It's giving date vibes.

Online comment by BookwormLily

Kate

The doorbell rang.

"I'm coming!" I called. I grabbed my rucksack, which felt surprisingly light now that it no longer contained my entire life, and went to the door. Grace and I both had the day off, and I'd asked if she wanted to go shopping.

"Hey!" I said when the door opened.

Grace grinned at me from beneath a red hat. Beside her stood a young woman in a mustard-yellow coat, and I instantly recognised her as Grace's twin—the resemblance was uncanny. They had the same brown eyes, the same blond hair, and the same even features with soft, feminine contours.

"Hi. I brought reinforcements," Grace said. "This is Amy."

Amy raised a hand. "Hey, it's nice to meet you."

"Likewise. I'm Kate."

Grace clapped her hands impatiently. "Can we leave?"

I nodded and pulled the door shut behind me. At reception, I handed Naomi my room key—for security reasons, keys had to stay on the premises. We left The Darlington through the underground car park, since the press was still camped out in front of the main entrance. I didn't know how they weren't getting bored. Once we were sure that the coast was clear and no journalists were about to pounce on us, we slipped outside and crossed the street, heading towards Soho.

Grace shoved her hands into her jacket pockets. "So, what are we shopping for today? Are you looking for something specific, or are we just window-shopping?"

"I need a dress for the Halloween ball," I replied.

Grace's steps slowed. "The masked ball?"

"Yes. Henry asked me to go with him."

I was pretty sure Grace's squeal could be heard two streets away. "Oh my god! Are you kidding? I knew it! He has little heart-emoji eyes whenever he sees you in the corridor."

I laughed. "No, he doesn't."

"He really does! Henry is totally into you." Grace sighed theatrically. "Oh, man. I like you, Kate, but I'm so envious. I want a hot billionaire to fall madly in love with me too, and take me to a ball."

"You could try your luck with Ethan," I joked.

"I doubt that devil's spawn is capable of feeling love. And even if he were, I'd rather spend the rest of my life living under a bridge than getting involved with *him*."

No, you wouldn't, said a voice in my head.

"I don't like the guy," Amy said, her chin buried deep in her scarf, her cheeks rosy from the cold.

"No one likes him," Grace clarified, before turning back to me. "Enough about Beelzebub and back to Henry. You do know that's a date, right?"

"Yes." I grinned.

"What kind of dress do you want?" Amy asked.

I shrugged. "No idea. A pretty one."

She laughed. "OK. And do you know where you want to go?"

My thoughts drifted to Henry's credit card, tucked into the sewn-in pocket of my leather jacket. Although it would get me into the most high-end, expensive boutiques in the city, I knew I wouldn't feel comfortable in them. Besides, I was paying Henry back, and I didn't want to waste my savings on a dress. I wanted to use that money to build something—my own life. I couldn't stay at The Darlington forever, after all. Sooner or later, I'd have to learn to stand on my own two feet.

"What about the secondhand shop at Seven Dials?"

"Good idea," Grace said, and we decided to walk the half hour to the shop.

Though it was cold and the wind cut through my leather jacket, the sun was shining and the sky was a brilliant blue. It struck me that I'd practically barricaded myself inside The Darlington over the last month. I had only left the hotel two or three times, usually just to buy snacks from a shop down the road. Otherwise, The Darlington had everything I needed, and everything I had craved: a warm bed, a clean bath, and privacy.

"Kate!" someone called behind us, and a chill colder than any gust of wind gripped me. I knew that voice and had hoped to never hear it again. "Kate! Wait!"

No.

No.

No!

What was Randell doing here? My stomach clenched, and I quickened my pace. It took all my willpower not to run like I used to. But Amy and Grace didn't speed up to match my pace. They slowed down instead, and I could feel their curious eyes on me. I had no answers for them.

"Kate!"

A hand gripped my upper arm, stopping me in my tracks. Dirty fingers dug into my skin—firm, but not painful. Still, I knew all too well how it felt to be beaten by those hands, and my body remembered the pain. My heart pounded fiercely against my ribs as I turned to face Randell, meeting the eyes I despised so much. He stared back at me, his pupils dilated.

I wanted to scream at him, curse him, wrench myself free, but doing so would have required an explanation. And if there was one thing I dreaded more than confronting Randell, it was Amy's and Grace's inevitable questions. I took a deep breath, filling my lungs, and forced myself to stay calm.

"Randell." My voice was cool. Detached.

He looked even worse today than he had the day I'd given him the money. As if he'd spent it all on getting high and drunk. The acrid stench of cigarettes hung over him like a cloud.

I looked at Grace and Amy. "Can you give us a moment?"

They looked worried—they must have noticed the stench of alcohol emanating from Randell—but I forced a smile that seemed to reassure them. They stepped back hesitantly, still not taking their eyes off us.

I turned back to Randell. It couldn't be a coincidence that he was here. London was far too big for that. He must have been lying in wait for me. He had probably got wind of the news that I worked at The Darlington. "What do you want?"

"Justice."

I snorted. Justice would have been Randell dead instead of my mum. Or at least Randell locked up in prison for what he had done to us. "Leave me alone, you bastard!"

I made to turn away, but Randell grabbed my arm again. It took every shred of self-control I had not to wince.

"What do you want?" I repeated.

He came closer. "Money."

"Do I look like a bank?"

"You owe me."

My face hardened. "I owe you nothing!"

"Oh, believe me, you do!" Randell hissed, spittle flying.

Disgusted, I wrinkled my nose. "I've paid off my debt."

Randell gave a grim smile, revealing a chipped front tooth. It looked like his face had collided with the edge of a table—or with a fist. I was betting on the latter. "You paid off your mum's debt, but not your own."

"And what debt would that be?"

"For the rent. And the food."

I rolled my eyes. He had to be kidding. The initial panic I'd felt at seeing him again had faded, replaced with a burning rage that coursed through my veins. "We gave you half the rent every month, and if any of us was buying food, it was me. Most of the time, you were both too high to go shopping. So don't tell me I owe you something."

"I need money," Randell hissed, ignoring my words. He knew I was right, but he was desperate and wanted to squeeze every last penny out of me. I refused to play ball.

I crossed my arms. "Then get a job."

"Or you give it to me."

"I don't have any money."

"Maybe you don't, but your rich boyfriend does."

I blinked. So that's what this was about. Not only had he found out that I was working for The Darlington; he'd also seen the photos of Henry and me together.

"Henry isn't my boyfriend. He's my boss. The only thing I get from him is my salary, and that money belongs to me."

"So you're going to leave me in the lurch?"

I didn't feel an ounce of sympathy, only satisfaction. "Yes. We've gone our separate ways, Randell. The only thing that ever connected us was my mum, and she's dead—because of you. Now leave me alone. My friends are waiting for me."

Without waiting for a reaction, I turned and made my way back to Amy and Grace, who had been watching our conversation from a distance. I could feel Randell's gaze drilling into me.

"See you soon, Kate!"

I ignored his threat. I was done with him.

"Is everything all right?" Grace asked when I caught up with them.

"All good."

"Are you sure? That guy was weird."

"Yeah. He was just an old friend of my mum's."

Amy glanced over her shoulder. "He doesn't look too good."

"He doesn't. But that's not my problem."

We walked, none of us saying a word for a few minutes, until I couldn't stand the silence any longer. I turned to Amy. "Grace told me you're studying medicine."

She smiled proudly. "Yeah, in my third semester."

"You need pretty good grades for that, right?"

"My twin is super smart!" Grace interjected, throwing an arm around Amy's shoulders. "She's always wanted to be a doctor. When we were kids, she'd make me pretend to be her patient. I usually survived, but sometimes, she'd make me die on the operating table. The little sadist."

"Hey! I only made you die when you talked."

"And I only talked when you were doing a crappy job."

Amy laughed. "Yes, but you weren't supposed to be able to talk. You were under general anaesthetic."

"It was boring to play a game where all I could do was lie there."

I smiled at their bickering and found myself wondering, not for the first time, what it would have been like to grow up with siblings. I couldn't rule out the possibility that I had some. Perhaps my dad had had impregnated other women, or he'd settled down and was living in a cute terraced house somewhere with his wife and my half-siblings, who didn't know I existed. But I had come to terms with that, because there was no point in mourning something I'd never had—or that perhaps didn't even exist.

Grace and Amy shared more anecdotes about their childhood and their brother, Jason, who was going through puberty and hated everything. They also talked about their parents. Their dad was a doctor, which had inspired Amy, and their mum was a teacher. I liked hearing their family stories, but it also stung a little, especially when they spoke about their mum. It reminded me just how much I missed my own. To distract myself, I told them about my plans to get a second job so I'd have more financial stability. I had already sent out a few online applications. Finding a job in this city wasn't easy—especially not for a high school dropout. I was willing to do just about anything, but I had no qualifications, and most companies required them—a lot of them. Simply because they could. London had a large job market, but the number of applicants was even larger. Every day, people with more impressive CVs were moving here.

We arrived at the secondhand shop where I had bought my leather jacket two years ago. Some items were pricey, but there were also some real bargains. The shop had a large selection, including a section for evening wear, which I made a beeline for while Amy and Grace drifted off in different directions.

I sifted through the dresses on the rack to get an overview. I didn't really know what I was looking for, except that I wanted something black. I'd need to wear a mask, and everything looked good with a dark dress. Grace disappeared into the changing room with a pile of clothes, while Amy rifled through the jewellery and accessories.

"What do you think about these trousers?" Grace asked.

I watched her twist in front of the mirror to get a better view of her bum, which looked incredible in the dark-green leather trousers she had tried on. "I think they look great."

"What do you think, Amy?"

"You should definitely get them!" she said, just as her phone rang in her handbag. She smiled when she pulled it out and saw who was calling. "Hey, what's up? I'm shopping with Grace and her friend."

I couldn't hear the person on the other end, but I saw Amy's smile falter until it disappeared altogether.

"Oh, OK. No problem," she said quietly.

". . ."

"I could come with you, if you want."

". . ."

"Of course. I get it. But Halloween is still on?" she asked hopefully.

". . ."

Her smile returned. "Cool. I'm looking forward to it. Have fun tonight. I love you."

She hung up and turned back to us.

Grace was still standing before the mirror, but her enthusiasm for the trousers was gone. Instead, she seemed annoyed. With her hands on her hips, she glared at her sister. "Please tell me that wasn't Garrett."

"It wasn't Garrett."

Even I could tell she was lying.

Grace groaned. "Did he cancel on you again?"

Amy shrunk into herself. "He just needs some space."

"Who's Garrett?" I asked.

"A loser Amy should dump," Grace replied.

Amy shot her a look far darker than I would have expected from someone with such a sweet face. "He's my boyfriend, and he's not a loser. He's just stressed."

"That's no excuse for treating you like crap," Grace said. Judging by the frustration in her voice, they'd already had this conversation more than once. "You're also stressed with uni, but you still make time for him. I'm not saying you should be together night and day, but it's not OK that he keeps cancelling on you last minute just because it's all too much for him. If he really loved you, you wouldn't be too much for him."

"What's that supposed to mean?" Amy hissed. She took a step towards Grace, who seemed unfazed. "That Garrett doesn't love me?"

"Maybe. I never think you're too much."

"You're my sister!"

"And he's your boyfriend," Grace snapped back. "I have to spend time with you, but he has a choice. And time and again, he chooses not to. And yet you're always waiting around for him."

Amy stared at Grace in silence for a moment. "That . . . that's not true."

Grace scoffed. "You tell yourself that, if you have to. But he's playing you, and you're letting him do it. And somehow, I'm the bad guy. Makes sense." She turned on her heel and stormed back to the fitting rooms, yanking the curtain shut with more force than necessary.

Amy didn't move. I took a cautious step towards her.

"Sorry you had to hear that. I shouldn't have come."

"It's OK," I said, and placed a comforting hand on her arm. "I'm glad you're here. Grace has told me so much about you."

"I hate fighting with her."

"Is some of what she said true?" I asked carefully. "Does Garrett cancel on you that often?"

Amy hesitated a moment. "Yes, it's happened quite a lot recently. But he's very busy. Grace doesn't understand. She doesn't know how exhausting med school is."

"He's studying medicine too?"

She nodded. "Yes, but he's ahead of me—he's already working in a hospital. We met at a faculty party and have been together since then. Grace has never really liked him."

"But you love him?"

Amy nodded.

I smiled. "Then I'm sure things will get better. Grace is just worried. Give her some time to cool off, and everything will be fine."

She sighed. "I hope so."

I was right. The tension dissipated a few moments later, when I stepped into the fitting room with a pile of clothes and put on a fashion show. Most of the dresses looked terrible on me. They were too long and I was too thin, and often they slipped off my shoulders. I had grown gaunt living on the streets, and even with the weight I'd gained in the last few weeks, I was still pretty skinny.

I slipped into another dress. It was the last of seven, and I was beginning to lose hope. Grace had picked it out—I never would have chosen it myself. But as soon as I pulled it over my head, my hope returned. I knew instantly that this dress was different. I stepped out of the changing room, excited. Grace and Amy were sitting on stools, and they looked up from their phones. Their eyes widened when they saw me.

"Oh my god," Grace whispered.

Amy grinned. "I think you've found your dress."

I nodded and looked at myself in the mirror. "I have."

34

Halloween Party Scandal at The Darlington:
Guests Dance on the Graves of Dead Morals!

INsider Headline

Kate

"Henry is going to lose it when he sees you."

Grace sat cross-legged on the bed in my hotel room and watched me with a smile as I stared at myself in the mirror. I hardly recognised myself. Who was this woman? The dress was the prettiest I'd ever worn in my life. It wasn't black but made of a light, silky fabric that hugged my body to create the illusion of curves. Thin straps gathered at the back of my neck, and while the neckline was relatively high, the cut left almost my entire back exposed. It was a stunningly elegant dress—but it was how Grace had transformed me that took my breath away.

She had brought makeup with her, along with the scissors Amy used to trim her fringe. For the first time in months, my hair was even, with Grace having fixed what I hadn't managed on my own. Afterwards, she had used her straightener to add soft waves to the ends of my hair. And she had made my eyes look sultry behind the gold mask, which covered only the top half of my face. The sides of the mask were adorned with delicate, white feathers, as if it had sprouted wings, or a tiny angel had landed on my face.

"I think I'm going to lose it too," I replied. This was yet another one of those times when I couldn't quite believe that this was my life now. I had experienced so many of these moments over the last few weeks.

Grace laughed. "You look amazing."

"Thank you." I gently ran my fingers over the silky fabric. I had the strange feeling that I moved differently in this dress. Maybe because, for the first time in months, I wasn't trying to be inconspicuous or invisible. I wanted to be seen, because this dress deserved to be seen. "For your help too."

"I expect a detailed report tomorrow as a thank-you."

"You would have received one anyway," I said, tearing myself away from the mirror.

Grace had risen from the bed to put on her shoes. She had the day off today and had come to the hotel especially to help me, but Amy was waiting for her at home because she had been stood up by Garrett again. The twins were having a film night instead, something I would have been jealous of were it not for the fact that Henry was picking me up at any moment. "I can't wait. Have fun tonight."

"Thanks, you too. Say hi to Amy from me."

Grace slipped on her coat, and we hugged goodbye just as the doorbell rang. She shot me an excited smile before she went to open the door.

My stomach did a somersault when I saw Henry. He looked as if he had stepped straight out of one of my romantasy novels.

Instead of a regular suit jacket, he wore a burgundy tailcoat adorned with black embroidery, paired with a matching waistcoat and elegant gloves. Like me, Henry wore a mask that concealed the upper half of his face. But while mine came from a supermarket's Halloween assortment, Henry's seemed custom-made. It fit the contours of his face perfectly and had two curved horns protruding from it. If this was what the devil looked like, I could hardly wait to get to hell. Or perhaps I was already there, given how hot I suddenly felt.

"Perfect timing, Mr. Darlington. You look great."

"Thank you, Grace." The mask gave Henry's smile an air of mischief.

"Have fun, you two, and behave yourselves." Grace smiled as she slipped out into the corridor, leaving me alone with Henry.

His full attention was on me, and the heat in my body intensified. His gaze swept slowly over me before returning to my face. My throat suddenly felt dry, and my heart pounded wildly as he approached slowly before stopping right in front of me. Even though I was wearing heels, he was still much taller. He looked down at me. His pupils were dilated, yet the blue of his eyes seemed even more intense than usual behind the dark mask.

I swallowed hard. "Hey."

"Hey," Henry answered. "You look stunning, Cupcake."

I suppressed a smile, not because I liked the nickname, but because he simply wasn't giving up—it wasn't in his nature. "Thanks. But please don't call me Cupcake, Mr. Darlington."

"Mr. Darlington?" Henry asked, bemused.

"Don't you like me calling you that?"

"Oh, I do. Far too much," he replied with a smile that made me want to say his last name more often. He took another step closer and raised a hand. His fingertips gently grazed my mask, then skimmed the ends of my hair before finally tracing my bare shoulder. My heart pounded even faster. "I have to admit, I slightly regret inviting you to this ball."

"Oh, really?"

"Yes. Now I'll have to share you with everyone else."

"We could always stay here, order pizza, and watch a film," I suggested, not entirely selflessly. As much as I was looking forward to the evening with Henry, I was nervous about diving deeper into his world. I had nothing in common with the people at this ball, and I had no idea what to expect.

Henry's fingers were still dancing lightly across my shoulder. "As tempting as that sounds, I'm afraid I need to make an appearance, if only for a couple of hours."

"Shame," I murmured.

His hand slid from my shoulder and trailed down my arm to my hand. Our fingers intertwined instantly in a way that felt completely natural. He gave me an encouraging smile, as though he could sense my nervousness despite my best efforts to hide it. I didn't know the other guests at the ball, but I'd dealt with plenty of absurdly wealthy people in the past few weeks. It was impossible to ignore how different I was—and they never failed to remind me of it. They exuded an old-money vibe that couldn't be imitated.

We took the lift down to the lobby, where voices and laughter filled the air. I had never seen it so lively before. Dozens of masked guests, dressed in elegant suits and gowns, made their way to the ballroom. Some outfits looked like they had come straight from a fairy tale—one woman even wore a tiara. The masks were colourful and varied, and it was clear that most people wore custom-made pieces like Henry rather than last-minute masks made of cheap lace and faux feathers like mine. Doubt crept in. Had I made a mistake by not taking full advantage of Henry's credit card? But it was too late for regrets now.

Henry gave my hand a squeeze and led me into the throng. Waiters from the restaurant, which was closed for the night, glided through the crowd with trays, offering guests flutes of champagne. Henry took one, but I declined, too nervous to drink on an empty stomach. It wasn't long before people began to recognise Henry. They nodded in greeting and smiled at him through their masks, while I drew curious glances as guests tried to place me. Although the mask didn't conceal much, the dress and makeup had transformed me from the girl in those McDonald's photos. It would probably take a while for them to connect the dots.

Henry steered me confidently through the lobby. The double doors of the ballroom stood wide open, and the air buzzed with anticipation and excitement. The ballroom had been completely transformed as well. When Henry had shown me the scratch on the floor, the space had been empty, every step echoing off the walls. Tonight, floral arrangements adorned pillars, and while the tables were still pushed to the sides of the room to create a big dance floor, they were elegantly set rather than hidden beneath sheets. Upholstered chairs were dotted around, offering people a place to rest their feet. A band played onstage, and although the evening had only just begun, people were already dancing.

"Wow. It's stunning," I said, brushing a strand of hair from my face. The downside to finally having a proper haircut was that I could no longer tuck it neatly behind my ears.

Henry smiled and gently nudged me into the ballroom away from the entrance. A waitress floated past with a tray of hors d'oeuvres. I grabbed two to line my stomach in preparation for the alcohol, and we went to find our seats. Most guests were milling around or dancing, but everyone had an assigned seat—it was probably expected at such an expensive event. No sooner had we sat down than a waiter appeared and asked if we wanted drinks. I ordered a colourful cocktail, and Henry asked for a glass of water.

"Good evening, Henry."

My shoulders tensed. I recognised Amanda Darlington's authoritative voice immediately. Of course Henry's parents were here. It was their ball too, after all. What else had I expected? My heart began to race when Mrs. Darlington stepped closer. She was wearing a cream-coloured gown that looked almost like a wedding dress and was accompanied by Mr. Darlington. I recognised his face from countless newspaper articles—and because, despite the mask, he was the spitting image of Henry.

Henry rose from his chair to greet his parents, and I quickly followed suit, assuming it was the polite thing to do. Maybe. I had no idea. "Hello, Mum." He leaned in to kiss her on the cheek before extending a hand to his father, shaking it with the formality of a business partner at a meeting.

Mr. Darlington ignored me. "Have you seen Ethan?"

"I don't think he's here," Henry replied.

His dad pursed his lips. "Why not?"

"It's not his kind of event," Henry said with a shrug. "If you wanted Ethan and his friends to be here, we should have thought about hiring strippers and serving weed."

I laughed, but Mr. Darlington clearly didn't find it funny.

"Who is your ravishing date?" Mrs. Darlington interjected. She smiled at me and held out her hand as if we didn't know each other. It dawned on me then that she didn't recognise me behind my mask.

Henry slipped an arm around my waist and pulled me close to him, but not even his proximity could calm my frantic flutter of nerves. "This is Kate. Kate, these are my parents, Amanda and Richard."

His mum's mouth slackened. "Miss Hamilton. I didn't recognise you for a moment. But I see it now," she added, wrinkling her nose as she looked me up and down, clearly unimpressed by what I was wearing.

I looked down and wondered once again if I should have spent more on my outfit.

"You've already met?" Henry asked, surprised.

"Yes, we met when she was *cleaning* the penthouse." She emphasised the word as if to remind Henry of my position at the hotel. "We had a conversation. But evidently, Miss Hamilton wasn't listening."

An unspoken threat lurked beneath her words.

Mr. Darlington, who had been sipping his whisky, paused mid-motion and lowered his glass. His eyes, just as blue as Henry's, narrowed beneath his mask. "This is the cleaning lady everyone has been talking about?"

"Yes," his wife answered curtly.

Mr. Darlington's gaze darted from me to Henry. While his mum's displeasure seemed to be directed at me, his dad looked disappointed in Henry. "Does Vivian know you've brought her with you?"

"No. It's none of her business who my date is."

"How is she supposed to do her job when you refuse to cooperate with her?"

Henry's jaw twitched. "It's her job to make you look like an innocent angel, not to judge my love life."

"It *is* Vivian's job if you turn up with someone like her," Mr. Darlington retorted, gesturing at me with his whisky glass, as if there were any doubt who he meant.

Ashamed, I felt heat rise in my cheeks, and I hastily tried to pull away from Henry. I didn't want him to fight with his parents because of me—it wasn't worth it. But instead of letting me go, his arm tightened around me like a noose. I glanced up at him, but he didn't return my look. His eyes were fixed on his parents, his expression darker than I had ever seen it. I was incredibly relieved to not be on the receiving end.

"I'm going to pretend you didn't mean that the way it sounded, because if you did, we'd have a problem," Henry said to his dad. His voice was calm—dangerously calm—giving me a glimpse of the man he became when he was at the office making million-pound decisions that affected dozens of employees. "I'm here to have a nice evening with Kate before I have to get up at the crack of dawn tomorrow to fix what you screwed up. If you can't give me this one evening and be kind to Kate, then it's best we don't speak at all."

A cutting silence followed Henry's words, broken only by the incongruously cheerful music of the band. I hardly dared to breathe.

Eventually, Henry broke the silence. "We're going to dance. See you later. Or not. That's up to you."

Before I could react, he took my hand and led me away from his parents. I glanced over my shoulder at Mr. and Mrs. Darlington, who stood frozen in place at our table, staring after us. If looks could kill, I would probably have dropped dead on the spot. But despite the tension and spiteful words, I felt strangely good. No one had ever stood up for me the way Henry had just done.

I shot him a furtive look. "Henry?"

"Yes?"

I wanted to address what had just happened, but I didn't know how. Instead, I said the first thing that came to my head: "I can't dance."

He laughed.

The moment we reached the dance floor, the upbeat song ended, and a slower one began. The couples around us inched closer together. Henry placed my hand on his shoulder while he wrapped his arm around my waist and rested his hand on my lower back. If he hadn't been wearing gloves, I would have felt his skin against mine, but I could still feel the heat of his hand through the fabric.

"Put your other arm around my neck," he said.

I obeyed, pulling us even closer together. His familiar smell washed over me, and though he hadn't asked me to, I instinctively rested my head on his shoulder. He pulled me closer, and it felt more like an embrace than a dance. We began to sway gently to the music as a whirl of colourful dresses and masks surrounded us.

"I'm sorry about that," Henry murmured into my ear.

I looked up at him. "You don't have to be sorry."

"My parents are sometimes . . ." He faltered and shook his head, words failing him. Despite how tenderly he was holding me, his eyes were hard behind his horned mask. He stared in the direction of his parents, though I suspected the dancing guests had already blocked them from view.

"Hey." I touched his cheek, gently turning his head to look at me. His expression softened instantly. I liked having that effect on him. I smiled at him. "Forget them. You said yourself that you're here to have a nice evening with me, so don't let them ruin it."

He sighed. "You're right. It's just . . ."

"Shh," I interrupted, pressing a finger to his lips. "Not another word about your parents. You can vent about them again tomorrow, but not tonight. We're at a ball now! A *real* ball. When I was a little girl, I dreamed of this. I wanted to be a princess."

I felt Henry's lips curl into a smile beneath my finger, which I took as a sign that he'd understood. I put my hand back on his shoulder. The rhythm of the music changed, although it didn't pick up pace. Henry turned us in slow circles, using only the slightest pressure to guide me. I had never danced to music like this in my life, but he made me feel like I knew what I was doing.

"You really wanted to be a princess?" he asked quietly. His hand glided up my back to my shoulder blades. I shivered as his fingers traced lightly over my skin, mirroring the slow rhythm of our movements across the dance floor.

"You sound surprised."

"You don't strike me as a princess girl."

"You might not believe it, but my life used to be quite normal," I said. "*I* was quite normal." It had been a long time since I'd allowed myself to remember life before Randell and even longer since I had talked about it. "I never had as much money as my friends, but I wanted the same things as them. In primary school, it was glittery pens; later, it was pretty clothes, cool makeup, and a cute boyfriend."

"And look at you now," Henry teased. "You have it all, glittery pens aside. But I'm sure we can fix that."

I lowered my gaze shyly. Was Henry aware that he'd just indirectly referred to himself as my boyfriend? I knew things between us weren't that serious, but the thought still warmed me.

"It's fine. I don't care about them so much anymore," I said quickly, trying to steer the conversation away.

"OK, but just say the word, and I'll call Rakesh. He'll take care of it." Henry's eyes sparkled playfully behind his mask, but his tone was serious.

"I can't tell if you're joking right now," I said.

Henry let out a deep, throaty laugh that sounded even more melodious to me than the music. "That was a joke. Rakesh deserves a break. I'd get the pens myself."

I was completely at his mercy. And I had no doubt that Henry would immediately set out to find me glittery pens if they truly mattered to me. Since we'd met, he had done everything in his power to make sure I was fine and that I had everything I needed. Right now, though, the only thing I needed was him.

I rested my head against his shoulder again. As if he had read my mind, he pulled me so close that not even the smallest gap remained between us, and we swayed together to the music. In Henry's arms that evening, I felt like a real princess. And he was my prince—not in shining armour, but dressed as the devil.

35

> The Darlington Hotel's masked ball is perfect! The music, the company—savour it, and leave the rest of the world behind. 🎭🥂🍾 #HighSociety #NoDramaJustFun #EliteOnly

Online comment by Emmeline Ridgewell

Kate

I hadn't known what to expect at the ball, but I hadn't imagined it would feel so ordinary, just in an outrageously fancy and criminally expensive way. Guests ate and drank. People talked, laughed, and danced. The band alternated between playing slow and fast songs. Henry told me that the real party wouldn't start until the band finished their set, the DJ took over, and everyone was tipsy.

I didn't feel uncomfortable, but I still felt out of place, even though Henry was doing his best to include me. Every few steps, someone stopped him to talk—and each time, he made a point of introducing me, all the while keeping an arm around my waist or holding my hand. But nobody talked to me, and I had nothing to contribute. The things these people were saying were so far removed from my reality that I couldn't even pretend I knew what they were talking about.

Henry was saying goodbye to Mr. and Mrs. Oldroyd, who had just spent ten minutes telling him about their horse racing track, when a bright voice called out his name.

"Henry! Finally!"

Henry turned towards the voice, but instead of shooting me an apologetic look as he had when the other guests had accosted him, something surprising happened: He smiled. Not the fake, formal smile he had given Mr. and Mrs. Oldroyd and the others, but a genuine one, the kind of smile he'd so far only given me tonight. "Hey! I was wondering where you were hiding."

"I've been looking for you two this entire time," replied one of the most stunning women I had ever seen, pulling Henry in for a hug. He let go of my hand to hug her back.

She looked vaguely familiar, but I couldn't quite place her. Her blond hair was styled in an elaborate updo, crowned with a tiara that sparkled as brightly as her midnight-blue dress, its bodice adorned with glittering diamonds. She wasn't wearing her mask like everyone else, but carried it attached to a short stick, ready to lift it to her face—an elastic strap probably would have ruined her intricate hairstyle.

The woman released Henry before doing something even more astonishing—she looked at me. After an hour of being thoroughly ignored by everyone, the weight of her green eyes on me was a shock. Just as astonishing was the embrace she pulled me into a moment later. "I'm so glad to finally meet you."

"Oh, really?" I asked, surprised, and patted her arm. I shot Henry a confused look over her shoulder, and he mouthed a name: *Olivia.* Oh, it made sense. And now I knew why she looked familiar. I had seen photos of her and Henry together, both online and when I'd passed newsstands.

"I'm a big fan," Olivia replied, letting me go. "I admire anyone who gets this sourpuss to smile."

"Sourpuss?" I asked. Sure, Henry was often stressed and frustrated by the situation the hotel was in—understandably so—but I had never thought of him as moody or bad-tempered.

Olivia nodded. "Yes. You can't imagine how miserable he's been in the last few months. But since he met you, he's a changed man."

"Olivia . . ." Henry warned through gritted teeth.

"What? It's the truth."

He rolled his eyes. "I hate you."

Olivia ignored him, focussing all her attention on me. "Henry has told me a lot about you."

"Really?" I knew they were close friends, but close enough for the truth? Or had he fed her the same lie he'd told everyone else? I looked questioningly at Henry.

He nodded. "Olivia knows."

"Yes. He can't keep anything from me."

"Oh, I can."

"You just keep telling yourself that," Olivia said. We'd met barely two minutes ago, but I could already see why Henry liked her. She had a radiance that drew people in and instantly made them feel welcome. "I'm really glad you're here tonight, Kate. And I don't want to be nosy, but I have a lot of questions. Perhaps we could meet for a coffee sometime?"

I nodded and tucked that annoying strand of hair behind my ear once again. "I'd like that."

"Can I come?" Henry asked.

"No," Olivia answered before I could respond. "It's a girls' date."

He glared at her, but she was unfazed. He'd probably given her many of those looks over the years. "You want to talk about me, don't you?"

She shrugged. "Of course. What else? But don't worry. I'll start with the less embarrassing stories. I don't want to chase Kate away, after all. I'll save the bad ones for later, when she's so madly in love with you that nothing can scare her away."

I laughed nervously, but I was also genuinely amused. I considered telling Olivia that even now, nothing could scare me away, but before I could open my mouth, a man joined our group. He had brown hair, cropped shorter at the sides than on top, and despite his mask, he was just as undeniably attractive as Olivia. He slipped an arm around her, and Henry's demeanour changed instantly. I could feel the tension radiating off him.

"There you are," the man said, kissing Olivia's cheek.

Olivia smiled. "I told you I was looking for Henry."

The man glanced from her to Henry, who looked anything but pleased to see him. Henry's lips were pressed together, and he glared at Olivia's companion from behind his mask.

"Hey, dude," the man said. "You good?"

Henry crossed his arms in front of his chest. "Yeah. And you, Marko?"

I trawled my memory for his name, but I was pretty sure Henry had never mentioned him. Still, I didn't have to be Sherlock Holmes to deduce that Henry didn't like him.

"I can't complain, not when I have such a hot date," Marko said, giving Olivia another kiss on the cheek. He was clearly tipsy already, despite the evening having only just begun.

"Olivia looks really beautiful," I agreed.

She smiled and looked like she was about to speak, but Marko beat her to it. "She always looks beautiful. It's a mystery to me why she would ever date a clown like Darlington." He laughed as if he'd told a hilarious joke, but no one joined in. Marko didn't seem to care. He sniggered again before turning his attention to the empty glass in his hand. "I'm going to get more champagne. Are you coming?"

Olivia shook her head. Marko turned on his heel without a word and disappeared as swiftly as he'd appeared.

Henry stared at Olivia as if she'd grown a second head. "Are you out of your mind? Marko Langston?"

"Who is he?" I asked, curious.

"Someone it's best to steer clear of."

"You're only saying that because he broke your nose back then," Olivia retorted. "He's nice, once you get to know him."

"He's drunk."

Olivia shot Henry a withering look. "He likes to party. So what? Just because you've become a bore doesn't mean the rest of us can't have our fun. And Marko is fun. A *lot* of fun," she said, her tone suggesting she wasn't just talking about partying.

Henry made a gagging noise. "I still don't like him."

"You don't have to," Olivia shot back. "I'm dating him, not you. And even you have to admit, he's ridiculously good-looking. It's worth it for that alone."

"He looks average at best."

Olivia scoffed. "If that's average, then every other man has already lost."

Henry rolled his eyes. "Fine, maybe he's above average, but there's no way he's better looking than me."

"Oh, but he is. Much better looking than you," Olivia said, patting Henry's cheek.

"Olivia, sweetie? Can you come here?" a voice called suddenly. I spotted an older couple who could only have been Olivia's parents.

She gestured to them that she was coming before turning back to us. "I have to go, but we'll see each other at our coffee date at the latest! Henry has my number. You can get it from him." She hugged first me, then Henry, before leaving to join her parents. She turned back once more to wave at us before disappearing into the crowd. By now, the ballroom was packed, and more and more people were flocking to the dance floor.

I looked up at Henry. "In case you need reassuring: *I* think you're more attractive than Marko."

His mouth twitched. He uncrossed his arms and reached for my hand again, as if it were the most natural thing in the world. My fingers felt warm and secure between his, like they belonged there. "Thank you," he said.

"Did Marko really break your nose?"

"Yes, but it must have been around seven years ago. We were drunk and reckless."

"And you don't like him because of that?"

"Yes. And because he's an arrogant arsehole."

I laughed. "I see. But Olivia is really nice."

"Yeah, she's the best. Far too good for someone like him," Henry replied, and we finally continued towards the bar. We had decided half an hour ago to get more drinks, but we'd been stopped several times along the way.

"Should I be jealous?" I teased, but I wasn't entirely joking. Olivia wasn't just nice; she was also exceptionally pretty, and she had known Henry far longer than I had—and knew him far better. It was only natural that I felt a twinge of insecurity, even if I hadn't sensed the slightest spark of chemistry between them.

"No, we're just friends."

"But you used to be together, right?"

Henry sighed, as if tired of the topic. "Not really. We went on a couple of dates years ago because our parents liked the idea of it and kept pestering us about what a great couple we'd make. So eventually we caved, but it never felt right."

We reached the bar, a dark wooden counter with a mirrored back wall lined with expensive-looking bottles. The lighting in this part of the ballroom was dim, casting a warm, golden glow. Behind the counter, bartenders worked tirelessly, juggling bottles and tossing shiny metal shakers into the air to entertain the guests as they waited for their drinks. Although Henry and I stood at the side of the bar, we were surrounded by so many people that we ended up pressed against each other again, just like we had been on the dance floor.

"So what went wrong?" I asked, unable to contain my curiosity.

"I love Olivia, but she's way too involved in all this," he replied, and gestured around the ballroom.

I raised my eyebrows behind my mask. "And you're not?"

"Sure, but not like she is. I'm a tiny part of this world, while this world is a huge part of her. If that makes sense." I nodded. "Olivia would do anything to belong. When we were dating, we argued more than we ever had before. Mostly about her desperate need to attend events like this just to be seen—whereas I just wanted to lie on the sofa and cuddle."

I couldn't help but smile. "Cute."

Henry shot me a sharp look. "Did you just call me 'cute'?"

Feeling momentarily bold, I stood on my tiptoes, bringing our faces close together. Lowering my voice so only Henry could hear, I said, "Yes, and there's nothing you can do about it, *Mr. Darlington*."

"Maybe I don't want to, *Miss Hamilton*." Henry's voice was barely louder than a whisper.

I shivered, and goose bumps prickled my arms. With his free hand, he tucked a rebellious strand of hair behind my ear, his gloved fingertips gently grazing my cheek. He looked at my mouth with smouldering eyes. A burning heat spread through me, and a jolt of deep longing tightened in my chest.

"Henry! It's so good to see you!"

"Fuck," Henry muttered. Regret flashed across his face, as if he wished he'd acted faster, and he squeezed his eyes shut. It seemed to pain him to let me go. His hand slipped from my cheek, but even without his touch, the spot where his fingers had been still tingled.

I sighed, trying not to sound too disappointed. "I think I'll freshen up," I said. I couldn't take another conversation about racetracks, estates, stocks, or the planned ski trip to Saint Moritz.

"Good idea. I'll wait for you here," Henry replied, before turning his attention to the man who had interrupted us. I smiled at him as I left, even while secretly cursing him.

To my surprise, there wasn't a queue for the restroom. The room was empty aside from a woman standing at the sink, touching up her makeup. In the stall, I lifted my dress, peeled down the tights Grace had made me wear, despite the dress being floor-length, and gathered the silky material around my hips. As I peed, I heard the woman leave the room, and two others entered. They didn't go into the cubicles, but lingered by the sinks. I regretted not bringing Grace's makeup with me. Powdering my nose wouldn't have hurt. Maybe I could borrow some from the women. I pulled the tights back up, adjusted my dress, and was about to flush when they started talking.

"I still can't get over the fact that Henry is here with his cleaning lady," one of them said.

I froze.

"I heard she's Richard's crisis manager."

"No, that's Vivian Edwards. Henry's date is a cleaner."

I shifted as quietly as I could, leaning forward to press my face to the crack between the door and frame, hoping to catch a glimpse of the two women. I could only make out vague figures—one of them wore a red dress, the other a blue one.

"You mean the girl from the photos?" the one in the blue dress asked.

"Yeah, the one wearing the tatty leather jacket," the woman in the red dress said, her voice dripping with disdain, as if she'd rather walk naked through London than wear my jacket. "I don't get why Henry's hanging out with her. She's not even particularly pretty. And have you seen her hair? It looks like she cut it herself with kids' scissors."

The woman in the blue dress shrugged and rifled through her makeup bag. "Perhaps she's amazing in bed and lets him do all kinds of really kinky stuff to her. I can totally imagine Henry being into that kind of thing."

"At least in bed, she wouldn't be wearing that cheap dress. It looks like she fished it out of some old charity shop donation bin. Isn't she embarrassed? She's humiliating Henry as much as herself."

My stomach clenched. I had felt pretty in my dress—until now. Now I felt foolish, like a kid playing dress-up. I had genuinely thought I looked elegant, but I'd clearly been wrong. Were the other guests thinking the same? Did they think my dress was fit for the bin? Were they secretly wrinkling their noses behind their masks, just like Mrs. Darlington? The thought made me feel sick.

"Totally. It's as cheap as it gets. But honestly? I bet it's all for show, to distract from Richard. I can't imagine Henry seriously being interested in someone like her. He's way out of her league."

My hands started shaking, and my heart fluttered as though it wanted to escape—to take off and fly away. I wished I didn't care about what the two women were saying about me and that I could brush it off like all the insults people had thrown at me when I was homeless. But I did care. The women's words confirmed what I had felt time and time again since arriving at the hotel: I didn't belong here, and I would never be good enough for someone like Henry. Everyone knew it. These women. Henry's parents. And probably every single guest at this ball. Sooner or later, Henry would also see how worthless I was and that I had nothing to offer him.

"Perhaps you should give him another shot, Em," the woman in the red dress suggested.

Em scoffed and put her makeup back in her purse. "Definitely not. I might have considered it before tonight, but it would just be humiliating now that everyone has seen how low the bar is. I'm not that desperate."

Her friend sniggered. "You could be the woman who makes a respectable man of him again. A real phoenix-from-the-ashes story."

"No, thanks. That ship has sailed. Perhaps I'll try my luck with . . ." The rest of her sentence was lost as the bathroom door swung shut behind them, cutting off their voices.

The room fell silent.

The only sounds were the faint hum of the ventilation and my shaky breathing. My eyes stung. I tried desperately to keep it together. I didn't want to cry. Not over this. But stopping the tears was incredibly hard. I had truly believed I could fit in for one evening, that I could pretend to be part of this glamorous world. Yet while I had felt like a princess in Henry's arms, to everyone else, I was just a dirty imposter. How could I have been so naive?

36

Have fun tonight. Let me know how it goes with Kate.

Message from Logan to Henry

Henry

"So, what is it like being the CEO of The Darlington?" Mr. Doyle asked. My dad would have called him a family friend, but to me, he was a vulture, circling events like this in search of the next piece of rotting meat to choke down.

"It's good."

"Really? A little birdie told me the hotel is struggling with declining numbers," Mr. Doyle said, which confirmed what I already knew. He hadn't approached me to make innocent small talk—he wanted something from me, and I was fairly certain I knew what. Mr. Doyle made his fortune buying up small and medium-sized hotels, absorbing them into his soulless empire. He preyed on desperation, purchasing businesses for a pittance. And apparently, he was deluded enough to think The Darlington would be his next victim. But he was biting off more than he could chew.

I warned myself to stay polite, though it became more difficult the longer I had to endure Mr. Doyle's sleazy smile, a smear of caviar clinging to the corner of his mouth. When would Kate finally return?

"The figures go up and down, but fluctuations are totally normal."

Mr. Doyle grinned and let his hand rove over his companion's back. She wasn't his wife, and judging by how fast she was knocking back her champagne, she would rather be anywhere but here. "Some wouldn't call a fifty percent occupancy *down* so much as *a deep abyss*."

What the hell? Where had he got that statistic from? That kind of information was for internal reports only, not for the public to know. I kept my face expressionless, refusing to give Mr. Doyle the satisfaction of a reaction. It was clear that by "some people," he meant himself, and that he was trying to unsettle me, all the better to pressure me into a sale somewhere down the line. But over my dead body would I let him have The Darlington.

"I'd call those people cowards with zero business sense. It might be a challenge, but it's hardly insurmountable—unless, of course, you're completely incompetent."

Mr. Doyle's grin faltered. "That's a pretty bold statement."

"No, bold would be suggesting those people have tiny dicks and impotence problems, but no one here is saying that," I shot back. His date choked on her champagne, but it was Mr. Doyle's face that turned bright red. "Please excuse me, I'm wanted elsewhere. Enjoy the rest of your evening. And do give my regards to your wife when you see her."

Mr. Doyle didn't reply, but his puce face spoke volumes. Glad I was finally rid of him, I scanned the ballroom for Kate. She had bravely stuck by my side all evening, probably bored to death by the conversations. Still, she hadn't complained once—she'd simply been there for me. But now, I realised I hadn't seen her in a while.

I set off to find her. I didn't want her to be alone—or worse, cornered by my parents. I silently cursed them both for having made her feel unwelcome when she was anything but. Not just in the hotel and at the ball, but in my life, regardless of what my parents or their friends thought.

I went to the bar first. On my way there, I was cornered by Shawn Wilders, an old friend of my mum's, but told him I would find him later. Kate was neither at the bar nor on the dance floor. I checked the restroom, but she wasn't there either. Finally, I went back to our table, though I was certain she wouldn't have sat with my parents of her own accord.

Unsurprisingly, her seat was empty. It was as if she had vanished into thin air.

I wondered if she'd had enough of the ball—but I was sure she wouldn't leave without telling me. Still, I wrote her a message, just in case she had gone back to her room. I put my phone away and was just about to do another round of the ballroom when I spotted Kate through the glass door that led to the balcony. The white dress with its deep-cut back was unmistakable.

She stood alone, gazing longingly out at the water. Fairy lights twinkled along the railings, and lanterns above her cast a soft glow, chasing away the darkness. Against the dimly lit backdrop of London, she looked like a figure from a painting.

I felt a tug in my chest. It almost hurt how beautiful she was, in every possible way, and I stood no chance against the overwhelming wave of affection that crashed over me.

37

> Henry took his employee to the ball as his plus-one! What was he thinking? Everyone's talking about her, but he seems completely oblivious.

Message from Charlotte Ashford to a friend

Kate

I was no longer alone. I had my back turned to the door, but I didn't have to see Henry to know he had joined me. His presence was like the sun—even with my eyes shut, I felt it on my skin.

With a soft click, the glass door closed behind him. The lively voices, the laughter, the music—all of it faded into the background. Only the sounds of the city remained. I kept my eyes fixed on the Thames. The lights of the surrounding buildings were reflected in the dark water, which lay still and peaceful below.

"I was looking for you," Henry said. Despite the balcony heaters, he took off his tailcoat and draped it over my shoulders. The fabric was warm and heavy, and smelled of him. The unfamiliar sense of security, overwhelming in its intensity, returned. "How long have you been standing out here?"

I wasn't sure. I only knew I couldn't bring myself to go back to the ball, unable to bear the thought of subjecting myself to the judgemental stares of the other guests. I hadn't wanted to leave Henry in the lurch either, so I had fled to the balcony, trying to muster the courage to go back in. But there was no way I could pretend I hadn't heard the spiteful things that had been said about me.

I pulled Henry's tailcoat tighter around me. "A while."

He leaned his hands on the railing, his right one only millimetres from my left. He playfully extended his little finger and touched it against mine. I smiled, reminding myself why I was still here. It would have made sense to leave the ball and accept that Henry and I were just too different, but I was incapable of making reasonable decisions about Henry. When it came to him, I couldn't think—I only felt, my heart overriding all reason.

"Thank you," Henry said unexpectedly.

I looked up from the river to him. He was gazing out at the Thames, his mask looking even more diabolical in the dim light on the balcony. He looked like he'd just stepped right out of hell. "What for?"

"For coming with me tonight. The conversations at these events can be pretty dull. I hope you aren't too bored."

"Not at all." But Henry's sceptical expression told me he clearly didn't believe a word. "OK, I was a little bored. But there's no one I'd rather be bored with than you, Snowflake."

He grumbled. "So we're back to *Snowflake*. What happened to *Mr. Darlington*?"

"I decided I didn't like it." His last name reminded me too much of who he was and what I wasn't. When I called him Snowflake, he wasn't Henry Darlington, billionaire heir—he was simply Henry. The man who ate pizza sitting on the floor, wore holey socks, thought dirty thoughts about me, and secretly bought my favourite book to read it himself. The man who, after months of uncertainty, made me feel like I'd finally found a place where I was safe.

"Kate?" His tone was sharp, but not demanding. When I looked up to meet his eyes, I realised he could see right through the carefree front I was putting on. "What's going on?"

"Nothing," I lied. "Why?"

Shit. Rule number one: Never ask why.

"Why were you out here alone?"

My mouth felt dry. Part of me wanted to tell him the truth, but I also didn't want to repeat what the women had said about me—which was presumably what everyone was thinking. "I just needed some fresh air."

"Why didn't you find me? I would have come out with you."

"I . . ."

I didn't want to interrupt your conversation.

I needed a moment alone.

I just wanted some fresh air, and I lost track of time.

But by the time I'd invented these lies, Henry had noticed my hesitation. His expression darkened. "Did my parents say something to you?"

"No, they didn't say anything."

"Someone else?"

God, I wished I had a glass of champagne to hold. I lowered my eyes, uncomfortable. Why did I feel so weak right now, when I had managed alone on the streets for months?

"Maybe."

"Who?" Henry demanded.

I couldn't keep up the lie. "Two women. I don't know who they were. I overheard them in the restroom. They had no idea I was there and could hear them."

Henry's jaw tensed. "What did they say?"

I really didn't want to repeat it, knowing it would make him angry, but it was too late to backpedal. "They said my dress looked cheap and that—that I'm ugly," I confessed hesitantly. "They think that you're only here with me to divert attention from your dad. They think I'm beneath you. And that I've lowered the bar for whoever you're with next."

"That's a load of bullshit."

"It's fine." I didn't want to ruin his evening.

"No, it's not!" he hissed, and I saw his hands clench into fists on the balcony railing, the skin of his knuckles turning white. "You really don't know who they were?"

I shook my head.

"That's a shame. I'd have thrown them out if you did. They don't know what they're talking about. You're not beneath me—they're beneath you. And you're not here as a distraction, but because there's no one else I'd rather be with."

I swallowed hard. "Really?"

"Really." He turned to face me, standing so close that our bodies touched. He had unclenched his fists, and with a tenderness that had been unimaginable just moments ago, he stroked my cheek. A hot shiver ran up my spine as Henry gently reached for my angel mask and carefully pulled it off my face, leaving me with nothing to hide my feelings behind. "Promise me something."

"Anything."

He placed my mask on the balcony railing and then touched my face again, gently tracing its contours with his thumb until he reached my chin. He gripped it with a tender firmness that made it impossible for me to look away. "Promise me you won't believe those women."

I wanted to reply, but I couldn't—Henry left me speechless. Maybe it was his words. Maybe it was the warmth of his fingers on my skin. Or maybe it was just the tenderness in his eyes, a look that was at odds with his devilish mask.

"Promise me," Henry insisted, pressing his thumb against my lower lip as if he could coax the words from me. "You can't believe it. They're wrong. You've never looked more beautiful than you do tonight. You're gorgeous. Your dress is stunning. And I have no idea how it's possible, but my tailcoat looks a thousand times better on you than it does on me. You could wear a bin bag, and you'd still be beautiful. There's nothing in this world that could ruin your beauty, my angel."

My heart faltered at the nickname, and the butterflies in my stomach intensified when Henry cupped my face in his hands. Without taking his eyes off mine, he leaned towards me. I felt his warm breath on my lips. My eyelids fluttered in response, mirroring the pounding of my heart, and then his mouth touched mine. I let out a sigh of pleasure. The kiss was everything I'd dreamed it would be—and more. It was sweet yet insistent, tender yet firm. It was as though Henry was trying to tell me with his body as well as his words that the gossip meant nothing to him. It didn't matter.

Only we mattered.

Henry and I.

A *we* I certainly hadn't seen coming when I had stolen his phone from his coat—one of the best decisions of my life.

I stood on my tiptoes, pressing myself against him, letting him know that while I appreciated his tenderness, this wasn't the moment for it. I had been craving his kiss for much longer than I wanted to admit, and I had no patience for his restraint. Emboldened by his words, I parted my lips for him. He didn't hold back, kissing me deeply, as if he had been just as impatient as I was. His tongue flicked between my lips, making me feel briefly but intoxicatingly dizzy, a sensation I felt all the way to my fingertips.

The taste of Henry was exhilarating: sparkling champagne and the thrill of something new. I wrapped an arm around his neck to press myself even closer, while his hands slipped beneath his tailcoat to touch my bare back, exposed by the deep cut of my dress. I cursed his gloves. I could almost feel his skin against mine, but it wasn't enough—I wanted more. Just ten minutes ago, I had regretted coming to the ball, but in this moment, my only regret was that we hadn't done this sooner. Kissing Henry felt overwhelming and was unlike anything I had ever experienced. I hadn't known it was possible to be kissed so all-consumingly.

His hands trailed down my back until they reached my bum. The long tailcoat he'd draped over me hid what was happening beneath. He gripped me, pulling me against his hips. I gasped, and a low growl rumbled in Henry's chest as my pelvis pushed against the unmistakable evidence of his arousal. He was hard. Rock-hard. And that was just from our kiss. Wow.

The molten heat spreading through me pooled between my thighs. I surrendered completely to Henry's kiss, only dimly aware of the balcony door opening. The sounds of the ball grew louder—but I didn't care. Nothing but the sensation of Henry's lips on mine mattered.

At least, not until Mr. Darlington's sharp voice sliced through the night. "Henry, get your arse back inside. You have guests!"

Henry muttered a quiet curse against my lips and kissed me again before pulling away. I loved that he didn't jerk back like a teenager caught doing something forbidden by his parents. And why should he? He wasn't a teenager, he was a man—the evidence of which I could still feel pressing against my hip. Henry met my eyes for a moment, assuring me silently that the kiss would be continued, before turning to face his dad. Richard stood impatiently in the doorway. I could only imagine how surly his expression was beneath his mask.

"I'm coming. Give me a minute."

His dad hesitated, as if considering insisting that Henry come immediately, but then he gave a curt nod and stepped back inside, leaving the glass door open as a pointed reminder. The moment when it had been just Henry, me, and the fire between us was over.

Henry turned back to me. His cheeks were flushed, his lips moist, and his eyes dusky with the desire that had overcome him. He didn't speak, kissing me again instead. This time, the kiss was slower, less urgent—he couldn't possibly rejoin the guests in the ballroom with an erection, after all. The thought of how outraged the people in their fancy designer gowns and tailored three-piece suits would be if Henry strolled through the ballroom like that made me giggle. That would be a true distraction from his dad's misdemeanours.

"What's so funny?" Henry asked, smiling as though simply seeing me happy was enough to make him happy too.

I grinned. "Nothing. Forget it."

"OK. But do you know what I won't forget?" His face was so close to mine that I could feel his breath and the hum of his words on my face.

"What?" I asked curiously.

"That you, my angel, didn't object to your new nickname."

"That wasn't really possible with your tongue in my mouth."

He shrugged. "Well, it's too late now to veto it."

I placed my hands on his chest and stroked the silky material of his vest. "That's OK. If you kiss me like you just did, you can call me whatever you like."

Henry inhaled sharply before breathing out with control, as if summoning every last shred of willpower to fight the urge to kiss me again. "I'll bear that in mind. But duty calls, unfortunately," he said, pulling his coat off my shoulders to go back inside. "How about you head up to your room? I'll stay for another hour, shake a few more hands, and then I'll join you and we can fulfil your pizza-and-film fantasy?"

I smiled. "That sounds perfect."

"See you in your room in an hour."

I nodded eagerly, grateful for the escape he was offering me. I wished I could be a better date, but under the circumstances, our plan seemed for the best. He pulled me close and kissed me one last time before pressing his lips to my temple. "I won't be able to think about anything else for the next hour except kissing you again, angel," he murmured against my skin before releasing me.

I left the ball with a wide grin.

Message from Kate to Grace

Henry

My dad glared at me reproachfully for the rest of the night, as if he'd caught me in bed with five sex workers, and not just kissing Kate on the balcony. He probably would have preferred the sex workers, as at least they would have vanished from my life without a trace—and with the discretion my money would have bought—after a few hours of fun. Kate, on the other hand, would stay for as long as she wanted, and my dad knew it. Judging by my mum's disapproving glare, which followed me around the ballroom, he had already told her.

I ignored them. They were the last people on earth who had any right to pass judgement on my love life. It still infuriated me how they had treated Kate. She may have no money and be different from Olivia and the other women I had dated before, but we weren't living in the eighteenth century. There were no rigid social hierarchies left requiring us to uphold appearances. And even if there were, it wasn't Kate who was sullying our family's reputation—it was my dad. Not that he could see it, blinded as he was by his own ego.

I would have loved to leave the ball with Kate, but it wouldn't have made a good impression. I had to be seen mingling, though my thoughts never strayed far from Kate. How could I have believed, until so recently, that I had the willpower to be just her friend, when every part of my body ached to be close to her? It was ridiculous.

To my frustration, what was meant to be an hour of handshaking became two, then three, and I was still nowhere near Kate. I was trapped in conversation after conversation, and it felt almost deliberate—as if my dad had conspired with his golf buddies to keep me away from her. Every time I attempted to slip away, someone reeled me back in.

I kept Kate updated, letting her know it was taking longer than planned. Just after midnight, she messaged to say she was going to bed, and that I could get her room key from reception and let myself into her room. It made me happy that she trusted me so much, but I hated that I had let her down. And as much as I loved The Darlington and wanted to save it, I couldn't help but wonder if it was worth the sacrifices I was making for it.

I finally left the ballroom shortly after 2 a.m., even though the party was still in full swing. The band had stopped playing two hours ago, and the DJ—alternating between playing rock classics and hip-hop—had gradually driven away my dad's friends. There was no one left to stop me from leaving. I picked up the spare key for Kate's room from reception before making a detour to my penthouse apartment, where I changed into my T-shirt and jogging bottoms. A dull pain throbbed at my temples. Massaging my head, I weighed up whether the pain was enough to warrant another pill, but decided against it. I had taken one just before the ball to make sure I got through the evening, and besides, it would be impossible to sleep if I took one now, and I wanted nothing more than to fall asleep next to Kate. She had kept me sane in the last few weeks, and after the commotion of the last few hours, I craved the calm she brought me.

In my socks, I padded to Kate's room on the first floor, unlocked her door, and slipped in. The only light came from the reading lamp, which cast a dim glow. Kate was already in a deep sleep, her eyes closed and her breathing shallow. There was a book open on the mattress beside her, as if she had fallen asleep while reading. I placed it on the bedside table and turned off the light. The room was instantly plunged into near-total darkness. I could see only faint outlines cast by the moonlight filtering through the curtains. Kate let out a soft sigh and shifted slightly, but her eyes remained closed. She looked peaceful, somehow even more beautiful than she had been in her stunning dress at the ball. I knew I shouldn't reach out and brush my fingers lightly across her cheek, but I did it anyway—I couldn't help myself.

"Henry?"

"Yes, it's me."

She let out a contented sigh and smiled gently, revealing her dimples. "Finally." Without opening her eyes, she reached out a hand for me—an unspoken invitation I couldn't turn down.

I slipped under the duvet to join Kate, and she nestled up against me. I wrapped an arm around her. She was warm, and the fresh, floral smell of lavender enveloped me. I buried my face in her hair and inhaled deeply. My body relaxed next to hers, the tension of the last few hours without her finally melting away.

"Goodnight, Snowflake," Kate mumbled drowsily against my T-shirt.

I smiled. "Goodnight, my angel."

39

BREAKING NEWS: Henry Darlington Kisses Hotel Employee on Balcony!

Online news story by the *INsider*

Kate

Henry.

He was my first thought when I woke. Had he really joined me in my room last night, or had I just dreamed it? He had been held up at the ball. I waited for him for hours, resisting sleep, but eventually, my exhaustion had got the better of me. The evening had been so tiring, emotionally as well as physically. There had been so many people. So many new faces. So many conversations I hadn't been able to follow.

Sitting alone in my room waiting for Henry hadn't helped. I hadn't been able to shake the words of the two women in the restroom—because they were true. Regardless of how you looked at it, I might belong to Henry, but not in his world—and I never would. He had enough money for both of us and could shower me with luxury—but I would never truly fit. The wealth, the extravagance, and the excess would never feel natural to me. Even if I had more money, I would still buy secondhand clothes, because that's what I had always done. I would always choose a practical rucksack over an expensive designer handbag. If I ever went on holiday, I would choose hiking and camping over sitting around some fancy ski resort. And I would much rather eat burgers at McDonald's or pizza straight from the box than swanky caviar hors d'oeuvres. These little things would always set my world apart from Henry's.

I yawned and stretched—and felt something warm and firm beside me.

Another body.

So it hadn't been a dream.

I opened my eyes. The first light of day streamed in through the window, illuminating Henry asleep beside me. He lay on his front, his face half buried in the pillow, his black hair tousled. I reached out a hand to brush a few strands from his face. He seemed tense even in sleep, as if his dreams were plagued with worries and responsibilities too.

I leaned forward and pressed my mouth gently against his, and his eyes instantly opened. He fixed a drowsy gaze on me, looking up from beneath half-lowered eyelids. The tension vanished from his face immediately, and his lips curled into a sexy smile. The fluttering I'd felt in my chest last night returned.

"Good morning," he mumbled, his voice rough and raspy with sleep.

I smiled back. "Good morning to you too."

"Did you sleep well?"

"Yes. You?"

He nodded. "Your bed must be magic. I never sleep this well in my own."

"Then you should sleep here more often."

"Perhaps I will," Henry hummed. He reached for my body under the blanket, pulled me close and kissed me as if it were the most natural thing in the world. Sighing, I wrapped my arms around his neck. His lips sent my pulse skyrocketing. His hands slid lower, slipping under The Darlington T-shirt I'd taken from the laundry room.

Last night on the balcony, I had wished he hadn't been wearing gloves so I could feel his skin on mine—and now my wish had come true. I shivered as his fingertips danced over my spine. A liquid heat coursed through my body, and I arched towards Henry. I couldn't get enough of him. Burying my hands in his hair, I pulled his face closer to mine. He moaned with pleasure as we kissed, and bit gently on my lower lip. No man had ever kissed me like Henry, with so much longing, and so all-consumingly—and I had never kissed back with such urgency. The kiss was intoxicating, robbing me of all sense of time. Nothing else mattered. I forgot last night's worries, and all my insecurities and reservations vanished.

Henry eventually pulled away from me, his chest rising and falling rapidly. I felt just as breathless. We looked at each other silently for a moment, too dazed to speak. My lips tingled from our kiss.

Henry lifted one hand from my back and gently brushed the hair from my forehead. I loved when he did that. "I'm sorry I couldn't make it earlier last night."

"It's fine. It's not like you stood me up on purpose."

"I'd never do that. I was thinking about you the entire time." He began planting tiny kisses along my neck. His warm breath tickled my skin, and the hairs on my forearms stood on end, as if they too wanted to be close to him.

"And I was thinking about you," I confessed, although it was difficult to focus on speaking. I tilted my head, offering up more of my neck to his lips. The buzzing of his phone vibrating filled the room, but we didn't react.

Henry kissed my throat, running his tongue over my skin, as if savouring my taste, before gently sucking at my neck. My breath hitched, and I couldn't help but wonder how it would feel if he did the same to other parts of my body. The thought sent a rush of nervous excitement through my veins, like the molten heat of lava.

"How can you possibly taste this good?" Henry mumbled against my skin.

"Water and soap," I replied, my voice throaty with desire.

He laughed, and I loved how the sound made my entire body thrum. A moment later, though, his phone began to vibrate again on the bedside table. His kisses slowed. I could sense that he was trying to ignore the interruption, but this time, he was unsuccessful.

"I'm sorry. I have to get that." He reached for his phone, and I saw Olivia's name on the display. He accepted the call.

Olivia's face appeared on the screen. She seemed briefly surprised to see me, then she grinned. "Hey, you two," she purred smugly.

Henry rolled over onto his back and pulled me with him so that my head rested on his chest. With one hand, he stroked the skin under my shirt. "Hey. Have you sobered up yet?"

Olivia waved a hand dismissively, still lying in bed with her hair twisted up in a messy knot. Even barely awake and without makeup, she was effortlessly stunning—and showed no signs of a hangover. "So-so. I woke up five minutes ago to go to the bathroom, and I was planning to go back to sleep when I saw that Shannon had sent me an interesting link."

Henry groaned. "What is it this time?"

Olivia's gaze flicked to me. "There are new photos of the two of you."

Henry stopped stroking me. "What? Where?"

"I've sent you the link."

Henry swiftly opened his chat with Olivia and tapped the link. It led to one of the *INsider*'s social media pages, where several photos of me and Henry on the balcony had been posted. Although the images were slightly grainy, it was unmistakably us. The photos had captured not just our kiss but also showed the moments leading up to and following it, including Henry removing my mask to reveal my face. Below the photos was a single sensational headline, as if the reporter had been too impatient to write a full article to accompany the images.

"Fuck," Henry mumbled, and returned to the call with Olivia. Her expression was concerned. "Thanks for the warning," Henry said. "I'll call you back later."

She nodded. "OK. But don't let this ruin your day. Fuck the paparazzi. You look happy, and I love that for you."

I smiled. "Thank you. See you later."

"Bye," Henry said.

He ended the call and flicked back to the photos. The post already had thousands of likes and hundreds of comments. I was curious about what people had written, but Henry didn't open the comments. He zoomed in on the photos, studying each one carefully. We looked very close. And in love.

"What do you think?"

I looked up. "About the photos?"

"Yes."

I wasn't particularly bothered by them. I found it slightly unsettling to know someone had been watching us kiss, but if people wanted to waste their time like that, it wasn't my problem. I was living my best life. "I think we look pretty good in them," I said with a shrug.

Henry laughed, and I could feel the vibration of his chest in my head. "We really do."

"Does it bother you that someone caught us on camera?" I asked, curious.

"It bothers me that those clowns don't give a shit about our privacy." Henry tossed his phone onto the bedside table with the carelessness of someone who could easily afford a replacement. "It was a private event, no press allowed, and they've got nothing better to do than hide in the bushes with a two-hundred-millimetre lens."

"Do you think you'll get in trouble?" I asked, tilting my head to look at him.

"Who with?"

"Your parents." I turned in his arms to see him better. He looked back at me, and his fingers began to move across my back again, tracing gentle circles that brought the heat flooding back. "I'm sure they won't be pleased."

"So what? I'm not pleased with them either."

"I just don't want you to be in trouble because of me."

Henry snorted. "I'm not afraid of my parents. And there's no way I'm letting a man accused of rape meddle in my love life—whether he's my dad or not."

"And this won't damage your reputation?" I couldn't forgive myself if Henry's image suffered because of me. A few wealthy snobs gossiping about me was one thing, but if the whole nation jumped on the bandwagon, that was something else entirely. "What if people think that you pressured me or forced me into something? Most of your dad's victims were hotel employees, weren't they?"

"True, but everyone with any sense will see that our kiss was consensual. And if anyone does kick up a fuss, you can always issue a statement as a last resort, though I'd rather avoid that."

I nodded. "All right. I just don't want us to damage the hotel's reputation."

Henry smiled, his expression full of unmistakable affection. "We won't," he assured me, continuing to stroke my back. "There are always headlines about Ethan or speculations about my love life. They don't mean anything, and they don't have any impact on The Darlington. In a couple of days, everyone will have forgotten about the photos. So please, don't worry about it."

I nodded hesitantly. "OK."

Perhaps the photos really weren't such a big deal. Who Henry spent his time with should have no bearing on the hotel or its guests. People were just bored and hungry for gossip. Besides, the press still didn't have a clue who I was. As long as nothing about my past came to light, we had nothing to worry about.

THE BLACKROOM

As we all know, a picture is worth a thousand words. Something Richard Darlington knows all too well. Three years ago, photos of Darlington allegedly harassing a woman on the dance floor of an exclusive club made the rounds on the internet. The photos mysteriously disappeared a few hours later and haven't been seen since. It looks like someone was keen to sweep the whole thing under the rug—but we won't be fooled. *The Blackroom* brings back the lost photos . . .

No way was that kiss real! Henry just staged it to get back at Olivia! #HenryDarlington #OliviaAsterdam #Asterdarling

Online comment by MeltXGlow

Henry

The photos of Kate and I spread fast. It wasn't the first time the press had reported on my love life, but it was the first time that the topic was so controversial. People had a lot to say about the fact that Kate worked for The Darlington and, by extension, for me. Some applauded Kate and saw our relationship as a modern fairy tale, while others were convinced she was using me for my money. Yet others argued I was abusing my power, which was ridiculous. Kate hadn't just stolen my phone—she had taken my heart. So it didn't matter how much more power, success, and money I had, because Kate already possessed the most valuable part of me.

I was scrolling through online articles when there was a knock at my door. Before I could respond, the door opened. It was no great surprise when my mum stepped into my office—I had expected her to show up much earlier.

I closed my laptop. "Hey, Mum," I said, and gestured at the sofa. "Sit down."

She ignored my invitation and sat on a chair at my desk, which told me all I needed to know. She smoothed her red dress. It was embroidered with silver thread, which gave it a Christmassy feel, but there was nothing festive about her expression.

"We have to talk."

"I don't have time." It wasn't a lie, but more importantly, I didn't *want* to talk to her. I already knew what she had come to say—she didn't like Kate. She had already warned me to stay away from her after the first photos had been posted. But her words had fallen on deaf ears then, and they would do so again today.

My mum fixed me with a glare. "Make time."

"I have nothing to say."

"Then listen to me," she demanded.

I stopped protesting. The quicker she got to the point, the sooner I could be rid of her and finish my work, so I could get back to Kate. I looked at my mum expectantly, drumming my fingers against the desk with impatience.

"You're meeting Daphne Walsh on Tuesday at 6 p.m."

"Mr. Walsh's daughter?" I asked with surprise.

"Yes."

"What for?"

My mum tutted, as if I was being deliberately obtuse. "To have dinner with her, of course. I've arranged a date for you. Miraculously, she's still interested in you."

Was she kidding? "No way."

My mum ignored me and kept talking. "Daphne looks absolutely striking with her new nose. Like a young Kate Moss, but without the drug problem and just as slim. And she has a spotless reputation. You'll like her."

"I don't want to go on a date with Daphne. Kate and I . . ."

"Forget Kate," my mum interrupted, eyeing me with pursed lips, as if she were taking stock of me. Judging by the faint wrinkle of her nose, she didn't like what she saw, though I couldn't tell if it was the dark circles under my eyes or the colour of my suit that bothered her. Not that I cared. "Daphne is a much better match for you."

"How would you know that? You don't even know Kate."

"No, but I know you, and what you have with her isn't going to last. She's exciting, an adventure. I get that—but every adventure comes to an end. Everything new eventually becomes old and loses its charm. And once that charm fades, you'll see that there's nothing connecting you."

"I'll be the judge of that."

My mum sighed theatrically, as if my lack of reason was giving her a headache. "Henry, please try to be sensible. You two don't stand a chance. Anyone can see that Kate doesn't belong here. It's pretty selfish of you to pull her into a world that doesn't have space for her."

"I'll make space for her."

"You will, maybe, but others won't," my mum said, her chin raised—proof that she was one of those *others*. "You have no idea how many people talked to me at the ball about the two of you. Not to mention the countless phone calls I've already received today about the photos. Kate is a bad influence on you. She would be on anyone."

"And a rapist is a good influence?"

My mum stared at me, affronted. I had never dared use the R-word in her presence, not wanting to hurt her, especially since I knew how much my dad's infidelities had wounded her. But I'd had enough of tiptoeing around the issue while everyone felt entitled to openly judge Kate.

"If you're talking about your father: That hasn't been proven."

I scoffed. "I was there when you first heard about the allegations. You weren't surprised or shocked. You knew immediately that it was true. Everyone knows it's true, and yet somehow, that's OK—something you and your *friends* can accept. But Kate not being born into money? That's unacceptable?"

"The situation with your dad is completely different."

"You're right. Dad committed a horrendous crime. Kate, on the other hand, has done nothing wrong. She's only guilty of having had less luck in her life, whereas your husband made a conscious decision to behave like scum."

My mother pressed her lips together furiously. She knew I was right. My dad might have been money-rich, but she couldn't deny that he was poor in other things—decency, honesty, and moral standards.

"Why do you put up with it?" My mum wasn't perfect, and she had her prejudices, but unlike my dad, she wasn't a bad person. "You're a smart, beautiful woman, Mum. Any man would be lucky to have you, but you stay with the one who deserves you the least."

For a brief moment, I dared to hope I was getting through to her. Her expression softened, and in it, I could see the pain she had to endure because of my dad. But in a flash, her face hardened again. She had perfected the act. "My relationship with your father isn't up for discussion," she said sharply. "And you can't compare him to Kate. He's an integral part of this society. Not just that, but he and his family have helped build it up. Kate, on the other hand, is an outsider. Different rules apply to her, whether you like it or not."

"I'm not giving Kate up."

"You're making a mistake."

"Maybe I am, but it's *my* mistake, so stay out of it."

My mum shook her head. "I will not. Your mistake reflects on me, your father, and the hotel. You can't truly believe that people will just accept you dating someone like Kate. It doesn't work like that."

Silence descended on the room.

I was certain that if we were quiet enough and listened closely, we'd both be able to hear the outraged pounding of my heart. I hated the double standards. I was livid—not at my mum, but at what she represented in this moment.

"What do you expect me to do?" I heard myself ask.

"I expect you to take responsibility."

My patience snapped. "*Fuck!* All I've been doing for months is taking responsibility!" I hissed, unable to keep my cool any longer. "Responsibility for this family. For the hotel. For all the shit Dad got us into that no one here is willing to talk about." My hands shook with rage. "While Dad is off playing golf with his mates, drinking whisky, and probably screwing Vivian behind your back, I've been busting a gut trying to ensure that the hotel survives next year. I'm racking up endless overtime to organise a gala that might be a flop—one wealthy donor after another is pulling out because they're afraid of being seen on the red carpet. Not because of Kate, but because of Dad. The rest of the world isn't blind, and people see him for what he is: a fucking rapist who belongs in prison. I haven't slept more than four hours a night in weeks. I have no free time, and I don't have any fun. I haven't seen my friends in forever, because my entire crappy life revolves around saving this hotel. My home. Something I get neither thanks nor recognition for from you or Dad. Instead, the only thing you do is criticise the one person who makes me happy."

My mum stared at me with wide eyes. I had never given her a piece of my mind like this before. The blood pounded in my ears, and a relentless headache pulsed behind my temples. I had no patience left for her imagined *social rules* or her elitist pretensions. All I wanted was to hold Kate in my arms and get my work done so that the hotel stood a chance of survival. And once we got over the worst of it, I would find a way to get rid of my dad, making sure he never had a say in The Darlington again.

I took a deep breath. "You should go."

My mum was smart enough to know that arguing was pointless. She got up, smoothed down her skirt, and turned away without a word.

Her fingers were already on the door handle when she turned back to me. Her expression was hard to read—a mix of regret, sadness and wounded pride. "You say you want to save the hotel, but you won't be able to do that with Kate by your side. You don't have to like the rules of our society, but you still have to stick to them. All of us do. Maybe Kate makes you happy right now, but what will be left of that happiness if you lose your home because of her?"

41

Dear Miss Hamilton, we regret to inform you that we cannot offer you a position at our branch at this point in time. Your application has been carefully reviewed, but unfortunately, you do not meet the required qualifications for the advertised position.

Rejection of one of Kate's job applications

Kate

The next two weeks flew by without me noticing. One day the Halloween decorations were still hanging, and the next, everything was strung with sparkling lights as the city prepared for Christmas, despite it only being the middle of November. People couldn't wait for the Christmas holidays. The Darlington was no exception: A five-metre-tall Christmas tree stood in the lobby, and stockings hung above the fireplace. Fairy lights adorned the facade, making it sparkle once dusk fell.

I used to love this time of year. My mum and I had never had much, but we'd always made sure we had a nice time during the holidays, making the most of London's winter offerings. This Christmas reminded me how terrible the last year had been, but it also made me see how far I had come in the last few weeks. There were many things to be grateful for—particularly that I now had a certain someone in my life.

I knocked at Henry's office door. He had sent me a message asking if I wanted to have lunch with him.

"Come in!" Henry called.

I pushed open the door and entered, wondering if it was strange that I hadn't been here before. The floor was covered in thick, red carpet, and dark shelves crammed with binders and old books lined the walls. A leather sofa stood in one corner, while a solid wooden desk commanded attention at the centre of the room. Henry sat behind it, his jacket removed and the sleeves of his shirt rolled up, as if he were preparing for physical labour.

"Hi," I said, closing the door behind me.

He smiled. "Hi yourself. Give me a minute."

I nodded and settled into one of the chairs in front of the desk while he finished typing up whatever he was working on. My gaze wandered around the room before landing on a magazine—with Henry on the cover. The photo showed him in a suit, leaning casually against the counter of The Darlington's rooftop bar. He held a crystal glass filled with amber liquid, his expression both seductive and slightly roguish. Behind him, rows of expensive bottles of spirits lined the wall. The headline read, "A New Luxurious Era."

I picked up the magazine. A Post-it note stuck to a page directed me straight to the feature article, a four-page interview with Henry. I skimmed it. The interviewer asked about his family and career, and focussed on his vision for advancing The Darlington as one of the youngest CEOs in the global luxury hotel industry. His responses were eloquent and passionate.

I looked up from the pages. "You didn't mention this."

Henry closed his laptop. "I forgot."

"You forgot you're on the cover of a magazine?"

"The photoshoot was three months ago." He stood and took the navy suit jacket from his chair. "Vivian talked me into it. If I could remember the interview, I would have retroactively changed some of my answers."

"Which ones?"

"I said that the BBC wanted to make a documentary about the centenary of The Darlington, which was a little premature. The filming was called off a few weeks ago because of the allegations. I also made a grand announcement that there would be no redundancies."

I raised my eyebrows. "And will there be redundancies?"

He gave a brief nod, slipped on his jacket, and focussed intently on straightening his cuff links, avoiding my gaze. "Since the allegations against my dad went public, around forty people have resigned. I'd hoped that the resignations would make up for the dwindling reservations, which mean there's less to do; apparently people prefer to stay in hotels that aren't run by rapists, not to mention ones that have more privacy and no press loitering at the entrance."

"How many people do you have to let go?" I asked.

Henry looked up, and I could see in his face how disappointed he was in himself. He was doing all that he could and more, but the allegations against his dad trumped everything. "It's not clear yet. We're still crunching numbers and figuring out the prognosis. We're thinking about temporarily closing one of the floors to save costs. Perhaps it will give us a little time."

"You could cut my pay," I suggested. It was more than enough that I could stay at the hotel and eat The Darlington Diner's leftover food. Besides, I had sent out a handful of job applications in the last few days. I had already received several rejections, but I wasn't about to give up.

"I'll cut my own salary before I stop paying you."

"That makes it sound like you're favouring me."

"You bet I favour you," Henry said. He came closer and put a hand on my waist.

My heart involuntarily skipped a beat, and I wondered if I would ever get so used to Henry's proximity that my body stopped reacting. I doubted it. In the last two weeks, the effect Henry had on me had only intensified. My body responded to every kiss, every touch, every soft whisper in the night—usually the only time we had together, because Henry had his hands full with the gala. Every so often, we'd cross paths in the hotel corridors during the day—but they were stolen moments, fleeting glances before Henry was pulled into his next meeting. Right now, though, it was just us.

"Don't tell the others, but I like you the most."

"I promise I won't," I said and stood on my tiptoes to gently kiss Henry's lips. He wanted to deepen the kiss, but I wouldn't let him. Instead, I reached into the bag slung over my shoulder and pulled out a wrapped present. I'd initially thought about giving it to him at lunch, but the moment was too perfect. "I like you the most too, so I have something for you."

Henry raised his eyebrows. "A present? It's not my birthday."

"It's to say thank you. I got my first paycheck a while ago and wanted to give you something in return for everything you've done for me," I said, feeling myself blush. Now that Henry stood in front of me in his fancy office, wearing his tailored suit and an outrageously expensive designer watch, the present I'd bought for ten pounds seemed ridiculous. It was a lot of money to me, but to

Henry, it was nothing. A part of me wanted to tear the present out of his hands again and return it to my bag, but it was too late. "I know it's not very much in light of everything you've done for me, and you probably could have bought it yourself. And I can return it if you don't like it, but . . ."

"I love it," Henry interrupted before I could finish the sentence.

I swallowed. "You don't even know what it is yet."

"It's from you, and that's all that matters."

He took a purposeful step towards me, put a hand on the back of my neck, and pulled my face towards his. I was expecting a soft, sweet kiss, but Henry had other plans—the kiss was intense and sensual, and almost instantly, I felt a searing heat in my chest that travelled down to my pelvis. I shut my eyes and leaned against his chest, my gift between us as he ran his tongue over my lower lip and then flicked it into my mouth. Henry clearly did nothing half-heartedly. He put just as much heart and soul into every kiss and every touch as he did into his work for the hotel. It felt like our lips were destined to be pressed together, but I couldn't forget the present squashed between us. I no longer found it silly—Henry had dispelled that worry with his kiss.

"I should give you presents more often, if this is the thanks I get," I whispered between kisses, stroking his shirt. I could feel that his heart was racing just as unsteadily as mine. "Open it."

Henry's beautiful blue eyes shone, and his lips were red from our kiss. He seemed reluctant to let me go, but then he slipped his hand from the back of my neck to open the present. Naomi had helped me wrap it, as I didn't have much experience with that. Nervously, I watched Henry tear open the paper to reveal a DVD of *Interstellar*.

"For your DVD collection," I explained, as if it weren't obvious. "I thought it would be nice if you had a film that wasn't *London Has Fallen*, and this is one of my favourites. I wrote you something in the case, like Logan always does."

Wordlessly, Henry opened the case to read my message. I had spent the previous evening searching for the right words, and until just now, I hadn't been sure I'd found them, but the look in his eyes assured me they were perfect. When he looked up at me, the affection in his gaze almost swept me off my feet. But even if it had, it wouldn't matter. I wouldn't fall—Henry would catch me. Or maybe we would fly together. At least, that's how it felt.

"Thank you, angel. It's perfect," Henry said. Once again, he leaned in to kiss me. This time, his kiss was sweet and achingly gentle, and my heart swelled, expanding with something I had never dared dream I'd feel. "You have no idea how much I'd love to cancel our reservation, order a pizza, and watch the film with you," he murmured against my lips. "But I'm pretty sure Logan would kill me."

The name piqued my interest, and I disentangled myself from him. "Logan?"

"Yes. I've reserved a table at The Meridian for us."

I was surprised and suddenly a little nervous. Logan was the only member of the family I hadn't met yet—and he was also the one Henry was closest too. I was eager to meet him.

We arrived at The Meridian in Covent Garden twenty minutes later. Henry parked his Bentley in a side street, and we walked to the restaurant in Floral Court holding hands. A passageway led to a small courtyard surrounded by houses that blocked out the hustle and bustle of the city. There were potted plants everywhere and fairy lights strung from house to house. But the most surprising feature of the courtyard was a sculpture of an elephant made from delicate wooden struts.

Logan's restaurant was located right on the corner of the courtyard. It had floor-to-ceiling windows, and tables had been arranged with visible care among the lush plants. Outdoor heaters allowed guests to dine alfresco despite the cold November air.

Henry led me to an entrance flanked by two large-leafed plants. He pulled the door open and waved me ahead. For someone who had turned their back on the luxurious lifestyle of The Darlington, Logan's restaurant was relatively upscale, with dark chandeliers hanging from the high ceilings. The walls were partially mirrored, partially decorated with opulent paintings. Creating the illusion of privacy, plants like those outside were strategically placed between the tables, almost all of which were occupied. Unobtrusive music played softly in the background.

"Hello, Henry," the hostess greeted him with a broad smile. "I haven't seen you here in quite some time."

"Hi, Sara. Yeah, there's been a lot going on."

"I'll let Logan know you're here. He reserved your usual table for you."

"Thank you," Henry replied, and with his hand at the small of my back, he guided me to a table with two dark wood chairs and a brown leather bench at the window. He let me choose my seat, and I slid onto the bench. I shrugged off my jacket and shoved it behind me as he hung his coat on a coatrack. A waiter approached with a carafe of water infused with mint leaves and poured us each a glass.

"What do you think?" Henry asked when the waiter had left.

I looked around. "I imagined it differently, after everything you told me about Logan. A bit more . . . simple."

Henry took a sip of his water. "The only thing that's simple here is the food. Logan has never been a fan of tiny, pricey portions that look pretty but barely taste like anything. He and Maxton wanted to combine classic dishes with luxury. You won't find a cheeseburger or pizza with better ingredients anywhere in London."

I was about to answer when I spotted Logan. I would never have recognised him on the street wearing jeans and a T-shirt, but his chef's uniform gave him away. Aside from his height, he bore no resemblance to Henry or Ethan. Logan clearly took after Mrs. Darlington with his brown eyes and blond hair, which he wore tied back, accentuating the shaved sides. His forearms were covered in tattoos. They seemed to extend beneath the sleeves of his white chef's jacket, over which he wore a black apron embroidered with The Meridian's logo.

"Hey, Buttface," Logan greeted Henry.

"Rather Buttface than Dickface," Henry retorted with a laugh, and they performed a well-practised handshake that made me smile—I could imagine them inventing it as teenagers. "Logan, this is Kate." Henry gestured to me. "Kate, this is Logan—also known as the unattractive Darlington brother."

Logan swatted Henry, although it had clearly been a joke. Logan was beyond handsome. Before I'd met Henry, he would have been just my type. A little rugged and serious, perhaps even slightly intimidating. He was the kind of man who might make you cross the street at night if you didn't know him—and a man who would make you feel completely safe if you did.

Logan shook my hand. "It's nice to meet you, Kate."

"Likewise. I've heard a lot about you."

"I'd love to say the same, but Henry hasn't been here for weeks," Logan said, giving his brother a reproachful sideways glance as he lowered himself onto the empty chair. He leaned his arms on the table and rolled up his sleeves, revealing more of his tattoos.

I smiled. "Your restaurant is beautiful."

"Thanks. Maxton did the interior design."

"Is he here today too?" Henry asked.

"No, he's out and about, checking out properties."

Henry raised his eyebrows. "So you're serious about the second location?"

"Yes. We're fully booked every evening until the end of the year, even during the day on weekends. We have reservations for March already," Logan answered. "We've been looking for a suitable property for a while now, but the pickings are slim."

"I can think of a rent-free location for your restaurant . . ." Henry said.

"Forget it."

"Why not?"

Logan shook his head. "I don't want to open a restaurant at The Darlington."

Henry examined his brother thoughtfully as he drummed his fingers on the table. "What if we run it independently of the hotel? Separate accounting, you keep the name and have a separate entrance that doesn't go through the hotel?"

"No," Logan replied without a moment's hesitation.

"Your food must be really good if you're so booked out," I said, trying to prevent the discussion from escalating.

It was fascinating—one brother loved The Darlington, and the other hated it. I wondered what had happened between Logan and his parents. Henry had told me that they had sent Logan to boarding school in France. But was that reason enough for him to foster years of resentment and turn down the offer Henry had just made?

"Our food is fantastic," Logan replied, shoulders squared. "We only serve simple dishes, but we use the best ingredients and prepare everything ourselves—it's all fresh and homemade. We even bought greenhouses last year, so we could grow our own vegetables to guarantee the best quality."

"And how long have you been doing this?"

Logan thought for a moment. "A few years. During school, I worked part-time in restaurants, and after that, I trained as a chef at Le Cordon Bleu. Then, when I came back to London, I worked at Sketch, the three-star restaurant on Conduit Street. I probably would have stayed there if Maxton hadn't . . ."

I didn't hear Logan's next words, because out of the corner of my eye, I spotted a figure in the courtyard. My pulse skyrocketed instantly. Was that Randell? I twisted around to see if it was him, or if my mind was playing tricks on me. Scanning the courtyard uneasily, my gaze flitted from passerby to passerby, but I couldn't see Randell. I had probably just imagined him. Still, I couldn't shake the feeling that something wasn't quite right. My skin tingled as if a thousand ants were crawling over me.

"Kate?"

Someone touched my hand. Startled, I flinched and looked up to see Henry's concerned face.

He studied me, frowning. "Are you OK?"

I blinked, still dazed from the brief shock. I glanced outside again, but there was still no sign of Randell. Perhaps it had just been someone who looked like him.

"Yes," I said, my voice shaking. "My blood sugar is probably just low. I haven't eaten today."

"That's my cue." Logan rose from his chair. I regretted not having heard the rest of his answer. "Do you have any allergies?"

"Peanuts," Henry said. I was surprised that he had remembered.

Logan nodded. "I'll get to work, then. I'll have someone bring you an appetiser. Perhaps we can chat later. It was nice to meet you, Kate."

"It was nice to meet you too," I replied.

Logan headed back to the kitchen, leaving me alone with Henry, who was still scrutinising me with a combination of scepticism and concern. He reached out for my hand again, and this time, I didn't pull away. My fingers felt like icicles against his warm skin.

"Are you sure everything is OK?"

"Yes, it's just my blood pressure," I lied. My forced smile felt shaky. Not because I was afraid of Randell, but because however desperately I wanted to leave that bastard and everything he represented behind, he was like a ghost from the past, constantly haunting me. No matter what I did or how hard I tried, I just couldn't shake him. He was a dark shadow trailing me through my life, and today, he felt particularly oppressive. However safe and settled I felt at The Darlington and with Henry, I hadn't forgotten what day tomorrow was . . .

42

> Henry dating an employee doesn't sit right with me, especially considering that his dad has assaulted several female staff members. Weird dynamic.

Online comment by Midnight Musee

Kate

Dark rainclouds blanketed London. That in itself wasn't unusual, yet it seemed to me that the city was even greyer and bleaker than usual, as if the world was mourning with me on the anniversary of my mum's death. She had died exactly a year ago, and the memory of her was particularly heavy today. Since waking, a crushing weight had settled on my chest, pinning me to the bed.

Motionless, I stared at the ceiling and fought the urge to message Henry. He would notice right away that something was wrong, but I didn't want him to worry or give him the feeling that he had to take care of me. I would get through this day without him. I could manage alone. That's what I told myself, even though I would have given anything right then for one of his warm hugs.

At least I'd had foresight enough to provide a distraction for today. I checked the time. I would have to get up now if I was going to make it. I had suggested to Tilly that I visit her at the Hope Harbour office, which would hopefully take my mind off things. I forced myself to get up and dragged myself to the shower. The warm water wasn't as satisfying today as it was on other days; I had no capacity for satisfaction today. My heart was entirely consumed by an overwhelming grief that I felt deep in my bones.

I checked off the steps of my morning routine absent-mindedly before examining myself in the mirror to make sure I hadn't forgotten anything. Hair. *Check.* Jumper. *Check.* Trousers. *Check.* Shoes. *Check.* Jacket. *Check.* Rucksack. *Check.* I looked the same as always, except for the pain in my eyes. But maybe I was just imagining that.

Before I left my room, I pinched my cheeks to make myself look less pale and joyless. I was no longer so sure it was a good idea to meet Tilly today. I wasn't myself at all, but then again, I didn't want to sit around in my room all day, running through all the what-ifs. It didn't matter what might have happened if I had managed to convince my mum to go to rehab. Or if I'd called the ambulance in time. She was gone, and no amount of fantasising or mind games would bring her back.

I crossed the lobby with my head down. Theodore, already sitting at the piano, greeted me, but I didn't greet him back. I couldn't. At reception, I wordlessly handed my key to Philippa.

Lost in my own grey world, I left the hotel through the back entrance and made my way to the closest station. I had treated myself to the luxury of an Oyster card a few days ago, so I could finally take the Tube again. I had spent the last few months walking around London, but I didn't have the strength today to trek through the city for an hour.

Twenty minutes later, I stood in front of Hope Harbour headquarters, an unassuming residential building with a light facade. Nothing about it suggested that it housed a charity organisation, but the name on the buzzer confirmed I was at the right place. I pressed the button. A buzzing sounded, and then Tilly opened the door. Her cheerful face felt like a punch to my gut.

"Hello, Kate!"

"Hi." I smiled wanly, trying to act normal. Based on her reaction, it looked like I had succeeded.

"I'm happy you're here. Come in!"

Tilly waved me inside, and I was grateful to skip the small talk and jump right in with the tour. As we walked, Tilly told me how she had come to work for Hope Harbour. I didn't have to say very much; I just listened as she explained the organisation's tasks and projects, introducing me to people behind their desks as we went.

Hope Harbour had few permanent employees and plenty of volunteers. Many of them were pensioners looking for meaningful work and community. The atmosphere was warm and friendly. Under different circumstances, I knew I would have loved being here, but the persistent ache in my chest kept bringing my thoughts back to my mum. It was around this time one year ago that I had spoken to her for the last time. I couldn't remember what she had said, but it had probably been something mundane, such as a reminder to take out the bin or buy pasta.

"That's Emanuel," Tilly said, pointing at an older man whose brown hair was peppered with grey. "He's been volunteering for Hope Harbour for two years, his main task being food procurement. We work closely with several supermarkets and even manufacturers who provide us with surplus goods—items that don't meet retail standards. Food with misprinted packaging, for example."

Emanuel glanced up from a computer that looked like a relic from the last decade and was in desperate need of replacing. He smiled at me, his leathery skin suggesting a life spent in the sun. "Hey, a new face. I didn't know we were expecting reinforcement. Welcome to Hope Harbour!"

I shook my head. He wasn't the first to mistake me for a new employee, although the idea was appealing after everything I had seen. Was Tilly hiring? Perhaps I would ask her about it later.

"No, I don't work here. I'm just getting a tour."

"Kate's from The Darlington," Tilly explained. "It was her idea for this year's Pearl Gala to support Hope Harbour." That wasn't entirely accurate, and I had corrected her more than once, but she stuck to this version of the story.

Emanuel's eyes widened. "That's amazing. Thank you!"

I smiled self-consciously. I would pass the thanks on to Henry. He deserved some praise and recognition, since he had been working tirelessly on the gala for weeks and wasn't receiving nearly enough credit.

Emanuel was the last stop on Tilly's tour before she led me to her small office. The furniture was old and scratched. Folders were crammed like sardines into the shelves, and a plant that looked like it was on its last legs stood on the windowsill, its leaves drooping.

"Take a seat," Tilly said, gesturing at the chair in front of her desk.

I sat down and cast an anxious glance at the clock. Only two hours had passed since I had left the hotel. I had hoped the tour would keep me distracted for longer. Tilly leaned back in her chair, studying me over the rims of her gold-framed glasses. My stomach clenched, and I forced my mouth to smile in the hope that I would look less sad.

"Henry and I discussed the Pearl Gala schedule a few days ago," Tilly said. "I don't know how familiar you are with it, but at some point during the evening, the organisation that the gala is fundraising for introduces itself. I'll give a short speech. To make sure it isn't too dry, I thought it might be nice to have someone with personal experience introduce people to the topic of homelessness. You came to mind straightaway."

I raised my eyebrows. "Oh. You want me to speak at the gala?"

Tilly nodded. "Yes. But you don't have to if you don't want to."

I tugged nervously at a loose thread on my leather jacket. "I'm sorry, but I can't. No one at the hotel knows that I was homeless, and I want it to stay that way for now. Having someone with experience speak is a good idea, though."

Although Tilly smiled, I could see she was disappointed. "That's a shame, but I understand. And don't worry, I've not told anyone here about your past."

"Thank you, and . . . I'm really sorry," I apologised again. The idea of revealing to all these ultrarich people that I'd once been ultrapoor was daunting. Still, I would have done it to support Hope Harbour, if the decision didn't affect Henry as well as me. I'd promised him I'd keep my mouth shut about my past, and I intended to keep my promise.

"Don't be sorry," Tilly said. "You've already been a great help to us."

I smiled tightly. I didn't feel like I'd been helpful. I hadn't contributed anything at all to the cause. The only thing I'd done was steal Henry's phone months ago. The more Tilly insisted she was grateful, the worse I felt—although that may have been because of what day it was. I couldn't stop thinking about my mum. About how I hadn't been able to help her. I had a lump in my throat, and my eyes burnt with unshed tears.

"Kate?"

Tilly was blurry when I looked at her. Shit. I blinked rapidly to get rid of my tears, but it was too late.

"What's wrong?"

"Nothing," I croaked thickly. "Everything's fine."

"Are you sure?" she pressed, unconvinced.

I nodded and wiped my face with the back of my hand to catch my tears, but they kept falling.

Tilly opened a drawer and wordlessly handed me a packet of tissues. I thanked her and took one. "No need to thank me." She smiled at me sympathetically, and I had to turn away. I couldn't bear her kindness.

I sniffed. "Sorry. I'll be fine in a minute."

"It's OK," she reassured me, and reached across the table to pat my arm. It was a tender gesture, one that reminded me of my mum before the drugs took over. A searing pain shot through me, and I knew I couldn't stay a second longer without breaking down completely and sobbing. I liked Tilly, but right now, she reminded me too much of my mum. They were even the same age.

I scraped my chair back and stood up. "I think I should go."

"You're very welcome to stay."

"I'm meeting someone for lunch," I lied, and shouldered my rucksack. Had it become heavier, or had I grown weaker? "Thanks for showing me Hope Harbour, and I'm sorry I can't help you."

Tilly returned my smile. "You know where I am if you change your mind. And take these, just in case." She handed me the tissues.

I pocketed them gratefully and said goodbye.

Five minutes later, I left Hope Harbour, relieved that I hadn't entirely lost it in Tilly's presence. I took several deep breaths, trying to get my tears under control, and then I started walking. The only problem was that I had no idea where I could go. I had nowhere to escape my pain and my memories.

> It was nice to meet Kate yesterday. She seems cool. I don't quite get what she's doing with a workaholic buttface like you, but whatever.

Message from Logan to Henry

Kate

I stared at the cast-iron gate. I hadn't been here since my mum's funeral. Over the last few months, I had kept vowing to visit her but had never been able to bring myself to go, always finding new excuses to delay my visit. But now here I stood, my heart pounding, holding a cheap bunch of flowers and trying to pluck up the courage to step into the cemetery. The clouds had given way to a steady drizzle shrouding London.

The gate to the cemetery swung open, and a woman dashed off towards the parking lot and her dry car. I wished I could also be somewhere dry. I wished I was at The Darlington. I wished I was with Henry. But I had to be here—there was no way around it.

Determined to get it over with, I opened the gate set into a sandstone wall. It creaked slightly. To the left, there was a small chapel, behind which lay the cemetery. The unpaved paths were slippery, and the wind had blown the autumn leaves from the trees. I made my way past the graves—some of them new, others so old that the gravestones were crooked.

Although I had only been here once before, I had no problem finding the small, inconspicuous grave at the edge of the cemetery's grassy area. Since I couldn't afford the funeral, the city had organised it. Randell had stayed out of it. He hadn't even had the decency to show up on the day, which made it abundantly clear how much my mum had really meant to him. He hadn't loved her; he'd loved the way he could control her.

I stopped at her grave and felt the lump in my throat grow bigger.

"Hey, Mum," I said. My voice was hoarse and barely audible, but that didn't matter. I could have yelled and she still wouldn't have heard.

I crouched down in front of the grave and laid the flowers down beside it, although I knew they would probably freeze during the night. There was no headstone, only a wooden cross. It already looked weathered, and I could hardly read the inscription on it anymore, but perhaps that was also due to the tears that blurred my vision. I wiped my eyes, and for a brief moment, the world seemed a little clearer, despite the rain.

Rebecca Hamilton
8th August, 1986—15th November, 2023

I stared at the engraving until it blurred again, and finally, the lump in my throat gave way to tears. I let out a soft whimper as they fell, then collapsed onto the ground. The cold dampness seeped through my jeans, but I barely registered it. All I could feel was a heavy pressure in my chest, as if the grief were crushing my heart.

"Shit," I murmured. I gasped for air and tried to stem the flow of my tears, but they continued to stream down my face relentlessly, silent sobs racking my body. I felt an urge to hold on to something, but there was nothing here to anchor me. I clutched my stomach in desperation, holding on to myself—holding myself together—but it only made me realise that the one person whose arms I wanted to feel around me right now would never hug me again.

Sometimes I forgot how final death was, because it was easier to repress the thought of it than confront my grief. But now the pain hit me, and it was unstoppable. I missed my mum. I missed her voice and her dark sense of humour. I missed cooking with her in the cramped, shabby kitchen in our old flat. I missed sitting on the sofa with her in the evenings, drinking tea together before bed.

I pressed my hand against the cold ground, hoping to feel a little closer to her, but my fingers met only damp soil. The worst part of it all was knowing that the version of my mum I mourned had been gone long before her death. And when she died, the last shred of hope that things could ever return to how they were before Randell came on the scene vanished. He had taken her away from me bit by bit, until there was nothing left.

Suddenly, I heard the squelch of footsteps behind me. I blinked away my tears and glanced around to see who else had braved the cemetery in the rain. A chill of terror ran down my spine at the sight of a dark figure. I leapt to my feet.

"What are you doing here?" I snarled. Was it a coincidence that the scumbag was here? Or had he followed me? I thought back to my lunch at The Meridian yesterday, and how I had thought I'd seen him. Had I not imagined it, after all?

Randell smiled, baring his teeth. "I'm visiting your mum."

I glared at him. "Piss off!"

He ignored me and came closer. His pupils were dilated, as if he were high, and there was a fresh scrape on his eyebrow. Had he got into a drunken brawl, or was he in serious trouble?

"You lied to me. I saw the photos of you and your *boss*," he said, his lewd tone sending a chill through me. "When you said you worked for him, I assumed you were cleaning at the hotel, not sucking his dick. But once a whore, always a whore."

I ignored his insult. "Why are you here?"

"I'm here because you're an ungrateful bitch," Randell replied, licking his lips, which were so chapped they looked like he'd sandpapered them. "I took you in after you and your mum lost everything. Without me, you would have become a dirty whore much sooner. You owe me for that."

"So that's why you're here? You want money?" I asked, my voice heavy with disdain.

Randell stared shamelessly right back at me. He nodded.

"Forget it!"

"Kate . . ."

"You're not getting a single penny out of me," I hissed. How dare he ask me for money? Here, of all places? Especially after everything he'd done to me and my mum. "Leave me the fuck alone, you prick."

Scorn flashed in Randell's eyes, but instead of leaving, he stepped closer. I took a step back—and another, and another, until eventually I bumped into the wooden cross that marked my mum's grave and could go no further. Randell stopped an arm's length away from me. The earthy scent of the rain mingled with the acrid stench of stale smoke.

He studied me. I hated the feel of his eyes on me.

"Does your lover boy know you suck dick for money?"

I gritted my teeth. I wouldn't waste my energy answering or correcting him. He wouldn't believe me anyway.

"What would he think of you if I told him?"

"Stay away from Henry!" I spat. I couldn't let Randell near him—he would ruin everything. Henry was already surrounded by the wreckage left behind by his dad. There was no way I would let Randell destroy even more. Henry had done so much for me already; I couldn't ask him to deal with Randell as well.

"What if I don't?" His lips curled into a sneer, and he stepped even closer. The smell of smoke grew stronger, and with every word he spoke, he exhaled alcohol fumes into my face.

I felt nauseous. "Why can't you just leave me alone?"

"I'll leave you alone when you give me what I want."

"I don't have money," I insisted.

"But your boyfriend does. Call him."

I shook my head. "No."

"Call. Him."

"I'm not going to do that."

"For fuck's sake, call him, you miserable bitch!" Randell roared, and I was sure I felt his spittle join the drizzle on my face. "Call him, or you'll regret it."

My stomach clenched as memories of all the fights we'd ever had flooded back. Each one had started this way. Any moment now, I would feel the sting of his blows—I was certain of it. But I had to stay strong. For Henry.

"No," I said, lifting my chin defiantly and steeling myself.

Instead of hitting me, Randell pulled out a switchblade from his jacket pocket. *Fuck!* The blade snapped out with a click. My eyes widened as he pointed the gleaming metal at me, a smug grin plastered across his face. "I warned you."

Randell tested the weight of the knife in his hand. Panic rose in my throat, and I wondered if I could run fast enough to escape before he managed to plunge the blade into my stomach.

"Call your boyfriend!"

"Randell, please." I hated how my voice was suddenly trembling. My rage had vanished, replaced by fear. My eyes locked onto the knife hovering just centimetres from my body. One stab, and everything would be over. I would bleed to death. There was no one here to save me. "Let me go."

"Are you deaf?"

"Haven't you caused enough damage?"

Randell pressed the knife into my stomach. He didn't stab me, but I felt the sharp point pierce the fabric of my clothes and press against my skin. It wouldn't take much more for the blood to start flowing. "Do you want to die?"

I shook my head.

"Then call him!" Randell screamed.

I stared at him, frozen. I could smell my own fear—a mix of sweat and something salty. Unshed tears burnt in my throat. I didn't know what to do. I couldn't think, my head clouded by the fear that I might die. I wasn't ready. But the thought of dragging Henry into this mess made my stomach twist. If Randell ruined Henry's life too, I would never forgive myself. I had already let him ruin my mum's.

"Let her go," a sharp voice suddenly hissed.

Henry!

Relief and panic crashed over me. I glanced sideways, not daring to move. Henry stood just a few steps away, gripping an umbrella and fixing Randell with a withering glare. I had never seen him this furious, not even with his father or when I had told him about Mr. Fleming. How had he found me?

"Looks like you can save yourself the phone call," Randell sneered.

"Get away from her!" Henry demanded. "Now!"

Randell didn't move. "What if I don't?"

"Randell, please . . ."

He ignored me.

Henry's hands clenched into fists. "Then we have a problem."

Randell gave a crooked grin and shifted his weight, making sure Henry saw the knife pressed dangerously close to my stomach. Henry's jaw tightened at the sight of the blade, but instead of the fear I had expected, his fury only deepened. Contempt darkened his expression, his anger burning even brighter.

Ignoring my head shake, Henry stepped closer. "If you hurt Kate, I'll kill you."

"Henry, get away from him!" I pleaded.

To my relief, he stopped moving.

"I want ten thousand pounds," Randell demanded.

Henry raised his eyebrows. "You want money?"

"Yes. Cash."

Henry didn't reply, seeming to contemplate the demand. He couldn't give Randell money. I didn't want to be even more indebted to Henry—but more importantly, I didn't want Randell to get ideas. Today it was ten thousand pounds, tomorrow twenty thousand, and then thirty thousand. Drugs were expensive, and he would always find new ways to blackmail Henry once he realised he could.

"I have a better idea," Henry finally said.

Randell raised an inquisitive eyebrow.

"I'm calling the police."

Randell stiffened beside me but quickly masked whatever fear the threat had stirred in him with arrogance. "Go for it. By the time they get here, I will have stabbed you both."

Henry raised an eyebrow. "Your tiny knife doesn't scare me. But if you so much as leave a single mark on Kate, I will destroy you. I'll hunt you down, wherever you are, and make your life a living hell. I'll make sure you never feel safe again."

Uncertainty flickered in Randell's eyes—he hadn't anticipated Henry's threats. But he stayed where he was, keeping his knife pointed at me.

"If you think I'm bluffing, you're mistaken," Henry continued. "This isn't a threat—it's a promise. Unlike you, you pathetic son of a bitch, I have unlimited resources to ruin your life. So let Kate go and put the knife away. Do me that favour. And more importantly, do yourself that favour."

I felt and heard my heart pounding in my chest as my eyes flicked between the two men. Randell returned Henry's withering look, but he said nothing. For a brief moment, time seemed to stand still—and then Randell finally stepped away from me. He retracted the blade with a click. At last, I could breathe again.

"Good decision," Henry said. "Now fuck off!"

Randell hesitated. I could see how much he hated this. He was used to getting his own way, forcing his will upon people like me and my mum, who couldn't stand up to him physically. But Henry was different. Still glaring at him, Randell moved away from me. I was afraid his retreat was a ruse and that he'd lash out at any moment, but he seemed to grasp that the situation wouldn't end well for him if he did. He turned and fled.

I didn't dare move. The blood was still thundering in my ears.

I felt movement beside me—Henry. I lifted my head and met his eyes. His expression was steely, but beneath the rage, I saw his concern. I must have been a mess—damp, dirty, and tear-streaked.

"Are you OK?" he asked, his voice thick with worry as he held his umbrella over my head.

"Yes," I croaked, fighting back a whimper, but the relief was too much. Tears spilled down my face, and I threw myself into Henry's arms. He caught me instantly, pulling me close. I clung to him, burying my face in his chest as sobs wracked my body. I couldn't believe Randell had threatened me with a knife. He would stop at nothing now. "I was so scared."

He stroked my back, his proximity calming my racing heart. "I know. But you're safe now."

Thanks to you.

"Did he hurt you?"

I shook my head, and Henry relaxed slightly. The rain intensified, but he didn't move, keeping me in the safety of his embrace. For a moment, I simply soaked up his reassuring presence, then he placed his hands on my shoulders and gently held me at arm's length to examine me. His blue eyes were clouded, as if he were struggling with his emotions too.

"Shall we get out of here?" he asked.

I nodded, eager to leave.

He took my hand, and we left the cemetery together. I cast one final glance over my shoulder at my mum's grave. Our footprints—mine and Randell's—were still visible. Not even in death was she free from that monster.

44

> Hey, I'm staying at Randell's tonight. There are leftovers from last night in the fridge for you to heat up. I hope you had a good day. Let me know when you get home.

Old message from Kate's mum

Kate

Henry opened the passenger door of his Bentley and gestured at me to get in. I hesitated—I was soaked through and my trousers were muddy, but what choice did I have? I couldn't walk back to the hotel alone and risk running into Randell again. He must be livid about the turn our encounter had taken. So I followed Henry's silent order.

He closed the door, walked around the car and slid into the driver's seat. Without a word, he turned on the engine and cranked up the heating. Warm air blew out at me. I shivered and sunk into the seat with relief. The confrontation with Randell had only lasted ten or fifteen minutes, but it had drained a week's worth of energy on a day when I was already feeling fragile.

Henry drove off, still not speaking. The silence between us felt deafening—or maybe it was just my own thoughts screaming at me. I glanced over at Henry uncertainly. His eyes were fixed on the road, his jaw tense. He had seemed relieved at the cemetery that I was OK, but now he seemed annoyed more than anything else.

"Are you angry at me?" I asked.

Henry didn't look at me. "No."

"But you seem angry."

"I'm thinking," he replied as we stopped at a red light. I waited for him to elaborate, but he didn't speak.

The light turned green, and we drove on in silence. I hated this tension—there had never been so much coldness and distance between us, not even during our first encounter in the park. I didn't blame Henry. He should have been in his office sorting out his own problems instead of getting dragged into my past and having to deal with Randell.

"I'm sorry," I said quietly.

He sighed. "You haven't done anything wrong."

"I just wish you hadn't had to witness that."

Henry abruptly pulled the car into a parking space at the side of the road and turned to face me. His eyes were piercing. "Do you have any idea how glad I am that I witnessed that? I'm not mad at you—I'm mad at myself for finishing some ridiculous email before I left. You can't imagine how scared I was when I saw you there with that guy. And the knife . . ." He shook his head as if trying to banish the memory.

I swallowed. "You . . . you didn't seem scared."

"Believe me, I was. I would never have forgiven myself if something had happened to you." He reached over the centre console for my hand and gently stroked his thumb over my cold skin. The tender look in his eyes tugged at something in my chest. Despite how much he had on his plate, he had dropped everything just to be there for me.

"How did you even find me?"

"Tilly called me and said you'd cried in her office. I was worried about you. The old iPhone I gave you is still linked to my account, and I tracked you using Find My," he explained hesitantly. "I've never checked up on you before, but when I saw you were at a cemetery after Tilly's call, I was worried. I wanted to make sure you were all right. I hope that was OK."

"It was." I wouldn't have called Henry, but I was still glad that he'd come. And it was nice to know that someone cared about me enough to worry. No one had looked out for me since my mum had fallen prey to Randell and the drugs.

"Good, that's a relief," Henry said with a smile. But instead of starting the engine and taking us back to the hotel, he got out and came to open my door.

I reluctantly left the warm car and stepped out into the cold drizzle. I glanced around. He had parked in front of a café called Better Days. The name was pretty ironic on a day like today.

"What are we doing here?"

"We're talking," Henry said. "Or rather, you're talking and I'm listening."

He took my hand and led me into the café. It smelled incredible—of roasted coffee beans and pastries. A young woman with pink hair stood behind the counter, carefully decorating cookies. She looked up as the bell above the door chimed, announcing our arrival. Her smile faltered at the sight of us—Henry in his elegant coat and tailored suit, and me in my worn leather jacket and mud-streaked trousers, both of us drenched to the bone.

The café was nearly empty, save for a couple and a blond woman working on her laptop—probably because most people were either at work or avoiding the rain in the comfort of their own homes.

"What would you like?" Henry asked.

"A tea." The cakes and cupcakes on display looked delicious, and on any other day, the selection would have cheered me up. But I had no appetite today, and I dreaded the conversation we were about to have. I had avoided talking to Henry about my mum and Randell so far, but he deserved the truth.

"Find us a table. I'll join you in a minute."

I nodded and chose a booth in the furthest corner of the café. The place had a cosy charm, with small tables and chairs, and comfy seating areas piled with colourful cushions. The walls were dark green, and standing lamps cast a warm, inviting glow, even on a gloomy day like today.

I watched as Henry chatted with the woman at the counter. Her eyebrows were knitted tightly together, her expression inexplicably sceptical. Was she upset with us for leaving puddles on the floor? They spoke for a moment longer, their conversation animated. Finally, she nodded, and he handed her his credit card.

He came to the table without our order while the woman approached the other customers. I watched curiously as Henry removed his coat and draped it over the back of a chair at the neighbouring table before slipping around to the bench to sit next to me. "What were you talking about for so long?"

"I asked Kaycee to close the café."

"Why?"

"So we can talk without being disturbed."

"And she actually agreed?" I asked, disbelief creeping into my voice as I watched the blond woman shut her laptop and the couple slip on their coats. None of them looked the least bit annoyed about having to leave.

"I said I would pay everyone's bill, and offered her a very generous sum as compensation for the next hour."

"That's really not necessary!"

"Yes, it is. I don't want anyone eavesdropping, or for more photos of us to end up in the news. This is too important," he said firmly.

The other guests left Better Days, and Kaycee flipped the sign on the door to "Closed" before returning to the counter to make our drinks. Shortly after, she brought us two cups of tea.

"There you go," she said with a smile.

I avoided her gaze, uncomfortable that Henry had paid for us to have the café to ourselves. Still, although I found it over the top, I preferred to have this conversation in private too.

"Thank you," Henry said.

"You're welcome. I'll be in the kitchen if you want anything else. Just use the little bell on the counter, and I'll come straightaway," said Kaycee, before disappearing through a door.

I took two packets of sugar from the stand on the table and tipped them into my tea. The entire time, I could feel Henry's inquisitive eyes on me. I felt uneasy. After all, there was a reason I had avoided telling him about my past.

He noticed my hesitation and touched my hand gently. Our fingers intertwined instinctively, and the gesture gave me the strength to speak.

"It's the anniversary of my mum's death today."

"Kate . . ." He sighed deeply, seeming disappointed that I hadn't shared the burden with him sooner. His fingers squeezed mine. "Why didn't you tell me?"

I shrugged. "You have so much on your plate. Things are really kicking off at the hotel, the Pearl Gala is just around the corner, and everyone wants something from you. I didn't want to make you worry about me on top of all that."

"I worry about you most when I don't know what's going on with you." The intensity of his gaze was overwhelming—my chest tightened, and I looked away, though I managed a nod. Henry raised our intertwined fingers to his lips and kissed the back of my hand. "Do you want to tell me who that guy was? He seemed to know you."

I hesitated, resisting my usual urge to dodge the topic, but Henry's gentle touch and steady gaze melted my resistance. "Randell was my mum's boyfriend. They met three years ago. Back then, me and my mum were living in a small apartment in Richmond. She was an amazing mum, and gave me everything she had to give, but she suffered from depression. She didn't have an easy life—her dad beat her when she was a kid, and she ran away from home when she was seventeen. Sometimes, her mental health made it difficult for her to work."

Henry listened intently.

I took a sip of my tea, but my throat still felt dry and scratchy, as if my body were trying to stop me from continuing. But I went on anyway. "Four years ago, she had a pretty bad depressive episode. She was unemployed, and we were behind on the rent. It really weighed on her. I dropped out of school to support her financially, but that somehow made things worse. She was in a really bad place until she met Randell at a mutual friend's party. At the beginning, I had no reason to question their relationship. Randell seemed to make my mum happy. She enjoyed his attention, and with the extra money I was earning, things finally seemed to be improving."

Looking back, I felt so naive. I had truly believed that things were getting better. Now I knew that those few hopeful days had just been the calm before the storm.

"A few weeks later, though, I realised that something wasn't right," I continued. "I was working at a cinema back then, and sometimes I stole from the customers. At least, from those who looked like they had a few pounds to spare. I stashed the money away in a drawer in my bedroom when I got home. After a while, though, I noticed that it kept disappearing. At first, I thought I was imagining it. But I couldn't shake the feeling that there was more to it."

Henry raised his eyebrows. "Your mum was stealing from you?"

I nodded. "Right after that, we got another warning notice from our landlord, even though the rent should have been covered. By that point, my mum wasn't coming home much anymore, and she stayed at Randell's place most nights. When I asked her about the money, she got angry, screamed at me, and stormed out of the apartment. That should have been a clear warning sign."

"You just wanted to see the best in her."

He was right. In my eyes, my mum could do no wrong for a long time. I had looked up to her and admired her strength. Because strength didn't mean you succeeded at everything—it meant getting back up and carrying on, even when you failed and life knocked you down. My mum had never given up. She'd always fought for us—at least until Randell had stolen her strength.

"After that fight, everything happened so fast," I went on, ignoring the tightness in my chest that came from knowing how the story ended—an ending I hated. "My money was vanishing. The warning notices kept coming, until eventually we were evicted. We moved in with Randell. I hadn't had much contact with him up to that point, and I thought it would be a good thing. Living in his bungalow seemed like a better option than living on the streets. But with the three of us sharing fifty square metres, my mum could no longer hide what was happening to my money. They'd been stealing it and spending it on drugs. Randell had been an addict for a while, and he'd dragged my mum into it. She assured me that they were just harmless pills to help her relax, and I was gullible enough to believe her."

Henry tensed beside me. I couldn't quite read the expression that flickered across his face. Worry? Panic? Guilt? Whatever it was, he quickly suppressed it. He seemed to know where the story was heading and took a deep breath, as if bracing himself for what came next.

"But it wasn't just the drugs that my mum had concealed from me. She'd also hidden the fact that Randell was beating her, just like her dad used to. She hadn't been spending six days a week with him because she loved him, but because she was ashamed and didn't want me to see the bruises. It didn't take long, though, for Randell to show me his true colours. One evening, after I'd come home from my shift at the cinema, he lashed out at me for forgetting to take out the rubbish. He beat me black and blue, until my mum stepped in to stop him."

"What a pathetic son of a bitch," Henry growled. His grip tightened around my hand, and his eyes darkened, matching the menace in his voice. His intensity sent a shiver down my spine. "Did that happen often?"

"All the time," I admitted. "Although it was usually my mum he beat up. She often protected me. I begged her to leave him, but she was dependent on him. He wasn't just her partner—he was her drug dealer too. She was so terrified of not being able to get the drugs anymore that she stayed with him, despite everything. At some point, she started taking more hardcore drugs, because it was the only way she could tolerate him. It was a vicious circle. I lost my job at the cinema because I had to take care of her and couldn't stick to a regular schedule. I threatened to leave so many times if she didn't get sober, but either she didn't care, or she knew I was bluffing." My heart clenched. It hurt to remember. "I kept trying to make her stop. I brought home brochures, showed her statistics. I hid my money and her drugs, but she always sniffed them out, like a bloodhound. Once, I even flushed the drugs down the toilet—and later that night, Randell beat me so badly I thought I was going to die. The hearing in my right ear never fully came back. He damaged something."

Absent-mindedly, I touched my ear with my free hand. I wasn't completely deaf on that side, and over time, I'd learned to live with it. But it had been a real disadvantage on the streets. I'd always had to sleep on my right side, so I could listen for danger with my left.

"Even that didn't open my mum's eyes. One evening, I came home and she was lying on the sofa, unconscious. I didn't think much of it—the drugs often knocked her out—and I went to take a shower. It was only later, when I was making myself something to eat, that I realised something was wrong. She hadn't moved an inch and was completely still. Too still. I called the ambulance right away, but it was too late. She was already dead."

My voice cracked, and my eyes burnt. I had relived that moment hundreds of times in my nightmares, but saying it out loud made it so much worse. Guilt and shame twisted inside me. As much as I blamed Randell, I blamed myself just as much—maybe even more. Because unlike him, I had truly loved my mum . . . yet I had still let her die.

Henry's fingers tightened around mine. "Your mum died of an overdose?" he asked, his tone a mix of horror and panic, presumably because this was yet another terrible secret from my past that would be best kept out of the public eye.

I nodded. "The worst thing is that I don't know whether she was already dead when I got home or if she was still alive, dying while I was singing Taylor Swift songs in the shower."

Henry's expression softened. "You did everything you could."

"Did I, though? I can't stop wondering if she would still be alive if I had checked on her right away. Or if I'd tried harder to get her off the drugs."

"You did everything you could," Henry repeated insistently.

"So why wasn't it enough?" I croaked. The memory of her lifeless body sent a fresh wave of pain through my chest. Tears welled up in my eyes again—as if I hadn't cried enough for one day. But I couldn't stop them. They came flooding out, loud and ugly. I squeezed my eyes shut and clamped a hand over my mouth, but it was useless. I whimpered, my shoulders shook, and an agonised sob broke the silence of the café.

Suddenly, warm hands cupped my face. I felt Henry's breath on my skin, then the soft press of his lips as he kissed the tears from my cheeks. Everything inside me tightened, pain and gratitude coming together with unbearable intensity.

"Don't blame yourself, angel," Henry murmured and rested his forehead against mine. "I didn't know your mom, but if she was even half as loving, selfless, and understanding as you are, she wouldn't want you to carry this guilt around with you. And I'm sure she was grateful for how long you fought for her, even if she couldn't tell you that. That's not something to be taken for granted, and it just shows how much you loved her."

I began to cry even harder. Henry's words had shattered something deep inside me, only to piece it back together again. He wrapped his arms around me, and I pressed my face into his chest to muffle the sobs that racked my body. He held me close, his lips grazing my forehead as his hands moved gently over my back. He murmured soothingly into my ear. His words, his warmth, and his voice grounded me; Henry was an anchor keeping me from being completely swept away by my pain and guilt.

I took a trembling breath and concentrated on his steady breathing. With every rise and fall of his chest, my tears slowed and the pain became more bearable, though it didn't disappear completely. It never would.

"Are you feeling any better?" he asked after a while.

I nodded, not yet trusting my voice.

He took his hand from my back, and a second later, he offered me a packet of tissues out of his pocket. I took one, and after I blew my nose, I dabbed at my eyes, though most of my tears had seeped into Henry's shirt.

I traced my fingers over his chest. "I really have to stop crying all over you."

"I like it."

"Strange kink, but OK."

He smiled. "I didn't mean it like that. I just meant that I like being the one to comfort you," he explained, stroking my cheek. His skin was warm while mine was cold. I leaned into the touch. It felt safe and familiar. "You have to promise me one thing, though."

"Anything," I said, and I meant it.

His gaze met mine firmly, not quite matching the softness of his voice. "Promise me you'll never hold back from talking to me just because you think I'm too busy to listen. It's true that I have a lot going on, but it's never so much that I can't be there for you when you need me."

A warm feeling spread through me at his words. Realising that what I felt for this man was so much more than gratitude. He had woken something in me that was both beautiful and terrifying. I saw nothing but warmth and affection when I looked into his blue eyes. I had been so alone in the last few months, but Henry had taken me under his wing without a moment's hesitation and led me out of that loneliness. I had left it behind a little more every day, and now it was so distant that I could barely see it. I saw only Henry.

"Do you know how incredible you are?"

He smiled. "Thanks. You're not too bad yourself."

"I'm serious."

"Me too. You're really not so bad."

I saw through his attempt to lighten the mood on this dark day—and it wasn't even necessary. With him by my side, every day felt a little brighter. Ignoring his teasing, I kissed him.

Our lips melted together. We must have kissed hundreds of times in the past few weeks, but this one felt different—deeper and more intimate. Sharing the truth about my past with Henry had revealed another truth. A truth I could no longer deny.

I, Kate Hamilton, was madly and hopelessly in love with Henry Darlington. And that was probably the most beautiful realisation of this terrible day.

THE BLACKROOM

Consequences—a foreign concept to people like the Darlingtons. Every problem is just a cheque away from being solved. But this one is a mess even they can't afford to make go away. The reservations at the luxury hotel are dwindling. The beautiful—and, more crucially, wealthy—guests who once queued up to stay at The Darlington are now steering well clear of the place, eager to avoid damaging their reputations.

Talk of layoffs and salary cuts is making the rounds. And to cover up how deep in the red the hotel is, Henry Darlington is allegedly planning to close the fourth floor of the hotel for "renovations." We've heard from a reliable source that this is just a ploy to cut costs. Is it time to say goodbye to The Darlington?

45

The Darlington in Crisis! *The Blackroom* Leaks Financial Reports.

INsider headline

Henry

I rubbed my face. My eyes were burning. The only sources of light in my otherwise dark office were my laptop and the desk light. It was already late, and I should have been finishing my work—but instead, I was fuming over *The Blackroom*. The site had somehow managed to get its hands on The Darlington's financial plans. Ever since it had started, the blog had been a thorn in my side. Our lawyers had been trying to get it taken down, but so far, we hadn't managed to track down the people behind it. Confidential information kept surfacing in their posts, information that wasn't intended for the public. It was a mystery to me how they had found out that the alleged reason for the planned closure of the fourth floor—renovations—was a lie.

I pushed my chair back with a sigh and walked over to the small coffee machine in my office. It whirred to life as I slid a capsule into the machine. While the coffee brewed, I pulled the small box from my trouser pocket and took a pill. A pang of guilt washed over me, but I forced myself to ignore it.

The machine announced that my coffee was ready with a beep. I took the cup and went back to my desk to answer emails. I had managed to work my way through most of my inbox, my focus razor-sharp, when my phone vibrated.

KATE:

I'm thinking of you.

The message was followed by a blurry photo of Kate. The lighting was dim, and I could make out many people behind her. She was holding a glass of beer and grinning at the camera. That morning, she had told me she would be going out tonight. Since the incident with Randell, she always let me know where she was, or where she was planning to go. I wasn't sure if she was trying to reassure me or herself. Either way, I wasn't complaining. I was still having nightmares about what had happened at the cemetery. Kate had told me afterwards that Randell had blackmailed and threatened her for months, and that she had used the four thousand pounds I had given her to pay off her "debt" so he would leave her alone.

In hindsight, I regretted letting that scumbag walk away. He didn't deserve to get away scot-free, not after everything he had done to Kate and her mum. I hated the thought that he could appear again at any moment to threaten Kate. I hoped he had taken my warning seriously, and that he would stay away from her from now on. If he didn't, things would get pretty ugly for him.

That bitch is crazy if she thinks I'm that easily intimidated! Her boyfriend doesn't scare me.

Message from Randell to Edwin

Kate

SNOWFLAKE:

What pub are you at?

I shared my location with Henry. After everything that had happened with Randell, it made me feel safe when he knew where I was. And even if he didn't say it, I could sense that he felt similarly. My confession about Randell had shaken him.

ME:

I'm with Rose and Grace.

SNOWFLAKE:

Is Rose the one who doesn't like me?

ME:

Yes, but I think it's mainly because she doesn't like your dad. Don't take it personally.

SNOWFLAKE:

Good to know.

ME:

Are you still at the office?

SNOWFLAKE:

Yes.

ME:

When are you wrapping up for the day?

SNOWFLAKE:

Why?

ME:

I don't want to miss you.

SNOWFLAKE:

I need at least two more hours.

ME:

OK. See you later!

"Is everything OK?" Grace asked when she returned to the table with a pint. It was Friday evening, and the pub was full to overflowing. The air was stuffy and stale, heavy with the smell of beer and greasy food. The music coming from the speakers was drowned out by laughter and conversations.

I put my phone away and shouted above the hubbub. My cheeks glowed, and although I was only on my second pint, I was already feeling the alcohol. "Yes! I was just messaging Henry."

"He should come if he wants!"

"He's still at the office."

"Really? It's so late."

"He always works late," I said, wondering how much Grace knew and if I could tell her just how badly things at The Darlington were going. But I didn't want to ruin the evening, so I decided against it.

"How's the hunt for a second job going?" Grace asked.

"I have an interview next week." It was the only positive response I'd gotten to my applications. Otherwise, I'd received only rejections. Either I was underqualified, or I wasn't flexible enough, thanks to my job at The Darlington. I wanted to ask Tilly about a position at Hope Harbour—my dream job—but I hadn't been able to get a hold of her by phone for days.

"Where?"

"A 24-hour corner shop," I replied. "They're looking for someone to cover the night shift. The pay isn't great, but the hours wouldn't be a problem." Except I'd probably see even less of Henry. But we would find some way to spend time with each other.

Grace made a face. "Sounds like a dangerous job."

"No more dangerous than . . ." I bit my tongue. I'd almost let slip that it was no more dangerous than sleeping alone on the streets at night. ". . . than going out clubbing at night. Anyway, I'm sure the place has CCTV, and it's card payments only. It'll be fine."

"If you say so," Grace said, still sounding doubtful.

I changed the topic. "Have you signed up for that dating app yet?"

"Yes! Do you want to see my profile?"

"Of course."

Grace moved Rose's bag aside and shuffled closer to me. While she opened the app on her phone, I glanced around for Rose. I spotted her almost right away. She was still at the bar with the same man, her hand resting on his arm, their faces just centimetres apart. I had watched Rose flirting hard all evening, but the sight still caught me off guard. She always seemed so reserved at the hotel, but here, she was anything but.

"Look!" Grace said, and held her phone in my face.

I took it from her and scrolled through her profile. It was a colourful mix of photos and entertaining facts about Grace. "Have you had any matches yet?"

"Yes, but none of them have really impressed me."

"What are you looking for? Maybe we'll find someone here for you," I said, only half joking. The pub was packed with men our age. A few of them had already checked Grace out, which was no surprise. She looked stunning—her long hair cascaded over her shoulders in waves, her lips were painted an alluring red, and she was wearing a black wool dress that emphasised her curves.

"I like tall men with dark hair and broad shoulders," Grace said, counting off the points on her fingers. "He should also have beautiful eyes. I love beautiful eyes. Especially blue ones."

I grinned mischievously.

She frowned. "What?"

"Do you know who you've just described?"

"Who?"

"Ethan."

"Darlington?!" she said indignantly.

"Yes," I said, and started counting off the points on my own fingers. "Ethan is tall, he has dark hair, and he's sporty. He has a great face and really beautiful blue eyes."

"You're only saying that because he looks like Henry."

"No, I'm saying it because it's true."

Grace snorted and started twisting the ring on her index finger. "Maybe, but he's still not my type. I don't like arseholes. I want a man who's nice to me and treats me like a princess. Not a knobhead who dumps rubbish at my feet and whose used condoms I have to get rid of."

"Gross." I wrinkled my nose. "Did that really happen?"

"Yeah. Sometimes when he's drunk, he just leaves them lying around. But at least he uses them in the first place. God forbid Satan's spawn spawns yet more demons." She shrugged, and I suspected that her indifference had a lot to do with the three pints she'd already downed. "Honestly, Ethan just isn't my type. Maybe appearance-wise, but I want a man I can fall in love with, not one to just sleep with—and Ethan isn't good for anything else. He has the emotional intelligence of a rock."

I didn't argue. If I was honest, I didn't want her getting close to Ethan, not even physically. Not because he was a loser, but because he very clearly was smoking weed, and I didn't want to watch Grace be dragged into the same mess my mum had been in. Ethan could do what he wanted for all I cared, as long as he stayed away from Grace.

We talked for a while about the dating app, with Grace showing me some of her matches, until Rose returned to the table and announced she was heading home with Shane. We told her to have fun and decided to stay a little longer. Grace and I played a round of pool with two men, and the cocktails they insisted on buying for us went straight to my head and made everything seem funnier. I hadn't laughed so much in a long time, and I loved the feeling of lightness and freedom the alcohol gave me. So when the men showed up with a tray of shots, I didn't say no. By the time the pub closed and the bartenders kicked everyone out, Grace and I were pretty drunk. The men asked if we wanted to go to a place a few doors down with them, but we declined and called a taxi. The driver dropped me off at The Darlington before taking Grace home.

The hotel lobby was quiet except for a few partygoers heading up to the rooftop bar. The restaurant had already closed, and most guests were either in their rooms or out enjoying London's nightlife. I picked up my key from Naomi at the reception desk, but I didn't head for the lifts. Instead, I entered the staff-only area at the back of the hotel. The sound of my footsteps echoed through the long corridors as I made my way to Henry's office. When I knocked on the door, the sound seemed unnaturally loud in the stillness.

"Come in," Henry called.

I pushed open the door and stumbled inside. The room was dim, lit only by the lamp on the desk Henry sat behind.

"Heeeeey," I said, drawing out the word.

Henry grinned. "Hi. What are you doing here?"

I leaned against the doorframe—standing upright was too much effort, especially with the floor shifting so unhelpfully beneath me. Did Henry know that his floor was moving?

"Picking you up. You have to take me to bed."

"Are you drunk?"

"No." I giggled. "Yes!"

With his eyes on mine, Henry closed his laptop and switched off the lamp, plunging us into a darkness broken only by the lights of the city outside. He came around the desk and stopped in front of me. My heart still raced every time I saw him. It was outrageous how good he looked after an absurdly long day of work. His hair was tousled from running his fingers through it, and he had taken off his tie and undone the top buttons of his shirt. I would love to undo the rest of them . . .

47

Ethan Darlington Kicked Out of Club! Drunk Heir and His Date Cause a Stir on the Dance Floor.

INsider headline

Henry

Kate's eyes were glassy and her cheeks flushed from the alcohol. She looked adorable. The distinctive smell of pub clung to her, reminding me of my wilder years. She gazed at me, eyes brimming with desire, even though she was struggling to focus. It was clear that nothing would happen between us tonight, even if the glow on her face did things to me I was better off not thinking about.

"Let's go," I said.

I still had a lot to get done, but it was late, and the thought of bringing Kate to bed was a lot more appealing than dealing with plans for the marketing budget. I wrapped an arm around her waist to support her, and we left my office together. I typed in a code to lock the door, and we headed to the lifts, Kate pressing herself close to me as we walked. When my stomach knotted, it was out of affection rather than desire—it meant so much to me to see how Kate trusted me, even in this vulnerable state.

"How was it with Rose and Grace?" I asked to keep her awake.

"It was nice," Kate said, slurring slightly. She grinned. "We drank shots. Just me and Grace. Rose wasn't there. I've never had shots! They burn in your throat."

I smiled, wishing I'd been there with her. Not to stop her from drinking, but to drink with her, to have fun with her, to celebrate. "Where was Rose?"

"She went home with some guy."

I pressed the call button for the lift. It took a moment to arrive. The shiny metal doors swished open. I scanned my ID card and pressed the button for the private floor. The lift sprung into action with a barely perceptible jolt, but it was enough to drain the colour from Kate's face. She pressed her lips together and clung fiercely to me. I drew her in closer, supporting her as she struggled to keep her balance.

A quiet *ding* signalled that we'd reached the top floor. It was completely silent. I led Kate down the corridor to my penthouse. A look of amazement flitted across her face, just as it had when I'd brought her here for the first time. Back then, I had wondered whether it was the right decision to bring her to my apartment instead of putting her in one of the empty hotel rooms. Today, I knew it had been one of the best decisions of my life. If I hadn't done so, we probably never would have grown so close.

"I still can't believe you really live here," Kate said incredulously, looking around my apartment in amazement, even though she had been here many times before. We spent most nights in her room, but today I wanted her to sleep in my bed. I led her through the apartment to my bedroom and manoeuvred her onto the bed. She looked up at me with her big brown eyes, wrapped her arms around my waist, and hugged my torso. Her face was far too close to where I had often wished it to be.

"I missed you today," she murmured into my thigh.

I stroked her hair. "I missed you too."

Her lips curled into a smile. "Really?"

"Really," I affirmed, and ran my fingers along her jaw.

She sighed and pressed her cheek against my hip. A jolt shot through me, and blood rushed down my body. I couldn't help it: I grew hard. I hoped Kate wouldn't notice in her tipsy state, but when she looked up at me again, I was pretty sure she had clocked the bulge in my trousers. Her eyes scanned my face and landed, with surprising precision, on my lips.

"Henry?" she whispered.

"Yes?" I whispered back.

She smiled. "Kiss me."

I leaned down and pressed my lips against hers but didn't let myself deepen the kiss, instead fleetingly savouring the taste of her lips. Kate made a frustrated sound and gazed at me with an intensity I hadn't thought possible in her state. Her cheeks were flushed and her mouth glistened.

"Kiss me properly!"

She looked so enchanting—and her expression was so hopeful—that I couldn't deny her request. I kissed her again, this time deeper and more fervently. She gave a satisfied sigh and threaded her fingers through my hair. I shivered as her fingernails raked my scalp. Kate pulled me down onto the mattress to lie on top of her with surprising strength. Propping myself up with my hands on either side of her body, I ran my tongue over her lips, tasting the alcohol on them. I felt drunk, although I hadn't had a drop to drink. Kate wrapped a leg around my hips, pulling me closer until my pelvis pressed against hers. My erection pushed at her, hot and eager. I gave a throaty growl, and my dick twitched with eager anticipation.

"We have to stop," I murmured against her mouth.

Kate made a protesting sound. "Why?"

It was a good question; the same one my body was asking. My blood simmered, and I wanted nothing more than to lose myself in Kate. "Because you're drunk."

"But I want you to kiss me. All over."

Fuuuuuuck.

I swallowed hard. My throat was suddenly dry at the thought of exploring every delicious centimetre of Kate's body with my lips. I wanted to know how she tasted when I made her orgasm with my tongue. My desire to do so had been building for weeks, but every time I tried to take our kisses further, Kate had hesitated. She clearly wasn't ready, and I would respect that, no matter how hard it was.

"I will kiss you everywhere, but not today. OK?" My voice was rough.

Hers, on the other hand, was soft. "Shame."

Impressed by my own restraint, I pulled back and sat up. Kate remained sprawled across the bed. I didn't want her to sleep in the clothes she'd been wearing—but instead of encouraging her to undress herself, my masochistic side decided to take on the task. I unzipped her leather jacket and slid it off her shoulders. Despite the cold, Kate was wearing only a thin jumper. I made a mental note to get her warmer clothes for the winter. I knelt down and removed her shoes, then her jeans, averting my eyes from her underwear. My self-control was hanging on by a fine thread, and I decided not to take off her jumper—it was clear from the way her hardened nipples pressed against the thin fabric that she wasn't wearing a bra.

I lifted the duvet. "In you go."

Kate obeyed and crawled under it. "Are you coming?"

"In a minute," I promised, and she sank deep into the pillow.

I switched on the lamp on my bedside table and turned off the overhead light before pulling shorts and a T-shirt out of my walk-in wardrobe. I headed to the bathroom. I was still rock-hard, but I couldn't take advantage of Kate in her current state. Which meant I had to take care of it myself. After getting myself off in the shower, I got dressed, brushed my teeth, and returned to the bedroom.

Kate had rolled onto her side, and her eyes were closed. I joined her under the duvet and turned off the light, despite not being at all tired. Exhausted? Yes. Tired? No. My body was still thrumming. I rolled towards Kate. She opened her eyes and looked at me sleepily. My heart pounded as her lips curled into a faint smile, as if she were happy that I was there.

I moved closer, draping an arm around her waist. A strange, warm feeling flooded my chest, spreading through my body and relaxing my tense muscles. My heart, which had been racing just moments ago, steadied. All because of Kate. Without any effort at all, she managed to stop my chaotic world from spinning.

"Henry?" Kate asked, her eyes already closed again.

"Yes?"

"I like you."

"I like you too."

"Yes, but I like you the most," she mumbled tiredly, and then she was asleep, her breaths deep and even.

I smiled and kissed her forehead—gently, not wanting to wake her.

48

Oh my god! Have you seen the interview yet? How are you? More importantly, how's Kate? He's such an arsehole!

Message from Olivia to Henry

Kate

My head buzzed as if an entire swarm of bees had taken up residence in it. What had I been thinking, drinking so much? The beer, the cocktail, the shots—they'd felt like harmless fun last night. Today, though, the effect of the alcohol was anything but harmless—it was painful. Groaning, I turned in the big bed. The sheets smelled of Henry, but he was no longer there. I usually woke up when he did, but the alcohol seemed to have knocked me out completely. I wondered if Grace also felt this bad.

I opened my eyes, grateful for the blinds that blocked out the daylight, and scanned Henry's bedroom. I spotted my phone on the bedside table, next to a bottle of water and a small box with a Post-it note attached. I switched on the lamp, enraging the swarm of bees in my head. Peeling the Post-it note off the box, I saw that it was a packet of painkillers. The note was from Henry. After several attempts, I finally managed to decipher the scrawl of his barely legible handwriting.

Good morning, angel.

I'm sorry I had to go to the office. The tablets should help with the headaches. And drink the water (the whole bottle!!).

Henry

PS: I like you the most too.
PPS: I'm looking forward to kissing you all over.

I felt suddenly hot. A memory of the previous night washed over me—how I had gone to Henry's office and practically ordered him to take me to bed. He had looked after me, and I'd demanded he explore my body with his lips before confessing how much I liked him.

I took two tablets from the packet and drank the entire bottle of water, just as Henry had instructed. I soon felt better, and the swarm of bees in my head gradually disappeared. My mind clearer, I reached for my phone to thank him, only to find the battery dead—it must have run out overnight. I stayed in bed a little longer before forcing myself to get up and find my clothes. They smelled unpleasantly of the pub, but I slipped them on anyway.

I left Henry's apartment and hurried to the lift, hoping to avoid encountering anyone, but my plan was foiled—I ran straight into Ethan. His bloodshot eyes, crumpled clothes, and the vivid love-bite on his neck made me think he was just getting home from a long night of partying. His eyes met mine, and his lips twisted into a grim smile.

"Hey," I said, my voice still rough.

Ethan's eyes flashed. "Hey, *Kate*."

There was something strange about the way he said my name, as if there were a hidden meaning I was supposed to catch. Maybe I was imagining it. Or maybe he was still drunk and it was an effort to speak, just as it had been for me the night before. A little unsettled by our odd encounter, I sidestepped him and headed for the lifts.

When the lift stopped at the third floor and a room attendant stepped in, I realised something wasn't quite right. Her eyes widened at the sight of me, and she muttered a quick, "Good morning," avoiding my gaze as the lift descended.

With an uneasy feeling in the pit of my stomach—one that had nothing to do with last night's alcohol—I stepped out at the first floor. In the corridor, I passed two guests who reacted to me just as strangely, eyes widening before they quickly looked away, as if the sight of me was unbearable.

"Is that her?" the woman asked as they passed.

"I think so," the man replied.

The hairs on my arms stood on end. What was going on? I quickened my pace, hurrying to the safety of my room. I was determined to figure out what was happening. Once inside, I rushed to the bedside table and plugged in my phone. Tapping my foot impatiently, I waited for it to charge enough to turn on. After what felt like an eternity, the display lit up. I had several missed calls and messages from Grace.

My heart did a somersault. What was Grace talking about?

ME:

What's happened?

GRACE:

Finally! Have you seen it?

ME:

What?

Grace sent me a link—a dreaded *INsider* URL. My stomach clenched. It could only mean that yet another sensational headline about Henry was making the rounds. I clicked on the link, but instead of an article, a video loaded. I froze, and an icy chill spread through me. It wasn't about Henry—it was about me. The thumbnail alone confirmed I was about to see something terrible: It showed the one person I had hoped never to see again—Randell Barker. The headline read,

The Truth About Henry Darlington's New Girlfriend!

"No, no, no, no . . ." I murmured. This couldn't be happening. I leapt from my bed, too panicked to sit still. As I paced the room, I tried to summon the courage to play the video. I didn't want to hear whatever "truth" Randell had told about me, but I had to know. There was no way around it.

I took a deep breath and pressed play.

"Hello, Randell. It's great to have you here with us today," William Hunt said.

"It's good to be here," Randell replied.

The two men sat opposite each other on a studio set. The makeup team had done a remarkable job on Randell—he looked considerably less greasy and, as a result, healthier than usual. His white shirt lent him an air of trustworthiness. When he smiled at the camera, though, I saw that they hadn't been able to fix his teeth—they were crooked, and yellowed from years of heavy smoking.

"Would you like to briefly introduce yourself to our audience?" William asked with a greedy keenness.

"I'm Randell Barker. Forty and single."

William chuckled. "I'm sure the ladies will appreciate that bit of information, but you're not here to make new friends, are you?"

"No, I'm here to talk about Kaitlynn Hamilton. The young woman who's been seen a lot with Henry Darlington recently. There are a few things about Kate that I think people should know."

I couldn't take any more. I stopped the video and took a deep breath. My lungs felt tight, as if something were sitting on my chest. This couldn't be happening. How the hell had Randell made it into William Hunt's studio?

The answer was as obvious as it was simple: money. Henry and I hadn't given him any, so now he was trying to profit off me in another way—by talking to the press. Bastard. I wanted nothing more than to throw my phone against the wall, but the interview was still out there, whether I watched it or not. It was better to know exactly what I was up against.

I pressed play again.

"Kaitlynn Hamilton. Finally! A name to the face!" said William, and photos of me and Henry appeared on the screen behind the two men—and not just those from McDonald's and the masked ball. There were new ones. One showed me at the pub with Grace and Rose, and the other had been taken outside Better Days. With my damp hair, sodden clothes, and mud-streaked jeans, I looked terrible—completely dishevelled and unkempt. "So," William began, "who is this Kate who has managed to wrap Henry Darlington around her little finger?"

"Above all else, she's a dirty whore," Randell said.

His last word had been bleeped out, but I had no trouble filling in the gap. My entire body was gripped by an icy chill. I desperately wanted to stop the video again, but I forced myself to be strong and listen to what else Randell had to say about me.

William gave an exaggerated laugh, as if the answer had taken him by surprise. "What?"

Randell grinned arrogantly, revelling in the attention. "You heard me right, William. Kate is a *****. She ***** men for money. At least, that's what she did before Henry became her sugar daddy."

"Unbelievable," William said, his eyes gleaming with excitement. He was clearly thrilled to have landed such a sensational interview.

Randell nodded. "You're right, it's unbelievable. And that's just the beginning. Kate's mother and I were together for a while. She didn't have enough money to support herself and Kate, so I stepped in and let them both live with me. Becca died of an overdose a year ago. I kept trying to help her get sober, but she wasn't interested."

A burning rage coursed through me. Randell wasn't just an asshole; he was a liar!

"Is Kate an addict too?" William probed.

Randell sighed, as if my well-being actually mattered to him. "I don't know, to be honest. I haven't spoken to her for a long time, but it's entirely possible. After her mother's death, she totally lost it. She moved out, even though she had no money and no job. She spent the last year living on the streets. I already told you how she got by." Randell made an obscene gesture to clarify.

"Wow." William exhaled heavily. "You just made some pretty shocking claims. So Henry Darlington is involved with a homeless prostitute who's after his money. Imagine that. How do you think they met?"

Randell raised his eyebrows. "Isn't it obvious?"

"Right, right," William replied, his tone heavy with feigned regret. "What else should people know about Kate?"

Randell pretended to think for a moment. He probably had a list in his trouser pocket, itemising the terrible things he wanted to say about me. "Kate dropped out of school when she was sixteen and started stealing. She was arrested multiple times, but nothing ever came of it. But apparently, theft eventually stopped being lucrative enough for her."

"So Kate isn't just a hooker—she's also a thief?"

"Yes. That girl is nothing but trouble."

William nodded. "Good to know. Thank you for your insights, Randell."

Randell smirked smugly. "You're welcome, William. I thought it was important for people to hear that, so they know what kind of person Kate Hamilton really is—a kleptomaniac ***** who should be handled with caution. Hide your money and your men."

The video stopped.

The interview was over.

I was done for.

49

> I just watched the Hunt interview. This shit is wild. The Darlingtons need their own reality TV show. #KeepingUpWithTheDarlingtons

Online comment by CoffeeAddict22

Kate

This couldn't be happening. It *couldn't*.

And yet, it had. My fingers clenched around my phone, and I fought back tears. I stood frozen in place, a storm of anger, fear, and despair raging within me. Had Henry already seen the interview? Surely. Everyone seemed to have seen it. It explained Ethan's grim smile and the stunned looks of the others. They had all heard what Randell had said about me—that I was a kleptomaniac sex worker with a possible drug problem who was just using Henry for his money.

Henry . . .

I had to go to him, but I couldn't move. I was paralysed and couldn't think clearly. It felt like someone was crushing my chest. No, not *someone*—Randell. I played the interview again, hoping that it would be less terrible the second time, but it was just as cruel. The last few seconds were interrupted by an incoming call. Grace.

I accepted the call but didn't speak.

"Oh my god, Kate!" She sounded relieved. "Did you watch it?"

"Yes," I answered. Was that my voice? I sounded cool and distant, as if the small world I had built with Henry's help over the past few weeks wasn't falling apart. He had asked me not to talk about my life, because he had anticipated the uproar it would cause. But now Randell had revealed it all—in the worst way possible, in a story filled with lies. Yet it was less my own reputation that I was worried about, and more Henry's and The Darlington's.

"How are you?" Grace asked cautiously.

"I don't know," I answered. I felt everything and nothing.

The line was silent for a moment, and I could practically hear Grace's unspoken questions. My stomach was tied in a nervous knot that grew tighter by the second.

She cleared her throat. "Who is this Randell guy?"

"He's my mum's ex-boyfriend."

"So that part was true?"

"Yes."

"What about the rest? The stuff about the sex and drugs?" Grace pressed. She didn't sound accusatory, just curious—and perhaps a little disappointed that I had kept it from her. I understood that. I would explain everything, but not now. First, I had to get to Henry and find out the extent of the damage Randell's interview had caused.

"Can we talk about this later?" I asked, already half out of the door. "I really have to talk to Henry."

"OK. Call me if you need anything."

"I will. Thank you, Grace."

We hung up, and I made my way to Henry's office. My heart was racing, and I felt like I might throw up. I took the stairs down and marched purposefully towards his door. My gaze fixed straight ahead, I ignored the people I passed in the corridor, even though their twisted mouths and disgusted expressions made it difficult.

My steps slowed the closer I got to Henry's closed office door. I could hear angry voices shouting from inside.

I didn't even have to make an effort to eavesdrop.

"I don't want to issue a fucking statement," Henry yelled. "I want us to file an injunction. Right now!"

"You can't afford to be associated with theft, prostitution, and drugs. It would be the end of The Darlington," a more measured voice reprimanded. "You have to distance yourself from that woman."

"The only thing I have to do is silence that son of a bitch."

"What good will that do? He's already said everything."

"You're the crisis manager, Vivian. You know how these things go. Tomorrow at the latest, that prick will be on some talk show mouthing off about Kate again. I won't let it happen. Either you support me, or you get out of my office."

"Henry!" snapped a man. It was unmistakably his father. "Could you stop worrying about that whore for one second? We have bigger—"

"What did you say?" Henry interrupted.

"You heard what I said."

Silence fell—a dangerous silence. A moment later, it was broken by the sound of footsteps, followed by Henry's voice. This time, he spoke more quietly, but his words were no less scathing—perhaps even more so. "Never call Kate a whore again."

"Or what?" Richard challenged.

"You'll see."

"Was that a threat?"

"No," Henry growled. "A promise."

"Hey!"

I flinched in shock when someone suddenly appeared next to me. I turned and found myself looking into Giulia's dark-brown eyes. I hadn't heard her coming—probably because I'd been too absorbed in the conversation on the other side of the door. She didn't seem to be judging me for eavesdropping. Her expression was soft and understanding, without a hint of disgust.

"You shouldn't go in there," she said.

"But Henry . . ."

"Can manage alone," Giulia reassured me gently before I could finish my sentence. "If you go in there now, you'll only be fanning the flames. And then Henry might really lose his temper. I've never seen him like this before."

Worried, my eyes darted to the door. The angry voices continued, doing nothing to ease the knot in my stomach. If anything, they tightened it.

Giulia placed a hand on my shoulder. It was a warm, consoling gesture that brought me close to tears. "Come on. You can wait for him in my office. They're so loud that you'll still be able to hear from there. And I have tea. You look like you could use a cup."

I nodded and followed Giulia, but my uneasy thoughts stayed with Henry.

Is it true that your brother's girlfriend is a hooker?!

Message from Charles Eddington to Ethan

Henry

"Was that a threat?" my dad asked.

I twisted my lips into a grim smile. "No. A promise."

We stood face-to-face in my office, neither of us backing down. The air between us was electric. It took every last bit of my willpower to not punch my dad in the face. He seemed to be practically begging me to do it, but I wouldn't stoop to his level. Besides, it wasn't really his face that I wanted to smash—it was Randell's. There weren't many things in life I truly regretted, but not calling the police that day at the cemetery was one of them.

"Calm down," Vivian said, pacing nervously. She had burst into my office unannounced this morning, interrupting a phone call to show me the interview. "This bickering isn't getting us anywhere."

"What do you suggest, Viv?" my dad asked.

Viv? I raised my eyebrows. That was new.

"That we all take a deep breath." She inhaled demonstratively.

I followed her lead and stepped back from my dad, though I kept my eyes fixed on him. He didn't have to love Kate, but in my presence, he had to respect her.

"Why didn't you tell me she's a prostitute?" Vivian asked once everyone had calmed down a little. She had stopped pacing and was scrutinising me reproachfully. "It's my job to keep these kinds of scandalous details out of the public eye. But I can only do my job if you talk to me."

I clenched my teeth. "Kate isn't a sex worker."

Vivian's eyebrows shot up. "So this Randell guy was lying?"

"Partially."

"What's that supposed to mean?" my dad growled. "That she's only half a whore?"

"Richard!" Vivian warned sharply, and for the first time, I thought I might actually like her. She sighed in frustration and rubbed her forehead, as if plagued by the same pounding headache I was. "Tell me how things started between you and Kate, so I know what I'm dealing with."

I had little desire to analyse my love life with Vivian and my dad, but I also didn't want to start another fight. I just wished they could see Kate through my eyes and not through Randell's lecherous perspective. "We met in St. James's Park. She was homeless at the time. I wanted to help her, so we went to get something to eat," I said. I left out the bit about the stolen phone. It wasn't important, and it would only give my dad even more reason to dislike Kate. "We got on really well. I liked her from the beginning, but after that meal, we went our separate ways—until that bad storm."

Vivian nodded, as if she remembered it.

"I couldn't bear the thought of her being alone out there, and I was afraid something would happen to her, so I went to the park and brought her back here. It wasn't my plan for her to stay at the hotel long-term. But we talked, and after everything she said, I couldn't, in good conscience, send her back onto the streets. So I gave her a room and a job."

"Did you pay her for sex?" my dad asked, his nose wrinkling in disdain.

I almost laughed. How could it be that the concept of sex work disgusted him more than the idea of forcing himself on a woman? If he had only chosen to go to a sex worker back then instead, we'd have far fewer problems today.

I walked over to the drinks cart. Though it was still early, I poured myself two fingers of whisky. "Like I just said, Kate isn't a sex worker. She used to pick pockets—that part is true. But she doesn't steal anymore, not since she started working for The Darlington." I sat down at my desk, wanting to create a barrier between my dad and me, and undid the top button of my jacket. "Regardless, I like Kate, and I'm not going to abandon her. So save your breath."

Vivian sighed again, this time with resignation. "Henry, I don't know Kate, and I'm sure she's a wonderful woman, but this isn't the best time for this kind of drama. You should really think about whether she's worth all this."

"She is. A hundred times over," I replied without hesitating.

My dad shook his head in disbelief and started pacing the room, just as Vivian had done earlier. "Are you aware that you're putting the hotel, our reputation, and your own future on the line for sex?"

I took a sip of my whisky, and it burnt my throat like fire. "No, Dad. *You* put those things on the line for sex. Nonconsensual sex, to be precise. I'm putting them on the line for love."

My dad swore.

Vivian's eyes widened. "You love her?"

"Maybe," I admitted. Kate was the first woman in a very long time who had made me even consider the word.

"All the more reason to let her go," my dad retorted. "Do you have any idea what you're doing to that girl? She was anonymous. A nobody. And now she's being dragged through the mud for the whole world to see. Because of you."

"That's why I want the injunction."

"I'll handle it," Vivian said to my surprise, a newfound determination in her voice. "It'll probably take a few days, but I've got good contacts at the *INsider*. I might be able to convince them to take Randell's interview offline, but it's going to be expensive."

Finally, a good suggestion. I nodded. "I don't care how much it is. I'll pay."

She nodded. "OK. I'll get to work."

"Thank you, Vivian," I said. And I meant it.

She smiled and left my office, her phone already in her hand. My dad stayed and stood in front of my desk with his hands shoved into his trouser pockets. He stared at me as if he could change my mind through the sheer power of his authoritative presence. It might work on others, but he couldn't intimidate me anymore. As a child, I had respected him, finding him imposing in his expensive suit. Today, that respect was long gone.

I met his gaze defiantly and raised a weary eyebrow. "Is there anything else you want to say?"

"It was a mistake to let you run The Darlington. I should have trusted my gut feeling instead of letting Vivian and the others talk me into it. I knew you weren't ready for it."

I stared at him incredulously. "Are you saying it's my fault that the hotel is doing badly?"

His nostrils flared. "Who else's fault would it be? I trusted you with The Darlington, and you've run it into the ground in just a couple of months. We'll have to close at the end of next year if you don't get your act together."

He had to be joking. "If *I* don't get my act together?"

"You're not at university anymore, Henry. This isn't a game, or some project for one of your classes. This is your life. Your legacy. And you should take that seriously instead of wasting your time with some homeless woman who's beneath you."

"You can't be serious."

"Of course I'm serious. Do you see me laughing?" my dad demanded. It would be more fitting if his blue eyes were black, like his soul—there was no understanding or kindness in them, only pure contempt. They fixed themselves on me icily. "You're gallivanting around with that woman while the hotel goes under, letting her take advantage of you at every turn. You're just a means to an end to her—a way to get money."

My hands clenched into fists. "No, Dad. *You're* the one using *me*. You're taking advantage of my passion, expertise, and love for this hotel to fix what you screwed up. And what do I get in return? Nothing! Absolutely nothing. Not even a thank-you. Only criticism and accusations, because the world refuses to buy your lies."

My dad tensed his jaw, and the vein on his forehead bulged like a third eye glaring at me. "Watch your mouth."

"I'm just speaking the truth. The Darlington wouldn't be in this mess if you'd kept your dick in your pants. Or at least had the decency to only sleep with women who wanted you, instead of forcing yourself on ones who didn't—like the perverted old man you are. How you can look at yourself in the mirror every morning knowing what you've done is beyond me."

"You can't talk to me like that!" my dad snapped, spit flying through the air.

I grimaced in disgust and rose smoothly from my chair. Planting my hands on my desk, I fixed my dad with a glare. "I can, and I just did. I'm so sick of acting like you're not the biggest pile of shit around here. Kate just did what she had to do to survive. You, on the other hand, did what you'd always wanted to do, with no regard for the consequences or for anyone else. I'm done keeping quiet about it," I said resolutely, my frustration ringing in my ears. "I won't let you and Mum sabotage my relationship with Kate. So either you get your act together and have my back, or you get lost and stop wasting my time. I have work to do."

I adjusted my jacket demonstratively, sat back down, and opened my laptop. I felt the intensity of my dad's glare but ignored it, knowing how much it would infuriate him. Several seconds passed before he turned to leave. His footsteps receded, only to stop once more.

"I hope you don't end up regretting this," he said, then shut the door behind him.

I exhaled loudly, leaned back in my chair, and closed my laptop again—opening it had just been a ploy to get him to leave. Ever since Vivian had stormed into my office this morning, I hadn't had a single moment alone to gather my thoughts—most of them about Kate. Had she already seen the interview? Or was she still sleeping? She had been in bed when I'd left for the office. Part of me wished I could keep the interview from her. She shouldn't have to hear what Randell was saying about her, even if it was untrue. He wasn't talking about the real Kate, but a version of her that she had been forced to become—both by life and by Randell himself, leaving her with no choice. It wasn't fair to throw that in her face now.

I speed-dialled Rakesh. The poor guy had just as little time off as I did these days. He answered after the first ring, as if he'd been waiting for my call.

"Hi, Henry. What can I do for you?" He sounded tense.

"I assume you've seen the interview."

"Yes."

"Do you know what it means?"

"More paparazzi."

"More paparazzi," I echoed. "Hire more security. I want every entrance monitored around the clock. No more press entering the hotel unauthorised. And make sure that our guests can come and go without being harassed. Make our chauffeur service available to them free of charge for the next few days."

I could hear the faint sound of Rakesh taking notes. "Will do."

"Thanks. That's all for now."

Rakesh said goodbye, and I ended the call.

My head was spinning, and although I'd slept well—as I always did with Kate beside me—I was exhausted. Not just from this morning, but from the past few months, which had completely shattered my nerves. I had no idea how to piece them back together, but now was not the time to dwell on that.

I reached into my pocket and pulled out the little box. I washed down a pill with the remaining whisky in my glass. Just then, my phone vibrated—a message from Giulia.

Kate was in her office.

British High Society in Shock! Scandalous Criminal Past of Henry Darlington's New Girlfriend Revealed!

INsider headline

Kate

The door to Giulia's office flew open, and Henry burst in, looking anxious and frazzled. The buttons on his jacket were undone, and his hair was dishevelled from raking his fingers through it. His eyes darted restlessly around the room until they landed on me. His entire body seemed to relax instantly. I attempted a smile.

I sat on a small sofa in the corner of the room holding a cup of tea, though I hadn't taken a single sip—I had been too preoccupied with eavesdropping on the conversation taking place across the corridor. The voices had eventually become too faint to hear, and after that, I had been too consumed by my worries. I still couldn't believe that Randell had gone to the *INsider* to sell them my life story.

"Giulia, can you give us a moment alone?" Henry asked.

She nodded and left the office.

Henry locked the door behind her and strode towards me. I felt like we had grown closer since I had told him about my past. Everything had been perfect—perhaps too perfect—but now this dark shadow loomed over us. The same dark shadow that had been responsible for my mum's death. I couldn't bear the thought of losing Henry to Randell as well.

"I'm sorry," I said quietly.

"Kate . . ." He said gently, sitting down so close to me on the sofa that his leg pressed against mine. He took my cup and put it aside—probably for the best, as my hands were shaking, and I was at risk of spilling tea onto his expensive suit. "You have nothing to apologise for. It was Randell who gave that interview, not you."

"But it's my fucked-up life that's now affecting you."

"Don't say that."

"Why not? I heard you arguing with your dad and Vivian."

"I argue with them all the time."

I felt tears well up in my eyes, but I didn't want to cry. There was just as much at stake for Henry as there was for me, if not more. At worst, I would lose him, whereas he would lose his life as he knew it. "But they were right, this time. The Darlington can't be associated with my past. You asked me yourself not to tell anyone, because you knew it would damage the hotel."

Henry looked at me, his pupils dilated—presumably from the adrenaline still coursing through him. "I asked you to do that because I didn't want you to get dragged into this mess my dad made. For me, it was always about protecting you, so please, let's not fight about whether or not the interview is your fault. It happened. We can't change that. All we can do now is come up with a strategy to contain the damage."

I nodded. Since overhearing Henry's argument with Vivian and his dad, all I could think about was how the last thing I wanted was to hurt The Darlington. If it hadn't been for the bad press elicited by Henry's dad, Randell's interview alone probably wouldn't have damaged the hotel's reputation. But under the circumstances, my past was another blow of a hammer to an already cracked pane of glass.

"You could release the statement Vivian asked you to," I said, even though doing so revealed that I had been able to make out some of their conversation. "Distance yourself from me. Tell everyone that you didn't know those things about me and that you can't be with me anymore because of them."

"No way!"

"I wouldn't mind."

Irritation flashed in his eyes. "But I would."

"It would just be for the press."

Henry's irritation turned to anger. He glared at me as if he couldn't believe I would suggest such a thing. "It's out of the question! We'll get through this together. I don't want to lose you."

My heart clenched. "You wouldn't lose me, Snowflake. It would be a white lie, just until everything has calmed down and the hotel has recovered."

"How do you envision that working?" Henry asked, still agitated. "If I were to make that statement, we couldn't be seen together. No one could know about us. If it came out that we were still seeing each other, it would start all over again, and it might be even worse because we lied. I won't hide you away for years and treat you like some dirty secret, Kate. You mean too much to me for that."

"Henry—"

"Your past won't just disappear," he said, cutting me off. "We have to face it—together. As long as you want that."

My heart wanted to shout from the rooftops that it was exactly what I wanted. We hadn't known each other for long, but I could no longer imagine life without Henry. But this wasn't just about what I wanted. This was so much bigger than us. For the first time since we'd met, I wished that Henry wasn't a Darlington, but some poor nobody. Then we could be together without the constant scrutiny of the press. I didn't need a luxurious room, fancy events, or more money than I knew what to do with. I only needed Henry. But it wasn't that simple.

"Can I ask you something?"

He nodded.

"But you have to promise you'll be honest with me—and more importantly, with yourself," I said. He held my gaze, and I interpreted his expectant silence as agreement. "Do you really think we have a future together?"

Henry pulled away from me—it felt terrible. He furrowed his brow as he looked at me, as if that was the last thing he had expected to hear. "Don't you?"

"Honestly? I don't know," I admitted. My voice was heavy with sadness, and I felt a sharp pang in my chest. "You're important to me, Henry. And there's no one I would rather have been with over the past few months. But you have to admit that we come from very different worlds, and I will never belong in yours. I'll always be the outsider. Your parents—and the people they surround themselves with—will never fully accept me."

"I'm not interested in what those people think."

"*Those people* are a big part of your life."

"They're not," Henry countered gently. "Most of the time, I never think about them. Whereas you've been on my mind constantly. So don't think they're better than you. You're far more important."

They were the most beautiful words spoken in the ugliest moment. I reached out and stroked Henry's cheek, his stubble tickling me as he kissed the palm of my hand. A shiver ran down my spine. "I just don't want you to look back on today a few months from now and wish you had made a different decision. What if you lose the hotel because of me? What if I'm the straw that breaks the camel's back?"

Henry shook his head. "I don't care about the hotel."

"That's not true, and you know it."

"OK, I do care about the hotel. But I care about you too. A lot. You matter to me, Kate," Henry said. His irritation and anger had vanished, and in his eyes, I now saw nothing but affection. "You matter so much. And I don't want to have to choose between you and The Darlington just because my dad screwed up. I want you in my life, and I'm prepared to fight for you. Are you prepared to fight?"

I saw the fear flicker in Henry's eyes. But it wasn't fear of what people might think, or what the press might report. It wasn't even fear for the hotel. He was afraid of losing me. And there was no way I would let that fear become reality, because he was just as important to me.

Henry suddenly felt too far away, even though he was sitting right next to me. I got onto his lap. He looked surprised—and then I leaned in to kiss him. The kiss was gentle and loving, passionate and deep. It was everything—and so much more. He wrapped his arms around me, and I melted into his embrace, holding him as tightly as I could. I never wanted to let him go. He had been there for me ever since we met, giving me a chance when no one else had believed in me. And in return, he had asked for nothing—which was probably why I wanted to give him everything.

"I'm ready to fight for it too," I murmured against his mouth. With the next kiss, I felt his smile on my lips. It warmed me from within and gave me hope. I was confident now that Randell wouldn't succeed in ruining my life again. I wouldn't let him. And this time, I wouldn't have to face him alone. I had Henry by my side.

> How are you? Let me know if I
> can do anything for you.
> Are we still on for our coffee date?

Message from Olivia to Kate

Kate

Once upon a time, I ran for fun.

Later, I ran to survive.

Today, I ran to forget.

I didn't want to think about how Randell had dragged my past into the public eye like a corpse—one that was now being eviscerated and dissected by the media. It seemed like all of England was talking about the homeless whore who had snapped up one of the most esteemed bachelors of British high society. Thanks to Vivian and a sum of money—the enormity of which I didn't want to think about—the video of Randell's interview was no longer online. Henry had paid for it to be removed, but the damage was already done. Every media outlet had picked up the story and run with it, and had started to dig deeper. They'd found old tourist photos from St. James's Park in which I was visible in the background.

And men who claimed to have been my clients shared their alleged experiences with me, all of them just looking for their five seconds of fame. It was creepy and terrifying. People kept making up more stories, because the worse I looked, the more scandalous and provocative my relationship with Henry seemed—and the more clicks the articles generated. There were now hundreds of them online.

"When can we stop?" Grace groaned on the treadmill next to me. We were at The Darlington's gym, which was technically only for hotel guests, but Henry had given me permission to use it as well. I had been working out a lot since the interview last week. I needed something to distract me from the chaos.

I looked at Grace. A strand of blond hair had already escaped her ponytail. Sweat glistened on her forehead, and her cheeks were flushed. "You can stop anytime you want."

"I want to do this in solidarity with you."

I had been grateful for our friendship before, but in the past few days, the feeling had multiplied. After my conversation with Henry, I had called Grace as I'd promised. I had answered all her questions and dispelled the lies Randell had spread in his interview. I had also told her the truth about how Henry and I had met. Instead of responding with anger or disappointment, she had shown nothing but understanding and support.

"You can be supportive while sitting down."

"Thank god!" Grace stopped the treadmill and dragged herself over to the bench where we had left our water bottles and towels. She took a sip of water and wiped her face. I could feel the sweat running down my back, but I wasn't ready to stop.

"Will Giulia let you start working again next week?" Grace asked.

"I hope so."

I had been determined to carry on as usual after the initial shock of the interview, but it quickly became clear that it was impossible. Before, the hotel guests had mostly ignored me and let me do my job. But now, they stared at me and asked inappropriate questions, to the point where Giulia had temporarily taken me off the work roster. My job interview had also fallen through. The owner of the corner shop had called yesterday to cancel because he didn't want *someone like me* working at the till. I had tried to explain, but he hadn't wanted to hear it.

"Maybe you can do something behind the scenes."

"Maybe. I'll talk to her." I smiled at Grace. "How's Amy doing?" I asked, hoping to distract myself from my own life.

Grace sighed. "Not very well. She spent half the night crying."

"Why?"

"Because of that loser Garrett, of course," Grace hissed, and aggressively screwed the lid onto her water bottle. "They had planned to go on a date yesterday, and five minutes before he was supposed to pick her up, he cancelled. He said he was tired and needed an evening to himself—again. But a few hours later, he was at a party. One of his friends tagged him in a photo, and naturally, Amy saw it."

"Shit. And then?"

"Nothing. She cried, as always. I offered to go to the party with her and confront him, but she didn't want that." Rage radiated from her. "That guy is the worst. Amy deserves someone better, and I'm not just saying that because she's my twin. She's the kindest person I know, and Garrett is a selfish bastard."

"Why does Amy put up with it?"

"I don't know. Garrett is her first boyfriend. It's probably a combination of denial, false hope, and low self-esteem."

"Bad combination."

"The worst," Grace replied with a sad smile, which turned into a disgusted grimace, as if she'd smelled something bad. "What is *he* doing here?"

"Who?" I glanced around to see Ethan. I hadn't seen him since our encounter in the corridor, when he'd smiled at me grimly. He wore black shorts and a dark T-shirt and had a heart rate monitor on his upper arm. "He probably wants to work out."

"But why here?" Grace groaned. "He has a gym in his apartment."

Until now, I'd been as invisible to Ethan as I was to the hotel guests, but now he noticed me. Our eyes met, and then, to my surprise, he approached me. I doubted I would ever get used to how similar Henry and Ethan looked. "Hey."

"Hi," I replied.

Behind me, Grace gave an irritated sigh, which caught Ethan's attention. He peered past me to look at her. "Hey," he greeted her.

"Go to hell," she growled.

"That's not very nice."

She snorted. "*You're* not very nice."

"How would you know? We don't know each other."

"Oh, we know each other!"

Ethan tilted his head, giving Grace a slow once-over. "Are you sure? I don't remember you."

Grace gasped in disbelief, her face flushing even redder than when she'd been running. "Yeah, arsehole. We know each other. I'm the one who's been cleaning up after you for months, because you aren't capable of doing it yourself with your delicate man-hands."

Ethan slapped the palm of his hand against his forehead, as if he'd had a revelation. "Oh, it's you, Claymore. Sorry. I didn't recognise you without a bin bag in your hand." He flashed her a grin that made it very clear he knew exactly who she was and was just trying to get under her skin. When Grace realised, she pressed her lips together and gave Ethan a look that could have killed. I caught myself thinking that he'd better watch out for death traps hidden around his apartment.

"Do you want something from us? Or is the universe just punishing us with your presence?" Grace snapped.

"Believe me, you're the last person I want anything from."

"Good, because I wouldn't touch you with a bargepole."

Ethan raised his eyebrows. "Who said anything about touching?"

"You did!"

"No, I didn't," Ethan said with a wink, before turning his back on us—he clearly wanted to have the final word. He headed for the weights at the other end of the room without sparing us another glance. Grace, on the other hand, stared furiously at his retreating back and flipped him a middle finger, adorned with a silver snake ring.

I sighed. "Do you have to provoke him like that?"

She lowered her finger. "What? He started it."

"'Go to hell'?" I reminded her.

"Oh, you're right. Sorry. Well, if he complains about me to Henry, you can just put in a good word for me. There must be some advantage to you sleeping with my boss."

I gave a tight smile as I ran. Grace seemed not to notice, but the mere thought of having sex with Henry made my steps falter. We hadn't slept together yet—not because of him, but because of me. I had no experience in that area, and I was nervous about disappointing Henry. But if there was one thing I had learned in the last few days, it was how much he wanted to be with me. Not even the chaos Randell had stirred up could make him break up with me. And the longer I thought about it, the more certain I became: I wanted my first time to be with Henry.

And hopefully, it would happen soon.

53

We're Worried About Henry Darlington!
Is Kate Dragging Him into the Drug Scene?

OK! Magazine headline

Henry

The reports about Kate kept coming. Although the interview with Randell had been offline for a while, dozens of new articles about her appeared every day, most of them spreading false information. And it wasn't just the media—my parents' snobby friends also had plenty to say. I had received at least two dozen calls asking indignantly whether the rumours were true. All they were concerned about was how it made them look, as if Kate's past would somehow turn the hotel into the nexus of a drug ring.

It was far from ideal, so close to the Pearl Gala. The charity event was taking place in three weeks, and the details hadn't been completely hammered out yet. Usually, I could take a back seat at this stage of the planning and let Rakesh handle the final arrangements. But this year, everything was different. There were dozens of unanswered questions, and ever since Randell's interview, the cancellations kept rolling in. Initially, I had been worried, but now it just made me angry. Some people were willing to turn a blind eye to my dad's wrongdoings, but not to Kate's minor transgressions. My dad had committed crimes just because he had wanted to, whereas Kate had stolen to survive. Besides, she hadn't destroyed anyone's life—she'd just stolen a few pounds.

A knock pulled me out of my thoughts. I glanced up. According to my laptop, it was already after 11 p.m. Shit. I had lost all sense of time again.

There was another knock.

"Come in!"

Kate slipped into the office wearing an old Black Sabbath T-shirt I'd given her a while ago, paired with the black trousers that were part of her Darlington uniform. She wore boots, though the laces were undone, as if she had dressed in a rush.

"Hey. What are you doing here?" I asked.

"Just checking in on my favourite person," Kate replied, pulling the door shut behind her. Her short, dark hair was slightly damp, curling at the ends. "I messaged you earlier, but you didn't reply."

"Sorry, I must have missed it." I glanced at my phone. Sure enough, I had several unread messages from her.

With her eyes on mine, Kate came around the desk to me. It had grown warm, so I'd taken off my jacket, loosened my tie, and rolled up the sleeves of my shirt. My hair was a mess from nervously running my fingers through it for hours.

"How was your day?"

Kate settled onto my lap and wrapped an arm around my neck. I instinctively placed a hand on her waist to steady her and slid my fingers under her T-shirt. I wanted to feel her skin against mine. She was soft and warm—she was everything I had missed today.

"Not bad. I had coffee with Olivia."

"Did you have fun?" I asked. I hadn't seen Olivia since Halloween. I was usually only free in the evenings after work, while her schedule was crammed with evening events—galas, receptions, and art gallery openings.

"I did. I can see why you like her. She told some pretty wild stories about you," Kate answered with a grin that spelt trouble. "Is it true that you dyed your hair pink when you were sixteen, and your dad forced you to shave it off?"

"I think I have to end my friendship with Olivia."

Kate laughed. "Please don't. I like her."

"I'm glad." I really was. I didn't really care about most people, but I cared about Olivia. She was my best and oldest friend, and it boded well that she and Kate got along. "Is she still dating Marko?"

"She mentioned him a few times, so probably."

I groaned. Olivia deserved so much more than that arrogant loser. Why couldn't she see that? She must have heard the rumours about him—why didn't they put her off?

"How was your day?" Kate asked. She ran her fingers through my hair in an unsuccessful attempt to tame it. The feeling of her nails on my scalp sent a shiver down my spine.

"Terrible, but it got better about five minutes ago."

A bashful smile crossed her face, as if she still couldn't quite believe how much better she made my life. "Oh, really?"

"Yes," I confirmed, burying my face into the crook of her neck and taking a deep breath. She smelled fresh, of lavender. I gave a satisfied moan and pressed my lips to the skin of her throat, savouring her.

With a sigh, Kate tilted her head back. I took up her silent invitation, trailing a path of kisses from her neck up to her chin and, finally, to her lips. Our mouths met, and my tension immediately melted away. When I was with Kate, my world shrank until it revolved solely around her—her sweet scent and warm body, the delicious taste of her. Everything else faded into the background. She was like an oasis in the desert, and I was parched. My burning desire to be close to her was more consuming than anything I'd ever experienced. I'd never felt for anyone the way I did for Kate.

She drew in a sharp breath as I cautiously slid my hand upward beneath the fabric of her T-shirt. Until now, Kate had kept a certain physical distance between us, but right now, I felt no resistance. The closer my fingers inched to her breasts, the deeper her nails dug into my shoulders and the more her body arched towards me. I ran my finger over her soft curves, where the skin seemed warmer than the rest of her body, and I felt a heat rising in me too. Kate moaned into my mouth as I ran my thumb over a hard nipple. I cupped her breast, kneading it gently, and a surge of blood flooded down my body. There was no way to hide from Kate how aroused I was, as my erection pressed against her bum.

"Is this OK?" I asked between two kisses.

She nodded eagerly, and my hand wandered from her left breast to her right. I took her nipple between two fingers and teased it gently. Kate pressed herself further into my touch, shifting on my lap and grinding against my hard-on. Fuck! I couldn't think straight. I wasn't even sure if she was doing it on purpose or if it was her subconscious making her body rub against me. All I knew was that if she didn't stop immediately, I would come much sooner than I wanted.

I pulled her closer to make her stop moving, and Kate made an impatient sound that felt like music to my ears. She wanted more, and I was ready to give it to her, because I had been waiting for this. Ever since the night Kate had asked me to kiss her everywhere, I couldn't think of anything else but exploring her body with my mouth. I was about to do just that. I trailed my fingers from her breasts down over her belly, stopping when I reached between her thighs. Kate gasped as my fingers pressed against her.

"Henry!" She spoke my name like a plea, a request and a command all at the same time. I started rubbing Kate through the fabric of her trousers, first with two fingers, then three, before touching her with the flat of my palm. Her breathing grew faster, and a sweet flush that took my breath away spread across her cheeks. Her eyelids fluttered as she fought to keep them open. It wasn't long before her body won. She closed her eyes and surrendered fully to the pleasure.

I kissed a trail from her lips down her neck, then lower, to her breasts. Through the fabric of her shirt, I took one of her hard nipples in my mouth and sucked it gently. Kate's head fell back with a gasp as I teased her with my teeth. My erection throbbed, aching for her.

I didn't know how this moment could feel so incredibly hot when we were both still dressed—but perhaps that made it even better. If foreplay with Kate felt this good, I wasn't sure I was ready to have sex with her. I would lose my mind. It would break me, ruin me for all other women. Not that I wanted anyone else. I only wanted Kate.

I rubbed harder, massaging her clit. Even through the rough fabric, I could feel her heat. She pushed herself against me, impatient, and I knew I could bring her to climax like this. But that wasn't enough for me.

I pulled my hand away from between her thighs. Kate's eyes flew open, and she stared at me, aghast. Pure desire was written all over her face.

"Get up," I demanded, my voice rough.

She hesitated, and for a fraction of a second, I was certain she would ask me to stop. She looked uncertain—but then she rose from my lap.

She stood before me, her legs trembling. I reached for the waistband of her trousers without breaking eye contact. When I smiled at her, she smiled back—shy and self-conscious in a way I had never seen her before. Yet she didn't stop me as I undid her trouser button, then pulled down the zip to reveal plain white cotton underwear. In theory, the sight shouldn't have been at all sexy, yet it was the most seductive thing I had ever seen. A jolt of longing tightened in my stomach, and I pushed my laptop aside to clear space on my desk. When Kate had sent me that photo of herself in the bath all those weeks ago and I had sat here fantasising about what her body looked like beneath all that foam, I'd never dreamed of finding out for real one day.

"Sit," I ordered, pressing a button under my desk to lock my office door.

With a little hop, she perched her pert bum on the edge of the desk. I took her right foot in my hand first, slipping off the boot, then did the same with the left. Kate watched me intently, her chest rising and falling rapidly as she bit her lower lip nervously. A thought—more of a suspicion—crossed my mind.

"Kate?" My voice was hoarse.

"Yes?"

"Have you ever done this before?"

She shook her head, which didn't surprise me. Yet despite her nervous anticipation, she looked at me with an expression full of trust. My own desire would take a backseat for now, and I would give her the pleasure she craved. But I wouldn't have sex with her in my office, though. Perhaps one day, but definitely not her first time. Kate deserved more than a quickie on my desk. I could wait.

I smiled encouragingly at her, and she returned my smile as I reached for her trousers, which I had already tugged down far enough to slide off completely. A shiver ran through her, goose bumps rising on her skin. My hands trailed up her bare legs until they reached the tops of her thighs. Gripping her hips, I pulled her to the very edge of the desk in one fluid motion. Kate's legs parted instinctively, making space for me. I drew in a sharp breath. Even in the dim glow of the desk lamp, I could see her wetness through her underwear.

Ignoring the throbbing ache of my erection, I focussed entirely on Kate. She watched my every movement. Although I wanted nothing more than to lose myself in her, I forced myself to stay in control. I stroked her legs gently and leaned in, giving her a slow, lingering kiss, grounding her in something familiar. I eased her nerves kiss by kiss, taking my time, until I felt her completely relax beneath me. Only then did I guide her body backwards with mine until she lay flat on my desk. All she had to do was let go and enjoy what came next.

"Do you trust me?" I murmured into her lips.

"Yes, but I'm a bit nervous," she confessed, her voice suddenly shaky.

"Why?"

She swallowed hard. "I . . . I don't know."

"Do you want me to stop?"

"No," she replied firmly.

I smiled and brushed a strand of hair from her face. "Then I'll carry on, but I won't do anything you don't want me to. I promise. Just say the word, and I'll stop."

"OK."

It was exactly what I'd wanted to hear. I kissed her lips one last time before slowly kissing my way down her body, lower and lower, until my face was nestled between her legs. Without taking my eyes off hers, I pressed my lips gently against her underwear.

Her breathing faltered.

"Relax," I murmured, pressing a kiss to the damp cotton.

Kate's hips jerked toward me. "Oh my god, Henry."

I teased her through the fabric with my tongue. "Does that feel good?"

"It really does!" she gasped.

I smiled and hooked a finger under the elastic of her underwear to pull it aside.

Damn. She was perfect, so ready for me that it was physically painful not to be inside her—but I was determined to stick to my plan and not take her right here on my desk.

I buried my head between Kate's thighs and kissed her, her underwear now completely out of the way. She gave another gasp, and like before, she gave in to the urge to close her eyes. I kept my gaze fixed on her as I dipped my tongue into her.

"How does this feel?"

"Good . . . Good . . . So good!" She gripped my hair with one hand, her self-control slipping. The way she pulled at me was almost painful, but it was a pleasurable pain—one that told me I was doing everything right. With every stroke of my tongue and movement of my lips, Kate's moans grew louder. I was glad it was so late that no one would pass by my office, because the sounds she was making could leave no doubt as to what was happening in here.

"Oh god, Henry!" Kate whispered hoarsely.

She gasped my name again and again, and I had to hold back from unzipping my trousers when suddenly her entire body tensed up and she came with a cry, bucking against my tongue. I could taste her climax. It was incredibly intoxicating. I would never again be able to enter my office without remembering Kate like this.

I didn't take my mouth off her until the waves of her pleasure had subsided, then I readjusted her underwear.

She released my hair but didn't move, lying there with her gaze fixed dreamily on the ceiling, breathing heavily. I gave her a moment before leaning over the desk to bring my face level with hers. Her skin glowed, and there was a delicate sheen of sweat on her forehead.

I kissed her. "Are you OK?"

"Mm-hm," she muttered, wrapping her arms around my neck. I straightened up, pulling her with me until she was sitting upright on the desk again. With her cheeks still flushed pink from her orgasm, she looked stunning. "I should distract you from work more often, if this is what happens."

"Or you could just ask me if I want to fuck you with my tongue."

"Oh my god!" Kate buried her face in my chest. "Don't say that."

"Why not? I mean it. You taste so good. I *really* liked doing that."

"Henry!" Kate cried, blushing. "You're making me feel flustered."

"And you . . . you make me feel happy."

My words made Kate look up. Her eyes met mine, and a shy smile crept over her face, deepening the two enchanting dimples in her cheeks. On the balcony at the masked ball, I had told her that she'd never looked more beautiful, but right now, she was surpassing her beauty on that night. Without makeup, her eyes shimmering and her cheeks flushed, she was the most stunning version of herself. She took my breath away.

"You make me happy too," she said softly.

I smiled. "I do?"

She nodded and gave me a brief kiss before drawing away, looking up at me from beneath her eyelashes. She bit her lower lip shyly, as if unsure whether she should say what was on her mind. "How do you feel about finishing up work for the day? Perhaps we could do something about *that* together." As she spoke, her eyes drifted to the bulge straining against the fabric of my trousers.

Fuck! "Are you sure?"

She nodded, nervous but resolute. "I want you, Henry."

I reached out to her and ran my thumb over her lower lip. She stopped biting it and looked at me, her eyes wide with expectation. I kissed her tenderly. "You already have me."

"Yes, but . . . I want more of you."

I took her hand, smiling. "Then let's go."

54

Kate is incredible. I really like her. She makes me feel things no one has ever made me feel before.

Message from Henry to Olivia

Kate

With weak knees, I followed Henry out of his office and to the lift. It was late, and not much was going on behind the scenes at the hotel. Still, I was sure that everyone we passed could tell, just by looking at me, what Henry had just done to me in his office and what we intended to do now. I didn't care. I needed Henry more than anything else. The thought of going even one more day without knowing what it felt like to be with him fully was unbearable. As soon as the lift doors slid shut behind us, our lips locked again.

He tasted of coffee, of Henry, of myself—a heady mix that made my head spin even faster than it had the night after the pub. He pressed me against the cool metal of the lift wall, his warm body flush against mine. As Henry ground his hips into me, his rock-hard erection pressed into my stomach. He moaned into my mouth—and I could feel that he was on the brink of losing control entirely.

Playing with fire, I ran my hands over his chest, undoing the buttons of his shirt one by one. At last, I could touch his bare skin. It was warm beneath my fingertips, his heartbeat pounding just as wildly as mine. Despite my nerves, I could barely contain my longing and anticipation. My body ached for Henry, and judging by his heated caresses and fervent kisses, he felt the same way.

I let my hand glide lower, first over his flat stomach, then down over the waistband of his trousers. Henry gasped as I wrapped my fingers around his erection through the fabric. He was hot. Hard. And big—impressively big. The thought of having him inside me both thrilled and terrified me. My fingers wandered to his zipper—but Henry caught my wrist before I could tug it down.

"Not here," he murmured, his voice hoarse. He took a step back, swiped his ID card, and pressed the button for the private floor. Woozy with desire, I hadn't noticed that the lift wasn't yet moving.

Heat rushed to my face. There were no words, only our heavy breaths and impatient glances. I didn't want to wait any longer.

The lift climbed agonisingly slowly, until the doors finally opened onto the corridor leading to Henry's apartment. He reached for my hand and pulled me along to his door, which he unlocked hastily. But instead of pushing it open so that we could pick up where we'd left off in the lift, he hesitated and turned to me. A fresh wave of arousal washed over me as his eyes met mine—his seemed to have grown even darker with lust.

"Nothing will happen in there that you don't want to happen."

I didn't answer. Instead, I grabbed the lapels of his jacket, which he had hastily slipped back on as we walked, and pulled him down to kiss me. Our lips melted together, and I made it clear that I wanted *everything* to happen. I didn't want to hold back any longer—I wanted to tear down the last barriers between us. My heart and soul belonged to Henry, and tonight, I wanted him to claim my body too.

My kiss was answer enough. He pushed open the door without breaking away from me and pulled me into his dark penthouse apartment. Pale moonlight spilled in through the floor-to-ceiling windows, offering what I knew must be a breathtaking view—but I only had eyes for Henry. Without turning on the light, he lifted me into his arms. I wrapped my legs tightly around his waist, his erection pressing fiercely against me. We groaned simultaneously, and though he had just made me come with his deft tongue minutes ago, I felt a fresh surge of longing.

Henry carried me effortlessly into his bedroom and laid me down on his bed. Without taking his eyes off me, he shrugged off his jacket, letting it fall carelessly to the floor. His shirt followed, slipping just as easily from his shoulders. In the moonlight, his silhouette was strong and sensual—but I wanted to see more of him. I reached for the bedside lamp and a soft glow flooded the room, illuminating his perfect body. Muscles rippled subtly beneath his smooth skin, his chest partially covered in dark hair that snaked down from his navel, disappearing beneath the waistband of his trousers. At eye level, his erection was even more pronounced, straining at the fabric.

I swallowed hard and reached for his zipper again with a trembling hand. This time, Henry didn't stop me. I unfastened his trousers and slipped them down, along with his boxers, in one fluid movement. His erection sprang free, and I gasped, which drew a self-satisfied smile from Henry. He kicked off his shoes and stepped out of his clothes—and suddenly he was completely naked before me. I was desperate to pull off my own clothes too—but first, I wanted to pay Henry back, even if I didn't have much experience.

I wrapped my hand around his hard-on.

"Fuck!" he groaned, his hips bucking towards me, which I took as a sign that I was doing it right.

I stroked him—slow at first, then faster, back and forth. The sounds he made sent shivers through me. Watching Henry lose control only fuelled the delicious ache between my thighs. I felt seductive and powerful, and gradually grew bolder. Again and again, I ran my thumb over the moist tip of his erection—which he especially seemed to like.

"Can I take you in my mouth?" I asked, my voice husky.

Henry cursed. "You can do whatever you want, angel."

Without breaking eye contact, I leaned forward and pressed a kiss to his stomach. He shuddered, his hips lifting eagerly to meet my lips. I trailed kisses down his body until I reached his erection, my body thrumming with desire as I finally took him into my mouth.

"Fuck, Kate!" he groaned, his voice thick with longing. A low, guttural sound came from his chest as his hand tangled in my hair. His fingers dug into my scalp, but he didn't guide me—he let me stay in complete control.

I licked and sucked him, letting his sounds direct me. He tasted salty and earthy—far better than I had ever imagined. A part of me wanted nothing more than to make him come like this, but a deeper, more insistent part ached to finally have him inside me.

I pulled back. When our eyes met, he seemed to instinctively understand what I needed. He leaned down, his warm breath brushing my lips before he kissed me. The kiss was tender and loving, with none of the urgency that had driven us until now. The throbbing heat between my thighs melted into a deep, pleasurable warmth.

My lips parted for Henry, and our tongues met in a slow, teasing dance, impossibly languid. I felt his hands at my waist, grasping the fabric of the old T-shirt of his that I was wearing. Interrupting our kiss for the briefest moment, he pulled it over my head. My body was so hot that the air in the room felt cool against my bare skin. But Henry's hands were anything but cold. They roamed over my arms, my shoulders, my breasts and my stomach, leaving a trail of fire in their wake.

I had already kicked off my shoes, and Henry slid my trousers and underwear effortlessly down my legs. For the first time, we were naked together. The moment was too precious—Henry's gaze too full of passion—to leave any room for insecurity.

I crawled backward onto the bed, and Henry followed, settling beside me. He kissed my mouth, then my cheeks, before trailing a path down my jaw to my breasts. I gasped as he took my right nipple into his mouth, sucking hard.

My eyelids fluttered. Without the barrier of fabric between us, the sensation was so much more intense. I arched my back, pressing myself against him. Henry groaned with pleasure. His tongue circled my nipple before he gently grazed it with his teeth. I moaned, surrendering to the hot tingle radiating deep into my core.

"Spread your legs for me," Henry whispered against my skin.

I obeyed, and he ran his hand down my belly, moving lower and lower, stopping only when he reached the space between my thighs. But instead of touching the part of me that craved him most, he traced slow, torturous strokes along the sensitive skin of my inner thighs, his patience endless. I bucked my hips feverishly, desperate for more, but Henry refused to be rushed. He savoured every second of the delicious torment he was inflicting on me. He lavished attention on first one breast, then the other, all the while denying me the touch of his other hand, until I thought I could bear it no longer. A strangled, incoherent sound escaped my lips when he finally touched me.

"Oh my god!"

Waves of desire coursed through me as he touched the throbbing wetness between my thighs. I felt him smile against my chest before he began tracing slow circles with two fingers, varying the pressure. I squirmed beneath him and pushed myself against his hand.

Henry's lips left my breast, and he looked up at me. His warm breath brushed over my skin, still damp from his kisses.

"Relax and take a deep breath," he instructed.

I did as he said, and as I exhaled, he slid a finger inside me. I moaned. The sensation was new—intense, incredible. Henry seemed to know exactly how to unravel me. He moved his finger, slowly at first, then faster, all the while circling my clit with his thumb. With every touch, I felt myself getting closer to the edge.

"Please, more fingers!" I gasped. Maybe I would be mortified about my words later, but right now, I was too consumed by lust to care.

"Are you sure?"

I bit my lower lip and nodded fervently. I whimpered softly as he pushed a second finger inside me. Henry kept his hand still, giving me time to adjust before he began moving his hand again. The muscles in my lower abdomen clenched and unclenched in sync with his touch. He kissed me, sealing my lips with his and swallowing the sounds spilling from me.

A bittersweet, burning pressure spread through me. My entire body was ablaze, my hips rising and falling to meet Henry's fingers as if of their own accord. A rushing sensation filled my ears, but each time I neared the brink of release, Henry changed his pace or the angle of his fingers. It was almost as though he didn't want me to come. He teased me to the point of desperation.

"Henry, please," I begged breathlessly.

He lifted his gaze from my breasts. "Please, what?"

"I . . . I need you."

His lips curved into a mischievous smile, as if he'd just been waiting for me to beg. Then, all at once, he withdrew his fingers and reached into the drawer of his bedside table. He pulled out a condom, tore open the packaging hastily, and rolled it on. Moments later, he was leaning over me, his lips finding mine again as he lowered his body onto me. The weight of him on me felt perfect. His erection nudged against my slickness, sending a shiver of longing—and a flicker of fear—through me. The very tip of him brushed against me before easing inside. I gasped, already overwhelmed by the intensity of the new sensation.

Henry's eyes burnt with unbridled desire, and I braced myself for his thrusts—hard and relentless after the patient torment of his fingers. But they didn't come. Instead, he held himself above me, his arms braced on either side of my head. In silence, we gazed at each other. We didn't need words. Henry could read my mind, just as I could read his. I gave him a shaky smile. He returned it, his eyes filled with reassurance as he eased deeper into me, inch by inch, until our hips met at last, the space between us closed completely. I tried to steady my breathing, but it was impossible. The sensation of being filled so completely was too intense, too consuming—and a little painful to be honest. Henry remained perfectly still above me, giving me time to adjust to the feeling.

"It'll feel better soon," he promised.

I nodded. I trusted him. Taking a shaky breath, I let myself sink into the sensation as Henry trailed soft, lingering kisses along my cheeks and neck. It didn't take long for the discomfort between my thighs to fade, replaced by the familiar tingling from before. Tentatively, I moved my hips.

Henry moaned. "You feel incredible, Kate."

Heat rushed to my already flushed face at his compliment. I didn't know how to respond, so I repeated the motion, drawing another sharp gasp from him. The muscles in his arms tensed, veins standing out along his neck—he was clearly holding back to keep himself from losing control. But that was exactly what I wanted.

I kissed him. "Let go."

He understood instantly. "But you'll tell me if it's too much?"

"I promise," I whispered hoarsely—and after that, nothing could hold him back.

Henry pulled out, only to thrust back in, hard and unrestrained. This time, there was no hesitation, no withholding—his movements driven by pure lust. Each deep, rhythmic stroke sent more tremors through my body. My limbs felt electric, and I pulsed with the buildup of an incredible pressure. I couldn't control the sounds spilling from my lips, though I wanted to tell Henry how incredible it felt to be with him. Both in a gentle, loving way and in this wild, animalistic way that was driving me mad.

"Fuck, Kate. I'm going to come," Henry groaned.

"Then come," I urged, wrapping my legs around his hips, pulling him closer, deeper, until there was nothing left between us.

He growled, and our mouths met in a clumsy kiss. I clutched him as he let go, his thrusts growing harder, more urgent. The pressure inside me coiled tighter, reaching an almost unbearable intensity. With every movement, Henry struck that perfect, electrifying spot deep inside me—

And then we both exploded—together. Everything inside me tightened as his hips bucked against mine, and I felt him pulse inside me until he had nothing left to give.

Holy shit.

Henry pulled out of me slowly, leaving behind a strange, aching feeling of emptiness. With the last of his strength, he removed the used condom before collapsing, spent, on top of me. But before his full weight pinned me down, he wrapped his arms around me and rolled us over so I was lying on top of him. A sheen of sweat covered his forehead, his cheeks were flushed, and his lips, like mine, were swollen from our kisses.

He looked at me, a contented smile playing on his lips as he brushed my sex-tousled hair from my face.

"That was really nice," I said, still a little breathless.

"No, it was incredible," Henry corrected. "Just like you, my angel."

I smiled and nestled closer to him.

For a few minutes, we lay in comfortable silence, catching our breath. The entire time, Henry traced slow, soothing circles along my back, while I pressed soft kisses to his chest because I couldn't get enough of him. This man meant everything to me—and more. I had once struggled to imagine living in his world, but even more impossible was the thought of living in a world without him.

Dear Henry,

Getting to know you is the best thing that's happened to me in the last few years. You've shown me that even the worst storm passes. You gave me a chance when no one else was willing to. And you gave me hope when I had lost mine. You're the reason I can dream again.

Kate's message in the DVD case

Kate

I opened my eyes at a gentle touch on my cheek. The bedroom was dark, but not completely—soft light filtered through the curtains, casting faint shadows across the room. Henry was watching me. As our eyes met, his lips curved into a slow, sexy smile meant for me alone. A delicious shiver ran through me as memories of last night came rushing back.

"Sorry, I didn't mean to wake you," he murmured.

"It's fine," I whispered. His breath was warm against my lips, which were so close to his, it was an effort not to close the distance and kiss him. "Did you sleep well?"

"The best sleep of my life," he said, his voice rough. His hand traced from my cheek to my arm, then down my back. In one fluid motion, he pulled me against him until my bare skin was flush against his. "And the best sex of my life."

I couldn't explain how, but I knew he was telling the truth. Henry would never lie to me. And besides, I had been there. I had nothing to compare it to, but even I had felt how special last night had been. "I thought it was incredible too."

"I was worried I got too rough towards the end," he admitted, his fingers tracing lazy patterns up and down my spine. A shiver of pleasure rippled through me, and I wrapped my arms around his neck. He pulled me even closer, and I felt him against me—already hard again. A delicious, searing heat shot through my belly straight to my core.

"No, not at all," I reassured him. "It was perfect."

"You're perfect," Henry murmured, holding my gaze. His blue eyes were stunningly clear this morning—open, unguarded. There was nothing left between us. No walls. No uncertainty. No secrets. I hadn't known it could be possible to feel so deeply connected to another person. And I couldn't imagine ever sharing this kind of intimacy with anyone but Henry.

"No, *we're* perfect," I replied, and kissed him.

Henry's hand slid to the back of my neck as he deepened the kiss. He shifted me effortlessly so I was straddling his lap. His erection pressed against me, firm and insistent, and a familiar ache bloomed between my legs. We both knew what we wanted—what we needed. And once again, we lost ourselves in each other.

After Henry had rolled on a condom, I positioned myself over him. Being on top felt different from lying beneath him, but no less incredible. I relished the sense of control, but even more, I savoured the way Henry devoured me with his gaze—hungry, reverent, completely undone. His hands explored every inch of my body, holding me close as I moved, driving us both closer and closer to release.

When it was over, I collapsed onto his chest, breathless. He wrapped his arms around me, holding me close as we basked in the warm afterglow. I never wanted to leave his bed, to leave him. But eventually, I untangled myself from his embrace, even though every fibre of me longed to stay.

He frowned. "Where are you going?"

"To the bathroom," I replied with a smile.

"OK, but be quick. I want a second round."

So did I. And a third. And a fourth. And a fifth, because I just couldn't get enough of him.

I swung my legs over the edge of the bed and headed to the bathroom, only to catch my foot on something. Henry's jacket, like the rest of our clothes, had been strewn across the floor. I bent down to pick it up—it was far too expensive to be left lying around.

"Don't—" Henry started, just as the small box of mints he always carried with him slipped from his pocket. It hit the floor, the lid sprung open, and dozens of tiny white tablets scattered across the floor. It took me a couple of heartbeats to realise I wasn't looking at mints, but pills.

I froze, blinking.

Henry leapt from the bed and was beside me in an instant. He snatched the box from my hand and dropped to his knees, hastily gathering up the pills. I didn't move. My mind raced to make sense of what I was seeing. Because something wasn't right.

"I told you not to touch the jacket," he said. His voice wasn't angry, but there was an edge to it—agitation, maybe even nervousness. It didn't make sense.

I crouched down and reached for one of the pills. The moment Henry realised what I was about to do, he lunged for it, but I was quicker. His eyes widened, shock flashing across his face. It didn't seem like a normal reaction. I examined the small pill in my palm. It was white and unremarkable—except for the *V* imprinted on one side.

"What's this?" I asked, my voice flat.

"Nothing."

I knew instantly that he was lying. His voice had never sounded like this before—tight with anxiety, laced with the desperate hope that I might believe him. But I didn't believe him. My stomach clenched.

"Henry, what are these pills?" I demanded, my voice strained. My chest tightened, as if there wasn't enough space in my lungs for air. This scene was all too familiar. Dark memories surged to the surface—memories of the beginning of the end, when my already miserable life had started spiralling into something even worse.

Henry stared at me in silence. He didn't answer—but he didn't need to. His silence spoke louder than words ever could. If he had pulled out a knife and plunged it into my chest, it wouldn't have hurt as much as the realisation that was slowly and inexorably dawning on me, despite my heart's desperate attempts to resist it. I couldn't believe—no, I didn't *want* to believe—that Henry had betrayed me like this. Not after everything I had confided in him.

"Did a doctor prescribe them to you?" I asked, clinging to hope as it slipped away.

Henry took a step closer. "Kate—"

I stepped back. Moments ago, we had been as close as two people could be, but now the last thing I wanted was for him to touch me. I snatched Henry's old T-shirt from the floor and pulled it over my head. "Answer me," I hissed, my voice shaking with fear and fury. "Were those pills prescribed to you?"

He stared at me, his face suddenly pale. "No."

An icy chill spread through my body. "Then where did you get them?"

"Does it matter?"

It shouldn't have, but I was grasping at straws, desperately searching for an explanation that wouldn't break my heart. I didn't want to hear that Henry had a drug problem, but how else could I explain this? He was taking pills—and not only had he not mentioned anything to me; he was actively trying to hide them. His reaction had made that painfully clear.

Henry swore and ran a desperate hand through his hair, as if he'd rather tear it out than have this conversation. "They're from Marko. We met at a party a few months ago, just after I'd taken over managing the hotel. Everything was a lot. The press was all over The Darlington, and I was overwhelmed. Everyone wanted something from me, and suddenly, I had to make all these critical decisions about the hotel's future. I was stressed and overworked—which was a nightmare, because people expected me to function at peak performance for sixteen hours a day, and every mistake could have cost me my home."

His Adam's apple bobbed nervously as he continued. "Marko noticed how burnt out I was and gave me a couple of Vitalyn pills. I didn't take them straightaway, but eventually, I caved, and . . . everything got easier. Suddenly, working sixteen-hour days, seven days a week didn't seem impossible. My mind was clearer, I was more focussed, less exhausted. The hours were still long, but pushing through didn't feel as impossible. After that, I went back to Marko for more."

Henry's words felt like more than just a punch to the gut—they were a fist driving straight through my entire body. The pain of betrayal radiated through my chest, spreading like poison and freezing the blood in my veins. It hurt. And suddenly, I couldn't breathe.

I.

Couldn't.

Breathe.

History was repeating itself, and I wasn't ready. A desperate sound escaped me, half whimper, half gasp. Tears blurred my vision. But these weren't tears of despair, grief, or even betrayal, all emotions that churned inside me. They were tears of rage. I was boiling inside. How could he have hidden this from me?

"How long have you been taking them?"

Henry had the decency to look ashamed, but that didn't make his confession any less terrible. He was addicted to a stimulant. I hadn't seen it coming, yet I wasn't surprised. Suddenly it all made sense—how he had endured the relentless pressure and an outrageous workload that would have destroyed most people long ago.

"Since April," he admitted.

"Fuck you!"

"Kate—" Henry reached out towards me.

I slapped his hand away. The room blurred before my eyes, my chest aching as if my heart were trying to break free.

Standing in front of me, still naked, Henry bent down to pick up his shirt. It was crumpled, like his face. He threw the shirt on and slipped into his trousers. "Please, let's talk about this."

"Talk? Talk!" I snapped. He was acting like I was the irrational one. Did he not understand what he was doing to me? He had let me run headfirst into my own personal hell. "You had weeks to talk. Months! You could have told me the day I told you how drugs killed my mum and ruined my life, for example. Did you really think I wouldn't find out?"

"I was waiting for the right moment."

"Bullshit!" I shoved Henry's chest, needing an outlet for the fury and pain threatening to consume me. "You didn't tell me because you knew I wouldn't stand for it. And because you can't stop. You're afraid I'll take away the thing you're addicted to."

"I'm not addicted."

"Sure. You've been taking them since April—just for a bit of fun."

"I can stop anytime I want."

"So why haven't you?" My voice shook, and tears streamed uncontrollably down my face. "Why haven't you already thrown them out? You should have gotten rid of them the day I told you about my mum, at the very latest. I would have. The fact that you didn't can only mean two things: Either I'm not important enough to you—"

"You are important to me!"

"—or you're addicted," I finished, ignoring Henry's interruption. My mum had loved me, but she'd still chosen drugs. Because her addiction hadn't left her any other option.

Henry took a step towards me. This time, I didn't flinch away. He raised a hand and tenderly wiped the tears from my cheek with his thumb—tears I was shedding because of him. His touch was a bittersweet torture.

"You mean the world to me, Kate," he said quietly, almost reverently. His voice trembled. "Not telling you was a mistake. If I could, I'd turn back time and never take those pills from Marko. But I can't. The only thing I can do is promise you that I'll stop."

My throat constricted. I wanted to believe him—but I couldn't. Not anymore. If I hadn't found the pills today, it could have been weeks, even months, before he told me about them. If he ever told me at all . . .

"I . . . I can't do this." The words barely made it past my lips. Just yesterday, I couldn't imagine living in a world without Henry. Now that world was on fire, and he was the one who had set it ablaze. If I didn't put it out immediately, I'd burn with it. I couldn't bear this pain a second time, and above all, I couldn't watch Henry slowly lose himself to his addiction.

He blinked. "What can't you do?"

"I can't do this again," I said, taking a step back. It was only a small step, but it cost me more strength than running a marathon. His hand slipped from my cheek, leaving a cold ache in my chest. It had probably been our last touch. I couldn't stand by and watch him head for the same abyss as the one that had taken my mum. As much as I loved him—and yes, I did love him—in this moment, I had to love myself more. Maybe things would have been different if he had confided in me, if he had asked for my help. But he hadn't. And that left me no choice.

"Thank you," I said softly. "For everything you've done for me. For your kindness and affection, and all the chances you gave me. But . . . I think it's best if I leave now."

The colour drained from Henry's face. He reached out as if to stop me, to hold on to me, but when he saw the silent plea in my eyes, he dropped his hand.

"Kate, please." His voice was raw, barely louder than a whisper. I had never heard him sound so vulnerable. "Don't go. We'll find a way."

"I have to," I said with a sad smile.

"I'll stop. I promise. Look!" Henry marched past me to the bathroom. He flipped the toilet seat up with such force that it slammed against the tiles, and then he dumped the contents of the pillbox into the bowl. He flushed the toilet. "See? All gone!"

Fuck. Fuck. *Fuck!*

I wanted nothing more than to believe him, but I couldn't—not after he'd lied to me for so long. Not with words, but with his silence. Besides, I'd hidden and thrown out my mum's drugs dozens of times, and nothing had ever changed. Henry could easily get more pills whenever he wanted and keep it from me. The thought of being betrayed like this again was unbearable. But even worse was the thought of watching him destroy himself.

I shook my head. "It's not that easy."

"Yes, it is." He was lying to himself now too.

"If it were, you wouldn't have been taking that stuff for months," I said, my voice and heart breaking.

A heavy silence fell over the room. He knew I was right. I could see it in his eyes, which were just as heartbroken as they were beautiful.

I took a step back. Then another, and another. My gaze swept over Henry one last time, trying to memorise every detail of his handsome, despairing face. I wanted to remember him—and the most wonderful weeks of my life—forever.

"Look after yourself, Snowflake," I whispered before turning my back on him.

My rage had long since faded, leaving only sorrow, pain, and confusion in its wake. It wasn't Richard and Amanda, or the rest of British high society, or even Randell who had stolen my future with Henry. It was Henry himself. A part of me still hoped he would say something, that he'd find the right words to make me stay. But I had no idea what those words could be. He hadn't just broken my heart; he had shattered something far more precious. My trust.

I heard you quit?! Is it true?

Message from Rose to Kate

Kate

I stared at the illuminated sign of The Meridian, trying to convince myself I was doing the right thing. The rucksack that once again held my entire life weighed heavily on my shoulders. After my fight with Henry, I had made the heartbreaking decision to leave The Darlington.

Henry had hidden his pill addiction from me, even though he should have known exactly how I would feel about it. I couldn't be with him under those circumstances, no matter how much I loved him. I couldn't bear the thought of one day finding him dead—just like my mum. Which is why I couldn't stay at the hotel. I was already dreading the day I might see the headline "Henry Darlington Dies of Overdose."

Cold fear crept up my neck, and tears welled in my eyes again. I blinked them away, surprised I had any left to cry. I had been sobbing nonstop since packing my rucksack and leaving the hotel. I had wandered aimlessly around the city, my red eyes and puffy face drawing stares, questioning my decision to leave Henry at least a hundred times. I already missed him, and the pain of losing him was almost unbearable. But I had to do this.

I *had* to!

Determined, I stepped into Logan's restaurant. It was cosy and warm inside—a welcome contrast to the frosty evening air.

"Welcome to The Meridian. Do you have a reservation?" asked the woman stationed at the entrance. She wasn't the same employee who had greeted Henry and me last time. Her gaze swept over me sceptically from head to toe, lingering on my tear-streaked face.

"No, I don't."

She smiled tightly. "I'm sorry, but we're fully booked."

"I don't need a table. I have to talk to Logan. Is he here?"

"He is. But as the chef, he's very busy. There's a lot going on tonight."

"It's important. Could you please let him know I'm here?"

"I'm afraid that's not possible."

My throat tightened. "It's an emergency."

She didn't budge. "I'm sorry. I can't help you."

"Please!" I pressed.

"Is there a problem?" a deep voice asked.

I looked up to see a tall man with curly, dark-brown hair and deep-set eyes. He was dressed entirely in black, but instead of the smart elegance of a suit that was expected in this kind of restaurant, he wore jeans and a T-shirt. Silver rings gleamed on his fingers, and he also had a nose ring.

"No, Maxton, everything's fine," the receptionist replied, finally forcing a polite smile. "This young woman was asking for Logan. I was just explaining that the chef is busy and doesn't have time for private conversations."

Maxton studied me, frowning slightly, and I noticed that his ears were also studded with silver rings. He didn't look like the owner of a fancy restaurant, but then again, neither did Logan with his tattoos.

"You're Henry's girlfriend. Kaitlynn, right?" he said.

"Kate," I corrected.

"I'm Maxton, Logan's business partner." He gestured for me to follow. "Come with me. I'll let Logan know you're here." Relief washed over me as I followed Maxton through the crowded restaurant. Every table was occupied, and I wondered whether Logan would even have time to talk to me. We headed towards the kitchen, where I could hear the clatter of pots and the harried voices of the kitchen staff. But instead of entering, we walked past to a door marked "Staff Only." Maxton held it open and led me into a break room.

"Take a seat," he said, motioning towards a chair. He smiled at me, and two dimples appeared in his cheeks. He seemed kind, and I could see why he and Logan were friends—though it was probably my tear-streaked face that prompted him to be so nice to me. "I'll let Logan know you're waiting here for him. He'll come as soon as he can. There are drinks in the fridge if you're thirsty."

"Thank you," I replied weakly, drained by the events of the last few hours. I just had to get through this one last conversation, and then I could find somewhere to sleep and nurse my wounds. The problem was, I had no idea where to go. My every thought was consumed by Henry, and even though I had spent almost a year living on the streets, I still felt just as lost and helpless as the day Randell had thrown me out. How was it possible that this was happening to me a second time?

Lost in thought, I stared into space as I waited for Logan. I couldn't be there and stay strong for Henry, but I still didn't want to leave him alone with his addiction. He needed someone by his side, someone in his corner to fight for him—and it certainly wasn't going to be Richard or Amanda.

Several minutes passed before the door to the break room swung open and Logan stepped in. A weight lifted off my chest. He was wearing the same white uniform as during our last meeting, which made his colourful tattoos look even more vibrant.

"Hey," Logan greeted me, his gaze attentive in a way that suggested Maxton had already filled him in on my state. Wordlessly, he pulled out the chair opposite me and sat down. "Is everything OK?"

I shook my head, choking back the tears that once again threatened to surface. But I couldn't cry now. "No. I need to talk to you about something important."

Logan's concerned eyes locked onto mine. "What about?"

"Henry . . . he . . . he has a drug problem."

Two hours later, Grace opened the door to her apartment in Shadwell. The news that I was no longer working at The Darlington had spread like wildfire among the hotel employees. I had barely finished my conversation with Logan when Grace had called to check on me. I hadn't been able to bring myself to explain over the phone, so I'd asked if we could meet in person instead. She had invited me to her apartment without a moment's hesitation.

Whatever she had heard, she clearly hadn't expected the state I was in.

"Oh my god, Kate!" Grace gasped in shock when she saw me. I could only guess how terrible I looked after the day I'd had, but one thing was certain—I felt even worse.

Fresh tears turned Grace into a blurry silhouette. I was exhausted and drained, and the only thing keeping me upright was a pain that refused to let me rest. It had settled deep in my chest, different from the grief I'd felt after my mum's death. This pain was more consuming, because my heart was torn—by my love and worry for Henry and the overwhelming, unshakeable sense of his betrayal.

"What happened?" Grace asked, her voice soft and compassionate.

I opened my mouth, but all that came out was a whimper that barely sounded human, as if I were a wounded animal. And like a wounded animal, I fell. Grace caught me, pulling me into a firm embrace. My arms hung limply at my sides—I didn't have the strength to lift them and hug her back. I buried my face in her shoulder and gave in to my tears once again.

57

Did Their Love Crumble Under Pressure? Insiders Claim Kate Hamilton No Longer Works for The Darlington.

INsider headline

Kate

The days and nights that followed were a blur. The world beyond Grace's bedroom ceased to exist. Everything had become meaningless—nothing made sense anymore to my broken heart. As much as Henry meant to me, I still couldn't be with him. My heart rebelled against this truth, while my mind tried to accept it. It was an exhausting struggle, one I could only lose, and it drained me of every last bit of strength.

Grace kept me company every free moment she had, and I didn't know what I would have done without her. We didn't talk much—mostly, we sat in silence on her bed, watching anime. I couldn't have recounted the plots afterwards even if my life had depended on it. My thoughts were everywhere and nowhere, inevitably circling back to Henry. I wondered how he was doing and what he was up to. Had he stopped taking the Vitalyn as he had promised? Or was he still on it now that I was gone? Had Logan spoken to him? If so, how had Henry reacted to me ratting him out to his brother?

I had so many questions, and I would probably never get an answer to any of them. Not only had I blocked Henry's number, but I had also deleted him entirely from my phone to stop myself from messaging or calling him in a moment of weakness. And unfortunately, there were far too many of those moments. Grace had assured me that it would get better, but the pain and longing seemed to grow worse with every passing day. I missed being close to Henry. I missed his voice and his laughter. I missed the way he had looked at me and held me in his arms at night. But most of all, I missed the unwavering sense of safety and comfort he had given me. Now it felt as if I were losing my way all over again, sliding back into an abyss he had only just helped me escape.

I poked my head cautiously through the doorway and glanced left and right. The corridor outside Grace's room was empty. Unmelodious piano playing drifted from her brother's room, but otherwise it was quiet in the apartment. The Claymores had been nothing but welcoming and understanding over the past few days, but I wasn't in the mood for small talk, so I did my best to avoid Grace's parents. I didn't always succeed, but often enough.

I crept quietly to the kitchen to find a snack. I'd had no appetite in the first few days after the breakup; though Grace had kept forcing me to eat a little, my stomach had been as paralysed as my body—most of the time, eating had just made me feel nauseous. But now, after about a week, my appetite was slowly starting to return.

I entered the kitchen, where Amy was sitting at the table. Her blond hair was tied up in a bun, and she was hunched over her medical textbooks, a marker pen in hand and a chaotic sea of notes surrounding her. She looked up at the sound of my footsteps and gave me a faint smile.

Amy knew I'd broken up with Henry, but she didn't know any details. I had only shared them with Grace, who was under strict instructions to keep them secret. The Darlington didn't need another scandal. If the press ever found out about Henry's drug problem, it would probably mark the end of the hotel.

I returned Amy's smile. "How's it going?"

She grimaced. "Don't ask."

"That bad?"

"I'm never going to pass this exam," she said with a groan and dropped her head onto the book open before her. "What was I thinking, studying medicine? Couldn't I have picked an easier course? Business management? Communications?"

I patted her shoulder and glanced at the notes scattered across the table. They were filled with Latin words that meant nothing to me.

"You can do it. And if not, you can always switch to business management."

She groaned. "But I don't want to study business management."

"You won't have to. You've got this," I reassured her. For the first time in days, I felt like myself again. It was the first proper conversation I'd had in a long time. "When are your exams?"

"In January."

"So you've still got a few weeks. I don't know much about medicine, but if you need help, let me know. I can test you or something."

Amy smiled. "Thanks. I might take you up on that."

I nodded, then pulled out the ingredients for a sandwich from the fridge. As I slipped two slices of bread into the toaster, I couldn't help but think about Henry's and my first night at the hotel—how he had cooked for me and made me toast with tofu scramble, as if taking care of me was the most natural thing in the world.

He was such a kind, thoughtful, and caring person that it was hard to see him as a drug addict—but that's exactly what he was.

I turned to Amy with a sigh. She had already returned to one of her medical textbooks.

"Can I ask you something?"

She looked up. "Sure."

"Do you know what Vitalyn is?"

"Yes, it's a medication. Why?"

I bit my lower lip, unsure how much I could say without her figuring out that I was talking about Henry. "Can you take it even if you don't need it?"

"You can take anything. The question is just at what cost," Amy replied with a shrug. "Vitalyn is . . . relatively harmless, if you want to put it that way. Which does not mean that you should treat it lightly! If you don't need the Vitalyn to treat the symptoms it's prescribed for, it can boost your concentration and stop you from feeling tired. That's why it's pretty popular among my classmates, especially around exam time."

I tilted my head. "What do you mean by 'relatively harmless'?"

"Well, Vitalyn is still a drug. You shouldn't take it if you haven't had it prescribed by a doctor, but you can't get physically addicted. You can develop a psychological addiction to it, though, if you start believing you can't function without it." She tapped her bottom lip with her pen pensively. "And there also can be unwelcomed side effects, of course, as with any medication—loss of appetite, for example, and headaches and nausea. In rare cases, heart rhythm disturbances. Most of my classmates just get insomnia."

It didn't sound so bad. I still hated the fact that Henry was taking it, and most of all, that he had hidden it from me. But the fact that a medical student said it was relatively harmless made me worry less about him.

"So you can't overdose on it?"

"You can overdose on any medication, but a typical overdose like you get with some other drugs is unlikely. At least, I've never heard of it. One of my classmates ended up in hospital because of Vitalyn once. It isn't healthy to pull all-nighters for days without taking a break—and eventually, your body gives up. But she was fine a few days later," Amy said. She gave me a sceptical look. "Just to be clear: I would definitely advise you not to take Vitalyn unless you have a prescription."

I smiled. "Don't worry. I hate drugs. I was just watching a TV series where someone took it, and I was curious," I lied before turning back to my sandwich. I wasn't sure if Amy had bought it, but she didn't press further and returned to her textbooks.

Not wanting to distract her any further, I headed back to Grace's room with my plate. I thought about what Amy had said as I ate my sandwich. Even if Vitalyn didn't carry severe risks, it was still a drug. And if Henry was willing to take it, he might also be willing to try other, harder drugs if he felt he had no other choice. That was what scared me. My mum's addiction had started with something relatively harmless too, and it had ended in tragedy.

I stared out the window. Rain pelted against the glass, and people with umbrellas darted down the street seeking shelter. They all seemed to know where they were going. I, on the other hand, had no idea. I wasn't really in the mood to make important decisions about my life right now, but I needed to start thinking about what to do next. I couldn't stay with the Claymores forever, after all. Sooner or later, I would have to leave the safety of Grace's bedroom—and then what?

I didn't want to live on the streets again. Not just because of the cold nights, the relentless hunger, and the constant danger, but also because I was afraid I wouldn't make it out a second time. Thanks to Henry, I finally had a bank account and a little money again, but it wasn't nearly enough to rent an apartment. Maybe it was time to leave London, to use the money to buy a bus ticket that would take me out of this city that had caused me more pain in the past few years than anything else. There was nothing left to keep me here except Grace, and in some other city, I wouldn't run the risk of running into Henry. Or Randell, even if I was pretty sure that his interview with William Hunt was the last I'd ever hear from him. He'd milked me of every last penny and used up all his ammunition, which meant he had nothing left to blackmail me with.

But if I was honest with myself, I didn't want to leave London. This city was my home and all I had ever known. I could apply for more jobs. Now that I was no longer working for The Darlington, I was more flexible, and if I played my cards right, I might even be able to get a reference from Giulia. I hadn't worked at the hotel for long, but I'd done a good job.

I was still lost in thought and running through my options when the door to Grace's room swung open, and she walked in. Her cheeks and the tip of her nose were flushed red, and the wind had whipped wildly at her hair, leaving it looking dishevelled.

"Hey! You look pretty alive today," she greeted me.

I made a vague gesture with my hand, but I knew what she meant. Over the past few days, she'd mostly seen me curled up like a shrimp in her bed. Today, I was sitting up, at least, and I hadn't yet cried. I probably would later, but for now, my eyes were dry.

Grace set down her bag. "How are you doing?"

"Better. I even ate something earlier."

"Glad to hear it," she said with a smile that faltered almost immediately. She turned her back on me to hide it, but it was already too late.

"What's wrong?"

She sighed heavily, her shoulders slumping. "It's nothing serious . . . Or perhaps it is. But you're feeling better, and I don't want to ruin it."

"Tell me. You're scaring me."

"Henry came to see me today." My stomach cramped at Grace's words. I looked at my friend uncertainly and waited for her to continue. "He asked if I knew where you were," she explained when I didn't speak.

"What did you tell him?" My voice sounded thin.

Grace's expression softened sympathetically. "I told him you're staying with me and he doesn't need to worry about you, but that you don't want to see him."

Relief washed over me. I wasn't ready to see him yet. Perhaps I never would be. The thought of being close to Henry without being *with* him was unbearable. "How did he react?"

"He didn't seem particularly happy, but he gave me something for you," Grace answered hesitantly. "I don't want to keep it from you, but I'm also not sure it's a good idea to give it to you."

I wasn't sure either. "What is it?"

"A letter." Grace pulled out a black envelope from her handbag. Just like the other letters Henry had sent me, it was sealed with gold wax. "You don't have to read it just because Henry wants you to. It's your decision. Just say the word, and I'll throw it in the bin."

I stared at the black envelope in Grace's hands. My throat suddenly felt tight, and a familiar pressure started building behind my eyes. So much for not crying today.

Grace stepped closer and held out the letter to me. I hesitated, torn between the desire to know what it said and the fear of finding out. But I missed Henry, and the thought of being close to him, even if just for a few seconds through his words on the paper, was too tempting to resist.

I broke the seal and pulled out the letter. I couldn't help but smile when I saw Henry's messy handwriting, which was barely legible even though he had clearly made an effort.

I started reading.

Kate,

I don't know where to start. A simple "I'm sorry" doesn't seem like enough, but I am sorry. I'm sorry I broke your trust. I'm sorry I did this to us. And I'm sorry I didn't tell you about the Vitalyn. That was a mistake, and I'm ashamed—most of all, of my own cowardice.

I've felt guilty about it since you told me about your mum, because I knew what I was doing would hurt you. I was determined to stop, but I kept finding reasons why taking another tablet was OK.

Stress. Exhaustion. Too much work.

That's probably why I didn't tell you about it. I kept telling myself that every time would be the last—and it never was. Looking back, I see that my reasons for continuing to take it weren't actually reasons but excuses. But I'm done with that now. I know you'll have a hard time believing it, because your mum never managed to stop, but I'm serious. I've thrown away every single Vitalyn tablet. I'm quitting because you are the most important thing in my life, my angel.

Yours forever,
Henry

How is Kate doing? I'm looking forward to our movie night later. Should I bring something? Chocolate? Ice cream?

Message from Rose to Grace

Kate

"What do you think about this one?" Grace asked, sliding her laptop towards me so I could see the job posting she'd found. We were sitting on her bed, Grace searching for jobs for me on her laptop while I scoured the internet on Amy's iPad.

I skimmed the posting, then shook my head. "They'll never hire me. They want at least five years of relevant experience," I replied, pointing at the requirements.

"Shit," Grace muttered. "I didn't see that."

I smiled, trying not to show how much the job hunt was wearing me down. I wanted to work, but it was sobering how slim my chances were. In a desperate attempt to get my mum off drugs, I'd put my entire life on hold. I'd dropped out of school early to take care of her, and now I was faced with the fallout of that decision. Perhaps that was part of why I'd been so afraid of being with

Henry, faced with addiction. I couldn't sacrifice everything for another person again, only to be left with nothing.

"And continuing to work for The Darlington really isn't an option?" Amy asked, sitting cross-legged on the floor as she rifled through the flashcards I would be testing her on later. "You liked that job, and you would get to keep working with Grace."

I shook my head, although I knew Henry would let me stay on at The Darlington. He had told me my position at the hotel wasn't dependent on our relationship, but I couldn't go back to work there. It would mean returning to Henry. His letter alone was enough to make me weak, because my heart wanted to be weak. It wanted to forgive him—until my mind reminded it that neither declarations of love nor promises were enough. It was easy to write that he had stopped taking Vitalyn, but staying clean was hard. And how was I supposed to believe him after he'd hidden his addiction for so long?

"If I were you, I wouldn't want to work there anymore either," Grace said, patting my shoulder sympathetically.

We spent a while longer searching for jobs—a sobering experience. What was meant to be a distraction from my heartbreak only reminded me that I had given up a perfect life others would have clung to for dear life. But I'd had to learn at far too young an age that life would never be perfect if you lived in constant fear for the person you loved.

19th December

Kate,

I miss you. It's probably not fair to write that after what I did to us, but it's the truth. I miss you, my angel. My parents think my life will be easier now that you're gone, but they're wrong. It has never felt harder, and that's not just because of the Vitalyn detox.

I want to be honest—it isn't easy. I've been clean for a couple of days, and . . . it's bad. But not being able to talk to you, touch you, or kiss you is a thousand times worse.

Yours forever,
Henry

"Hope Harbour, Gallagher speaking," Tilly finally answered the phone. I'd been trying to get a hold of her for a while to ask about potential jobs, but we'd somehow kept missing each other. I really hoped she'd have something for me—I was starting to get anxious.

"Hi, Tilly. It's Kate."

"Oh, hi, Kate. How lovely to hear from you. Is everything OK?" Tilly asked, her voice filled with concern. "I saw the interview and wanted to call to ask how you're doing, but I didn't want to intrude."

"You wouldn't have been intruding," I assured her, pacing around Grace's room restlessly. "I'm OK. What about you?"

"I'm good. Just a bit stressed about the Pearl Gala next week. I still don't have a dress. It's hard to find something that looks elegant but doesn't break the bank. Do you know what you're going to wear yet?"

I shook my head before remembering Tilly couldn't see me. "I'm not going."

There was a brief silence.

"What? Why not?"

"Henry and I broke up."

"Oh, I'm so sorry."

"It's OK," I said dismissively. It wasn't OK. *I* wasn't OK. But I hadn't called Tilly to talk about my messy love life. "There's actually another reason I'm calling. Maybe it's a little presumptuous, but I thought I'd give it a shot."

"Shoot," Tilly encouraged.

I took a deep breath, my heart pounding, even though I knew nothing bad could happen. "I'm looking for a new job. I don't want to work at The Darlington anymore . . ."

"Understandable."

"Hope Harbour came to mind. I've never worked for a charity organisation before, but I do have experience with homelessness and poverty. I know what homeless people need and how to help them, and I hoped that with the funds from the Pearl Gala, you might soon have the budget to offer me a job."

The words came spilling out of my mouth. I was desperate to say my piece before Tilly could interrupt with a rejection. There was a silence on the line after I finished, and I could hear the blood rushing in my ears.

"That's an interesting idea," Tilly said at last. She didn't sound opposed, but there was hesitation in her voice. "But I can't make that decision alone. I'm the head of the Hope Harbour foundation in London, but personnel decisions have to be approved by the main office in Glasgow. I'll happily ask, but I'm afraid I can't make any promises."

"No problem," I said, doing my best not to sound disappointed. "Will you let me know as soon as you hear something? I can send you my CV and cover letter, if that helps. But if I'm being honest, they're not exactly impressive."

"That's not necessary. I know you're qualified to do the job, and the rest you can learn. Before Hope Harbour, I had no idea how charities worked either. And if the head office needs your documents, I'll let you know."

"Thanks, Tilly."

"No need to thank me yet," she said, a smile audible in her voice. "I'll let you know as soon as I hear back."

We said goodbye, and I wished Tilly luck in finding the perfect dress for the Pearl Gala.

Excitement fluttered in my chest as I set my phone aside. I didn't want to get my hopes up, but a job working for Hope Harbour would be perfect. Not only would it solve my problems, but I would also be able to contribute something valuable to solving those of others.

24th December

Kate,

Not getting into my Bentley and driving to you has never felt as hard as it does today. I miss you, and would do anything to see you—but it's your decision when, or if, you want to see me again.

Still, I won't give up hope.

The Darlington's doors remain open to you, just like my heart. I'm here whenever you want to talk to me again—whether that's today, tomorrow, in a month, or in a year. I'll wait for you.

I hope you have the most wonderful Christmas with Grace and her family.

Yours forever,
Henry

It was the third letter in ten days—and it arrived the day before Christmas. Henry had given it to Grace early because she was off for Christmas until the Pearl Gala. I both loved and hated Henry's letters. Every time Grace pulled a black envelope from her bag, my heart began to race, and my hands started sweating. I had hesitated before opening the first letter, but now I could hardly break the wax seal fast enough to see what he had written.

The first letter had made me sad.

The second had stirred longing in me.

The third made me doubt my decision to leave Henry.

It would have been easier for him to forget me, but he refused to give up. He kept fighting for me despite all the hurdles, and his loving words got under my skin—just like his relentless determination to win me back.

Looking back, I had to admit that I had acted more emotionally than rationally on the day I'd found his pills. I had been so afraid of someone I loved choosing drugs over me for the second time that I had lashed out in panic. It hadn't been fair to Henry. Until the moment I had discovered the Vitalyn, he had never given me a reason to doubt him. Every day, he had made me feel how important I was to him—with his words, actions, touches, and kisses. They had flowed through me, from the top of my head to the tips of my toes and straight into my heart.

I rubbed my chest. My heart was beating hard—because of Henry, for Henry. I felt a strong impulse to go to The Darlington and not leave him waiting any longer. I wanted to hold him in my arms and talk to him: to try, together with Henry, to rebuild the trust he had broken. After my discovery, that had felt impossible, but that had changed with a little distance. If Henry was serious—and it seemed he was—we could overcome his addiction. Together.

I flinched as my phone rang, and I felt a surge of hope that it might be Henry. But it couldn't be—I still had his number blocked.

I grabbed my phone and saw Tilly's name on the display. "Hey, Tilly!"

"Hi, Kate. Do you have a moment?"

"For you, always," I replied eagerly. I had been waiting for her to get back to me for days, and had almost given up hope of hearing from her before the end of the year. "Please tell me you have good news."

She hesitated, and my heart stopped. "I have . . . news."

"Okaaaaay," I drew out the word. "What kind of news?"

"I had to do quite a bit of convincing, but after some back-and-forth, the main office agreed to create a position for you."

My heart started up again.

"You can start working at Hope Harbour in January."

I squealed with excitement. For a brief moment, I had been genuinely afraid. "Oh my god! Thank you, Tilly. Thank you, thank you, thank you. A thousand times, thank you! I promise you won't regret it. I'll work harder than anyone you've ever seen."

"I believe you. But there's one more thing."

"What is it?" I asked, although I didn't really care. I had a job. A real job with proper pay. I wouldn't have to go back to living on the streets or start pickpocketing again!

Tilly took a deep breath. "The job comes with a condition . . ."

59

Do you need a Vitalyn restock?
I haven't heard from you in a while.
Or are you pissed because of the thing with Olivia?

Unanswered message from Marko to Henry

Henry

My right eye had been twitching nonstop for days. It was driving me up the wall, but at least it distracted me from the headaches and sporadic hot flashes that had been plaguing me for weeks—ever since I had stopped taking Vitalyn. I had read online that these were normal withdrawal side effects, as was the nausea, which, luckily for me, at least wasn't accompanied by vomiting. Still, I felt terrible. And I would have been lying if I said the thought of taking a pill hadn't crossed my mind. But I fought against the urge with all my might, knowing it was mostly in my head.

Take the pills, and the pain will stop.

Take the pills so you can concentrate.

Take the pills; the hotel needs you to think clearly.

Take the pills—just until the Pearl Gala is over.

Excuse after excuse haunted my thoughts, but all it took to silence them was the thought of Kate—her sweet voice, her sparkling laughter, and the soft feel of her skin beneath my fingertips.

I unlocked my phone, opened the photo gallery, and tapped on the last photo of Kate. It had been taken on the rooftop terrace of The Darlington. After the *INsider* had agreed to take down Randell's interview, we had gone up to the bar to toast the small victory. We had snuggled up together next to a heater, sharing a blanket.

In the photo, I had my arm around Kate, and she was nestled against my chest. Her hair was tousled from my hands, and her lips were slightly flushed from my kisses. And though I had been horrendously stressed that day, I was smiling blissfully at the camera. All because of Kate—because she was with me.

I heard a knock. For a brief moment, I thought it was just the pain hammering in my head, but then I realised someone was actually at the door of my apartment. I had left work early, the withdrawal symptoms having got the better of me, and had asked Rakesh to cover for me. I'd told him I was coming down with a cold, and he had believed me without question—probably because I looked just as exhausted and wrecked as I felt.

There was another knock.

I groaned as I pushed myself up, and debated whether I should open the door. I wasn't in the mood to deal with my mum, much less my dad. I'd barely seen him since our fight about Kate, but I wouldn't put it past him to turn up and make my life hell just for daring to take half a day off work—especially so close to the gala.

The charity event was only three days away. Things were finally coming together—from the decor and catering to the stars we'd booked for the red carpet. Everything was organised, even if this year's celebrity lineup was far less impressive than in previous years.

This time, the knock, when it came, was more forceful and insistent, as if someone were trying to break down the door.

"Are you having a wank, or why aren't you opening up?" said a deep, muffled voice.

I froze. "Logan?!"

"Yes!"

I leapt to my feet—a mistake. Everything went black, and for a moment, I felt like I was falling back onto the sofa. But then my vision cleared, and I steadied myself before hurrying to the door and opening it. Although I'd heard his voice, I was still surprised to see Logan standing there. Were hallucinations a side effect of withdrawal? He stood in the corridor outside my apartment, wearing dark jeans and a brown leather jacket. His blond hair was tied back in a ponytail, and his undercut had been freshly shaved.

"What . . . what are you doing here?"

"Making sure you're still alive. You haven't been answering my messages."

"Sorry, I can't look at screens for long right now." It wasn't a lie—screens made my head explode, like striking a match near a gas canister. Though that hadn't stopped me just now from staring at the photo of Kate.

Logan grunted and pushed past me into my apartment, looking around with curiosity. He had never been here before and only knew my penthouse apartment from the photos I'd shown him. His gaze landed instinctively on the shelf with my *London Has Fallen* DVD collection, which triggered a small, self-satisfied smirk. Kate's DVD was in my bedroom next to the bed, where I kept rereading her words.

"You're at The Darlington," I said, stating the obvious.

"And I'm not happy about it," Logan replied dryly. He hadn't set foot in the hotel for years, rejecting every invitation I'd ever extended. I had been certain I'd never see him here again, in this place filled with so many shared memories. But he was here now, despite his aversion and reservations—because he was worried about me.

"How are you?" he asked.

"Shit," I answered bluntly.

Logan knew everything. On the day Kate had left me, she had driven to see him and told him about my problem. That same evening, Logan and I had met at a pub. At first, he had ranted furiously about how reckless I'd been, but then we'd talked. For a long time. Eventually, he had understood—mostly. I'd had to promise him I would stop taking Vitalyn, which I had already planned to do anyway. If I wanted a future with Kate—which I did, more than anything in the world—I had to get clean. I couldn't put her through the same hell she'd endured with her mum. I wanted to make her life easier and brighter, not fill it with worry and pain.

"Because of the withdrawal or Kate?" Logan sank onto the sofa with the ease of someone who had done so countless times, as if him being at the hotel right now weren't a total mindfuck.

"Both. The withdrawal is killing me here," I said, pointing at my head, "and the situation with Kate is killing me here." I gestured at my heart, which hadn't stopped hurting since she'd left The Darlington. I'd been through a few breakups, but none of them had felt this bad. I may have been sad afterwards, but I'd never felt so lost, as if someone had removed a part of me.

"So she hasn't been in touch?"

I shook my head. I didn't even know if she was reading my letters. Grace had promised to give them to her, but whether Kate opened them was another matter.

"You know where she's staying though, right?"

I collapsed onto the sofa next to Logan. My exhausted body relaxed. I felt like a man in his sixties, not mid-twenties. I wasn't even sure if it was the withdrawal or if the exhaustion of the past few months was catching up with me now that the Vitalyn was no longer keeping me going.

"Yes. In Shadwell, with one of the other room attendants."

"Why don't you go and see her?" He asked the question as if I hadn't considered it myself a hundred times.

"I don't want to bother her. I hurt her pretty badly, and she needs time to process everything. She'll come to me when she's ready to talk. Until then, I'll just keep sending her letters."

"It might take more than a few letters."

I raised my eyebrows. "Intrusive visits?"

Logan let out a low, throaty laugh. "No, but as far as I understand, her biggest fear is that you'll end up like her mum, who never managed to get clean."

"What are you suggesting?"

Instead of answering, Logan reached into the inside pocket of his leather jacket and pulled out a piece of paper. It wasn't until he handed it to me that I realised it was a brochure for a private rehab clinic. "Don't just talk. Do something. Show Kate how serious you are."

60

Boycott against The Darlington: Many stars are staying away from this year's Pearl Gala, but politicians such as cabinet member Lawrence Eddington and members of the royal family are also refusing to attend the charity gala.

INsider headline

Henry

My heart was racing. I wasn't sure if it was from excitement about the Pearl Gala or lingering withdrawal symptoms—perhaps both. I stood off to the side of the red carpet, watching the flurry of camera flashes as photographers scrambled to get shots of Hollywood darling Kayden Bradley. A lot of journalists had turned up to cover the gala, possibly even more than last year. Presumably, they were all hoping for a new Darlington family scandal, but they wouldn't get one—I would make sure of it.

Someone tapped me on the shoulder.

I spun around to see Rakesh. He wore a suit and clutched his beloved tablet, looking just as harried as I felt. His cheeks were flushed, but at least his hair was holding up—slicked into place with what looked like an entire pot of gel.

"You're up in a moment."

I nodded. "Is everything going to plan?"

"Yes." He tapped away on his tablet. "We've had four last-minute cancellations, but not from anyone important. The last limousines for the red carpet should be arriving any moment, and the catering staff is about to start serving the aperitifs."

I let out a relieved sigh. Finally, some good news. "Thank you, Rakesh. Really. I couldn't have pulled this off without you."

"I'm happy to help. But do you know what's even better than thanks?"

"A raise?"

"A raise," he confirmed with a grin.

I laughed and made a mental note to arrange it, even if accounting would kick up a fuss. The Darlington couldn't afford to lose Rakesh—especially not now that I was planning to take a step back. Without the Vitalyn, I couldn't keep working a hundred hours a week or more. Right now, every hour felt like one too many. But I hoped that time and support would get me back on track.

"You're up," Rakesh said, patting me on the shoulder.

I resisted the urge to make a face and took a deep breath instead, adjusting my jacket before stepping onto the red carpet. Dozens of cameras shot up in the air, and blinding flashes engulfed me. It wasn't my favourite part of events, but it came with the territory.

"Henry, look left!"

"Henry, where's Kate?"

"Henry, don't you have a date tonight?"

"Henry, what happened to your girlfriend?"

"Henry, what can you say about Olivia Asterdam's relationship with Marko Langston?"

"Henry, give us a smile!"

The photographers called my name, and I followed their directions and demands, but didn't respond to their questions. I didn't want to talk—or even think—about Kate's absence. A small part of me had hoped we would make up before the gala, but I'd been fooling myself. She hadn't answered a single one of my letters. Even so, the next one was already sealed in its envelope, waiting in my office.

I finally stepped off the red carpet two minutes later, although it felt like it had been twenty. Rakesh smiled at me from across the other side of the carpet, and I made my way into the ballroom.

The Darlington exuded elegance and luxury year-round, but in December, it took on a special kind of splendour. The holiday decorations—the grand Christmas tree in the lobby and the countless tiny fairy lights, which took many hours of meticulous work to arrange—totally transformed the space. I had always loved this time of year at the hotel. A wave of melancholy washed over me as I considered the possibility that this might be the last time I saw it like this. The future of The Darlington was still hanging in the balance. I would do everything in my power to save it, but there was only so much one man could do.

The ballroom was also lavishly decorated. Lively voices filled the space, mixing with the live music. A digital display above the stage showed the donations. The figure currently stood at £5,423,050—not a record high, but still an impressive sum.

A waiter approached me with a glass of champagne, which I politely declined. I was trying to stay sober in every sense of the word. I made my way to the bar and grabbed a glass of water before mingling with the guests.

The attendees were a colourful mix of high society, including celebrities, politicians, aristocrats, and a few influencers Vivian had insisted on inviting. I spotted Aliza Malik and Fiona Harrison, whose videos Olivia enjoyed watching. I introduced myself to them, but quickly excused myself to continue shaking hands and encouraging people to donate. Occasionally, someone would ask me about Kate, but I avoided the topic, using the question as an opportunity to excuse myself.

The ballroom gradually filled until every table and chair was occupied. Last week, Rakesh and I had made some last-minute changes to the seating arrangement, and as a result, it was hardly noticeable that this year's gala had a third fewer attendees. The dance floor was larger, and we had added an extra bar. Everything was going to plan. I was rarely fully at ease at events like these, but I felt myself loosen up a little.

"Henry!"

My shoulders tensed again. So much for loosening up. I turned to face Vivian as she strode towards me in high heels. She was wearing a green suit that perfectly matched the branding of this year's gala.

"It's time for the family photo. Come on!"

Her commanding tone left no room for debate. The sooner I got the photo over with, the sooner I could start avoiding my parents for the rest of the night.

I followed Vivian as she led me to one of the many photographers documenting the event. My parents were already there, posing for photos.

My mum's eyes lit up when she saw me. "Henry, you look wonderful."

I kissed her on the cheek. "Thanks. So do you."

"Did you see who's here tonight?" she asked with a smug smile that turned my stomach to ice. I had already spotted Daphne Walsh in the crowd and suspected my mum was trying to set me up with her. Although she didn't know the details of what had happened between Kate and me, she hadn't failed to notice that we'd broken up.

I feigned ignorance. "No, who?"

"Daphne!" My mum clapped her hands gleefully. "You absolutely must ask her to dance later. I'm sure she'd be delighted—even if your date back then didn't work out. Anything could happen!"

"I don't think so."

Her smile faded. "Why not? She's a great woman. Pretty. Smart. Educated. And after that homeless girl—"

"Kate," I corrected.

She rolled her eyes, as if I was being pedantic for insisting she use Kate's name. "Now that Kate is no longer in the picture, it's time you started looking for a woman who's more suitable—both for you and for this family."

"I'm not interested." Not in Daphne nor in any other woman. My feelings for Kate hadn't changed just because she was gone. It would probably take an eternity to get over her—which, truthfully, I didn't want to do. On the contrary, I wanted her back. She was a truly special person, something my mum had never been able to see.

"Henry . . ."

To my surprise, my dad came to my defence. "Leave the lad alone. He doesn't want to date Daphne. Anyway, he'd be doing us all a favour if he focussed on the hotel for the next few months instead of on his love life."

I would decide what my priorities were, but I let my dad's comment slide, because I didn't have the energy to argue with him. And because some battles just weren't worth fighting.

Vivian returned with Ethan in tow. He held a cocktail glass in his hand, which Vivian practically had to wrestle away from him.

"Stand next to Henry," she ordered, pushing Ethan towards me. "And smile, please. You're thrilled to be here tonight."

"I guess so," my brother mumbled, smelling strongly of alcohol.

I wrinkled my nose. "How are you already drunk?"

He shrugged. "It's my god-given talent."

"Pull yourself together," my dad hissed through clenched teeth, forcing a smile. The photographer had already started taking pictures, even though it must have been clear this wasn't a conversation we wanted captured for posterity.

"I wouldn't have to pull myself together if this gala weren't so fucking dull."

"This is a charity fundraising event, not some party where you can get wasted," I pointed out.

"But it could be one. I bet that would really get people feeling generous."

I rolled my eyes, but instead of answering, I plastered on the best fake smile I could muster. The photographer took photos of us from every possible angle and in various groupings. Those few moments dragged on even longer than my time on the red carpet, but eventually, it was over.

Ethan let out a relieved groan, grabbed his cocktail glass from Vivian, and returned to his friends, who had been watching our photo shoot with amusement. I made my own escape before my mum could get it into her head to start introducing me to women I had no interest in dating.

I grabbed another glass of water and asked the bartender to keep an eye on Ethan, cutting him off if necessary. The event had to stay drama-free, and that included ensuring Ethan and his friends behaved themselves. It was one thing when the four of them went overboard at the club—that was old news, since it happened every weekend, and rarely attracted press attention—but this was a different story.

I visited Olivia at her table. She had come with Marko as her date again, but fortunately, he was nowhere to be seen. I despised him, mostly because he knew about my Vitalyn addiction. I still didn't know whether he took it himself or just sold it. I'd have to tell Olivia about it eventually, but not tonight—not with Marko and all these other guests around.

"How are you doing?" Olivia asked after we had said hello. She looked stunning as always in a cream-coloured Valentino dress. I couldn't help but remember how I'd felt after we had broken up—how easy it had been, and how different it was from what I was going through with Kate.

"I don't know," I replied truthfully.

Olivia reached out to pat my hand. "You know that you can always talk to me."

"Thank you. Right now, I just need some time for myself."

"OK, but just know that I'm here."

I nodded. "Maybe we can meet for a coffee soon. We haven't done that in ages, and there are a couple of things I want to talk to you about."

She looked at me attentively, her curiosity piqued. "And whose fault is that, Mr. Busy?"

I pulled a face. She was right. I really had neglected her over the past few months—partly because of Kate, but mostly because of work. But that was about to change.

"I'm sorry," I said. "Let me make it up to you. Forget coffee. Dinner. You pick the place. My treat."

Olivia grinned and clinked her champagne flute against my water glass, as if to toast the idea. "Sounds good. Apology accepted."

We talked until Vivian came back to fetch me. All the guests had now arrived, and it was time for the evening's official programme to begin. By now, the donations had surpassed seven million pounds. The band played their final song and left the stage—it was my turn. The conversations grew quieter until they eventually stopped altogether.

I squared my shoulders and walked onto the stage with decisive steps that concealed how fast my heart was racing—both from nerves and excitement. Against all odds, the Pearl Gala was clearly going to be a success. And this year, I had the honour of delivering the welcome speech for the first time. Although I had been organising the Pearl Gala for a while, my dad had always insisted on handling this part. Tonight, it was my turn.

I stood behind the podium and let my gaze sweep over the crowd. All I saw were friendly, curious, and open faces—devoid of the hatred and prejudice that had made my life hell over the past few months.

I cleared my throat. "Ladies and gentlemen, my name is Henry Darlington, and it is my great pleasure to welcome you all to The Darlington's forty-fourth Pearl Gala. This event is the highlight of my year and one of my personal favourites. Founded by my grandmother, Selma, the Pearl Gala has always aimed to help those who cannot help themselves—whether people or animals." I paused briefly for effect. "This year, the Pearl Gala is raising funds for a special organisation very close to my heart: Hope Harbour.

For years, Hope Harbour has been fighting homelessness in the United Kingdom. They lend a hand where others look away, giving a voice to those who are all too often ignored and overlooked. Tonight, we all have the oppor—"

I fell silent. The last syllables caught in my throat when, to my surprise, I spotted Kate in the crowd. She was here! My heart stopped. My breath caught in my throat. Kate was really here. She stood at the back of the hall with Grace, standing out like a diamond in a heap of coal, even though she was wearing neither an elegant dress nor a smart trouser suit. Instead, she was in tattered jeans and her old leather jacket. She stared at me with her big brown eyes, robbing me of both my breath and my words.

The hall had fallen deathly silent. Everyone was waiting for me to continue. I tried to remember what I had wanted to say.

". . . the opportunity," I managed, but my throat was suddenly dry as dust. I swallowed hard. "The opportunity . . . to make a difference. Each of us can contribute to ensuring that Hope Harbour can continue their work. And . . . and . . ."

My mind went blank. I couldn't remember another word of my two-page speech. All I could think about was Kate. She was here. What was she doing here? I had to talk to her—immediately, before she disappeared again. This might be my only chance to tell her, face-to-face, how much I loved her and how terribly sorry I was for how things had turned out.

"And now, Matilda Gallagher will tell you more about Hope Harbour's mission," I said, abruptly cutting my speech short. "Please, put your hands together for Matilda!" I clapped, then left the stage as fast as I could.

Tilly took my place behind the podium, looking slightly taken aback by my sudden departure—I was supposed to stay on stage with her. Instead, I hurried across the hall towards Kate. But she was no longer there. I looked around frantically. My nervous movements had begun to attract attention, but I didn't care. Where was Kate? She had been standing right here—I was sure of it. I hadn't imagined her. Had she already left? She couldn't have!

"Turn around," a familiar female voice said.

Grace. She stood just a few steps away, pointing at something behind me.

I turned, and my heart started pounding. It was Kate—and she was stepping onto the stage.

Henry was completely speechless when he saw Kate. OMG! They're so cute together. I wish a man would fight for me like Henry has fought for Kate. That's what true love looks like.

Message from Grace to Rose

Kate

All my attention was focussed on Henry. I wasn't aware of anything or anyone else around me—only him. I didn't feel the gaze of the crowd on me, and I didn't hear what Tilly was saying, which led to me missing my cue. She nudged me gently in the side, and I stepped up to the podium. I would have been completely lost without the notes I'd made on Amy's flashcards. On autopilot, I delivered the speech I had prepared with Tilly over the past few days. This was the condition of the job at Hope Harbour—I had to attend the Pearl Gala and share my experiences of life on the street, using my personal story to encourage people to donate more.

When Tilly had initially asked me in her office if I wanted to give a speech, I had declined because I had promised Henry to keep my past a secret. But thanks to Randell, the cat was out of the bag. I had nothing left to hide. Better yet, I could perhaps even correct some of the lies Randell had told about me.

The guests hung on to my every word, but my eyes were fixed on Henry. He stood on the other side of the ballroom next to Grace. The sight of him made my knees weak. In his three-piece suit, with his jet-black hair and piercing blue eyes, he looked devastatingly attractive. Even from afar, his gaze was so intense that I could almost feel it on my skin. Every nerve in my body tingled.

Unlike Henry, I had been able to prepare myself to see him again, because I had known he would be here tonight. And yet, I still wasn't ready. Nothing could have prepared me for the massive storm that brewed inside me at the sight of him. It was even more powerful than the one that had driven Henry to search for me in St. James's Park that night. It whipped at my thoughts—and even more so, my emotions—and left me reeling. Only Henry could catch me.

I spoke at double speed, just wanting to get it over with so I could go to Henry. I wanted to tell him how much his letters meant to me and that I had acted rashly, driven by fear.

Applause filled the ballroom. My speech was over, and I hadn't been conscious of a single word that had come out of my mouth.

Tilly hooked her arm through mine and whispered, "Well done," in my ear before we left the stage together to make way for the band. I glanced over my shoulder at the donation display. The total had risen from seven to eight million during Henry's speech. During mine, it had jumped to twelve million. Twelve! Twelve million for the homeless in London. That amount of money would make a huge difference. It would change lives—improve them.

People approached us, wanting to talk to Tilly and me, but I had to find Henry. I slipped away from Tilly, who gave me an understanding look, and made my way across the hall. A deep longing in my chest drew me towards Henry. When I reached the spot where I had just seen him with Grace, I spotted her immediately—but Henry was nowhere to be found.

"Where's Henry?" I asked Grace.

"He just left. I thought he was looking for you."

Damn. Had we missed each other? I craned my neck, scanning the crowd towards the stage, but I was too short, and the sea of heads blocked my view. I had to find him. But just as I was about to walk away, I sensed movement beside me.

I turned—and there he was, cheeks flushed, eyes shining.

Suddenly, I could barely breathe. "Henry . . ."

My voice wavered, but before I could say another word, he rushed towards me and pulled me into a fierce embrace. He practically squeezed the air out of my lungs, yet nothing had ever felt better. Enveloped in his familiar scent, I felt the full weight of just how much I had missed him. Tears welled in my eyes as I buried my face against his chest, holding him as tightly as I possibly could. I had no intention of ever letting him go again.

"I'm so sorry," Henry murmured in my ear, his voice so soft that only I could hear. "I'm so incredibly sorry for hurting you, angel. I hope you can forgive me."

I lifted my head, resting my chin against his chest as I gazed up at him. "I'm sorry too. I shouldn't have just left. I was scared for you, and terrified that I'd have to relive all the awful things I went through with my mum. I didn't mean to abandon you. I panicked."

Henry gently stroked my hair. "If I'd been in your shoes, I would have reacted the same way. I should have told you about the Vitalyn much sooner. I swear this was the first and last time I ever keep anything from you."

My heart pounded wildly. "Yes, you should have talked to me. But if you promise to stop, I'll believe and support you."

"I've already stopped. I've been clean for three weeks, and it's going to stay that way," Henry said firmly. He reached into the inner pocket of his jacket and pulled out a black envelope with a gold seal. Another letter. He handed it to me, and for a brief, electrifying moment, our fingertips touched.

"Have you been carrying this around with you the whole time?"

He laughed—god, how I'd missed that sound. "No, I just fetched it from my office. I was going to give it to Grace tomorrow, but now that you're here . . . please, read it."

With trembling fingers, I opened the envelope and pulled out the letter.

Kate,

I hope you had a lovely Christmas. I spent mine with Logan and Maxton—they did their best to distract me and keep my mind off things. But not an hour has gone by in the past few weeks where I haven't thought of you. I never wanted to hurt you, and I hate myself for having done so. You shouldn't have to go through anything like what you endured with your mum—especially not because of me. Which is why I've decided to start therapy. I've spoken to the Harmony Rehabilitation Centre here in London, and beginning in January, I'll be having sessions twice a week. Not just to get clean, but to stay clean. So I can be the man you deserve.

Yours forever,
Henry

I'm proud of you for taking this step.

Message from Logan to Henry

Henry

I didn't take my eyes off Kate for a second as she read my letter. After Logan had handed me the brochure, I had called the Harmony Rehabilitation Centre—not just to get help for myself, but to prove to Kate that my words weren't empty promises. That she could trust me.

She looked up from the letter. Her eyes shone, and her cheeks were wet, but she looked overwhelmed by emotion rather than sad.

"You're going to rehab?"

"It's more therapy than rehab, but yes. I want to show you how serious I am. I need you, Kate. More than Vitalyn. More than The Darlington. And more than my next breath. I love you with all my heart, my angel."

My heart pounded as I waited for Kate's response. She stared at me for a moment, then suddenly, a smile spread across her face, bringing out her dimples. When our eyes met, all I saw was affection.

"I love you too, Snowflake."

I froze and blinked.

Once.

Twice.

Three times.

I swallowed hard. "You . . . you love me?"

Kate's smile widened, her dimples deepening. "Of course I do. How could I not? You're amazing. And it was wrong of me to judge you for my mum's mistakes. You're nothing like her, and my reaction says more about me than it does about you. I never really got to process everything that happened last year, and when I saw the pills, it all came flooding back. That wasn't fair on you. And I'm sorry for abandoning you."

"So . . . does that mean you forgive me?" I asked, cautious but hopeful.

Kate nodded emphatically.

I wanted nothing more than to grab her and kiss her—really kiss her—but I wasn't about to put on even more of a show for the guests already watching us. Instead, I reached for her hand, interlacing my fingers with hers. It was a small touch, but it felt monumental. Then, without a word, I led her through the ballroom towards the balcony where we'd shared our first kiss.

A blast of cold winter air greeted us as I held the door open for her. We stepped up to the railing, the glow of the heaters warming our skin. Fairy lights sparkled like stars above us, and the city before us shimmered, quiet and serene.

I turned to Kate. She smiled, and I smiled back, my heart feeling like it might explode with joy. Stepping closer, I raised my hand and gently brushed her cheek, never breaking eye contact. She held my gaze, unwavering. God, I was so in love with this woman.

"Will you kiss me now?" Kate asked softly.

"Only if you want me to."

"More than anything."

I leaned in and kissed her—tender and loving, yet no less heartfelt. Kate sighed against my lips and kissed me back with the same abandon.

Finally holding her in my arms again after three long weeks felt incredible. Her body relaxed against mine, and I could feel her letting go. What we had was more than just love—there was trust too. It was delicate and fragile. Not quite what it had been before, but it was there. And I would do everything in my power to rebuild it, until it was strong and unshakeable. Day by day, for the rest of our lives—or however long Kate would have me. Hopefully forever.

The balcony door was flung open, and a wave of déjà vu hit me, pulling me back to my first kiss with Kate. I broke away from her and turned—but this time, it wasn't my dad who disturbed us. It was Rakesh, clutching his tablet so tightly that his knuckles had turned white. His face was pale, and a strange, desperate expression darkened his features. It didn't bode well.

"What's wrong?" I asked, my arms still wrapped around Kate.

Rakesh swallowed hard, as if choking back tears.

A knot tightened in my stomach. Something was very, very wrong.

"There's been . . . an accident," he said, his voice unsteady. "Someone has died."

THE BLACKROOM

On the evening of the Pearl Gala, tragedy struck near The Darlington Hotel. A 22-year-old woman was hit by a car on a side street near the venue and died at the scene. The driver fled, leaving her without assistance.

The exact circumstances of the accident remain unclear. Police report that there are no leads on the identity of the hit-and-run driver, despite the numerous surveillance cameras at the scandal-ridden hotel that should have captured the incident. Strangely, no evidence has been recovered . . . Sound familiar? Is The Darlington covering something up—yet again?

We hope justice is served and the driver is held accountable. Our thoughts are with the victim's family.

Rest in peace.

Henry's Favourite Songs

Lorna Shore—Of the Abyss
Sleep Token—The Summoning
Knocked Loose—Don't Reach for Me
Bring Me the Horizon feat. AURORA—liMOusIne
Spiritbox—Rotoscope
Zeal & Ardor—Götterdämmerung
BloodMagic—Death/Rebirth
Graphic Nature—Human
Linkin Park—Waiting for the End
Bad Omens—Dethrone

Kate's Favourite Songs

Taylor Swift—Vigilante Shit
Doja Cat—Demons
Olivia Rodrigo—bad idea right?
Paramore—Misery Business
Billie Eilish—bad guy
Sabrina Carpenter—Taste
Ashnikko—Daisy
Rico Nasty—OHFR?
Soap&Skin—Me and the Devil
Selena Gomez—Bad Liar

ABOUT THE AUTHOR

Laura Kneidl was born in Erlangen in 1990 and studied library and information management. Inspired by her favorite books, she began working on her first novel in 2009 and hasn't stopped writing since. Today, the author lives in Leipzig with her three cats, where her apartment resembles a library. On social media, she shares insights into her daily writing life and enjoys connecting with readers—so feel free to reach out!

CONTENT WARNING

(and spoiler warning!)

This book contains potentially triggering content.
This includes

Overdose
Death of loved ones
Substance abuse and addiction
Sexual harassment and abuse
Domestic abuse

The following topic is also addressed:

Homelessness

We know that the world is a fast-paced place to be right now, and everything can quickly become too much. During times of stress, the pressure to continuously achieve more can be overwhelming. While the drug mentioned in this book, Vitalyn, is a fictional creation, real substances with similar effects can have serious health consequences and lead to physical and psychological dependence.

If you're feeling stressed or overwhelmed, please seek healthy ways to cope, and don't hesitate to seek professional support if needed.